MORTAL ENEMY

LEGENDS of GRIM #1

A NOVEL BY

NICHOLAS RYAN HOWARD

PRAISE FOR MORTAL ENEMY

"We read to explore, to live tales and build worlds grander than our own. *Mortal Enemy* does this and much more—original, complex, and fiendishly twisted."

- Pierce Brown, author of the *Red Rising* trilogy and *Iron Gold*

"Nicholas Ryan Howard delivers an epic adventure that rivals the storytelling and addictive reading you would encounter with *Harry Potter*, *Game of Thrones*, and *Star Wars* hooked with the dark and gritty lure of these classic tales. *Mortal Enemy* is relentlessly intriguing while maintaining deep character backgrounds and even deeper plot twists. Absolutely a future household name in dark fantasies and probably a seat in the Comic-Con hall of fame. And I mean it. Mark my words."

- Keegan Allen, author of *life.love.beauty* and *Hollywood*

"Nicholas Ryan Howard's *Mortal Enemy* will draw you in immediately with its vivid language and detailed characters, and keep you there with the magnificently built worlds. It all feels so different—yet eerily, so similar—to what we are experiencing today. This is a story that sticks with you. A jolt to the imagination."

- Meagan Adele Lopez, author of *Three Questions*

"*Mortal Enemy* immediately swept me up with its pacing—there was no time to think much about it—the ride had already started! From beginning to end it was no dull experience. The writing is light yet evokes the dark pits of being human. It's full of depth while maintaining humor and wit and quirk. Bizarro characters fill a world that doesn't feel so very different from our own. A downright freaky and timeless tale."

- Mel Banick, *reader review*

"There is no other book like *Mortal Enemy* on the shelves right now. Both in terms of story and writing style, Nicholas Ryan Howard presents a book with a wholly unique voice. If you're a sci-fi or fantasy fan looking to shake things up, read it immediately."

- Billy Henehan, *reader review*

"*Mortal Enemy* was the epic fantasy adventure I didn't know I was looking for. It depicts a world that satisfies your imagination and character development that exceeds your expectations. You'll laugh, you'll cringe, and you'll cheer, until the very end. Instantly one of my favorite books."

- Renee Buckley, *reader review*

ISBN: 978-0-9993468-0-8
KDP - Standard Edition - Paperback - v05
Copyright © 2023 Nicholas Ryan Howard
All rights reserved

Story edited by Babar Peerzada
Edited by Joel Drazner and Rebekah Hendershot
Additional edits by William Rowel and Rosa Nadine Xochimilco Sánchez
Artwork by Nicholas Ryan Howard with photography by Joseph Rubinstein
Author photo by Keegan Allen

MORE ABOUT THE AUTHOR
www.NicholasRyanH.com
@NicholasRyanH

MORE ABOUT THE NOVEL
www.LegendsOfGrim.com
@LegendsOfGrim

THE AUDIO EXPERIENCE

This book is also available as an immersive audio experience featuring an extraordinary cast of performers, multidimensional sound, cinematic-quality effects, and a spectacular orchestral score.

Narrated by Reid Scott (*Venom*) and Devin Kelley (*Frequency*).

Performed by Eric Christian Olsen (*NCIS: Los Angeles*), Troian Bellisario (*Pretty Little Liars*), Chris Pine (*Wonder Woman*), Keegan Allen (*Pretty Little Liars*), Patrick J. Adams (*Suits*), Sarah Wright Olsen (*American Made*), Brett Dier (*Jane the Virgin*), Christa B. Allen (*Revenge*), Brendan Hines (*The Tick*), Adetokumboh M'Cormack (*Castlevania*), Jamie Harris (*The Prestige*), Robert Pine (*Frozen*), Neal Bledsoe (*The Man in the High Castle*), Robert Baker (*Supergirl*), and many more.

It is available to purchase on all major audio platforms, and streams for free on many of them. To locate it in the format of your choice:

> SCAN HERE >

OR VISIT

AUDIO.LEGENDSOFGRIM.COM

In the bitter cold... in the vicious winds... in the harshest snow... only one hunter has the skill to survive.

Skii Tavee.

Gifted beyond her years, she has become emboldened by her abilities. An unmatched prowess in tracking, stealth, and hunting has assured her status as an asset to The Grizz, the tribe of warrior nomads who have offered her amity. However, her fierce independence and remarkable aptness in the wild has given rise to an uncertainty: does she need them as much as they need her?

Find out in this exciting companion story that may be read either before or after *Mortal Enemy*. Get it now, absolutely free:

TABLE OF CONTENTS

For Simon

PART
ONE
FORSAKEN

The ball of fire in the sky scorched the desert wasteland...

C H A P T E R

The Curse and the Cavern

The ball of fire in the sky scorched the desert wasteland. Unrelenting heat seared the sand. A speck in the vast nothingness, like a pitiful bug, inched closer to nowhere.

This speck was a man. Known as Vant Hu'l.

He was tall and sinewy, but ravaged. Weathered. Wilted by the merciless hell on earth that beat against him with all its fury. Scalding temperatures... a bitter dryness... vicious winds... the elements assaulted him without reprieve. They had all but eradicated any traces of vitality that proved this was once a vigorous young man.

Vant's sandpaper tongue ran over cracked lips, aching for a moisture long since vanished. Desperate for relief, he pulled his hood over a wiry mess of sun-charred hair. His cloak, once a flowing masterpiece of craftsmanship, was now no more than tattered rags. It dragged behind him, scraping against the sand as he extended one decrepit boot after another in an arduous slog through the desolation.

This plight was not by choice.

Vant was cursed.

A plague festered inside of him, one that held a relentless dominion over his volition. It appeared years ago, and its dictatorial power had escalated over time. It took hold of him, gripped his nervous system, and became his captor. His enslaver. A demented beast urging him on, stabbing at him with a branding iron if he moved in any direction other than forward. Always forward. The only way to pacify the affliction was to submit, and to trek toward an endgame that only it knew.

Besides the torturous curse, Vant bore one more burden through the desert. Strapped to his back was a satchel containing an item of significance—and heft. Though oppressive, he endured the encumbrance as a punishment earned. The object was a cherished trapping and, in many ways, it had come to define him.

It was a weapon. The last of its kind.

The wind, one day, died out. The sand and rolling dunes ceased, replaced by a hard-packed gravel. Stillness dominated all. An emptiness filled the environment, an absence, as if every possible shred of life had been leeched dry. Nothing existed but a silence, disrupted only by the reverberations of Vant's rhythmic footsteps.

The terrain, almost imperceptible, soon began a downward slope. Vant looked ahead and spied something in the distance. Something unexpected. Something unfathomable. In the dead center of the wasteland, surrounded by thousands of lifeless miles sprawling in every direction...

...was a hole.

A hole like a puckered mouth. It appeared responsible for the total destitution of the surroundings. Like it had sucked in everything living, and left nothing behind but decay.

And Vant was headed straight for it.

Anxiety-fueled heartbeats slammed against his chest; the curse had, for reasons unclear, brought him to this forsaken place. Vant hoped the veil blinding him as to why he had been torn from his home, his life, and his love would at long last be lifted. Yet, the closer he came to the unholy orifice, the more he was overcome by an intense foreboding.

He dug in with his heels to stop his movement—and a wave of ferocious pain blasted through his physiology. The teeth of invisible demons gnashed at his nerve endings. Visceral throbbing jackhammered against his skull. Vant collapsed to the dirt and convulsed from the unendurable torment overrunning his senses.

He shivered as his skin was clawed by spectral fingernails and pleaded with his body to break free from its cursed bonds. Desperate syllables of protest sputtered from his mouth, but there would be no emancipation from this terror. This was a pain beyond any. A pain that could never be endured.

Vant surrendered, submitting to his bane's assertion. He moved forward once again, headed for the very place he otherwise would never have gone. The venomous discontent, pleased with the onward momentum, subsided. Vant lowered his trembling body beneath the edge of the crevice.

And entered into the hole.

Blackness enveloped him. His lungs filled with dust. He struggled for breath. Only his fingertips could guide him through the dark. He was gentle; particles of sediment rained down from overhead, threatening a cave-in.

His eyes adjusted, finding a hint of contour. A glimmer of detail. The blurred outlines of the interior soon came into focus and revealed a hallway running deep underground. He continued inward, downward, and entered into a chamber.

Faces were carved into the walls—mutilated faces, each sculpture a hideous rendering of torment. Hordes of the torrid statues decorated the circular tunnel. The suffering faces, though made of rock, seemed to be inhaling; echoes of asphyxiation accompanied gusts of air flowing into their mouths.

Vant took a step inside—and felt a dreadful texture underneath his boot. It was coarse, cracking beneath his weight and crumbling into dust. He looked down... he had stepped upon a pit of dried-out bodies. Ancient corpses, hundreds of them, were decaying in a mass grave.

Sounds of desecration echoed through the tunnel as Vant traversed the pit. The sculpted faces now surrounded him, inhaling deeper and harder the farther in he went. Their gasps grew increasingly aggressive, then turned desperate when he did not suffer the same fate as had the deceased beneath his feet. But after the last few steps—and to the wheezing dismay of the sculptures—Vant made it to the end of the tunnel, alive and breathing.

He descended an incline and entered into a cavern. A horizontal vertigo took hold as he peered down a seemingly endless corridor. The interior was rugged. The ground uneven. Stalagmites and stalactites jutted from its claustrophobic walls.

The passageway stretched on with no exit in sight. The more Vant progressed, the more jagged the rock protrusions became. Their edges seemed to grow finer. Their tips sharper.

In a moment of carelessness, Vant's arm grazed against one of the stalagmites. At first, he thought it was nothing, just a scratch. But on closer examination...

...it had cut an inch-deep slit in his flesh.

He cradled his arm and backed away. Another stone dragged against his calf. It opened a flap of skin on his leg.

Vant cursed under his breath—but quickly froze his movements. He assessed his predicament: the outcroppings were surrounding him. Pointing at him. He was ensnared, tangled up in a bizarre limbo. He searched for stable footing but lacked dexterity due to his depleted physical condition. He wanted nothing more than to back away, knowing further movement into the maze of razor-sharp rock would be insane. But the curse would not let him retreat.

With no choice, he pressed on.

His cloak and satchel repeatedly snagged stone tips, throwing off his balance. Each step resulted in an additional slash, gash, and slice of the skin. A sound filled the cavern, a trickle, like water into a basin. Vant's stomach lurched with the realization that it originated from *him*. Blood from his lacerations was dribbling onto the floor.

He contorted himself, attempting to ingress. Each movement was a desperate exercise in discipline. His strength waned. His muscles burned. His mind clouded. Consciousness was slipping away. He scanned every direction, but the intertwining of jagged rocks blocked every conceivable path through.

Yet... one option remained.

Vant navigated his hands behind his lower back. He dared not move his head—several spikes tickled his hair and ears, threatening impalement. He maneuvered his shaking fingers into his satchel, then into a pair of oversized gauntlets. He grabbed hold of them—but forced suppression of the sigh of relief that wished to follow. Inflating his lungs would have meant a punctured chest.

Donning the fist-shaped iron gloves, a flicker of strength reappeared inside of him, a nostalgic euphoria of power. He flipped hidden ignition switches inside the hand holes.

The weapons roared to life.

Flashes illuminated the cavern from the pebble-sized turbines lining the armaments. A melodic pulsing of power cells accompanied the thrusters as they rotated in sync with the embedded gyroscopes. The stabilizers and propulsion systems worked in tandem to make the heft of the gauntlets inordinately light.

Vant steadied himself, then shoved his weight forward. The knuckles of the weapons shattered the nearest spikes. He whittled himself enough space to adjust his body, then pulverized another set of spikes. And another. And another. Vant reveled in the destruction; after so many years of restraint, to let loose again felt sublime. He drank in the catharsis and freed himself from ensnarement by carving a path through the passage. At long last, he found a small opening. And dove into the crevice.

On the other side, the terrain gave out. He tumbled further into the unknown, into a darkness so thick he could feel it against his skin. He huffed for oxygen, but breath eluded him. The air was impossibly thin.

Vant righted himself and walked. He heard no footfalls; the void was suppressing all acoustics. This place was something unnatural. Ghostly. A stronghold of shadow.

He ambled on. The inky nothingness proved near impossible to navigate. His attempts to discern direction were useless; there were no landmarks, no echoes to serve as makeshift sonar, no marks in the ground, and no tracks to follow. His only guide was his gut, which he second-guessed with every step.

His intuition turned on him, arguing that going straight was somehow incorrect —*it would be so much better to pivot left or right*. With apprehension, Vant relented. He turned, but did he make a quarter-turn, or a full one? Was he now moving toward his destination or was he now further off course? All the while, he leaked blood. This had become a race to find the finish before his wounds emptied his precious life force onto the dirt.

His mind spun. His wits were abandoning him. He was losing himself in the black. He scoured his brain for an explanation for this, and for all he had experienced within the catacombs. He reflected:

A hallway that siphons life... a cavern of spikes... a labyrinth of blackness... these are more than devilish traps. They're mysteries to be solved.

Vant halted with a revelation: winding left or right brought no response from the curse. He could turn again.

This had to be a piece of the puzzle.

Had to be.

A riddle of hypothetical nature emerged in his mind:

If asked to design the most vindictive maze imaginable, where would the endpoint be?

He pondered.

Of course! At the start!

He did a swift turnaround and, sure enough, a shape materialized in the distance. He walked on.

The mass became larger. And more pronounced.

It was... a face?

Deep shadows resembled eye sockets and highlights accented a nose. It *was* a face... the face of an ominous monolith rising high into the blackness above. As he moved closer to the solemn visage, it revealed its massive dimensions. And its purpose.

The monument was a gate, and its open mouth a doorway. Vant had found the end of the labyrinth. He glimpsed what was on the other side: such perfect, *perfect* oblivion. Yet, in the furthest reaches of the emptiness, something stirred. Something tiny. Something white—

A meteor-like mass impacted with the ground in front of Vant. He scrambled away, wrestling to control his adrenaline. He rose, gathered himself, and took in what blocked his path:

A hulking golem composed of stone. No, not stone—*bone.*

The beast lumbered toward Vant. It moved as if awakened from eons of slumber.

"What—what are you?" Vant stammered. In his long life, he had seen his fair share of the bizarre, but nothing like this. Nothing he would categorize as supernatural.

The golem hobbled like an overgrown child. Its face, same as the monument, was devoid of expression. Any notion that this creature was a manifestation from delirium faded when it reached out its pillar-like arms to strike. Particles of debris wafted across Vant's face as he evaded.

He tried to reason with it. "I mean you no harm."

Hands of boulder struck ground. As Vant leapt aside, a sad, guttural moan came from the creature's innards.

"Calm down. Take a breath."

Vant had no idea if it even could. It gave no indication of comprehending his words. And instead, it took another swipe, this time twice as angry and with double the force.

"Listen, fella. I've never beaten up a... *whatever* you are. But I'll damn well start today."

It plodded on, preparing again to attack. It had one clear purpose: flatten the intruder.

Vant raised his iron fists, then jolted them downward. Two steel whips uncoiled from the knuckles of each gauntlet. Their tips stung the ground, creating a shockwave of reverberation.

He squared off with the golem. Taunted it. Flicked the lashes of his whips, which licked the dirt with a mesmerizing crackle. Combat was nothing new to Vant; he had taken apart his fair share of foes with his whip gauntlets. But a creature made of bone? *There's a first for everything,* Vant thought.

The brute charged. Vant took a well-timed dive to the side and flicked his right wrist. A whip skimmed the soil and—*crack!*—it locked around the leg of the beast. He pulled the slack taut, yanking its footing out.

The creature collapsed.

Vant jumped onto its torso. He pushed the propulsion in his weapons to *pound, pound, pound* at the golem. Its body split apart until nothing was left but a cloud of particles floating over bony rubble.

Vant blew dust off the knuckles of his gauntlets. The corner of his mouth threatened to let slip a grin; in the heat of battle, a long-lost brashness had returned.

But, within the eye sockets of the monument, viscous clumps of bone built up like tears. Another grumpy moan came from the formation.

And another.

The formations grew and grew until...

They dropped, touching down in front of the effigy's entrance. Two more golems.

Both charged. Vant slid between them. He flung his whips backward at the beasts—*thwip-crack!*—and felt the tension twist around their midsections. He shoved his hands forward. The torque lifted the golems off their feet. They collided midair in a satisfying explosion of debris.

"I could do this all day!" Vant said—but he choked on his words. Four more golems dripped from the monument's eyes.

Vant smashed. Dodged. Fought the beasts with a combination of whip work and power thrusts. But with every skirmish won, his strength waned. And with every destroyed opponent, twice as many appeared.

Another riddle?

The swarm was relentless. He had to regroup, had to get some tactical distance. After avoiding a boulder-like fist swinging past his head, Vant sprinted away from the monument...

...but his body involuntarily jackknifed.

The curse would not let him retreat. It clenched his muscular system in its claws and squeezed. The agony brought Vant to his knees.

He saw it coming, but there was nothing he could do: a golem's fist collided with his chest. The blow hurled him backward, sending him farther from the monument. The curse became enraged. Every fiber in Vant's nervous system exploded from its wrath. He hollered out in anguish.

Vant wrestled to his feet. Dozens of adversaries blocked his path. The last thing he wanted was to move *closer* to the creatures, but the vehemence of his affliction was too oppressive to endure.

He had no choice. He had to go through them.

He spat out a few choice obscenities, took a deep breath, and forced himself toward the effigy's open mouth. He pushed his gauntlets to their limits and shattered several golems, but more appeared in their stead.

He darted into the mob—the gate was in his sights. He juked around a beast. He faked out another. The monument grew near.

Two golems lunged. He avoided them, but, in doing so, he cut an angle too close to a throng of enemies lurking at the side.

Vant suffered a fist to the ribs.

A snapped leg.

An inverted elbow.

A head-butt.

He fell.

They dogpiled.

He lay limp on the floor. His spine was bent in a zigzag. Bodily fluids pooled underneath his mangled limbs.

His one good eye—the other was bashed in—tried to see something, anything, inside the mouth of the effigy. Vant knew it was the solution to the puzzle. The answer to all of the twisted riddles. The explanation for the cavern, of his forced march through the wasteland, and of his bastard curse. He had to know what lay beyond the gate. He had to.

Inside...

There was a glowing particle of purest white.

Vant heard a sound, ever so subtle, like the shifting of weight.

Then, the illumination seemed to move. And grow.

Heavy footfalls displaced gravel.

The golems, penitent and frightened, retreated.

The white grew larger... and larger.

Whatever it was, it took its time.

The footsteps grew louder as it drew closer.

And then, that which dwelled in the dark made itself known.

The white was a mask. A mask with the same expressionless face of the monument, and of the bone golems. The owner of the guise had the shape of a human—albeit a colossal one. Beneath a hooded cape, its body was wrapped in layers of fabric secured by tourniquet-tight straps. The living form inside was bound and sealed, with not a shred of skin exposed.

The figure crouched. It prodded Vant's disfigured body in a violating evaluation. Vant tried to speak, but failed. He managed only a fleshy lip smack.

The being rose, decisive. It kicked Vant's weapons out of his hands. He felt the crush of emasculation as his whip gauntlets tumbled across the dirt. Stripped of them, and all they represented, a solitary tear ran down the tip of his busted nose.

Vant tried to mouth the words *Who are you?* But nothing close came out.

Yet the figure nodded, knowingly.

And then... it spoke. The voice was raw, as if unused for the last eternity.

"Who am I?"

Vant wanted to know. *Please,* he emoted.

It shook its massive head. Futility seized Vant at his core. He tried again to mouth a phrase.

"What am I?"

Vant nodded.

A terrifyingly beautiful resounding filled the space. The ringing of a perfectly sharpened blade separating from a sheath.

The being answered:

"Death."

A scythe sliced through the air.

It cut through Vant's neck.

He felt the ripping sensation of becoming untethered.

His head rolled across the floor.

"Who am I? What am I?"

- Death

251 YEARS PRIOR

Of Heir and Allegiance

The storm raged. Wind slapped against the tent. Blades of sleet and a howling gust announced the arrival of Agmar, First Prime of the Knights of Rights. He gripped a scimitar in one hand, and a baby in the other.

"So it's true?" his voice boomed.

A husband and wife, warming by a fire, nodded.

"Show me!"

The woman delicately unwrapped a bundle in her arms. Blankets parted to reveal another baby, a boy, born to her only moments ago.

Agmar's blade clanged to the floor.

"I'll be damned! The same day as my son! The very same day!" He snatched the child away from the mother and danced, the infants bobbing in his rock-like arms. His own son cried. The other was silent.

"Never before have two of my Warrior Primes created a child together. Do you know what this means?" The parents held their tongues; Agmar rarely sought input from his subordinates. "It means your child is thick with fighting blood! He will make a fierce warrior, the perfect guardian to protect my heir!"

Agmar scrutinized the newborn. For a moment, it appeared he would not return the child to his rightful parents. But he did—forcefully. "Don't coddle him. Not even for a second!" Agmar ripped the blanket away, exposing the baby's naked body to the frost in the air. "He has a duty, and he must be ready to perform it. My son has arrived to lead, and yours to protect. These two will be raised together. They will train together. They will fight together. And yours will ensure the legacy of mine, Agmar-Burrian Terriforn, future First Prime of the Knights of Rights."

"Knights of Rights," the parents responded, as was custom. It was a sign of acknowledgment. A sign of subordination. A sign of allegiance.

"Tell me now. What is the name of this child?"
"Vant," said the husband.
"Vant Hu'l," said the wife.
"Protector Vant Hu'l," said Agmar. "Welcome to the war."

"I don't care if you *are* Death. No one cuts off my head
and gets away with it."

- Vant Hu'l

CHAPTER

The Beast and the Bidding

Blackness.

Then:

Vant shot upright. He sucked air in a panic. His heartbeat thudded against his ribcage. Nothing made sense.

He inspected his body with trembling hands. His spine was straight. His limbs were whole. His eyeball functioned.

He rubbed his face, working through layers of accumulated dust. Then he ran his fingers across his neck—and discovered a strange blemish. A scar lined its circumference, a perfect circle, going all the way around.

His mind swam with visions and sounds and screams and...

...the mask.

The expressionless guise of piercing white was burned into his psyche. He attempted to shake the haunting image from his mind when something became clear: the mask was not only in his thoughts—*it was in front of him.* What he had assumed to be a residual vision was, in fact, real. It was hovering inches away, studying him and attempting to lock eyes.

"Get away from—"

Two behemoth gloves wrapped around Vant's cloak and lifted him off his feet.

"Welcome back," Death's voice rattled. His face followed Vant's, every twitch and shake, like an intuitive mirror.

Vant closed his eyes in protest.

"Open them," Death demanded.

"Breakfast first?"

Death flung Vant across the chamber. Weightlessness. Then came a bone-rattling collision with the ground. The air raced from his lungs.

In seconds, Death was again on top of him.

"Get the hell off—"

Vant was thrown once again. A violent crash landing sent him into a roll. His body crumpled and went limp. He dry-heaved into the dirt.

"This pain is your choice," Death said.

Vant failed three times to get upright. On the fourth, he caught a glimpse of something in the dark. A glint. A few feet away...

His whip gauntlets.

Vant dove onto them. A flash of light strobed the fiend's monstrous silhouette as he activated the weapons. "I don't care if you *are* Death. No one cuts off my head and gets away with it."

And then, a surprise: "Meh-heh." An arrogant little laugh slipped from Death's throat.

Vant charged. He swung an iron fist at the creature, who seemed to vanish into the black. He threw a right cross, but hit only air. Another overzealous attack sent Vant to the floor. The damned thing moved insanely fast. It was impossible to get a bead on.

Vant's pupils darted left to right. Searching. Scanning. His eyes adjusted and the surroundings materialized. He was in the interior of the monument; the cavernous scale of the room was dizzying. A series of carved pillars, coated in centuries of accumulated dust, melted into the vastness above. The expansive realm was a palace.

Death's palace.

Wind brushed across Vant's face as his adversary stalked him. He clanged his iron fists together. "Come on!" Vant shouted.

"Meh-heh!"

Death swooped underneath Vant's feet, launching him ten feet high. *How is he doing this?* Vant pondered, before a collision with the floor interrupted the thought. Death's gigantic hands then clamped his skull and raised him up to eye level. The tender skin began pulling apart at his scar, stretching... stretching...

"It took a significant amount of time for your head to reattach itself to your neck," Death said. "Are you sure you want the two separated again?"

Vant thrashed in defiance, gurgling blood flooding into his esophagus. In a moment he would be headless. Again. He beat against Death's arms. "I'll kill you! Let me go!"

Death released his grip. Vant slammed back to the ground. He dropped his gauntlets and clutched his neck.

"Kill me?" Death said. "You misunderstand. I am the end of all things."

"You are the end of a prick."

Vant knew this was the wrong move.

Death kicked him. Hard. Vant skidded across the ground.

Then there was the sound—the terrifyingly beautiful sound—of the perfectly sharpened scythe sliding from its sheath. Though Vant tried, scrambling away was futile. Death was already upon him.

"There is nothing alive that can withstand the edge of this blade. Nothing. Yet, here we are. I watched you writhe back to life. I watched your muscles twitch while your spinal cord reconnected to your comatose brain. It was fascinating to behold. As you can imagine, distractions are sparse down here. Things can be a little... *bleak*."

The blade entered Vant's scar. The incision was skilled. Surgical. An inch of flesh opened up. Then two. Three.

"Ending your life may not be possible, but destroying your body most certainly is. As you do not wish to behave, I suppose I shall do so again. Perhaps the next time you awaken, you will appreciate me. If not, well, I have all the time in the world."

The scythe's tip hooked a vein in Vant's neck. Death manipulated it with delicate precision, tugging at it without severing it.

"Mercy!" Vant said. "Mercy."

"Mercy is *exactly* what I am. Now open wide, little immortal, and let me gaze into your soul."

Vant relented. Death's hulking frame enveloped him as the mask settled next to his face. The luminance was blinding, but Vant did not waver. He returned the stare into the creature's eye sockets. A connection between them formed, and Vant fell into a state of surrender.

His spine iced over and tingles danced across his skin. Invisible hands entered through his eyes, went past his brain, moved into his lungs, and wrapped around his heart. He sensed he was being seen—truly seen—for the first time. Not for what was on the surface, but for what lay dormant in the furthest reaches of his subconscious. He experienced perfect vulnerability, as if his insides were being outwardly exposed.

When the deed was done, Death casually tossed Vant aside. Physical-world reality returned with a crash and, once again, Vant found himself collapsed on the ground.

"I have seen through your eyes," Death said. "I have seen your weaknesses. I have seen your misunderstandings. And I have seen your misinterpretations of reality, which are extensive. It must be quite atrocious, to exist as you do."

"Thanks," Vant muttered, short on breath.

"To be the person you think you are, to live the way you have lived, to hold on to so much... I would rather *die* than trade places with you. And that is saying something. However, I have looked deeper, past the feeble clutches of your mind. I have seen all of which I needed to see. I have decided... you'll do."

"I'll do?"

"You'll do... my bidding."

Vant stood on wobbly legs. "Come again?"

"I have chosen you because of your particular... *sensibilities*. You are an ideal candidate for my needs. You have been made immortal, and you shall remain so, until you fulfill your purpose."

"I want no part of this. Whatever this is."

"It is too late. You and I are tethered. Your anatomy longs for death, which is what pulls you to me. It will never stop, no matter how much you resist."

"So you've doomed me? Take it back! Let me go!"

"If you wish to be free, you must placate the urges inside. I shall provide you with ample opportunity to do so. Do as I command and the leash will loosen, so to speak. Fail to do so, and things will become... *worse*."

"No. No chance. I didn't choose this."

"Ah, but you see, you *did*. You are here because of what you have done. Because of what you are capable of. Because of what you *really* are. As of this moment, you belong to something... *else*. You *will* do my bidding. I am quite certain of this."

"You're wrong. I refuse. You've got nothing on me. There is nothing you can take from me that hasn't already been taken."

"A foolish thought. You see, it's not what I'll *take* from you..." Death gently took Vant's hands in his own. "...it's what I'll *break* from you." He snapped them backward. A juicy crunch of bone mixed with Vant's shrill screams. His hands flopped loosely at the wrists.

"You son of a bitch!"

"Hold your tongue, lest I rip it from you!"

"I've suffered enough! End this already!"

"Choose your words carefully. I am *exceedingly* literal. Do you desire an end to your everlasting life?"

"Yes!"

"Your lack of gratitude is tantamount to stupidity." Death turned his back on Vant. "Have you any idea what your soul went through to gain entry to the physical realm? What unfathomable pieces had to fall into place to manifest you in this organic form?"

"How would I know that?"

"One may assume," Death looked over his shoulder at Vant, "it was substantial. How very cavalier of you to toss it all away, as if it meant nothing."

"Toss it away like you keep tossing me around this room?"

"I will confide in you. I do not take very good care of my... *things*."

"Your things? I have a name! My name is—"

Death swatted Vant onto his back and pinned him to the ground. "I loathe being interrupted. Call it a... *fatal* flaw of mine. To save us from future outbursts, I shall have to gag you."

Death lowered the scythe handle to Vant's face. The base of the shaft, jagged with splintered lumber, kissed Vant's lips. His eyes flared with terror as Death applied pressure. The rotted wood tore into his lips, and the shaft worked its way toward his flailing tongue.

"A name is meaningless," Death hissed. "Identity is the veil of the underdeveloped. I tolerate you not for what you call yourself, but solely for your inability to expire." He pushed the scythe handle lower; Vant's teeth bent, clinging to their roots. More pressure was applied. More. Teeth split from gums. Vant choked, spraying red-stained saliva from the corners of his cheeks. His body convulsed. The lumber pressed his tongue down his throat.

Death continued, "Exhaustion, hunger, thirst, and suffocation did not end you. You did not perish in my torturous tunnel. You were not pierced in my passageway. You did not lose yourself in my labyrinth. My guardian golems did break you, and I myself removed your silly little head, yet still you arose, still impetuous, still not humble before me. But, for all your bravado, make no mistake, you *will* do my bidding. Refuse, and I shall use you as my... *entertainment*. I will break your bones, remove your skin, and torture you in any way that so intrigues me. Know this... I can be quite creative."

Death ripped the scythe butt from Vant's mouth. Bloody spit fountained from his lips. "Now, before I was so rudely interrupted, you had something on your mind?"

Vant had no way to form words from his fleshy soup of oral faculties.

"Go on. I insist," Death said with a fiendish mock.

Vant hacked up bile and teeth, spasming with trauma.

"Pitiable immortal. May this serve as a reminder that nothing—*nothing*—will hurt you the way that I can. I have seen into the darkest reaches of your subconscious and I know which parts of your body you most fear to lose."

Vant quavered.

"Alas, the choice is now yours. Suffer an eternity of disfigurement by my hands, or do my bidding... out *there*." He waved brazenly, indicating the outside world.

Vant heaved. Tried to speak.

"Come again?" Death asked.

Vant managed to form two words: "Pain... stop..."

"I take those words as a confirmation of our arrangement. I shall stop your pain, tiny immortal. I shall stop your pain. They say time heals all wounds, do they not?" Death palmed Vant's head. "Let us find out."

He smashed it into the floor.

Vant fell unconscious.

"Now open wide, little immortal, and let me gaze into your soul."

- Death

243 YEARS PRIOR

Of Knights and Rights

"Go ahead. Pick my gun. For luck."

Vant, still so little, looked up at his father's arsenal. The polish of each firearm seemed to shine just for him.

"This one?" he asked.

"A shotgun. Good for close quarters. If someone creeps up on me, then boom! *They don't stand a chance. Bad for distance, though. I'll have to get right up close and personal."*

Vant scrunched his face, then pointed at the adjacent weapon. "That one?"

"Assault rifle. Much better at a distance, and it's really powerful. Downside, it's a heavy bugger."

"What about that one? The oozer."

"Ooh-zee! Uzi!" Vant hid his eyes, embarrassed by his father's chuckles. "Super-light, super portable. Shoots fast and mean. Accuracy isn't great, but if there are ten foes coming after your dad, then ten are going down!"

"That one," Vant said. "The ooh-zee."

"Get it for me, son."

Vant bit his lip with concentration and carefully lifted the machine gun off the rack. He was ashamed it felt so heavy when his dad had said it was so light.

"Good boy." He took the weapon from the child's hands.

Vant's mother spanked her son on the rear. "Out of the way, little warrior!" She removed the shotgun, the assault rifle, a magnum, and a hunting knife from the collection.

Vant's father widened his eyes for his son's amusement and said, "Your mom doesn't know how to pack light!"

"When will you be home?"

"Hard to tell. We're headed to Banker's Hollow. It's not far from here."

"Is it dangerous?"

"It is. But it won't be a problem for your mom and me."

"Why not?"

"Because of our cunning. No one can sneak up on us. Not even little snakes like you, Terrii!" He hoisted Agmar's son from a pile of fabrics.

"Lemme go! How did you see me?"

"I didn't see you, I could hear you breathing!" He dangled Terrii upside-down by the ankles and tickled him, the boy's shirt falling over his head.

"Put me down! My dad will punish you for this!"

"Ask Agmar who saved his life twice last week. Fair is fair. You're mine now!"

"Oh, put him down," Vant's mother said with assertion—but her eyes betrayed her amusement.

Terrii was returned to his feet. The boy returned the nicety with a kick to the shin.

"Hey! Get back here!"

Terrii hid behind Vant. "Get him!"

Vant puffed out his chest, but relented. Instead, he asked his father, "Who will you be fighting?"

"Bad guys."

"Why are they bad?"

"Sometimes people do bad things. The Knights of Rights were formed to stop them. You must always do what's right, Vant. Don't forget that. Ever."

"Yes, father," he said.

"That goes for you too, Terrii."

"Fine. Then I'm telling my dad about this!"

Vant's father reached toward an axe on the wall. Terrii and Vant ran from the tent, screaming and squealing with laughter.

"That curse. That damned curse. Ripped me from my love. My life. My home. The years... the years. How many lost?"

- Vant Hu'l

CHAPTER

The Wanderer and the Wilderness

Vant woke.

He snorted some dust that had built up on his whiskers. And sneezed.

He scraped crust from his eyes and, when they regained focus, he oriented himself to his environment—including the bed of bones on which he lay. In his blackout, he had been deposited in Death's torturous tunnel, near the entrance to the cavern. The carved faces of misery surrounding him gasped for breath. "Anyone else hung over?" Vant asked them.

He assessed his condition: hands healed, teeth back in, no unsealed holes in the skin... all essentials appeared to be in working order. *Could use a haircut, though,* he thought. *Definitely a shave.* He ran his fingers across his neck and tickled his battle scar, the perfectly symmetrical scythe mark. It served as a staunch reminder that something horrid—that *Death*—had, in fact, cut his head off.

Several failed attempts to right himself on the pile of corpses caused the scraps to displace. Among the depths of decay, he noticed a twinkle. It was a familiar—and very welcome—sight: a Corpo-Capsule. He dug into the heap and unearthed the pellet.

It sparkled green when cleared of a coat of grime. Vant shoved it into his mouth, but there was no saliva to help him swallow. He spat it out and scrambled through the bones looking for another pill, which he soon found. This one sparkled blue. He popped it into his mouth, bit down, and enjoyed the greatest sensation he had known in ages: moisture. Vant savored the luscious wetness of the capsule as it worked its miraculous science inside of him. Blue Corpo-Capsules, when ingested, sparked a controlled reaction which bonded the hydrogen and oxygen present within the pockets of a living body to create water.

With his thirst quenched, he tried the green pill again. This time, it slid down his lubricated throat. Sheer bliss. Energy capsules were packed with synthesized proteins, vitamins, amino acids, and a high volume of calories to provide nutrition and restore vitality. The topper was a gas that expanded inside the stomach to create the satisfaction of fullness after only one dose.

After this feast of a lifetime—or a few lifetimes, in Vant's case—he shoveled through the heap in search of additional flickering treasures. The remains contained a hidden stockpile of Corpo-Capsules scattered among the expedition gear of the dead. He connected the dots in his mind: the adventurers who had travelled this far into the wasteland would have required nourishment and, unlike Vant, not everyone had the convenience of immortality. Light and portable, Corpo sustenance and moisture pills would have been the best solution. With only a grip of them, a traveler could sustain life for months—even years—instead of having to lug around a perishable supply of food and water. Had Vant been given notice that *his* trip would have gone on for so long, he, too, would have carried a supply.

Readying to depart, Vant discovered his satchel beside him. He noted how polite it was for Death to have wrapped up his weapons, *but he didn't pack me a lunch,* Vant thought. The capsules would suffice. He tossed an excavated handful into his pack and set off.

As Vant approached the exit, golden sunbeams poured in from the world outside. His prolonged sojourn in the darkness of Death's cavern had made him alien to the light. He shielded his eyes from the sting of brightness and crawled out onto the surface.

He inhaled his first breath of fresh oxygen. The unexpected purity of the atmosphere, in contrast to the stale air underground, caused him to gag. Dust and muck poured out of his nostrils. He coughed up mucus and dried blood, heaving until his lungs were finally functioning again.

Vant stood. He stretched his atrophied limbs and let the sunlight blast him in the face. The sun's cleansing rays ran over his skin. Sweet liberation hugged his heart as he stepped away from the hole. After so much time shackled to the will of the curse, he again had the ability to walk wherever he wished. As promised, Death had calmed the malady; Vant celebrated by moving in any direction he chose. He even hopped backward a few times, just for kicks. His first nibble of free will in ages tasted damn good.

Yet along with the newfound freedom came significant confusion on what exactly he had agreed to—or what he had been *forced* to agree to. Apparently, he had made some sort of deal with a demon, but he would be damned if he knew what his end of the bargain was.

"You'll do... my bidding."

Death's voice echoed through his head as he internally re-experienced the horrors of the catacombs he had just endured. Shivering from the thought, he took a firm stance against going back to ask for directions.

Instead, he exercised his long-lost right to autonomy and began the journey out of the desert. He might have a new job working for Death, but, right now, he would make his own choices. No scythe was being held to his neck at this moment. So he put one foot in front of the other and followed his makeshift compass, his shadow, away from Death's lair.

The familiar, rhythmic chant of footfalls splashed up from desert grit. But, something was different this time. The weight of his pack seemed off. And, something was knocking around inside.

He searched the satchel and found...

Death's mask.

He ran the artifact through his hands. It was smooth. Cool to the touch. Masterfully crafted. Almost paranormal in its expressionless perfection. It was the purest of white, although it did not glow, as it had when worn by Death.

Vant's fingers brushed across the soft, inviting texture of the underside. He inched the mask toward his face. When close, it leapt from his hands and latched onto his skin. The icy chill Vant had experienced when Death gazed into his soul returned to his body.

The world became inky black, yet somehow, he could still see—*feel*—the environment around him. The contours of the sand, the outlines of the clouds, the stone and gravel... everything took on an otherworldly, ethereal quality.

Vant was captivated by his arms, which left multicolored trails in their movement. The mask was reacting to him, and to the world around him, but what *exactly* it was trying to say was lost on him. *Some bidding,* Vant thought, in regard to Death's cryptic guidance. He tugged at the mask, which had fused to his skin at the edges. It disconnected, but it did not relent easily. It *wanted* to be on his face.

Vant hiked on. He rolled the mask around his fingertips and pondered his new life under Death's charge. *"You must placate the urges inside,"* he had said. What would be required of him? What did this mean? Would the curse someday return? Would he ever be truly free?

He hiked with his legs on autopilot, frequently glancing down to stare into the void of the mask's eyes.

He did this for the next several months.

One day, there was grass. And eventually, plants. Trees. Green never looked so golden. The first flower Vant laid eyes on, a pink and yellow thing, captivated him for close to an hour. Color had new meaning after his time spent in the beige bleakness of the wastes.

Upon arrival at a stream no more than a foot wide, Vant lay down and let the water roll over his hair. Heaven. Soon enough, he located a river to bathe in, berries to munch on, rocks to cut his beard with, and small woodland creatures to chat with

—and subsequently kill, cook, and eat. His first solid meal, flame-roasted frog, ran through his digestive system without so much as a pause in his stomach. But Vant kept trying, and, at last, his anatomy accepted tangible proteins again.

With the restoration of his physicality, mental musings and internal self-talk also returned. Feelings followed. He experienced the damp of depression upon remembering his last days in Land Escape. The sting of grief over a peaceful life long gone. The pain of heartbreak when forced to abandon his beloved.

His beloved... desire for her turned into longing. Then anger.

That curse. That damned curse. Ripped me from my love. My life. My home. The years... the years. How many lost?

The thoughts could not be contained. They rushed like rapids through a decimated dam.

Death stole me. Tortured me. Has me by the balls. Fine. He can have me... but not yet. I'm going home, to see my beloved. I'll find a way to set things right. Somehow.

First stop, Land Escape.

The return trip progressed. Once near the habitable areas, Vant raised his guard. He was well aware of the risk of walking through open spaces during the day, and even more when carrying valuables (his weapons, the handful of Corpo-Capsules, and a relic given to him by a demigod certainly counted). In the wild, hijackings by nomads were serious business, and often fatal.

For an additional precaution, Vant shifted to a sleep-by-day, hike-by-night routine. This provided no guarantee of safety—nomads were skilled hunters at any hour—but he assumed it hedged his bet at least a touch.

While he based his navigation upon celestial objects and topographical patterns, it was a sound that confirmed he was heading in the right direction: the subtle yet unmistakable *shoom* of a Corpo-Bot in flight. The presence of the bot hinted at a nearby township, one that utilized Corpo and its fleet of robots for delivery services, commerce, and goods. The automatons were wondrous devices, marvels of technological craftsmanship and impressive in their versatility. They flew with immediacy and most deliveries were done in minutes due to their efficient network of hubs. Resembling a scarab when in kiosk mode and a praying mantis while in flight, each was constructed with the iconic brass that represented Corpo, the grand robotic city.

He increased his pace toward the reverberation. While this bot was most certainly not from Land Escape, following its trail would lead Vant into the habitable zones, the area of land where most of civilization lay. He remained alert, knowing that the closer he got to the township the robot came from, the more palpable the danger of nomad attacks would become.

Sure enough, he located the structure. Townships, from the outside, were mysteries. No one knew what treasures—or perils—waited inside. Vant had enough experience to know that Land Escape, the last dogma-free township, meant safety, while any other, such as this one, could very well suck him up and never spit him out. Over the years, many a wanderer had been seduced by the possibility of a warm bed or hot meal, only to fall victim to indoctrination, imprisonment, or an even worse fate.

The hexagonal structure before Vant looked as if it had been air-dropped into the isolated pocket of land. While the building was nonconforming to the rugged surroundings of the wilderness, the township's once-white walls were now coated in dirt from a substantial period of neglect. As this one did, townships often displayed iconography to convey the nature of their prevalent beliefs. This served the purposes of either attracting wanderers who would be welcomed as potential converts, or frightening away any unwelcome guests.

The renderings on this particular township's walls were simple and sterile, neutral but welcoming. Basic shapes indicated sickly people being cared for, and injuries being treated. Dogmatic societies dedicated themselves beyond the point of obsession to one methodology—and only one—as their solution to life extension. This township's dogma was clearly that of medical science as the hopeful path to everlasting life.

Although its philosophy seemed sane enough, Vant was still skittish. No dogmatic township was to be trusted, as their psychoses often ran deep from vast numbers of years spent toiling in isolation. Even dogmatic societies with the best of intentions were feverishly protective of their ways of life. Yet, more than the town's belief system, there was something else triggering Vant's nervous intuition. The culprit was the front door—or lack thereof. It had been pulverized, and all that remained was a mess of concrete and rubble.

Someone or something had attacked this town. *Impossible,* Vant thought, even though the evidence was right there in front of him. His mind could not comprehend it; wars of any kind, even small battles, had been nonexistent for more than a century. Nomads, of course, were a threat to any township, but they were, by nature, disorganized. They had nowhere near the wherewithal to launch an offensive attack of such a scope. While another township could have been responsible, the dogmatic simply had no reason to go after one another. Resources were abundant thanks to Corpo, and land was plentiful in the habitable zones. But, even more so, dogmatic societies considered contrarian beliefs to be a hindrance. As such, they all existed in unwavering, unconditional isolation.

Eerier still: this place, at a glance, seemed empty. Vant listened for any indicators of life and heard nothing. He knew he should have been able to hear something—*anything*—past the entrance, but it was silent.

The indicators of conflict were far too great to ignore; Vant, who had been present for the final conflicts after The Shift, knew this attack held a tremendous significance. Ignoring his curiosity would have been an impossible battle; the fighter's blood within him *had* to see what was going on.

He entered the keep.

Immediately, the deeply self-important mindset of the township arose. *In Meddia, All Are Cured,* read an elaborate mural in the lobby. Marble-like statues displayed people in various states of sickness with god- and goddess-like saviors treating them. Several of the sculptures had been damaged, as had the wall separating the lobby from the main crux of the township. As if the invaders had carved a path right through.

Deeper inside, the structure reeked of chemicals and disinfectants. The temperature regulation chilled Vant's skin. Chambers and chambers of cleanrooms dotted the encampment; each was full of elaborate devices designed to remove, manipulate, or repair human anatomy. Crystalline readouts projected intricate diagrams of the body; many of the images showed the human form in positions it was not intended to be in, missing key body parts, or with invasive-looking devices placed inside questionable areas.

Vant could see winding stairwells leading to lodgings, as well as dedicated areas for dining and quarantine. He peered down a hallway filled with laboratories where, behind the glass of each room, he could make out mechanical devices for the purposes of experimentation. Most featured scalpels, corkscrews, and cutting devices. All of the rooms had shackles for restraining patients.

Evidence of conflict was everywhere: shattered glass, discarded weapons, and scorch marks from firearms. His inquisitiveness was running wild, but Vant had seen enough. He knew it was unwise to linger even one moment longer than he had to, so he darted back outside and into the woodlands. Protected again by cover, he considered the implications of this discovery.

Why the invasion? he wondered. The attackers did not hold the township for their own purposes, so territorial possession was clearly not the goal. Similarly, all of the equipment inside appeared undisturbed. Unless they were after something small and specific, this was not a robbery. If it were a righteous thing, certainly those responsible would have burned the place to the ground or left some kind of message. All of this added up to a seemingly senseless assault. Nothing seemed missing except for the people, though Vant assumed they must have fled when the township was compromised. *But no dead bodies? he thought. Not even one?*

He moved on from Meddia and the mystery, though it travelled with him in his mind.

Shoom.

After another Corpo-Bot passed by overhead, Vant set course due north, underneath its trajectory, following its lingering smoke trail. This meant he was navigating in the direction of Corpo, which served as the perfect landmark. The automated city was roughly a thousand miles away but, if he headed in that direction, his route would eventually intersect with Land Escape.

Vant traveled for another week before he spotted a clear indicator confirming his course. A small clump of vegetation on the forest floor held a bluish tint; it was faint, but detectable to savvy eyes. The foliage around Land Escape featured this unique coloration, so Vant knew the deeper the saturation became, the closer he drew to the township.

Then, one day, as the sun rose, there it was.

The city was not hidden; it was far too expansive to hide. Yet painted blue patterns camouflaged the walls, matching the surrounding brush. The scope of the structure and the sounds of liveliness inside hinted at the thriving metropolis behind its grand walls, walls that encompassed the city in a perfect circle and angled inward to an open apex. The fortifications were just steep enough to make climbing into the city an impossibility, though they allowed an abundance of sunshine and fresh air to stream in, along with Corpo-Bots. Upon sight of the township, Vant became sentimental; Land Escape had sheltered him and been his home for many, many years.

Still a good distance away, Vant circled the city until he located two massive trees carved into pillars: the symbolic barrier between Land Escape and the outside world. Two hundred-foot-high steel doors rose up from behind the redwoods, like giant protectors of the city. And, before them lay a thicket that represented a safe zone within the town's perimeter of protection.

As he approached, his intuition overrode his senses: nomads *had* to be nearby. This was their way, lying in wait for travelers arriving to the city, or pouncing on deserters leaving it.

Vant stopped, lowered himself, and scoured the surroundings.

Nothing.

He had to get to the protected area, somehow. Any nomads would know better than to cause trouble within that perimeter, as bored city snipers could be itching for some target practice.

An idea came to Vant.

He quietly tucked into his satchel and located Death's mask.

Let's see what this thing does when there are people around, Vant thought.

He put it on.

Ice coated his insides as the mask bonded to his face. The environment shifted into darkness, as it had in the desert. The bluish greenery turned ghostly black.

But Land Escape... it was different. Something *phenomenal* was happening behind its walls. Particles of luminescence beamed from inside the city. The glowing silhouettes of a thousand or more people combined to create a gigantic mass of glowing light. It was astounding. Beautiful, even to Vant, who rarely appreciated beauty. Peaceful, even to Vant, who had known peace only once in his entire life.

He was entranced by the ripples of light that moved through the township, but he managed to pull his focus back to the forestry surrounding the city. Sure enough,

Vant could identify the glowing shapes of nomads concealed among the brush and branches.

Right there, he thought, noticing a weak spot where the concentration of bodies was thin. *There's my way in.*

Vant removed the mask and took a steadying breath. He sped through the unprotected pocket and crossed into the open. He was now exposed—but safely inside Land Escape's perimeter of protection. He heard a curse from a nearby tree. Then another. Then a barrage of threatening taunts.

Vant held his ground. He dared not speak, not to the nomads, and not to the Land Escape gate guard now most likely observing him. He knew the protocol; he needed to be on the good side of whatever watchman was currently on duty. Whoever manned the door was the last word on whether a person was in, or out.

After a few minutes, static, a hiss, and a voice sounded over loudspeakers. "Nomad or wanderer?"

"Wanderer," Vant said.

"Deserter or cast-out?" the guard asked over lip smacks. Vant, it seemed, was disturbing his breakfast.

"Deserter." Specific answers to this test were essential. Vant knew a wrong one meant he would be denied access to the township, and the nomads in the trees would be granted their opportunity to attack.

"From?"

This was a problem. Vant's only option was to lie. If he admitted to deserting Land Escape years ago, he would be rejected outright. No second chances, with townships.

"Strata," Vant made up.

"Dogma?"

"None."

"Tribute?"

This was new. Once a sanctuary for those who had escaped the clutches of dogmatic townships, Land Escape, it now seemed, charged admission.

"Tribute?" the voice asked again.

"Pills," Vant answered. "Corpo-Capsules. A handful or so."

Branches rustled in the nearby trees. Vant imagined the hidden wildlings salivating at the thought of his loot. To the faceless guard enjoying his meal, Vant mumbled a silent plea to hurry the hell up.

"Show 'em."

May as well taunt starving bears with a steak, Vant thought. This had the potential of turning sour, fast. *But what choice do I have?* He removed the pills from his satchel and held them up.

He heard the tension of an arrow drawing in a bow. A gun loading. A knife whetting. Several voices, in hushed tones, conspired to attack.

Too much time was dragging on. Vant was about to bail when, at last, the guard spoke, giving a canned speech with his mouth full:

"Deserter, upon admission, you will be subjected to a full-body search. You will renounce any civil rights you may have had in any other townships, and you shall hereby relinquish any entitlements that may be interpreted as a threat to the liberty of Land Escape. You will, without protest, turn over any material goods until such time it is decided you are not harboring malicious intent. Those items may or may not be returned to you, depending upon multiple criteria. If we determine at any point during the interview process that you are a menace to our peaceful way of life, you will be immediately cast out, your belongings will be forfeited, and you will be permanently denied re-entry into Land Escape."

The guard slurped his beverage.

"Now, this next part isn't in the book, but I like to say it anyway. If you so much as *look* at one of our citizens in a way I don't approve of, you will be gunned down without discrimination by one of our marksmen. Some of them have pretty good aim. When they're sober."

A camouflaged sniper on the wall fired off a warning shot. A flock of birds scattered from the trees. Vant almost lost control of his bladder, the gunfire was so sudden and deafening.

Hilarious, boys. Hilarious. "I understand. I agree," Vant said.

The sound of a crumbling wrapper indicated the completion of the guard's meal. "Security team, prepare for deserter entry and immediate processing. Turrets active. High alert. Threat level... medium."

A symphony of guns powered-up. Targeting lasers peppered Vant in dots.

"Deserter, approach the doors."

He did, arms raised.

"Deserter, halt. Deserter, remove all equipment and personal belongings and place them in the scanner."

Vant dropped his satchel and robes into the chute, experiencing relief. Unless the nomads had an interest in his ratty undergarments, he was now safe from raiders.

"Deserter, step away."

Vant stepped to the side. The enormous steel doors protecting the township cracked open—but only enough for a lone person to walk through. It made sense as to why, but Vant felt it quite anticlimactic for them to open only a few feet wide.

"Deserter, enter and submit."

Vant walked through the entrance.

"Deserter, on your knees."

He knelt.

A detail of guards surrounded him.

They pointed firearms at his head.

The door slammed shut behind him.

"If you so much as look at one of our citizens in a way I don't approve of, you will be gunned down without discrimination."

- The gate guard of Land Escape

PART
TWO

E S C A P E

"I'll bring you some grub."

- Kryystin

CHAPTER

The Homecoming and the Heartbroken

The Land Escape guards led Vant into an office building. In stark contrast to the wilderness, the indoors were unfamiliar. Confining. The air felt processed and had an aroma of stale coffee.

They proceeded to a holding area. The guards indicated a chair for Vant to sit in, which he did. They posted up at the door and watched him; Vant stared straight ahead, on his best behavior.

No one said a thing.

After a time, a rotund, uniformed man walked into the room with a bundle of documents under one arm and Vant's belongings in the other. He handed back Vant's robes and plopped down at a desk. Vant dressed silently.

The man thumbed through the stack, then slid over a translucent, paper-thin sheet. Vant looked into the crystalline display and saw a visual of his own face staring back. In the image he was clean-shaven, bright-eyed, and handsome—not the bearded, sunken-eyed husk currently slouched in the holding chamber. The visual was from long ago, when he once held residence in Land Escape.

"Records say that's you," said the man. "That you?"

Vant kept his poker-face, but ran hundreds of possible responses in his head. He settled on the least clever of them all: "Nope."

"Kinda looks like you." He raised the sheet up to Vant's face, studying the resemblance. "Used to live here, kid?"

"No, sir."

"Records say so."

"Records must be wrong."

"Not likely." He squinted at Vant. "How old are you?"

Vant had no idea. His body had ceased aging as a young man—ceased the day he died for the first time. He lied, "Twenty-nine."

"You sure? Says here you're a hundred-twenty." Vant swallowed the lump in his throat. "And, it says you deserted Land Escape twenty-three years ago."

Vant went dizzy. Twenty-three years. He had been away for twenty-three years. He had no idea it had been *anywhere* near that long.

He wrangled his composure and responded, "As you can see, I'm definitely not a century old."

"If you were, I was going to ask you, 'What's your secret?' My receding hairline could use a few tips!"

Vant fake-smiled.

The guard rifled through Vant's satchel. He fished out the Corpo-Capsules and placed them to the side. He removed the rest of the contents and said, "Got some weird stuff in this pack of yours, kid. Gloves and a mask? Masquerade ball I don't know about?" He fiddled with the whip gauntlets but did not discover the hidden activation switches. Instead he turned his attention to the mask. And started to put it on.

Vant's stomach dropped. He prepared to tackle the guard but then the unexpected happened: nothing. The man pressed it against his face for a few seconds, then put it aside. Vant concealed a sigh of relief.

The guard imprinted several sheets with finger swipes and stood up out of his chair. "Your lucky day. Gonna let you in. Word of advice? Behave yourself. We don't mess around. One step outta line and..." he whistled and made a gesture like he was tossing something over a wall.

Vant raised an eyebrow.

"Okay, fine. Not like we have a catapult or anything. But cause any trouble and we'll shove you out the door and let the nomads have you. Oh, and one more thing..." Vant scratched his forehead in a preemptive strike to kill off a bead of nervous sweat that was forming. "I'm taking a small 'processing fee.' Gotta update my records. After all, as you say, they're wrong." He snickered, handed back Vant's satchel, and pocketed the handful of Corpo-Capsules.

"Welcome to Land Escape, kid."

Vant walked past a few patrolmen who politely acknowledged him; the civil servants' attitudes were much friendlier now that he was a citizen. He went through the final security checkpoint and climbed the stairs leading to an atrium, the entranceway to the central hub of the city.

The view was magnificent. Lush. Dotted with the bluish-green trees so iconic to the township. He took a moment to drink in the homes, parks, buildings, and shops protected by the township's walls. Overhead, Corpo-Bots rhythmically flew into and out of the open-air roof, as did birds and fireflies.

And the people...

The place bustled with spirited townspeople going about their days. They were decent souls living a free existence in a city that protected them, cared for them, and afforded them the opportunity to pursue lives away from the threats of extremist dogmatism and nomad savagery. A kind of buzz emanated from them, a calm, warm buzz created by the mishmash of cheerful voices. Vant soaked up the serene spectacle for quite a while; the citizens' joy, hopes, and laughter—in stark contrast to his own years of isolation—created a feeling of blissful overwhelm within.

But the faces... none of them were the same. Vant had spent more than two decades separated from civilization, and now he recognized no one. The children he once knew would now be adults. The adults he once knew would now be seniors. If any of them were people with whom he was once acquainted, they were all now unrecognizable.

Vant succumbed to a loop running in his brain: *Twenty-three years. Twenty-three years. Twenty-three years.*

His love would be in her forties now, yet he retained a physical appearance the same as the day he was forced to abandon her. He wondered where she was, and what kind of a life she had made for herself. Had she gotten married? Or had she spent every waking moment staring out her window, tragically awaiting her lost lover's return? Maybe she had come to despise him. Or, perhaps, she had chosen a path of celibacy. *Hopefully,* Vant thought. The possibilities spun in his head.

He took the walkway into town. In a shop window, he glimpsed his reflection. It was... not good. Tattered robes, a mangy beard, covered in dirt... he thought better of reconnecting with her in this disheveled state. She had waited this long; what was one more day? He made the decision to rest up, clean up, and make himself presentable for a very strange homecoming, indeed.

Vant took a flight of steps into the shadiest side of town, the quiet and least occupied portion closest to the wall. He entered the first public lodging he came across. It was a nice little place. Quaint.

As he walked through the door, an old lady greeted him with a kind, but careful, grin. "Deserter, huh? Well, welcome, stranger. Whether you were born here or escaped here, here you are. It's all the same to me. No judgment, business is business! So, what can I do for you?"

"Would kill for a bed," Vant said. The lady looked at him sideways. "Oh! Not that I will!"

"Phew! You never know, stranger. Sometimes deserters need an adjustment period to adapt to our 'no-killing' lifestyle!"

Vant went red, ashamed of his social awkwardness spawned from years of isolation. "I have—er—I *had* money. The guards took it as my entry fee. Can I pay you later? I've got capsules saved up with Corpo." It was the truth. Every person was entitled to one green and one blue Corpo-Capsule per day, retrievable at any Corpo-Bot. As they were accruable and Vant had not accessed his share in years, he would have no problem settling up with the innkeeper.

She waved off Vant's worry. "Head on over to room twelve, it's clean and waiting for you. Why don't you pop in the shower, get rid of that odor—no offense—and I'll bring you some grub. Oh, and toss your clothes in the hallway and I'll have 'em cleaned."

Ashamed, Vant looked down at his cloak. "Can I promise you some extra pills to drop them off at a Corpo-Bot to be mended? I'm afraid they're all I have, so I'll be stuck in my room until they're tidy. I don't think I should walk around in the buff on my first day in Land Escape."

She covered her face. "A naked man running around? How horrible! Oh, my virgin eyes!" After they shared a laugh, she said, "I'll send 'em off to Corpo and bring 'em back when they're done. Call it six-green-four and we're square for everything."

Vant, taken aback by her kindness, said, "I'm good for it, I promise. You're an angel. Thank you."

"And I'll flirt back with you after you've scrubbed off that grime! No offense! Can't really tell if you're cute under all that muck, stranger!" She laughed as Vant, well aware of his revolting appearance, winked, and headed off to his lodging.

Entering number twelve, he was amazed at how quiet a room could be. The silence was deafening, in a good way. He stripped, tossed his clothes into the hallway, and barely made it to the bed before twenty consecutive hours of nonstop snoring commenced.

He dreamed of Death.
Behind his back.
In front of him.
Everywhere.
Nowhere.
The laugh, "Meh-heh."
The scythe.
A flash of steel.
His head, off.
Its eyes blinked.

Vant jolted awake.

He was drenched in a freezing sweat. He wrestled for control over his heartbeat. He breathed... breathed.

He massaged the scar on his neck. *I'm alive,* he thought. *Just a nightmare. Nightmares I can handle.*

He stood up. Stretched.

Outside his door, Vant discovered a brand-new pair of boots—a gift from the innkeeper—as well as his robes, restored to perfection. He had all but forgotten the masterful craftsmanship of the hand-sewn construction; the thick yet pliable black fabric had a brilliant sheen, and he enjoyed the subtle details such as the double-enforced stitches and the multilayered panels tailored to his fit. He reflected on the last time he saw them in this magnificent state—then experienced a stab of emotion as the memory was pulled from his subconscious. His cheeks tingled and his eyes welled, signaling an incoming wave of emotion.

He rubbed the cloak on his face and sobbed into the sleeve.

It was all too much.

Vant gave himself a thorough bathing, scouring himself raw. He shaved off his beard and his crispy hair—and even had to prune his rotted eyebrows. The layers of crud, dead skin, ticks, and blisters made a mess. *I'll have to leave a good tip,* he thought.

As if on cue, there was a knock at the door, followed by a delicious smell that buckled his knees. He stuck his head out and discovered a serving tray with food that had been prepared by the innkeeper.

It lasted twenty-two seconds and never made it into the room. Best meal he ever had, no question.

Vant dressed and exited the room a new man.

His robes swished as he walked; they no longer scraped against the floor, as his posture was tall again. He passed through the lobby, hiding an embarrassed smile when the lady who ran the joint hooted, hollered, and catcalled. He winked at her again, to which she replied, "Gonna need more than a wink to settle your tab, handsome!"

The day was astonishing. Crystal clear. He moved through the energetic city and marveled at how little had changed since he had been away. Same stores. Same streets. A few new odds and ends, but nothing major. Same clothing styles. Same feel. *You don't mess with the classics,* he figured.

Vant arrived in the town square where he could run an important errand. He approached a cluster of docked Corpo-Bots awaiting customers who required information, who came to withdraw their daily allotment of Corpo-Capsules, or who wished to exchange pills for goods or services. Nearby, a group of local children huddled by the bots.

"Kick it!" the leader of the youths demanded of the littlest kid.

"Fine!" He nudged the machine with his foot.

"Warning," a polite voice emitted from the robot.

"Again! Again!" the other kids chanted.

The peanut trembled. The bot just sat there. Its brass pipes hugged its frame in brilliant ways and glinted in the sun.

"Do it!" the bully commanded. The small child tapped it again.

"Final warning," the bot said. The head of the automaton, a glassy dome, pivoted toward the child. A door in its chest slid open and a weapon barrel telescoped out. The other bullies jumped back, cheering in amusement.

"One more time! One more time!"

It was unwise to taunt a Corpo-Bot three times—that much was common knowledge—but few knew what happened when you did.

Vant walked up to the leader of the pack and shoved him in the forehead.

"Hey!" the bully protested.

"Need to use this bot," Vant said.

"Use a different one!" he barked like a tiny dog.

"Oh, this is yours? My mistake. Here, I'll help you." Vant picked him up by the collar. He held his face in front of the bot's barrel, blocking it from aiming at the little one. "Hey kid," Vant said to him, "go ahead and kick it now. Let's see if this thing is smart enough to shoot through your buddy, here."

"No! Don't!" the bully whined. He wet his pants.

Vant dropped him, repulsed. "This little twerp pissed himself!" The flock of youths laughed and scattered, abandoning their leader.

The bully, in between sobs, yelled at Vant. "You can't hurt a kid!"

"I can do whatever I want. See?" Vant whacked him in the back of his head with his right hand. "Works the same with the other one, too." He slapped him with the left. "Want to know why? Because I'm bigger than you. You know how that goes, right? I'll make it clear... you ever torment that little guy again, I'll beat the crap out of you. Understand? Oh, and don't mess with the bots, or I'll feed you to them. They gobble up kids and turn them into robots, did you know they do that?"

The bully sniffled, holding back tears.

"He worships you, you know. He was going to follow your orders—no matter how stupid they were—to his death. You're wasting a loyal ally, moron. You only come across that once in a lifetime, if you're lucky. Now go on, get gone. And take your scrappy soldier here with you."

The kids ran off together.

Vant eyed the Corpo-Bot still in defensive mode, and wisely opted to use a different one, a few steps away. "Public records," Vant said. The machine chirped an acknowledgment. "Rii Tavee..." he took a deep breath, "...living or dead?"

The bot chirped, then spoke. "Rii Tavee, deceased."

All of the warmth in Vant's body transformed into ice.

All ambient sound disappeared.

He felt like he should weep. But he didn't.

After a while, he asked, "Living relatives?"

"Skii Tavee. Daughter. Living."

Rii had a daughter. Did that mean... *he* had a daughter?

"Where is she?"

"Incarcerated. Land Escape Detention and Rehabilitation Center."

Vant became lightheaded. His legs wobbled. He fell forward, catching himself by bracing against a Corpo-Bot.

"Warning," it said.

"Warning."

- Corpo-Bot

243 YEARS PRIOR

Of Friendship and Fealty

Vant and Terrii lay under bearskin blankets. They poked a metal rod at a pile of embers that used to be a fire. They whispered to each other. It was late.

"What did it feel like?" Vant asked.

"Kinda weird," said Terrii.

"Weird how?"

"I dunno. My dad did most of it. I just held the handle while he pushed it in."

"Did you feel bad?"

"Naw. It was only a boar. Who cares, right?"

Vant's eyes were wide, his curiosity nowhere near satisfied. A coal popped in the fire pit. They both jumped, startled.

"Did you feel its life go away?"

"I guess. I felt a funny crunch when the knife hit bone. It was gross. But it made Dad happy I did it."

"You're brave. I wonder if I'll be able to do that someday. And to a person, too."

"You better! It's your job to protect me!"

"I know." Vant rubbed his nose. "Some bodyguard I am. I haven't even killed anything yet."

"Don't worry. You'll kill something soon."

They watched the coals. A hypnotic orange wave swam across the pebbles. They let their minds drift.

"Terrii? Do you think we'll be great warriors?"

"We kind of have to be. I mean, I'm the son of Agmar, so that's a given. And you, you're pure-blood. Your mom and dad are both Primes, so you're going to be the strongest Knight ever. That's what everyone is saying."

"Not stronger than you."

"My mom was just a nurse or something dumb. But both your parents can fight." The words held a tinge of envy.

"What do you think our first battle will be like?"

"I hope I get to lead it."

"I hope so, too. I'll watch your back."

"You have to! You don't have a choice!"

"I won't do it because I have to. I'll do it because we're friends."

There was a commotion outside.

The boys silenced themselves, covered up, and pretended to sleep.

Six cloaked figures thundered into the tent.

"There he is," said Agmar. *"Wake him."*

"And your son?"

"Wake him as well. He should witness this."

"No one has seen as much as me."

- Skii Tavee

CHAPTER 5

The Survivor and the Stolen

Vant wandered in a daze. He had decided to meet this girl, Skii Tavee. What would he say to her? What *could* he say to her? He rehearsed out loud, each attempt worse than the last.

Before he had even the semblance of a plan, he found himself at the far end of town, face to face with the detention center. The modest jail, built into the township wall, seemed none too foreboding.

Vant entered the lobby. A guard greeted him with lukewarm deportment. "Help you?"

"I'm here to visit an inmate."

"Nature of visit?"

"Conjugal."

The guard squinted at him.

"Kidding," Vant said.

The guard un-squinted.

"Visiting a friend of a friend," Vant continued. "Guess she fell in with the wrong crowd. I'm going to set her on the right path."

"You a holy man?"

"Yes, sir. A man of faith. My boss is the big guy." *But not the big guy you're thinking of,* Vant thought.

"Prisoner name?"

"Skii Tavee."

"Ah. Her. Drop your equipment in the storage bin. I've got to search you. Turn around, let me pat you down."

"I told you, it's not a conjugal visit!"

The guard re-squinted.

"Just trying to keep it light," Vant said while placing his satchel in the container. A thought appeared: *Nothing suspicious is going on, and I'm not doing anything illegal. So why does it feel like I'm about to?*

The guard checked Vant for concealed paraphernalia, then led him through a hallway to the cellblocks. Although Land Escape embodied the modern with its foundations built on Corpo energy, this jail was basic: steel bars, analog locks and keys, and minimal surveillance. Vant figured he would see energy grids, motion detectors, protection bots, and other high-level technologies, but, essentially, the detention center was a drunk tank. Those who broke the more serious laws were simply jettisoned into the wilderness. Easy as taking out the trash.

They passed a dozen or so prison cells in the sparse cellblock. It was peppered with petty criminals, wayward miscreants, and sobering-up detainees. "Here we are, number eight," said the guard. "Skii Tavee."

And there she was.

Tiny. Ragged. Seventeen years old, if that.

She sat cross-legged at the edge of a bed. Streaks of copper hair fell over one eye while the other was unobstructed, free to examine her new guest. Her elbow rested on her knee. Her head rested on her palm.

"You've got five minutes," the guard said as he walked away.

Vant approached. Fidgeted. He attempted to speak, but he found himself mute. Skii did not move, but she raised an eyebrow as if to say, *Yes?*

Finally: "My name is Vant. Vant Hu'l. I'm—what I'm about to tell you is..." She raised her other eyebrow. "I'm your father."

She blinked twice.

He continued, "I know. I can't believe it, either. But there you have it. I'm your *father*. I know I've been gone a while... your whole life... but I promise to make it up to you. All of it. All the time we've lost. I'm sure we're not so different, you and I. Same blood in our veins, and all. And hey, look at that. We kind of look alike. Besides our hair color, I mean. And our complexions. And, uh, our eye color too, I guess."

No response.

Vant went on, "I know how hard it must have been growing up without a father figure—well, maybe you did have a father figure—but you didn't have your dad. Not your *dad*, Skii. That's me. I'm here for you now. And, for my first fatherly act, I'm going to get you out of here. Because... because that's what a dad would do." An awkward pause threatened to go on forever. "Right?"

She blinked a few more times, then hopped off the bed. She clipped the dangling strands of hair behind her ears and approached. Vant got a better look at her, including her charcoal-smudged eyes. Her clothes were gnarled, but their style was deliberate: ripped stockings beneath a ripped dress, aggressive combat boots almost comedic in their size, and a woven shirt covering one arm, leaving the other—a tattooed one—exposed. The skin decoration flowed from shoulder to wrist with wandering lines, colored dots, and spirals intersecting at seemingly random points.

She put her hands on the bars and peered up at Vant. He towered over her, but his height did not intimidate her, not one bit. She beckoned for him to bend down to her level. Which he did.

She spoke, "Okay... *Pops*. But there's one small problem."

"What's that?"

"You're not my dad."

"I am."

"No, you're not."

"I'm—well, I'm pretty sure—"

"Two things. First, you're way too young to be my dad."

"I'm older than I look—"

"Second, I knew him. He raised me. And you don't look like him. And you don't talk like him. And you certainly don't smell like him."

Vant glanced down at his armpits, which he had *thought* he cleaned—

"So, unless you're about to tell me a fascinating story that's gonna blow my mind, I'd say you've got the wrong gal, guy."

Vant's jaw dropped. This may have been a miscalculation, and a large one at that.

"Oh. Well. Okay, then." He turned to walk away.

"Wait! Where do you think you're going? Get me out of here!"

"No way. I had second thoughts when you *were* my daughter. But now? Forget it. Sorry, kid. You're on your own."

"Hold on! Somewhere you gotta be? Why don't you tell me what's got you cruising jail cells looking for daughters?" Skii's eyes narrowed and she took a step back. "Oh, it had better not be like *that*."

"What? No!" Vant raised his hands to demonstrate his non-lascivious intentions. "I know your mom." His eyes fell. "Knew."

"I figured as much, since you thought I was the byproduct of you 'knowing' her."

Vant fumbled for an explanation.

She added, "How would that even work? What were you, the world's most charming eight-year-old?"

"I'm older than I look."

"Yeah, you said that."

"Here's the thing..." But then, his cautious side interjected. He rethought telling her anything more. "Seems to me," he rapped on the cell door, "I have something you want. The chance to get out of here. Tell me what I need to know, and I'll do my best to get you sorted out. Deal?"

She did not have much of a choice. She was a prisoner, and Vant was a possible key to freedom.

"Fine."

"So, your mom. When did she...?"

"Years ago. I was a kid. My dad and I were traveling the outskirts when..." the words hesitated on her lips. "...when she passed."

Vant sunk to the floor and leaned against the cold brick. He nodded for her to go on.

"She was ill. Doc said she was a hopeless case. My dad... he was out of options. Every day she suffered more and more. So, we deserted Land Escape. We went looking for a cure, for anything that could help her." She scratched her scalp, a nervous tic helping her through an uncomfortable subject. "She died while we were gone."

Something piqued Skii's curiosity. She moved to the bars and dropped to her knees, studying Vant. He looked away toward, well, nothing. "You loved her," she said.

"Yeah."

"I'm sorry, guy."

"Thanks." Vant picked at his fingernails. "Sorry to you, too."

"Yeah, well..."

They shared a moment of silence.

"And your father?"

"What about him? He was what he was."

"Was? He's gone?"

"It's complicated. Let's just say we're no longer in touch. After we separated, I traveled around, made my way, and finally came back to Land Escape. Now, here I am, talking to my mom's former boy toy."

"I'm older than I look."

"Yeah, I got that."

The cellblock door opened. The guard stepped through. "Time's up."

Vant got to his feet.

Skii spoke in a hush, so the guard would not overhear, "I need a favor. Spring me? They sentenced me to two years of confined rehab, which really puts a damper on things. I gotta get loose, or I'll go crazy in here. Be a pal? I mean, we're kind of related."

They weren't. She was working him.

"Not interested," Vant said. "I mean, you're kind of the living reminder that the love of my life had 'relations' with another man."

"Maybe I have something you want?"

Vant raised an eyebrow.

"Don't be skeevy," she said. "What I meant was, how can I help you?"

"You can't."

"Try me."

"In a million years, you wouldn't believe me."

The guard was getting antsy. "I said, time's up! Out you go!" He was still out of earshot, but barely.

"Have to go, kid."

"Where are you headed?" Skii would not let up. "Sticking around Land Escape?"

"Not for long."

"Then lucky for you, I'm your best bet."

Vant looked skeptical.

"No, really! See?" She pushed her arm through the bars.

Vant studied her tattoo. "This is—"

"A map. All the places I went with my dad." She rubbed it with her palm. As she did, a phosphorescent glow appeared from within the ink, illuminating the strokes and symbols. To solidify the tantalization, she added, "I am the world's leading expert on the outskirts. No one has seen as much as me."

Vant eyed the guard, who was now in motion, lifting his lazy back from the wall he had been leaning against. Vant said to Skii, "All right, well, either I cut off your arm..." Skii recoiled, "...just a joke, or we make an agreement. Here's what I propose. I'll get you out of here and, in return, you take me where I need to go."

The guard cleared his throat in the most obnoxious manner possible.

"Deal?"

Skii answered quickly, "Deal. Anything beats two years of boredom."

"Guardsman! How much is bail?"

He laughed. "You couldn't afford it, deserter."

Vant scrunched his face at Skii. "That sounds like a *lot*."

"Don't you dare leave me!"

"Not so bad in there. Guess you could stay a *little* while longer, right?" Vant started to walk away, following the guard toward the exit. He asked over his shoulder, "What are you in for, anyway?"

Skii stared bullets, then flopped onto her bed in protest. "Grave robbing," she said. "Hers."

Once in the lobby, the guard pointed a finger in the direction of Vant's satchel. It was sprawled across a desk like it had been assaulted. "Those are pretty fancy," he said, referring to the gauntlets.

"Glad you helped yourself to a look. No need to have asked."

"I coulda kept 'em if I wanted," the guard sneered. "But hey, only babies need mittens to keep their pretty little hands warm, right?"

"Ha!" Vant fake-laughed. The sarcasm flew over the guard's head.

"So, why would a deserter lug around a couple of back-breakers like these? Just dead weight, as far as I can tell."

"Keeps me in shape."

"They got power cells in 'em. I checked. But I couldn't make 'em do anything."

"Like you said, the power's for the hand warmers. Want to try? Here, I'll show you."

The guard showed a tinge of suspicion, but he shrugged it off. Like he had anything better to do.

Vant held the gauntlets out. The guard slipped them on, his doughy arms hanging limp by his sides.

"Now what?"

"Now, you're an idiot." Vant elbowed the man in his temple. He collapsed, unconscious.

Vant lifted a key ring off the guard's belt, recovered his satchel, packed up his whip gauntlets, and returned to Skii's cell.

"Oh, good, you're back," she muttered, alongside an eye-roll.

"Brought you a present," Vant said, dangling the keys from his fingertips.

Her eyes lit up. She sprang to her feet. Vant tossed the key ring to her—but she botched the catch. They hit the floor.

Vant shook his head. Skii made a very impolite gesture.

Recovering the keys, she said, "I have to make a stop before we get outta here. It'll be fast." She turned her attention to the lock.

"What are you talking about? If you hadn't noticed, we're kind of in a rush, here."

"Sorry, Pops. Not up for discussion. I've got to rescue someone."

"Rescue someone? Who?"

"Cassidy. I can't leave without her."

"Cassidy? Who's Cassidy?"

"My friend."

"Your friend?"

"My teddy bear."

"Your *what?*"

Skii celebrated the discovery of the correct key as the cell door slid open. She tossed the key ring in an arc to Vant. He lunged to catch it, which he did, but not gracefully.

"Aren't you a bit old for toys?" he asked.

"I am *not* leaving here without my bear!"

"Fine! Where do they keep confiscated teddy bears in a prison?"

"The armory."

"Oh. Of course. Makes total sense."

Skii darted out of the cellblock and into the holding area. Vant followed. She hugged a corner and peered around the wall. "Coast is clear," she whispered. "We gotta stay silent. One wrong move and this place will be crawling with—"

"Freeze!"

Two guards drew their firearms. One rubbed his temple, where Vant had elbowed him.

"They didn't see you yet!" Skii said to Vant. "Get lost!" She inched toward the floor, making them come to her. *Clever girl,* Vant thought. He slipped away as she said to the guards, "You got me! I'm going to lay down on the ground and put my hands behind my head!"

"Uh, yeah!" a guard responded. "Yeah, that's right! Lay down on the ground and put your hands behind your head!"

Vant strategized. Maybe he could flank them before they called for backup—

"This is Thiio. I've got a situation here. There's a prisoner out of containment. Repeat, prisoner out of containment."

Guess not. Vant ran back the other way.

The other guard spoke to his colleague, "Thiio, we can handle this. It's just a little girl. Do we really need backup?"

"It's not just her, there's someone else. He looks like a bald, gothic priest. He's around here, somewhere." Into his walkie-talkie, "Send everyone you got to the prison. This is not a drill. Repeat: this is not a drill."

Skii snuck a peek at Vant. He shrugged at her. She rolled her eyes. Three sentries in body armor joined the ranks. They activated stun clubs and moved in on Skii.

"Eek!" A squeak as Skii panicked, leapt to her feet, and blew past Vant. She was heading back toward the cages.

"Where are you going?" Vant whisper-yelled.

"Back to my cell, where it's safe!" Skii closed the cellblock door behind her. Then she opened it again. "Can I have the keys?"

"No!"

"Fine!" She slammed the door shut. And re-opened it. "Pretty please?"

"Here!" Vant tossed the key ring to her. She caught it this time. And curtsied.

The guards discovered Vant in the hall. "There he is! Get him!"

Vant powered up his gauntlets. The thrusters bellowed down the hallway.

He squared off with the five guards. Sized them up. *Two at the front with firearms,* he strategized. *And three at the rear with stun clubs.*

"Get down on the ground and put your hands behind your head!" a guard ordered.

"Guys, here's the thing. I just got my clothes laundered. I don't want to get them dirty—" *Crack!* The tips of Vant's whips latched onto the guards' pistols. He snapped the slack backward. The firearms flew from their grips and slid behind him. The bewildered sentries stared at their empty hands.

The three guards with stun clubs charged, closing the gap through the narrow corridor. There was no room for clever whip tricks; Vant retracted his whips and raised his fists.

The guards swung their weapons with assertion. Their electrified tips left glowing trails with every swipe. Vant parried the clubs—sparks flew from the gauntlet knuckles with each block.

Vant continued to parry, parry, parry their swings. They advanced with force and pushed him into a corner. He watched their movements. They were committed, but slow. Out of practice. Out of shape.

Out of breath, one of the men hesitated. Vant smacked the tip of the guard's club, showering him with disorienting sparks. Then, Vant took a powerful swing. The blow connected with the breastplate of the guard's armor. The force launched him backward, taking out the sentry next to him as he reached out to brace himself.

Three left.

In his periphery, Vant saw Skii peeking her head out of the door. She noticed the guns on the ground, and snagged one.

"No, wait! Don't shoot!" Vant said. The truth was, these guards were not the enemy; they were simply doing their jobs. Vant could take on a dozen foes at a time —that was not the issue—the issue was suppressing them without making them dead. He had enough blood on his hands already. He did not need theirs.

Vant ducked another attack, a close call, then laid out a guard with a jab to the gut.

Two left.

The last enforcers charged into the fray. Skii flipped off the gun's safety. "You sure?" she asked.

"I can handle—oh, *hell.*"

Eight reinforcements arrived.

"Set it to non-lethal!" Vant shouted.

"There's a picture of a moon and one of a hammer! Which one is it?"

"I don't know!" A club whizzed past Vant's face. "The moon? That probably means sleep!"

Five guards aimed their pistols, preparing to fire. The others converged with their stun clubs.

"A moon could mean eternal sleep!" said Skii.

"Who would think that? Has to be the moon. No, wait—the hammer!"

"Oops!" Skii fired the weapon. Vant dropped to the floor. A burst of projectiles hit the fighters on the front lines. They toppled backward into the rest.

Vant and Skii caught their breath. They approached the pile of subdued guards and stared at the steam rising from their body armor. They were knocked out—stunned, but breathing.

"Nice shooting. Which one did you go with?" Vant asked.

"The moon. I think the hammer was actually a shovel. For digging a grave?"

"What's so hard about this? Skull and crossbones, and a person sleeping. Done. End of story. Problem solved."

"How would you know the person's sleeping and not dead? Still confusing."

"Well... I mean... little Z's coming out of his mouth?"

"I'm not convinced."

"Here's a tip. Always agree with the guy who broke you out of prison. Come on, let's get moving."

They ran through the corridors, looking for the armory. Outside the locked warden's office, Skii fumbled with the keys, searching for a match.

"I'm coming, Cassidy! Hang in there, pretty girl!"

Vant shook his head. *All this for a stuffed bear?*

"I'm sure there's a key here, somewhere."

"Let's try mine." Vant charged the thrusters in his weapons. They made a kinetic hum, then—*pow!*—the door crumbled with one punch.

"Whoa, those are awesome! Unless you need to use your fingers." Skii tossed the key ring to Vant. The gauntlets had no movable digits—they were solid chunks of iron—so the keys bounced off the knuckles and landed on the ground. She found this wildly amusing.

Skii entered the office, located the vault, and hopped up and down in front of its door. "This one! This one! Open it! Open it!"

"Move!" Vant shouted. "Damn, calm down, weirdo!"

"Sorry! I got a little stir-crazy, what with being in prison and all. After you." She moved aside and "politely" invited Vant to step on up. He charged the gauntlet thrusters and pounded the door until it bent, dented, and buckled. It gave Skii just enough room to squeeze through to the other side.

"Hurry," Vant said, detecting confused voices in the hallway. "More guards are on their way."

There was an excited squeal from inside the vault, followed by a one-sided conversation. She was talking with her toy. The opposite of hurrying.

"Skii! Move it!"

"Freeze, deserter!" Five guards with guns. "Lay down on the ground and put your hands behind your head!"

"Easy, boys," Vant powered-down his weapons and moved to the floor. "I don't want any trouble. My friend was just looking for her teddy bear—"

A sonic explosion erupted from the warden's office. A blue shockwave collided with the guards. They were lifted off their feet and slammed into the wall behind them, leaving body-shaped imprints in the drywall.

Skii grinned ear to ear, brandishing a pump-action shotgun with a fluffy teddy bear shell. The stuffed animal decorating the freakishly large firearm was not in great shape; it was oily, mangy, and a little cross-eyed. An aqua-colored haze—not quite smoke, more like dissipated energy—rose from the "mouth" of the bear, the barrel.

"That's Cassidy, I take it?" asked Vant.

"I told you I needed my teddy bear!" she giggled.

"She's got one hell of a bite."

"That's nothing. You should see her *growl!*"

"I'm sure it's impressive. Let's roll, Skii."

She did not move. Frowning, she looked at her stuffed friend with sad eyes. "Aren't we forgetting someone?"

"Oh. Sorry. You too, Cassidy."

"Give her a kiss."

"What? No way."

"Kiss her!"

She held the barrel up to Vant's face. The not-crooked eye of the bear stared him down. Its open mouth steamed with energy. "Skii, we just met. This is exhibiting a lot of trust—"

"Do it!"

Vant pecked the stuffed animal on the tip of the nose. Skii smiled, then skipped out of the room, cocking the pump handle of the weapon with a satisfying *shlick-shlock!*

They hopped over the unconscious guards and took the last turn of a corner toward their freedom. They burst into the lobby...

...where twenty riot officers awaited them, firearms drawn.

Vant threw his hands up. Skii did not. She raised Cassidy.

"Drop it!" an officer shouted.

"You first," said Skii.

"Put it down, or we'll take you down!"

"Let's all take a breath," Vant interjected, doing his best to exude calm. "Let's talk this out. Should we share our feelings? I'll start. Some days, I feel sad inside. I think it has to do with my childhood—"

"You have three seconds!" The squad member yelling at Skii was young. Nervous. The kind of guy who accidentally pulls a trigger.

Vant tried again, "This is all a big misunderstanding."

"Only way I'm going back to that cell is if you drag me there!" Skii shouted.

"Take it easy—"

Vant was interrupted.

The ground shook with an ear-churning rumble.

Everyone was puzzled. The riot squad members looked at each other.

"What just happened?" one of them asked. "Did you feel that?"

"Felt like an earthquake," Vant said. "It is earthquake weather..."

A transmission burst into the room from the communication devices on the officers' belts. "All city defenders! All civil agencies! Report to the front gates immediately! Repeat, get to the front gates immediately!"

One of the squad members lowered his gun and raised a comm to his mouth. "Uh, we've got a situation over at the detention center—"

"Situation my ass! Drop whatever you're doing and get out here, right now! Repeat, *situation my ass!*" Then, there was the unmistakable sound of gunfire, followed by a burst of static.

The transmission went dead.

"Detention center to headquarters," said the guard. "Come in, H.Q. Anyone?"

"I don't like this," said the squad leader. "I don't like this one bit." He thought, but only for a second. "You heard the man. Let's go."

They all filed out—except for the young one with the shakes. His gun remained focused on Skii.

"Calm down," Vant said to him. "Let's let this one go, huh? She's just a kid."

"Correction. Kid with a shotgun." She cocked Cassidy.

The rookie swallowed. "I—I can't let you go. My boss will fire me if I do. I have to take you back to your cell."

"Not going to happen," Vant said. "You can tell your boss you captured us. Tell him there was a big fight. Tell him we escaped later. Tell him anything you want. But lower the gun, friend. This is how the wrong people get hurt."

Another resounding—like a sonic boom—shook the prison.

"Sounds like they need you out there," continued Vant. "We're harmless. Just a couple of deserters who didn't play nice. We're nobodies, I swear."

"Okay... okay." He lowered his gun. "Don't tell anyone. Promise?"

"Promise."

He ran out the door to rejoin his force. Vant reflected on how the greenhorn was more afraid of his boss than of the weapon pointed right at him. Vant could relate. He had a terrifying boss, as well.

Things had taken a turn for the eerily quiet. Something was going on in Land Escape—that much was clear—yet the prison was far enough from the front gates that the source of the commotion had not yet reached them.

Vant kept his gauntlets activated and Skii's shotgun was primed. They tiptoed through the containment checkpoints and peered around corners.

No one was coming for them.

They looked at each other and shrugged. There were no guards. No reinforcements. Nothing.

Then, they heard it.

A scream.

Then another. And another. From outside.

"Umm—?"

"No clue. Freaking me out."

They moved across the abandoned lobby to the exit. Skii reached for the door—but Vant stopped her. "Wait. Let's be smart about this." He thought for a moment. "The roof."

They ran back through the prison and sprinted up a stairwell. A few flights later, they took a passage to the outside.

There were sounds of panic.

Chaos.

Pandemonium.

Vant and Skii approached the edge of the roof and peered down into the streets...

...where a full-scale invasion was in progress.

Forces of an unknown origin marched through the town. The invaders were adorned in glistening suits of armor, protection of the highest caliber. They exerted their will through sheer might and vast numbers, converging upon Land Escape's citizens.

Below Vant and Skii, several innocents—a few women and older men—ran from a battalion of the armored soldiers. The cowering civilians took shelter behind the prison guards—the ones who had let Vant and Skii go. The guards let loose their firearms; the blasts ricocheted off the soldiers' armor. The squadron kept firing, but their pistols were nowhere near powerful enough to slow the onslaught.

Bludgeoning batons slid out from the soldiers' armored forearms. Ruthless strikes immobilized the guards. Blows to their faces. Their arms. Their ribs.

But no fatalities.

The invaders wanted them alive.

Vant pulled Skii from the ledge, silencing her protests with a downward gesture. She got the hint: the prison below them was being infiltrated.

They ran to the other side of the roof. Vant noticed someone on the street, huddled in a trash heap. The person let slip an accidental whimper—three armored soldiers about-faced and marched to the disturbance. They reached into the pile of garbage and removed a child, the peanut Vant had rescued from the bullies at the Corpo-Bots earlier that day.

A second child jumped out of a bin, defending his friend. The rotund kid—the bully who had originally taunted the younger one—was now protecting him. A soldier gripped the youngsters by their legs and started to drag them away, kicking and screaming.

"Hey!" Vant slid down the fire escape to the sidewalk. The abductor, startled, dropped the children. They ran to Vant, who was standing tall against the troops. "Get out of here!" he yelled to the kids. He thumped the larger one on the back of the head with his elbow and added, "Hide somewhere *way* better than the trash!" It was not lost on Vant that this was the *second* time he'd had to bomp this kid on the head to get him to think straight. With some sense knocked into him, he took his little friend by the arm and they disappeared down the alleyway.

The soldiers advanced on Vant. Each was burly, roughly the size of two men packed together. Vant had only a moment to study them: *Clones? Possibly. Robots? Not likely.* They moved independently, like humans, with their armor granting both substantial protection and, somehow, deft maneuverability.

Whips shot out from Vant's gauntlets and twisted around the legs of two soldiers —*thwip-crack!* He yanked hard, collapsing them onto their backs. The third one charged, swinging a baton in an overhand arc. Vant dove to the side—there was a vaporous explosion where the weapon met concrete. It was not smoke—the steam gave off an almost musky scent. This was a unique technology, something Vant had never seen before.

He retracted his whips and backhanded the soldier, knocking it down and buying himself space. The other two were on their feet, and closing fast.

Let's see how well they learn, Vant thought.

He flicked his whips, again at their legs. They hopped over the lashes, signaling they had the capacity for logic. *But how smart are they?* He flicked the lashes back the other way—they did not anticipate the follow-through. The whips twisted around the midsections of the soldiers. Vant tugged hard, crashing them together. The third soldier lunged as Vant dove out of the way. A violent metal-on-metal collision left all three in a tangled mess.

"Skii!" Vant shouted to the rooftop, "let's roll!" He whipped a pillar next to her. The length of the lash was impressive, as was Vant's near-perfect control of it. Skii gave him a polite finger-to-palm soft clap in appreciation.

She threaded Cassidy over the whip and slid down the makeshift zip line, landing with poise.

"Thanks, Pops! The hell's going on out here? What *are* those things?"

"No idea."

The three armored troopers in the pile attempted to untangle themselves and break free.

"What do they want? Why are they terrorizing these people?"

"Let's find out."

One of the soldiers rose. Vant cold-cocked it in the face. He whipped a second one around the torso and flung it down the alleyway. He focused on the final foe, which struggled to stand. Vant used the thrust of his gauntlet to pin it to the pavement. The soldier flailed, but he kept the thrusters lit to restrain it. Skii secured its baton with her boot.

"Who are you?" Vant asked. He pressed harder on the thruster. "What do you want from these people?" The suit creaked from folding metal.

Apprehension fell across Skii's face as the soldier thrashed. She and Vant observed no cries, pleas for mercy, or moans, even though it must have been in tremendous pain from the collapsing armor. Vant released his left gauntlet and attempted to remove the combatant's headgear with his bare hand. He could not. The helmet was welded to the neckline.

"This suit is completely sealed. Whatever is inside must be trapped in there." He noticed the silent operation; surely if it were cybernetic or robotic, electronic sounds could be detected.

"Something is seriously off here. Leave it," said Skii.

"But—"

"Leave it!"

"Yeah... yeah. I think you're right."

Vant eased up. He said to the soldier, "Don't you dare follow us." There was no indication of acknowledgment. "You hear me? Stay put!" He revved the thrusters in his weapons as a warning.

Vant and Skii took a few steps away. The soldier leapt up and lunged. Vant threw his shoulder into a punch, splitting the soldier's armor from the force of the blow. Spray shot out from the seam and metal chips flew. It landed several feet away on its back, liquid pooling underneath its broken shell.

"That's not blood," Skii said. "Is it—?" She approached, touched the wet excretions, and sniffed her finger. "I think it's water."

"Come again?"

Skii ran the fluid through her fingertips. Then dabbed a drop on her tongue.

"Don't do *that!*" Vant freaked. "That's vile!"

"It's salt water," she said.

"I can't believe you tasted it! Disgusting. Wait. Hold on a second. I just thought of something."

Vant removed Death's mask from his pack.

Skii took a step back. "Whoa. What is that?"

Vant inched it toward his face. His hand had a faint tremble. "You should get ready to run."

"Why?"

"Because—I don't know. Just be ready. In fact, move ten feet away." She did. "Maybe twenty."

"Just put on your creepy mask already!"

Vant raised it to his face. It snapped onto his skin. Land Escape morphed into blackness and its buildings, streets, and scenery became outlined with shadow. But Skii... she exuded a calm, white luminescence. It was peaceful to look at her. Comfortable. He remained fixated on her.

"Can you hear me?" she asked. "Your eyes are black, and your mask is glowing. This is *so* skeeving me out! Should I run?"

"Huh? Oh. No. Don't run. This is wild. You're just... vibrating."

"I am? Well, what's *he* doing?" She pointed at the destroyed soldier floating on a liquid pool near her feet.

He saw an abominable red flashing within the armor. A visceral, epilepsy-inducing strobe. Vant was overrun with an impulse... the desire to mercilessly kill. The overwhelming urge to destroy what lay before him.

So he did.

He activated his gauntlets' thrusters and punched at the mass with a rhythmic *pound-pound-pound*. Soon, nothing remained but a mess of shrapnel and liquid. The red strobe waned, softened, and eventually dissipated.

Vant exhaled.

Skii was mortified.

"What happened to you? What *is* that thing on your face?"

"Wait here." He whipped the highest pillar he could find and propelled himself to a higher vantage point. From this perspective, he saw thousands of torrid red shapes throughout the city overtaking the peaceful white ones. It was all so obvious what was happening. It was all so awful. Through Death's eyes, the situation appeared clear as day, while simultaneously dark as night. Corruption was dominating tranquility. Hideousness was overpowering grace.

Vant felt an urge. A desire. A need to destroy them all.

Death's bidding.

Vant rappelled to the ground. He freed a hand from a gauntlet and tugged at the mask. The relic separated from his flesh, but not without pulling a few hairs and skin cells from his face. From the pile of wet metal that was once a sentient being, Vant picked up a loose scrap of its armor. It was a fascinating material—not quite silver, not quite gold—and it glimmered with multihued tinges. *Some sort of thallium,* Vant thought, recalling his studies in metallurgy. He pocketed the sample for safekeeping, then took off down the alleyway. Skii trailed behind.

They stayed low. Ducked in and out of cover. Arriving at the center of Land Escape, they found it inundated with the soldiers.

Battalions were sweeping the town with martial precision. They walked five by five, ten by ten, or however many could file down a path. They approached structures, separated from their packs, stormed interiors, and returned with armfuls of sobbing women, cowering men, or innocent children. None were spared.

Hopeless rebellions continued to break out. Some of the braver, yet misguided, citizens brandished makeshift weapons or basic firearms. They lasted only moments longer than the unarmed ones, silenced mercilessly by a baton launched from a thallium soldier's wrist or a swift strike to the head. The forces manhandled the townspeople like mere objects, kicking them, shoving them, and dragging them to the center of the city. The victims cried out, but their cries became wails of holy terror when they saw what they were being herded into...

A massive hose, like a gigantic earthworm, snaked through the streets and ran out the main gates of the city. Person after person was forcefully shoved by a soldier toward its opening as the overpowering suction lifted them off their feet and pulled them inside. Their bodies twisted in awkward ways and their screams traveled with them as they flew through the tube leading out of Land Escape.

"What the hell!" Skii was losing her grip.

Vant shook his head to scatter the cold shivers created by the mortifying sight.

"We gotta get out of here," Skii said.

"I can't. I have to watch them. Maybe follow them."

"Are you insane? Screw that!"

"Stop. Think for a second. If you're captured, what good will you be to anyone? I can't let you go."

Skii cocked her shotgun and aimed it at Vant's head.

"Point taken. Do what you want. But no matter what, stay out of sight."

"Oh, no. Look. Over there." Skii pointed at Land Escape's graveyard, which was full of the thallium soldiers.

The troops held smaller hoses, ones that were attached to the massive one. They were pointing them at the grave plots and sucking up chunks of dirt, grass, bone, corpse, and coffin.

Vant took Skii's arm to usher her away from the gruesome defiling. She resisted. "They're sucking up the dead people! My mom is in that graveyard!"

"Skii, walk."

"Oh, this is... I can't... Mom!"

"I won't tell you again! Walk! Now!"

She obliged, barely coherent enough to put one foot in front of another.

Whether or not she meant to, her boot grazed the casing of a fallen thallium soldier. A piece of its shell skidded down the pavement.

Vant, in his fury, pounded the rest of the armor into the ground.

"Something is seriously off here."

- Skii Tavee

243 YEARS PRIOR

Of Innocence and Execution

Agmar fell into his armchair. He rubbed his temples with his palms. They were covered in blood.

A knight ushered Terrii away from his friend. Two more stood behind Vant. He noticed his father's uzi had been placed on a table next to Agmar. It was isolated. Like it had an illness.

"Vant Hu'l," Agmar said.

"Yes, sir?"

"Your parents are dead."

No one moved.

"Your father killed an innocent." Agmar's eyes fell upon the uzi, betraying it as the murder weapon. "Splash damage. After it happened, he continued to fight bravely. He never once let down the order. He is a man of honor. Was a man of honor."

Terrii spoke. "Dad—"

"You will shut your mouth, or I will shut it permanently!"

Terrii slunk back into the corner.

Agmar continued, "Your father knew the price of his carelessness. After the battle, he submitted to me for sentencing. But your mother..." He wiped his bloody hands on a rag and threw it to the ground. "She betrayed us all. She tried to stop the execution. So I gunned her down. Her, and your father."

Vant trembled.

"Hear this, child. I am First Prime of the Knights of Rights. I have taken an oath, I must always do what's right. This is why I tell you the truth... the truth about your father's mistake. And your mother's treachery."

Vant could not speak. He dared not speak.

"Do you seek retaliation, Vant Hu'l? Do you wish to destroy me for the executions I have carried out in the name of our order?"

Vant looked at Terrii. His friend's tears mixed with the snot from his nose.

"No," said Vant.

"Any person would. Even one of your age."

"I don't. They took an oath. We can't break our oaths. They told me that."

"Who do you blame, then?"

Vant pointed at the uzi, which looked greasy. It repulsed him. "That."

Agmar studied the child.

Finally: "Return to your tent. You are now an orphan, and must fend for yourself. For that, I am sorry. If your mother had just—" he stopped. He rubbed his beard. "Out."

Four knights escorted Vant outside. Through the falling snow, Vant heard Agmar say one last thing, something not meant for his ears.

"That boy... he will seek his revenge."

Vant was returned to his tent and placed in bed. One of the knights squeezed his shoulder with compassion. "You'll be fine, little warrior," he said. "You're a strong one. Real strong."

Vant was left alone. It was cold. There was no fire.

He went to the corner farthest from his parents' bed and cocooned himself into a blanket.

So no one, in case they walked in, would see him crying.

"Now *there's* something you don't see every day."

- Vant Hu'l

CHAPTER 6

The Terror and the Taken

Land Escape was conquered.

It did not stand a chance. The peaceful city had existed in isolated harmony for more than a century, and its defenses were designed to protect against only moderate external nuisances—thieves and nomads—not armies. Once inside the main gates, the invaders overran the township with ease.

Vant and Skii avoided capture through sheer tenacity and perpetual movement. They reached the town's entrance undetected and surveyed the situation: the once-proud gates that had protected Land Escape had been forced open. Vant deduced that the violation of the massive steel doors was the source of the quake they had felt while inside the detention center.

And that which had done the deed, it now stood before them...

A thallium titan.

The monstrous overseer of the army towered over everything, save for the tallest buildings. Pacing the streets in a relentless vigil, each footstep crumbled the pavement and sent rumbling tremors through the town. Its hands, shaped like hammers, leveled obstructions to clear paths for the soldiers.

Vant's eyelids spread open in disbelief. Skii buried her face in Cassidy's fur.

Breaking free of his shocked stasis, Vant whipped the crossbeam of a building's exterior and propelled himself to a higher vantage point. He traced the foot soldiers' movements in his brain and identified a methodology to their sweeps. Not a moment too soon—the pattern indicated they would be upon him and Skii in moments.

He unraveled a whip to the ground. Skii wrapped it around her hand. Retracting the slack, he gently slung her up to another crossbeam where she sat uncomfortably, but safe.

They voiced their astonishment in whispers:

"Now *there's* something you don't see every day," said Vant.

"That thing's *huge!* What are we gonna do?"

"Escape's out of the question. The way out is blocked by that giant. And any direct attack on the soldiers would be suicide—there's too many of them. We'll have to wait them out."

"What if they stay forever?"

"I don't think they will. They're going door to door. I saw evidence of it at Meddia, a medical township near the badlands. It was the same—bashed-in door, stolen people, aftermath of a battle... Also, look how quickly the forces are moving. This is model efficiency." He traced their routes with a gauntlet, explaining, "They're organized and efficient. Systematic. No reinforcements have been posted for occupation. This is a snatch-and-grab job. They're going to fill their pockets and move on. For whatever reason, they're snatching bodies, the living *and* the dead."

Skii cringed.

"They don't want the town," Vant said, in finality. "They want the townspeople."

"You've got a knack for this stuff."

"I've been in a fight or two. It's smart to know your enemy. Amazing how they act when they think they're alone. Ever seen people walking down the street who think they're by themselves? Nine times out of ten, they pick their nose. That's what we're waiting for, a nose pick. Settle in, it may be a while."

Skii tried to make herself more comfortable on her tiny ledge. Vant loosed a bit of slack in his free gauntlet and handed her the coil. "Safety harness?" she asked.

Vant nodded.

She tied it around her waist; if she fell asleep, it would be a long drop to the pavement.

"So..." she began.

"So..." he answered.

Skii eyed the symmetrical laceration on his neck. "What's with the scar?"

"What's with the smirk?"

"Well, this is off to a fine start." Searching for something to do, she toyed with a ring on a chain around her neck. She rubbed it between her fingers.

"Rii's?" Vant asked.

"Yeah. It was buried six feet under with her. I liberated it. Cost me a prison sentence." She held it up.

Vant studied the beautiful circle, an engagement band made entirely of diamond. "So, she and your father?"

"No, she never married him. He tried. He handed her this ring every day for years. But she never accepted."

"Why not?"

"After I was born, she got really sick. Sorry, Ma. Hope I was worth it. But that didn't stop my dad. Every day he proposed to her, even though she always refused. She said no man should marry a dying woman. When I was about four, he couldn't cope anymore. I mean, she was suffering. Losing her mind. She couldn't even recognize me. I cried so much... I used to wipe my tears on her hand. I thought maybe if she felt how sad I was, she'd get better for me."

Vant remained respectfully silent. The sun set behind the Land Escape canopy as the soldiers persevered in their harvest. Their suits reflected the burgundy hues of the sky. The chaos was subsiding. The skirmishes were waning. The streets were growing quieter.

"So, one day, he put the ring on a chain, and put the chain around her neck. He told her to hold onto it until he came back. He said he'd bring her a cure, and, when he did, she'd have no reason to say no to him any more. We deserted Land Escape that very day to search for anything that could save her life." She ran her fingers around the spirals of her tattoo and paused at the dots. Vant assumed each one represented a township visited.

"You must have seen some bizarre sights."

"I saw a ton of the outlands, but Dad never let me inside the townships. I was too young. But he went into every one. He'd sneak in, like a ghost. He'd scale walls, go underground, use subterfuge... whatever it took. He'd disappear inside for what seemed like ages, then come back out, always empty-handed. And, no matter how much I asked, he never, ever told me what went on inside."

"I don't blame him. They're not the friendliest of places. I've been to a few, deserted them all. I'm lucky to be alive."

"Yeah, I would see it in his face. Each time he'd come out, it was like something died inside him. Worse, the lost time meant wasted life to us. Every failed attempt at finding a cure meant more time away from Mom. We looked for years." Her eyes darkened, and her tone shifted. "But hey, now the secret's out, right? Apparently, there was another man. Maybe *that's* why she never married my dad."

Vant held his tongue. Partly because he was caught off-guard. And partly because she may have been right.

"Why did you leave, if you loved her so much?" Skii asked.

"I was pulled away on business."

"Are you messing with me?"

"No."

"Well? I'm all ears."

Vant swallowed. "I was forced to go. I didn't have a choice. My boss can be very persuasive. Seems like Rii got over me, though. You're pretty clear evidence of that. She probably forgot all about me. I left her a long time ago."

"How long?"

"Twenty-three years."

"That doesn't add up. Look at you! I don't understand—"

"Shh."

"Don't you shush me—"

"Shhhhh!" Vant kicked her in the shin and widened his eyes. Skii took the cue and looked down. A dozen soldiers swept the streets below them.

Then: commotion in the central hub.

Three Land Escape rebels who had managed to avoid capture worked their way up the fortifications on the city walls to the defensive turrets. In a coordinated attack, they opened fire on the thallium titan. Bullets plinked like pebbles off its armor. The giant charged the wall, but the gunners held steady, assaulting it with everything they had.

The attack against the titan was a diversion. Ten men and women who had been concealed in a maintenance tunnel made a break for it, sprinting full-tilt toward the open gates.

The titan first focused on the gunners. It approached the wall, drew back its arm, and rammed the structure with a hammer-hand. The rebels in the turrets lost their footing. One grabbed a ledge as he fell, dangling from his fingertips.

Again, the giant punched the wall. The tremor destabilized the perches. The two other rebels dropped, falling hundreds of feet to the pavement. Another punch and the last rebel lost his grip. His helpless body met concrete.

The fleeing citizens neared the doorway. A battalion of the nearest thallium soldiers raised their arms, aimed, and fired batons from their wrists. The weapons flew like javelins and thudded against the backs and necks of half the townspeople. The other half seemed to have a clear path out of town, when...

The hand of the titan pounded the earth. The blow shattered pavement and the escapees were lifted off their feet by the shockwave. They smacked back down to the ground and scrambled to get up. But it was too late.

The titan reached the gates in two massive strides. Its limbs, like enormous pendulums, swatted the people back toward the squadron of foot soldiers. The innocents tumbled across pavement—bones broke, skin scraped, and flesh tore from the friction. The soldiers shouldered the broken townspeople, hauled them to the tube, and then tossed them inside.

The collecting of bodies continued for another hour. Soon, the township grew still. The soldiers convened around the tube, and a few manipulated it until a wheezing sound could be heard. A gust of wind poured out of the opening. The machine went from suck to blow.

The hose spat a group of townspeople back out into the center square. Twenty young adult males and twenty young adult females shot out, skidding across the ground. Their journey into the tube and back again had resulted in torn clothes and bruised bodies. It left them in a state of traumatized confusion.

With the expulsion completed, the thallium soldiers about-faced and began their exodus from Land Escape. The wailing of the helpless victims was drowned out by the rhythmic marching of the departing army. Rumbling vibrations emanated from the titan as it thudded into the center square, lifted the tube, and dragged it away.

By the gates, the monstrosity paused to take one last glance around. Vant scrutinized the titan as it studied its own handiwork; he detected an air of pride in the body language of the metal juggernaut.

Vant spat in disgust.

He watched the towering enforcer shrinking into the distance, along with its army, aware that he was losing his chance to pursue. He knew if he followed them there might be an opportunity to rescue the captives, but if he let them go there was no guarantee he would ever see them again.

Dammit, Vant thought. *Stay or go?*

He looked at the shell-shocked townspeople. If he abandoned them, they would be on their own, exposed to nomads and the dangers of the wild. Leaving them alone meant letting them die.

Dammit, Vant thought again.

He took a grounding breath, then made his decision.

To stay.

"Why did they do that?" Skii asked. "Why did they bring those people back?"

Vant had understood the moment he saw them reintroduced to the town. "Virility," he said.

Skii looked puzzled.

"Do I have to spell it out for you?" He yanked her off the ledge. She yelped, surprised. He lowered her to the ground, then dropped down beside her. "They took what they needed, then left candidates to re-up the numbers. Think about it... these people have been given a second chance at life. It won't take long for their primal instincts to kick in. There's no aphrodisiac quite like a near-death experience."

"So they're—"

"Cattle."

"Whoa."

"That army will be back when Land Escape's got a whole new herd of livestock. But I wouldn't worry about them returning."

"Why not?"

"Because I'm going to stop them."

"You're going to—*what?*"

He charged off, leaving her bewildered. She shook it off, then caught up.

Vant approached the shivering mass of discarded humans. At the sight of him, one of the townspeople panicked, creating a ripple effect of hysterics.

"It's okay," Vant said as he removed his weapons. "I mean you no harm." Assorted cries still indicated mistrust. He tried again, "You don't understand. I'm here to help. I'm here to avenge you. No, wait—is that right?" He thought out loud, "Do I avenge you? Or avenge *for* you?" Blank stares. "I feel like I should know this. Anyone?" More blank stares. "Never mind. Let's get you to safety."

Vant and Skii tended to the victims, most of them still catatonic with fear. It was a slow process, checking their injuries and getting them to their feet. But they managed. Vant asked if anyone had a shelter large enough to hold the whole group, and one man offered up his home.

They moved through the empty streets as a unit, then piled into the house. The opulence of the dwelling provided a much-needed grounding to those still disturbed. The host, a wealthy local, lit fires and handed out blankets and medical supplies to those in need. Water, food, and a welcome bit of booze were also distributed, bringing everyone a step closer to calmer mental states.

Skii had a natural way about her while tending to the more delicate personalities. She showed them Cassidy, did horrible impressions of the armored soldiers, and gave extra attention—by way of hugs and hair braids—to the most affected victims. Morale was on the cusp of rising, but it came toppling down again when a woman went into a seizure. Skii instinctively shoved her fingers into the woman's mouth to prevent her from biting off her own tongue—she gritted her teeth and endured the pain until someone found a cloth for her to use.

They held the woman down until her state subsided.

"You'll be okay," Skii said to her. "Just relax."

"My family. My husband. My children!"

"Don't worry about that right now. For all we know, those sparkly soldiers were rounding everyone up for a party, and they'll all be back in the morning."

"But they're gone—"

"Naw," Skii said. "Just misplaced."

On the other side of the reactionary line, several townspeople began forming a militia. They vowed to find and fight the army themselves, no matter what the odds. The leader of the mob stormed about the house, riling up the constituents.

"I'm going after those bastards! Who's with me? You? How about you?" He shook some of the people out of their stupors and barked orders. "You! Help me find whatever weapons you can. And you! Start collecting pills from everyone. We leave immediately!"

"The hell you do," Vant said.

"Excuse me?"

"You heard me. You're not going anywhere. You wouldn't last five minutes out there. Not against that army. Not against the nomads. Not against a damn rattlesnake. Here's what you're going to do. You're going to calm down, and sit tight until morning. Then, we're all going to work together to secure Land Escape. That's priority one."

The others in the room grew anxious from the tension unfolding between the two men.

"Who are you to give us orders?" the man asked Vant.

"He's the guy who took out a bunch of those... *things!*" Skii interjected.

"Bullshit," the man said.

"It's true! I saw it! He beat the stuffing out of them!" Skii was on her feet, fists clenched.

Vant waved her off. "What's your name?" he asked the man.

"Chaaris," he said.

"Chaaris, listen to me. Rushing out there is just going to get you killed. For now, we need to regroup." And then, to relax the tension, Vant addressed the rest of the townspeople. "I'm going to set this right. I'm going to find your loved ones. You can count on me. I promise."

Turning away dismissively, Chaaris said, "Who died and made you leader?"

Vant grabbed his arm, leaned in, and squeezed hard. He whispered, "So many people. But there's always room for one more."

Vant's eyes told no lie. They cut through every last layer of Chaaris' bravado. Everyone in the room witnessed a very definitive shift of power as Chaaris sat down and took his place with the others.

That's better, Vant thought.

"Tomorrow, Chaaris, you're going to prove how strong you are by protecting every single person in this town. Land Escape's vulnerable and, before we know it, every nomad for miles is going to stream in here to loot, pillage, riot, and rape everything in sight. So, it's up to you. You're going to lead a team to restore our defenses. You've got one mission, and *everything* depends on it... secure the gates."

Chaaris nodded. Then he started to open his mouth—but shut it quickly and nodded again.

Thereafter, a surge in spirits came in the form of two children who had survived the attack. The troublemaker from the Corpo-Bot kiosks and his scrappy little friend showed up at the door—the very kids Vant had previously rescued from abduction. The townspeople welcomed them as if they were their own children, even though the boys' actual parents were, in fact, missing.

The rascals had taken Vant's advice and remained hidden during the raid, swimming to the center of a pond. "The creeps looked like they'd sink!" the larger child said, trumpeting his cleverness. When it was revealed that Vant had needed to knock sense into the kid *multiple* times since they had first met, it earned him the nickname "Bomp." It seemed a bomp on the head was what it took to get him to use his brain. The other child became affectionately known as "Fray," as his cuteness inspired an uncontrollable impulse to muss up his hair and leave it frayed.

While spirits partially recovered, weeping and tearful concern for missing friends, family, and loved ones still permeated the house. During a mournful moment, Vant noticed a man who, though he seemed to have his wits about him, kept to himself in the corner.

Vant approached. "What's your name?"

"Jiino," he answered.

"Jiino, can I ask you a few questions?"

"Sure. Don't know how much help I'll be, though."

"What happened in that... tube?"

"Not exactly a smooth ride. Kept slamming into the walls." His eyes rolled back, thinking. "Got to the end."

"That's what I need to know. Where did it take you?"

"Big room. Holding area, or something. Thought I could smell the ocean."

"You've been to the ocean before?"

"No," he said. "But that's what the smell made me think of. Salt and fish. We get fish from Corpo, and when it's raw and sits out a while, same smell."

"The ocean..." Vant muttered to himself. "The ocean..." He was thinking aloud, but nothing was happening. *Maybe if I repeat it one more time?* "The ocean..."

Nothing.

"Then, they tossed some of us back in the tube. Don't know why they picked us, but they did. Now, here we are."

"Here you are," said Vant. "What did the the holding area look like?"

"Big," he said. "It was dark. Didn't see much. Before I could get a good look around, *poof,* I'm back in Land Escape."

Vant studied him. "You all right?"

"I'm fine. Do I not look all right?"

"That's what worries me. You seem just fine. Which, for some reason, makes me think you're *not* just fine."

"Oh," he said. "Got no family. Got no gal. Didn't really lose much today, except some piss on my way down the tube. Awful for them, though." He glanced toward the others. "Wish there was something I could do."

"There is." Vant put his hand on Jiino's shoulder. "Get some rest. Tomorrow, you're leading a team to sweep the streets for survivors."

Jiino nodded. "Can do. And you? What are you going to do?"

"Avenge."

"For whatever reason, they're snatching bodies, the living *and* the dead."

- Vant Hu'l

239

YEARS PRIOR

Of Cloaks and Masters

"No!" Cloakmaster Gordone bellowed at the child. *"No, no, no! Why on earth would you back-step if your adversary advances from the side? I swear, their skulls thicken by the day."*

Terrii threw down his wooden sword in defiance and snapped at the old swordsman. *"Are you calling me dumb? If my dad hears about this—"*

"Here we go again. Stow it, Terrii. Who do you think trained your father how to use his scimitar, hmm? Agmar told me himself, 'No special treatment for my seed!' Now pick up that sword, unless you want to hold it from your rear for the rest of your life!"

Several course-mates snickered. Terrii turned beet-red. "When I'm First Prime, the first thing I'm doing is firing you."

"I'll be dead long before then. Rest assured, I'll roll in my grave when that day comes. Now straighten up and meet your opponent in combat!"

Terrii retrieved his weapon and faced Vant, his sparring partner. They clunked swords a few times and went through the motions. Their teacher was not fooled by the charade.

"Pathetic!" Gordone spit on the ground. "This has gone far enough. I'm sick of the laziness, Terrii. And you, Vant. Shame on you. Cutting your friend slack will only place him in danger when the real battles come. This ends today. Let's see what you two are really made of."

Their course-mates inched forward, intrigued.

"You're going to spar for a prize. Terrii—since you despise me so—if you win, you may bypass my teachings for the rest of your life. Vant, if you are victorious, you may skip any course you wish with any Cloakmaster of your choosing. Let's see how you two perform when there's something on the line!"

They looked at each other. There was no way out of this. They would have to fight.

Plus, there were girls watching.

Vant and Terrii raised their swords.

Before Cloakmaster Gordone could signal the start, Terrii charged. Vant pivoted to the side using the footwork they had been practicing and Terrii flew past him. With his timber blade, Vant lightly slapped Terrii across the shoulder. The fight was over.

"I knew you'd betray me!" Terrii said. "My dad said so! As soon as you had the chance, you'd turn on me!"

Vant was stunned. "Terrii—"

"He was right! You still blame him for the death of your parents!"

"Enough!" The Cloakmaster's voice was an icy blanket extinguishing the flames. "Terrii, you lost. And your 'enemy' here, whether you like it or not, just saved your life. I'd bet my right eye you'll never fall for that again, and certainly not when in battle! So thank your opponent. Do it! Say, 'Thank you for saving my life!'"

Terrii stared at the ground. His course-mates held their breath, waiting to see how he would react.

"Thank you for saving my life," he mumbled.

Vant replied with delicate silence.

"Class dismissed. Go home."

They walked.

Neither spoke.

Finally:

"Sorry to bring up your parents like that. I... I didn't mean to."

"Terrii, I'm sworn to protect you. You're my best friend. I'll never raise my sword to you. Ever." Vant paused. "Unless..."

Terrii looked up at Vant. Terrii was tall, but Vant was taller.

"...unless it means getting out of another class."

Terrii socked Vant in the shoulder. They laughed, then went to find more trouble to get into. The day was young, yet.

"Even in the wilderness, never sacrifice fashion for comfort."

- Skii Tavee

CHAPTER 7

The United and the Unseen

Two weeks flew. Every ounce of physical, mental, and emotional strength was poured into repairing Land Escape's defenses. Through nonstop vigilance, gallons of elbow grease, and dashes of creative ingenuity, Vant, Skii, and the fifty-seven remaining men, women, and children managed to close and secure the front gates, re-calibrate the turrets, and patch the town's damaged infrastructure.

Once stability had been restored, the manic pace slowed. The townspeople turned to reflection, and many to isolation. Grieving had begun once reality had set in: their loved ones were lost, stolen away by a mysterious evil.

The city was empty, filled only with a somber serenity. One could travel from one end of Land Escape to the other without seeing a single living soul. The atmosphere was coated with a dizzying silence and loneliness permeated every square block. The metropolis desired to be full of life but it was, instead, comatose.

With every passing day, Vant knew the likelihood of a successful rescue decreased. The army that had abducted Land Escape's people had left no remains, no trail, and no hints as to its point of origin or next destination. In hopes of locating them through forensics, Vant brought the small piece of shrapnel—the one that came from the armored soldier he had destroyed—to a Corpo-Bot in the center of town. He inserted it into the bot for identification and, sure enough Vant's theory had been correct. It was, indeed, a type of thallium, a specialty composite known as "thallium vorax." It featured dynamic properties and extreme malleability, but without the natural toxicity of thallium. This made it ideal for applications such as robotics and power conduction.

Vant asked the bot to identify anyone or anything that may have recently purchased large quantities of the thallium alloy but, after emitting a rude tone, it noted that all sales transactions were private. Next, he requested geographic coordinates containing the highest concentration of the substance, but was answered by the same tone. He tried several more inquiries in the same line of questioning, and each time he came up empty.

The thallium army, along with its titan, had vanished.

Skii's voice emanated from a device on Vant's wrist. He mashed buttons on the communicator bracelet in response, searching for the right one. Vant needed a way to be in constant contact with Skii and key townspeople, so they scrounged up enough capsules to make a sizable purchase from a Corpo-Bot: "Bracelets for group or one-on-one communication. They should fit any size wrist, from a small child to an obese adult—or even a gauntlet. Lightweight. Easy to use. No more than an inch thick. Easily removable. Black."

Vant learned long ago to be specific when ordering from Corpo. Oftentimes a consumer, after receiving an item, would have to drop whatever they just bought back into the bot for a costly amending of some too-literal interpretation of the request. For example, Vant once ordered a "box of chocolate hearts" for his sweetheart, only to receive an ugly canvas container containing anatomically correct human-heart-shaped chunks of chocolate. Corpo-Bots were amazing, efficient, and, for the right price, could construct anything one required (except for weapons), but the downside was their astoundingly literal functionality.

Vant found the correct button and spoke into the wrist-comm: "Hello?"

"We did it!" Skii's voice rang from the speaker.

"You got in?"

"Sure did! Wasn't easy. Floo's arm is gonna be in a sling for a while, and Lyyra's gonna have a limp, but the vault is ours! I'm officially a bank robber. How great is that?"

"Nice," Vant said. Once the township had been secured, this was the final task that required completion before they could depart. "How big is the score?"

"Rough guess? A million billion pills. Seriously, I've never seen this much loot before. Looks like the town got invaded right before the deposits were going to be sent off to Corpo. Perfect timing! So, what do you want me to do now? Sit here and stare at all this loot? Because I'm fine with that."

"Grab enough for basics and emergencies." Vant heard a disapproving huff on the other end of the communicator. "That currency belongs to the townspeople. We only need enough to sustain us. And for incidentals."

"Yeah, yeah. And to buy me a new dress!"

"Fine. *And* to buy you a new dress. Not that Corpo knows a damn thing about fashion."

"It's all about the boots, anyway."

"Take a few capsules and do what you want, then deposit something modest at a bot for our trip. When you're all done, well, let's get going."

"Good," she said. "This place gives me the skeevies. I can already feel the guys wanting to 'rebuild society,' if you catch my drift."

"Make our investment, then meet me back at the homestead."

"Yep. Skii out. *Whee*—!" her voice cut off with a joyful squeal. He imagined her diving head first into a vault of Corpo-Capsules as if it were a pool.

Before their rendezvous, Vant decided to take a detour—though he dragged his feet in getting there. He headed past the repaired main gate. He meandered across a park dotted with neglected playground equipment. He wandered through the shopping district, filled with empty storefronts peddling wares he did not need, sold by merchants nowhere to be found.

He passed by the ransacked cemetery. Desecrated graves, unearthed soil, and broken tombstones littered the fields. It was not his destination but, near a pristine plot of grass, he noticed a townsperson kneeling in front of a handmade headstone. They met eyes. Vant nodded an acknowledgement.

The man stood, and approached. He appeared an honest-work, manual-labor type of guy with piercing, moist blue eyes. "Ho, there," he said.

"Hey," Vant responded. "Did someone in town pass away?"

"No, no. It's for my wife. She got taken in the invasion. Thought I'd put her to rest. Or something like that."

"She's still alive," Vant said quickly. "If they wanted everyone dead, they would have just done it."

"Figured as much. Guess I just needed somewhere to think about her. And talk to her. If that don't sound too silly."

"It doesn't. I've been known to do the same, from time to time."

"Graveyard seemed the best place to do it. And it gives me a head start if we get bad news. At least I found her a good spot, before the other ones get taken."

"I hear you." They both fell into a moment of silence. Then: "We haven't been formally introduced. I'm—"

"Yeah, I know who you are. 'Course I do. I appreciate everything you and the girl have done for us. All of us do. Pleasure to formally make your acquaintance. I'm Saamii Fraam."

"Vant Hu'l, now it's official." Vant bowed his head in respect to the memorial. "And your wife?"

"Laam Fraam." Vant raised an eyebrow. Saamii smiled. "Funny name, huh?"

"Heh, yeah."

"She was Laamlielle Ayway. Beautiful name. She hitched with me, married a Fraam. Folks started calling her 'Laam Fraam,' for short. Just think, gorgeous name turned ugly the day she said 'I do.' Poor gal." They shared a chuckle.

Saamii seemed to shake off a wave of emotion coming in hard and fast. "Heard you're going after that army. Need a hand?"

"Not yet. First, I have to find them. Then, I have to know what we're up against. In the meantime, we need decent men keeping order here. A rescue won't mean a thing if there's no home to come back to." Saamii appeared disheartened, but understanding. Vant added, "I promise when it's time to pick a fight, you'll be the first guy I call."

"Works for me." The men shook hands. "Been a pleasure chatting with you, Vant Hu'l. Thanks again. Laam Fraam thanks you, too, wherever she is. No matter how things turn out for her."

Somehow, the conversation gave Vant the final push he needed to complete his task. He continued on his detour toward a quiet pocket of cottages and turned a corner onto an unassuming pathway.

There, before his eyes, lay the former home of Rii Tavee.

He sat down on the lawn, leaned against a tree, and stared at the house.

It was smaller than he remembered.

He picked blades of grass and tossed them, letting the wind take them away. He tried to recall some of the many visits to the home; they all kind of blended together. He pushed his mind harder, but his subconscious was stingy with granting access to the particulars. It was protecting him from hurt by keeping the memories locked away. His head provided only fragments of recollection, so, instead, he turned to his heart. It reminded him, by way of feeling, of the love that had been his, a lifetime ago.

He drifted for a while.

"Surprised to see you here," Skii's voice appeared from over his shoulder. "When you said 'meet at the homestead,' I didn't think you meant mine." Skii allowed Vant a moment to piece together the reason for their accidental meeting, then added, "Weird, huh? We both spent plenty of time here with the same woman, but in completely different ways."

"Yeah... yeah." Vant wandered around in his own head some more.

"It was kinda small anyway. I got used to sleeping under the stars, traveling with Dad. Guess I'm about to get my fill again."

"Skii... about that. I know we had an agreement, but are you sure you want to leave Land Escape? Maybe you're better off here."

"I survived in the wild for years. Don't worry about me. You should be more worried about you. I know I am."

"I don't like forcing you somewhere you don't want to be."

"You saved my life. If I was stuck in that prison when the invasion hit, I would have been snatched up, too. I owe you."

"I don't know."

"A deal's a deal. I'm looking for my dad anyway, and you need to know what he knows. No one's more familiar with dogmatic townships than him. He may have seen that thallium army. And trust me, that's the only way you're going to find them. I went outside the gates and checked for a trail... don't ask me how the snick they did it, but they covered their tracks to *perfection*."

Skii hushed up suddenly. And scrutinized Vant.

"What?" he asked, uncomfortable.

"If I take you to my dad, you have to promise me something. That this isn't just some lover's quarrel. I know he ended up with your gal—*and* he made *me* with her—but you have to swear you're not looking to start trouble."

"It's the furthest thing from my mind." It wasn't. But, Vant really did require the man's information. He changed the subject: "I've been marinating on our plan. Are you certain about our destination?"

"It was the last place I saw my dad. He might still be there. If not, maybe someone there knows where he is."

"We'll need to move fast. The army may be headed their way. That town should be warned. Everyone deserves a fighting chance. Even them."

"Looks like we're going on a hike together. Lucky you!"

"Lucky me. Come on," Vant said as he stood. "Let's get moving."

They packed lightly for their trip—that is to say, they packed practically nothing. Skii carried only her pill purse, a canvas blanket, and Cassidy strapped to her back. She wore her new dress, a custom order from Corpo, created from a dark, synthetic material. It was practical—sewn-in gloves, completely waterproof, sleeves and leggings that could be rolled down for warmth—but also reversible into a bright blood-red-and-orange color for special occasions. "Even in the wilderness, never sacrifice fashion for comfort," she said to Vant when he paid her a backhanded compliment on the purchase. When he pressed harder, she insisted a dress was the perfect clothing for travel. "To see which way the wind is blowing, all I have to do is look down."

Vant shouldered the satchel containing his whip gauntlets, a pill pouch, and Death's mask. He considered loading up on material goods—hunting equipment, torches, and a tent—but Skii vetoed them all. She had traveled for years in the wild and had this to say on the topic: "Each additional thing you carry is something someone will want." Outside the walls of any township meant danger, and most deserters lasted mere moments before being sabotaged by nomads who held extreme advantage in the wild. Skii added that the wilderness provided for every basic need—fire, food, shelter, water, and weapons—if one knew where to look. So, no supplies. Their plan: don't be a target. Stay hidden. Appear to prying eyes as if they had nothing of value.

They had one thing going in their favor: the city had recently crawled with maniacal soldiers, so the nomads who usually stalked their prey outside Land Escape's walls had fled. While their absence would not last forever, Vant and Skii were currently afforded a clear exit out of town.

They said their goodbyes to the townspeople who had amassed to see them off. Vant and Skii agreed to keep in contact via wrist-communicator and provide updates on their progress. A few of the ladies hugged Vant for longer-than-necessary amounts of time; Skii over-dramatically gagged in a public display of pure tact.

"Take care, Vant Hu'l," said Saamii Fraam. "We're all with you. Even though we won't be *with* you."

Vant gave him a hearty handshake. "Keep the faith," he said. "Someone has to."

"Don't you worry about a thing," said Chaaris, dripping with snark. "The town's in good hands. If I'd have gone after that army like I wanted, our people would probably be home by now. But no matter. I'm sure you'll do fine."

Saamii and Jiino rolled their eyes. It made Vant crack a grin—a rarity. He slapped Chaaris on the shoulder and said, "I'll see you soon. Count on that."

"You troublemakers gonna behave while we're gone?" Skii asked Bomp and Fray, each of whom were holding furry friends in their arms. Bomp held a puppy, and Fray a couple of snowshoe hares. Skii had put them in charge of rounding up the orphaned house pets and consolidating them into one place. "Bomp and Fray's Zoo," it was affectionately called.

"Behave? With a whole empty town to run around in? Yeah, right!" said Bomp. Skii hissed at him like a cat and swatted at his head. He apparently needed another bomp to help him to think clearly. "I'm kidding, Skii!" he said, defending against her onslaught. "I'll be good."

"Just for that, I'm putting Fray in charge."

"Okay!" Fray said, nuzzling the big-eared hares in his arms.

Vant and Skii were not very impressive champions— a lanky maverick and a tiny teenager—but they were the best the citizens had. They set off; warm applause accompanied their walk toward the main gates.

"Wait," Skii said. "Thought of something." She approached a Corpo-Bot and said, "Leave a message for Gyse Fliyr." The bot chirped an acknowledgment. "Dad... we need to talk... if you're even alive." She paused. Thought. Opened her mouth to say something profound, then changed her mind. Finally, "Maybe I'll see you in Crash Town. End message." She rejoined Vant. "Let's go."

They crossed through the cracked gates.

The door sealed behind them.

They hiked through the blue forest and into the adjoining arbor fields. Lumber farms existed before Corpo had rendered the forestry trade obsolete, and before it had become too dangerous to develop industry outside the township walls. The terrain stretched on for a mile or so.

At first, Vant trailed behind Skii. She repeatedly threw looks over her shoulder to ensure he kept up. He tried to walk alongside her, but she insisted his loud breathing was an annoyance. No matter what their formation, their rhythm was all out of whack.

"Stop that," she grumbled.

"Stop what?"

"You're walking at pace with me."

"I'm what?"

"When I walk, you walk. You're at pace with me. It's like I have a gangly man-shadow."

"When I walk too fast, you get upset. When I walk too slow—"

"Figure it out. You're a smart fella."

With effort, Vant discovered a passable placement a few steps shy of Skii and slightly off to the side. It seemed the winning combination. Except...

The map on Skii's arm was too enticing to ignore. When she was unaware, Vant would steal glances at her tattoo in an attempt to pick up tidbits about their trek. But the design bounced up and down with her strides, so maintaining a clear view became a nauseating affair.

"Hey!" Skii came to an abrupt halt.

"What?"

"I'm on to you! You're fixated on my tattoo!"

Busted. "I'm not!"

"I told you, I know the way!"

"I trust you. I *do*."

"If you're trying to memorize my map and ditch me—"

"No! Why would I do that?"

"You're never gonna figure it out. My dad used a system that only he and I understand. The colors represent things you wouldn't expect. The swooshes are paths, but certain ones are decoys. The dots and symbols all mean something they shouldn't. And it's reversed and backwards, but only in parts. You can stare at this thing for hours and it would never make a lick of sense. Unless you know how to decode it."

Vant conceded, "Your dad was pretty smart."

"Something like that. Plus, this is only half the map. It only tells half the story."

"Where's the other half?"

"Like everything else in my life. Gone."

They continued walking.

"I wasn't going to ditch you."

"Save it."

Vant stayed quiet. He made a concerted effort to not walk at the same pace as she did. It was hard to do.

After a time, "Sorry," Skii offered. "Touchy subject."

"I understand." He kept his mouth shut for a while. Which was for the best, as they were entering into more dangerous territory.

They traveled for a dozen hours, nonstop. Skii had insane stamina; the girl never rested. She never stopped to admire the sights and never stopped to catch her breath. The outlying areas were her turf; she was home, though it was a home she had never wanted. Her and her father's predicament had forced their hands; they had left the comforts of Land Escape to endure the uncertainty of the outside world. And, in surviving its dangers, she had become an expert on it.

The hike was unrelenting. They moved as if an adversary secretly stalked them. Each deliberate step felt like a gamble, like it had the potential for drawing unwanted attention. Skii walked on the brink of a run, her breathing rapid, yet mechanical. She kept her heart rate up and her awareness piqued. She never scaled obstacles; she always circumvented them. Approaching a fallen tree no more than two feet thick, she took the long way around instead of making a quick hop over the trunk. Vant had no idea why. The noise? Disruption of the rhythm of her movement? Fear of spraining an ankle or leaving a trail? The rationale escaped him but, although grueling, he did as she did. Vant was an experienced journeyman—hell, he had trudged for years across a desert wasteland—but he had never moved at such an intensive pace for such a substantial duration.

After sunset, they slowed their strides and backtracked. They zigged and zagged and ducked and weaved through the brush in silence. She led them more than a quarter-mile out of their way to ditch any potential hidden threats.

When night fell, they made camp in a nondescript plot of forest. The location held no strategic advantage other than its total randomness. Skii found an elevated plot of dirt, sat upright with Cassidy on her lap, and entered into a state of deep concentration. Her posture spoke for her; she was scanning the forest with her senses for any unnatural stimuli. Vant did the same, mirroring her every move, attempting to absorb her skills through muscle memory. After a solid hour—which tested Vant's patience and the strength of his back—Skii disengaged from her intense focus. She gifted herself a cat-like stretch.

No ceremony, celebration, or comforts of any kind were to be enjoyed at the day's end. Skii nixed a campfire, a hunting expedition, and a leisurely bathroom break by way of her unyielding silence. Her nonverbal demeanor also asserted that there was to be no talking, no exceptions. A word, whisper, or even a cough meant someone a half-mile away might detect the vibrations, thereby making them a target for predators.

Vant picked up on her cues. Skii knew this world far better than he did, and many of his instincts were ill-considered, compared to hers. Case in point, he had opted for nighttime travel and daytime sleeping in his prior journeys, which, in retrospect, was a terrible idea. First, this meant movement and noise when nocturnal hunters were at their peak, and second, during the day, travelers were exposed and easily spotted anyway. That was the time to be in constant motion. Fine-tuned during her formative years, Skii had perfected this rigorous methodology designed for one purpose: non-detection.

Vant felt sympathy for her. To live like this as a young girl—an entire existence dedicated to remaining unseen—and with a sick mother motivating every step... his heart sank. And it dropped even further when he viewed a bittersweet sight that evening, at bedtime.

Under her canvas blanket, Skii hugged her teddy bear shotgun with vise-like arms. The embrace was so tight that, were Cassidy a real bear, she would have been strangled to death. Vant pieced together the puzzle: her dad, clever man that he was, must have wanted his daughter to protect herself at all times. So, he made her a defensive weapon, a concussive shotgun, that repels instead of kills. He would have insisted she carry the armament everywhere and even sleep with it at night for safety, so he gave it a personality. Something she could adore.

Skii's "bed" looked impenetrable, shutting out the cold and the noise of the forest and making her near-undetectable to prying eyes. The day of traveling had drained Vant's energy, but he stayed awake a touch longer after she fell asleep. He reflected on their first day and tried to figure out his unlikely companion, this gifted survivalist and daughter of his departed beloved. He also wanted to feel useful, as if he were protecting *her*, even if only for a few moments. So, through heavy eyes, he watched the wilderness.

Soon, however, he wrapped himself within his cloak and, helpless to sleep's onslaught, he succumbed.

He dreamed of Death.
Among clouds of smoke.
Violating.
Forcing.
Torturing.
Laughing, "Meh-heh."
Manipulating.
A pool of blood.
With jagged teeth.

Vant was jarred awake. Skii's boot was tapping against his temple.

"Can you poop?" she asked.

He was not quite sure what she was asking. All he could manage was, "Huhrgh?"

"Can you poop? If so, poop."

He sat upright, wiped the dry crusties from his eye sockets, and looked at her quizzically.

"We're a half-mile from our route," she said. "Better to jettison here what you'll eventually have to. Don't want to leave a trail."

No detail ignored. He obliged while she ran off to stretch and pinpoint their location. He noted the milestone marked by this final bowel movement: for the remainder of the journey, they would be living off Corpo sustenance capsules, which did not generate solid digestive waste.

After this important business was completed—and subsequently buried—they began hoofing it again. A few quiet hours later, they entered into a dry canyon. Skii explained that the rocks would dampen their noise, so the next several miles between the gully walls would be safe to talk. To be certain, Vant verified their safety by briefly donning Death's mask, which revealed a lack of hidden threats.

After some conversation false starts, Skii paused to investigate some geology.

"Remnants," she said, running some pieces of material between her fingers.

"Of what?"

"Roadways. Bridges. Something overhead, hundreds of years ago. Man-made, see? Nature wouldn't make this."

She handed the pieces to Vant, who studied them. They were like concrete, and they left a tar-like residue on his fingertips. "The world before The Shift," Vant said.

"You really are older than you look. Only old farts talk about that. And even *they* don't know much about it."

Vant said nothing.

Skii continued, "Dad suspected the material meant links between the townships. Though I don't know why they ever needed to be connected. They all believe in such different things. Or so Dad said."

"He would know. Sounds like he's seen a ton. That must have been hard on you, to wait while he went inside all those places."

A flock of birds flew in and out of the ravine. Skii spent a few moments identifying them, which gave her information about the geography that went over Vant's head. She pushed her finger to her lips to shush him as they tiptoed, careful to not startle the birds. An explosion of flutters rising into the sky would betray their location.

When clear of the chirping threats, Skii picked up where she had left off. "Yeah, it was rough. But to cheer me up, he'd say, 'We always have hope. There's one for sure who can fix Mom.' He'd tell me stories of a man who had the magic powers to save her."

"Magic powers?"

"I was a kid. I believed everything Dad told me. He said there was a magician who could heal her. 'The World's Best Magician.'"

"'World's Best Magician,' huh? Never heard of him. And I've been in the world for quite a while."

"He was a local myth. A celebrity that everyone in Land Escape knew of, but no one had ever actually met. They loved to tell stories about him. 'Don't worry,' Dad would say, 'we'll find the World's Best Magician, and he'll fix Mom right up.' And one day, heh, we found him."

"No. Really?"

"Yeah. We came across a caravan while camping in the outskirts. I mean, you could hear them a mile away. So we followed the noise and discovered a whole entourage. A circus, no joke. Like they used to have at Land Escape, but bigger. Horses, tents, animals, and an entire military protecting them. Tanks and guns and bodyguards, totally unreal. And, all over the carts and machines were these weird symbols..."

Skii picked up a branch and drew an emblem in the dirt. It read, *W8M*. She explained, "It stands for W—World's, 8—Best, M—Magician. See the illusion? You can turn W8M upside-down and it still says W8M. They had the marks all over their gear, and in all kinds of colors and patterns."

She reached down to scatter the remains of the logo—but paused. For a moment it looked like she was going to leave it—like she wanted to leave it—but she didn't. Her survival instincts overrode her whimsy and she wiped clean the patch of dirt. "We trailed them for days, along with tons of other curious strays. None of us had seen anything like it before. The security was crazy-tight, and they wouldn't let any of us within twenty feet of the convoy. The magician never showed his face, and we didn't know which cart he was in. If we had, Dad would have stormed the thing. We just followed and followed, hoping to get an audience with him at some point. We tailed the caravan straight to the gates of Crash Town."

"Plenty of money there to collect," Vant said. "Tons of people, and all that."

"That's what we figured, too. So, hundreds of us made camp around the edges of Crash Town while a bunch of others followed the circus inside. Dad left me with the crowd outside, which was safe, and kind of a party. I had been traveling with him a long time at this point, so I knew how to take care of myself. He trusted me to get away if things got weird. He kissed me, told me he'd make sure it was okay for kids, and said he'd get us tickets to the magic show. I'd never been more excited in my life. Dad's eyes were all lit up, too. I hadn't seen him that optimistic in, well, ever. So, yeah. He went in. And that was the last I saw of him."

"How long did you wait?"

"About a year."

"That's awful."

"A lifetime for a little girl." She paused. "There were okay moments. Made friends with a group of wanderers. But, one by one, they started leaving, giving up hope. The thing was, once anyone entered Crash Town, we never saw them again. Dad had been inside tons of townships and he always came back out, but this time, time really dragged on. Things turned desperate when pills ran low. Water grew scarce. The situation got tense. The outsides turned violent again. So, I split."

Vant picked up on a detail she had glossed over. "Alone, or with others?"

Skii did not answer. Vant had stumbled upon another uncomfortable subject. He chose to let it go. They walked.

A restlessness traveled with them on their voyage... a voyage that would take them so far out of their way, through so much danger, and toward a destination with so few guarantees. Still, Crash Town was as good a place to start as any. Vant and Skii had a symbiotic arrangement for the time being: Skii could seek out her father for some unfinished business, and Vant could meet a man with knowledge of the foes he might soon be confronting. Gyse Fliyr had first hand experience with more dogmatic townships than anyone on the planet, so if there was someone who knew about wicked water-filled soldiers made of thallium who vacuumed up humans, it would be him.

"It stands for W—World's, 8—Best, M—Magician. See the illusion?"

- Skii Tavee

PART
THREE
CRASH

"I changed my mind. I'd rather wait outside."

- Skii Tavee

C H A P T E R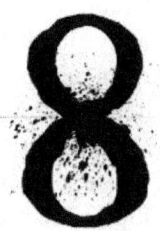

The Sinful and the Smug

They smelled Crash Town before they could see it.

Vile.

Putrid fumes wafted from within the deteriorating stronghold. A wretched odor of sweat and smoke, refuse and bodily fluids contaminated the air.

The look of the town was as foul as its stench. Rumored to have once been the most luxurious of all the Townships, Crash Town's heyday was long gone. The exterior walls were reddish-brown, rusted and filthy. Entire chunks of concrete were missing and lightning-like cracks ran from its base to an enclosed rooftop. Easily three times the size of Land Escape, its superstructure was bloated and swollen, having gone through several haphazard expansions over the years.

It was a citadel that the devil himself would deem a fixer-upper.

A siren song of thumping bass beckoned Vant and Skii to the township. As they closed the gap from the wilderness to the megalopolis, the pulsing beats melded with the din of the crowd inside. From a concealed position, Vant and Skii studied the entrance. Two garish, tacky pillars rose up from the turf and held the chipped gold signage of the township. Faded letters spelled out its original name, *CASH TOWN*. Yet, between the *C* and the *A,* a vandal had painted an *R,* changing the moniker to something infinitely more suitable.

The skewed dogma of the township was something of a legend, told mostly as a precautionary tale. In its inception, Crash Town promised the elongation of life through the alleviation of conscience. It was believed that surrendering one's burdens and committing to a guilt-free existence was the path to a longer lifespan and a more pleasurable way of being. Every passing year, droves of people flocked to Crash Town to escape whatever dogmatic rule they had been trapped in, for the lifestyle Crash

Town promised. It had become a beacon of hope for the hopeless. A final destination for the disenfranchised.

But this was no Eden. It was a sanctuary of sin. It offered no more than the chance for countless people to fill their lives with prurient distractions—and then experience the famous "crash" that followed. Every person who stepped foot inside the township was eventually hit with a harsh reality: they had escaped whatever hell they were trapped in only to have inadvertently discovered a new one.

Crash Town seduced them, broke them, and kept them.

Vant inhaled to clear his head—and choked on the stink. Skii's pointed look said it all: they had come so far undetected; they did not want to blow it now. All they had to do was slip inside the city without being spotted and they would be free of nomad threats.

Although the entrance was open to outsiders, they scanned the exterior in search of an alternative way in. Frankly, they were stalling. Skii's father had vanished into Crash Town years ago, and the reason for his disappearance was a mystery. Had he been murdered? Robbed and left for dead? Got lost in the madness? Skii shook off a shiver—Vant assumed she was warding off any nightmarish visions in her mind.

Vant, too, was skittish. Though a warrior—one who had battled Death himself and lived to tell the tale—he still felt his heart palpitating. What disturbed him most was the unpredictable nature of the place. He had heard stories of the temptations, tricks, and titillations that lay behind the city's walls, and he had no idea how he would hold up against them. He was, after all, a man... and one who had not experienced the touch of a woman in an astonishing number of years. Vant had a disturbing thought: he felt empathetic toward Skii's father, should he have fallen victim to the seductions of Crash Town.

After using Death's mask to scour the trees for camouflaged nomads—of which there were *hundreds*—Vant and Skii quickly strategized the safest route into town. Still concealed, and with the noise of the city masking their voices, they plotted their path to the front door.

"You ready?" Vant asked.

"Nope."

"You don't have to go. I'll go alone."

"Trust me, waiting outside is worse."

"Here's the plan. We get in, we deliver the message about the army, we find your father, and we get out. Agreed?"

"Agreed." She scratched her scalp a bunch, then pinned back the loose strands of her hair. "Okay. Ready."

"After me?"

She raised Cassidy. "Ladies first."

Skii moved with immaculate stealth. Vant followed at her feet, too tall for his own good and half as quiet. They hit a divergence point and split up; bodies clumped together would have made for one big target but apart they were two, smaller and faster.

They tucked in, dug deep, and sprinted hard.

They crossed the gap into open air.

Voices shouted from the trees. Curses and rustling branches betrayed the hidden nomads, surprised by the prey darting into the city. They scrambled to load their weapons and fired before acquiring solid targets.

Arrows stuck into dirt behind Vant's feet. Skii sidestepped a net launched from a canon. Bullets chewed the walls next to Vant's head.

Risking a backward glance, Vant saw ten pursuers on his trail. Another ten converged from the front. Beyond them, he saw Skii zip between the pillars and leap into Crash Town's entrance. *Damn she's fast,* he thought.

And then: *Wait—did she just leap?*

Vant neared the entrance. He noticed the flanking nomads disengaging. They brandished machetes and knives, but they did not attack.

What are they waiting for?

He was at the pillars. His instinct kicked in, overriding his brain. He did as Skii did, taking a running leap into the entrance.

Snap! A jaw-like trap buried in the ground snapped shut on the leg of a nomad trailing him. The man cried out, and the remaining pack stopped to free him.

Vant and Skii were inside the keep, safe from outside threats.

They steadied their breathing.

They collected their wits.

And walked through a turnstile.

It smelled like urine.

A narrow tunnel, once a processing zone of some sort, led them to an abandoned greeting center. The area featured an elaborate mural of the town that was heavily defaced with vulgarities. A "Welcome" sign greeted them, but it was missing key letters. It now simply read, "come."

A few more steps brought them to a broken moving walkway. They proceeded along the stationary conveyor until they arrived "outside" to a disorienting illusion.

The town was encased by an artificial sky. It glowed a nighttime violet-black in parts and a bright daylight hue in others. Either the holographic ceiling was meticulously designed to create a combination of simultaneous day and night, or it was malfunctioning. In a corner of the "sky," a pink sun rose above a cluster of buildings, surrounded by woefully inaccurate celestial objects. Projected clouds moved overhead, but disappeared into solid-gray areas where the roof was not working.

They stepped off the walkway onto the main street leading into Crash Town proper. And for the first time, they took in the sight of the thoroughfare.

It was not as bad as they thought.

It was *worse*.

Naked, greasy pedestrians lined the street. Some had vacant stares. Some were tweaked-out on chemicals. Others lay limp—sleeping, passed out, or possibly dead.

Mere feet from them, a teenage boy—missing an arm and coated in excrement—approached a motionless lump of a woman. He kicked her. When she did not respond, he mounted her.

A man snorted at their feet. Two hook-like syringes dangled from his nostrils. He was working on inserting a third.

To the side, a woman grunted in discomfort. Three children clawed at each other, fighting to breastfeed on her massive body.

Vant took it all in with stunned overwhelm. Skii choked on her emotions. "I changed my mind," she said. "I'd rather wait outside."

A handful of vagabonds noticed the new visitors in town. They rose with varying degrees of success, tripped over themselves, and approached with outstretched hands. They mouthed whatever words they could find to beg for whatever Vant and Skii had to spare.

Skii was visibly concerned, but also nauseated. She reasoned with them, "I'm sorry, I don't have anything—"

"Shut your mouth!" Vant snapped at her. Her words were drawing the attention of more husks of men and women. They approached with quivering hands and exposed genitals. Her naiveté was making her an easy mark.

A gooey tub of man lumbered toward Skii. He had an illness—his purple tongue flopped out of his mouth, and he stumbled over gangrenous legs.

"Get behind me," Vant said.

When the fiend was close enough, Vant booted him in his doughy chest, collapsing him onto his rear. Like a turtle on its back, he struggled to get up.

More junkies zeroed in on them. With her shaking hands pawing at Cassidy, Skii wrestled with whether she should start blasting or turn tail and run. She twisted around and yelped; no escape would be found back the way they came. A dozen of the strung-out beggars had converged from behind.

A bead of sweat rolled down Vant's cheek. It was one thing battling warriors, golems, or even Death himself... but the sick and desperate? He tickled his satchel with his fingers; he knew if he removed his gauntlets, blood would surely be spilled. He had no clue what the hell to do. Escape? Reason? Run? Kill? All seemed like crap options. "Crash Town," he concluded aloud to Skii, "sucks."

Dozens of junkies appeared from the walkways and alleys. A disgusting pile of skin charged, panting and violently scratching an infected wound on his forehead. He lunged at Skii, who evaded. Vant balled up his bare fist and smashed the guy in the face. A stream of pus emptied from his nose. Gagging with revulsion, Vant used his cloak to wipe the slop off his knuckles.

Vagabonds poured from the windows of adjoining buildings onto the street. There were thirty of them. Then fifty. Then a hundred.

An addict apocalypse.

"Ass down!" Skii yelled. She kicked Vant in the rear.

He dropped to the pavement.

She cocked her shotgun—*shlick-shlock!*—and took aim at the largest group. A blue blast exploded from the teddy bear's mouth with her trigger pull. The shockwave knocked the derelicts back a dozen yards. She fired at another pack, creating a sprawled pileup of bodies. Another discharge from Cassidy and three shiv-wielding women flew backward, arms flailing.

"Skii, you're pissing them off!" Vant elbowed a skinny miscreant with the shakes who had managed to sneak up behind them. The crowd's agitation was escalating and the chaos was attracting more curious strays into the mix. Their demeanor turned riotous. Hundreds of grimy fingernails and fouled appendages were upon them.

"Stay down! Cassidy's pissed, and she's gonna growl!" Skii pulled the weapon's slider back—*shlick*. A glow on the shotgun's barrel formed as she held down the primer. Air flowed into the nozzle as the size of the glow increased, and an ascending charge grew louder and louder. When it was fully primed, Skii let go of the slider—*shlock!*—and squeezed the trigger.

A burst of light.

A vigorous thrum, like an animal snarling.

A hemisphere of sapphire energy fountained from Cassidy's mouth, creating an impenetrable shield around Vant and Skii. They huddled together underneath the dome.

The vagrants attempted to penetrate the repulser shield. Upon contact, they were forced back by kinetic discharge.

Vant, in the blue sanctuary, experienced a moment of relief—followed by concern. "How long will this last?"

"Cassidy's got about thirty more seconds before she'll need a rest."

"That's *it?*"

"I'd like to see you do better!"

"Guess I'll catch a nap. Wake me up when we're being molested."

A bony *crunch*.

A spray of blood splattered on the shield.

The fluids sparked in a disgusting light show.

Vant peered through the semi-transparent energy field, trying to decipher what had happened. All he could see was some kind of metal contraption operating a few feet away. It had made a mess.

"Come on out!" an amplified voice boomed. "You two, huddled in blue! Yer safe now!"

The addicts panicked and scattered. Cassidy's shield fizzled out—an almost embarrassed sound sputtered from her mouth as the gun ran out of energy.

The metal leg of a mechanized biped—a walking tank—filled their vision. The chipped paint of its exterior was peppered in splotches of red. It lifted its appendage and scraped it against the curb, attempting to get the gunk off. It had squashed a vagrant underneath its massive foot.

"'Scuse the mess, folks!" The voice emanated out of embedded loudspeakers at an unnecessarily loud volume. The machine's posture was proud and arrogant, standing near twenty feet tall. "Welcome ta Crash Town! Pleased ta meetcha! I'm the keeper of the peace in this here settlement! They call me The Mayor! Pleasure, pleasure!"

The body was expressive and shockingly agile, moving with humanoid precision. A huge robotic hand extended to Vant, but he remained motionless. Skeptical. The hulking enforcer peered at him with a visor of glassy black eyes—sensor panels—that hid the contents of the cockpit.

The Mayor re-extended his hand in a demand for decorum. The whir of complex mechanics underscored his insistence. Vant patted the tip of the robotic index finger, a finger nearly as large as Vant's entire body.

Then, to Skii, "Li'l lady! Charmed!" It politely bowed. "My, my, my, the women of the world jest keep on gettin' purtier, don't they?" Was the machine... flirting with her? "Anyhoo, y'all picked the worst way ta introduce yerselves ta Crash Town. Most everyone knows the best way ta make an entrance is... ta make a *hell* of an entrance! Gotta scare off the roaches, make 'em scatter!" He lunged at one of the junkies who had gotten too close for comfort. The Mayor scooped him up into a clenched fist. The victim protested as mechanized fingers squeezed and squeezed until... *pop!* The beggar burst like a pimple. Skii averted her eyes in horror.

"Hey!" Vant bellowed. "Was that necessary?"

"Why surely, stranger! Gotta teach the damned dopers ta be polite! Otherwise, how we gonna let fresh *blood* in the door? Now, my friends, yer free to play in Crash Town! Know yer way around? Ah, well, hell, 'course you don't! I'll be more'n happy ta point ya in the direction of whatever dings yer doodads! But heck! What *am* I thinkin'? First, we got one *tiny* thing ta chat about..."

Uh oh, Vant thought.

"...the small matter of payin' yer taxes."

"Our what?" Vant felt lame playing dumb. He knew where this was going.

"Come now, we can't jest protect and serve fer free, ya know? This here metal beast needs power, polish, and paint! It don't lick itself clean, after all!" The Mayor shoved a bloody finger in Vant's face and waved it around. Skii looked nauseated. "Don'tcha fret, sweet thing! I ain't gonna squash ya! Yer safe with me. But ya gotta pay the piper, ya know how it goes. Here in Crash Town it's either business or pleasure. And yer pleasure is my business!"

"What do you want?" asked Vant.

"Well, let's see... whatcha *got?*"

Vant knew he was being robbed, but no alternatives sprung to mind. He was staring at a homicidal metal maniac in a sea of strung-out zombies. He looked at Skii and shrugged. She rolled her eyes.

"Corpo-Capsules." Vant removed the pouch from his satchel. "I'll give you half."

"Tsk, tsk. If you only wanna gimme half..." a compartment opened in the automaton's shoulder and a gatling gun raised out of the slot. The barrel spun and pointed at Skii. "...I guess we only need half of ya."

"Thought that may be the case," Vant grumbled. "But I should get something for my money. Let's make a deal."

"Talk, son."

"You're the head of this town? You keep order here?"

"Sure do, friend! M'self and the rest of the Peace-Keepers!" His steel fists pounded his torso. The implication that there were more of these machines gave Vant the willies.

"Then, we have to talk. We have a situation. I was a few townships over and saw some things... look, I can't explain it staring at a machine gun. Let's have a sit-down and chat man to man."

The "eyes" of the behemoth, the opaque glossy panels, appeared to be reading Vant.

"This a game, stranger? Not gonna try to get yer li'l pill-purse back, are ya?"

"No," Vant said. "A handful of capsules won't matter, what with the hell-storm headed this way."

"Sounds fascinatin'! Okay, pal. Yer on. Meet me at my mansion around suppertime. Ask anyone, they'll point ya in the right direction. We'll have some grub! Dinner's on you! After all, ya jest got stuck with the check! *Hyick!*" A self-indulgent guffaw came from The Mayor's loudspeakers as he stretched out an open palm. Vant emptied his pill pouch into an opening in the wrist—the machine was optimized for receiving handouts. Skii did the same with her capsules, then blew a dangling strand of hair out of her face in defiance.

They followed The Mayor past the addiction zone into the corrupted, polluted heart of the city. A mixture of rumbles and rattles posing as music thumped out of timeworn woofers. Trinket shops, fetish boutiques, swap-meet booths peddling bizarre wares, and thousands of people filled the metropolis of filth.

Every turn revealed a disconcerting sight. A four-year-old was getting her face tattooed on the sidewalk. A woman ate what appeared to be fried toes on a stick. A vendor was selling pocket-sized genital guillotines. There was no end to the debauched lunacy on display.

Massive buildings lined the streets, decorated with illuminated signs and image projections, some working, most broken. "Casino" was common, but so, too, was "Live Debasement," "Pleasure House," and "Fancy Massage." One sign cryptically read, "Happy Chunks." Vant pointed it out to Skii as if to say, *Interested?* She punched his shoulder. He shrugged, "Can't hurt to ask."

They wandered without a plan. Invasive eyes scoured them wherever they went. They were obviously new in town, and their stares from shocking sight to shocking sight confirmed the locals' suspicions.

Winding paths through the vast township led to dedicated areas for particular sensibilities. Their attempts to avoid the red-light districts were pointless—*every* district turned out to be a red-light district. The question became: what kind? Due to their manic salaciousness, certain zones practically begged to be kept a distance from.

But preventing the frenzy from bubbling over into total madness were sporadic patrols by the burly metal bipeds, the Peace-Keepers. Some were involved in disputes between citizens; others engaged in crowd control. Some twitched as if malfunctioning, and others people-watched. A few sat motionless: out of order? Taking a nap? While each had a different routine, they all had one thing in common: the townspeople despised them, and gave them a wide berth.

When passing through yet another red-light district, this one rife with denizens clad in fuzzy animal costumes up top but no clothing down below, Vant pointed out a section of Corpo-Bots to Skii.

"We're going to need pills to pay for shelter. There has to be a lodging around here, somewhere. Something we can use as a home base. Hopefully something sterile."

She nodded, walked up to a bot, then looked at Vant, waiting for a prompt. He answered, "Oh, um, pull out twenty-twenty. That should be enough. You've got that amount in your account, right?"

"Forty-forty," she requested from the bot. It chirped an acknowledgement and dispensed forty blue and forty green capsules, wrapped in bundles. "Two rooms, big guy." She was about to walk away, but the brass scarab sounded a distinct musical chime. "Message for Skii Tavee," it stated.

She looked at Vant for answers. He had none. "Have a pen pal I don't know about?"

"I used a bot in Land Escape. There were no messages. Someone must have recently sent this."

"Well, let's hear it. Right?"

She swallowed. "Bot, what's the message?"

"Message playback," it responded. "Message sent from *glurberfurbervish*. Message sent on *fligabligaboor* at *churglebaugreag*." The information was either scrambled, or the Corpo-Bot was malfunctioning. A small lens cap popped open, then holographic imagery beamed into the air—a cryptic mix of data, numbers, static, and strobes. The phenomenon lasted about ten seconds before, clear as crystal, words materialized:

"GET OUT. NOW."

The words faded. "End of message," the bot chirped happily.

"So, *that's* fun," said Skii.

"Yeah. Real nice," Vant agreed, sarcastically.

Skii scratched her scalp. "Bot, who sent that message?"

An abrupt tone, followed by, "No messages."

"Hey dummy, who sent the message you just played?"

The same tone, followed by, "No messages."

"What the hell? Bot, replay that message!"

"No messages."

"You just played it five freakin' seconds ago!"

"No messages." Skii kicked the leg of the robot with her boot. "Warning," it said.

They stared at the machine until Skii broke the silence. "Any ideas? I've never seen a busted bot before."

"I don't think it's busted. I think it's been hacked. Someone knows you're here. And they're warning you."

"Warning me? Sounds more like they're threatening me."

"No, that doesn't make sense. Why would someone give you a heads-up if they were coming after you? This is anonymous protection."

"Oh, good. A secret admirer. That's comforting. Whatever. Let's get moving. Skeevy message or no, we've got stuff to do."

"You sure?"

"Definitely. When you think about it, the message is telling us one thing for certain. We're on to something. Here's a thought... think maybe my dad sent it? Think he heard the message I sent to him in Land Escape? Hey, bot?" It made a friendly chirp. "Has my message to Gyse Fliyr been accessed?"

A sad tune, then, "Message unread."

She sighed. "Was worth a shot."

"No arguments here. But, look. We need to get off the streets. I saw far too many drooling mouths from Crash Town's finest when you withdrew those pills. And I don't know about you, but being robbed once a day is plenty for me."

"Agreed."

They left the bots and traversed into the upper echelons of the city, where the true wealth of Crash Town amassed. Grand casinos featuring death-dealing machines lined the thoroughfare. In the gambling houses, customers sat at tables, betting on their own or others' lives. There were amusements where blades struck out at random and money traded hands for every fatal blow. Devices that lowered people into acid while they played number-crunching games to slow their descent. Patrons betting on how long a victim could withstand the stings of poisonous insects. If an activity was violent and had the potential to be wagered upon, there was a good chance a casino offered it.

Deeper into the borough, they came across advertisements for live shows and entertainment, though most were long-since expired. Following the trail of promotions, Vant and Skii arrived at the base of a massive arena: The Spectorum Maxima. The forum more than lived up to its showy name in size, but its appearance was downright appalling.

It had been ravaged by the townspeople. No monument in history had ever been this viciously sullied. Years of hatred had been etched into the walls, and enraged malevolence had been slopped onto every inch reachable by human hands. One particular symbol served as the defacement of choice, repeated over and over and over...

"W3M."

Whether inscribed by blunt objects, blood, or bodily waste, it recurred hundreds of thousands of times. Clearly, making this mark was the "thing to do," some sort of Crash Town tradition handed down over the years. Vant and Skii let their eyes move up from the sea of vengeful scribblings to a mural—a near-impossibly sized mural—that ran to the very top of the arena.

It depicted The World's Best Magician, a handsome mustachioed man in a dapper top hat and cape, with hands emitting beams of light in the shape of his W8M logo. However, the painting had also been vandalized. The word "Best" was painted-over with the word "Worst," and half of the 8 was blotched out, creating a sideways W.

Skii's disappointment in seeing her hero portrayed in such a way was impossible to conceal. Vant opened his mouth in search of consolation, but Skii did not give him the chance. Feigning strength, she said "My dad was obsessed with the guy. At some point, he must have gotten hold of him. Maybe he knows something."

Vant nodded, studying her face.

But it held less hope than before.

They pressed on.

For shelter, they settled on a place that appeared sane enough. A "love hotel." It was moderately populated and decorated with paintings of hearts, breasts, hand bindings, impossibly intertwined bodies, and assorted phallic objects. At least it was clean. After a small discussion with the clerk about whether they needed the lodgings for a couple hours or all night, they paid for the accommodations and went to their rooms. Vant, filled with mistrust, lay down with his satchel under his arms and his mask under his pillow.

Sleep came fast.

He dreamed of Death.
Holding him.
Squeezing him.
Crushing him.
Draining him.
Laughing, "Meh-heh."
He saw himself.
He saw himself, as he should be.
He saw himself, dead. Melting away.
Melting away.

Vant arose in a panic. The abrupt awakening disoriented him and the lack of clocks, coupled with the schizophrenic holographic sky outside his window, left him uncertain as to the time of day. It could have been weeks later, for all he knew.

He cleaned up the best as he could in the communal bathroom, though it was difficult without a mirror—he noticed that he had not seen even one since stepping foot in the township. He soaked his face in cold water, then sped through a sponge bath.

He knocked on Skii's door a dozen times. She grumpily opened it—he was interrupting her marathon nap—and then she turned right back around and flopped face down onto the bed.

"I have to go see The Mayor," Vant said, "to warn him about the thallium army. While I'm there, I'll ask about your father. Stay here, okay?"

She mumbled incoherently into the linens.

"Skii, groan once if you can hear me and you promise to stay in your room."

She responded with a string of obscenities muffled by the pillow pressed against her face.

"I'll take that as a yes. Contact me via wrist-comm if anything comes up. I'll call you if I need you. Don't go anywhere, I won't be long. You getting all this?"

No response.

What could he do? It was dinnertime.

"Most everyone knows the best way ta make an entrance is...
ta make a *hell* of an entrance!"

- The Mayor

234

YEARS PRIOR

Of Admiration and Preparation

Three converged on Vant. He had no time to think. His training took over.

He threw his shoulder into the knees of the first attacker, toppling him over his back. He grasped a loose appendage of the second adversary and used his force against him. The third was nowhere near a threat; one hip throw later and he too was sprawled out on the turf.

Threats subdued.

Terrii yawned from the sidelines. He offered an unimpressed, slow clap.

Vant helped up his wrestling partners and shook their hands. The duration of Vant's spars was becoming shorter and shorter, no matter how many combatants were in the mix. The truth was, Vant excelled faster than his teachers could teach him and his course-mates could push him. As a pupil, he was even more advanced than many warriors in the Knights of Rights—in all areas except firearms, which he refused to study.

Vant rubbed a cloth over his sweaty body, which was chiseled and getting harder by the day. One of his many admirers, a mousy but bold coursemate named Shyyla, worked up the courage to ask him an important question.

"Vant," she began, "what are you doing tomorrow night?"

"He's busy!" Terrii slapped Vant on the back. "Protecting the future head of the order. You know, me!"

She looked at Vant. He shrugged. "Guess I'm busy."

"Shyyla, that reminds me," Terrii said, "I have a question for you, as well. What are you doing tomorrow night?"

"Oh, please." She turned her back on him and walked away.

Terrii used the opportunity to admire her backside. "Now there's *something you don't see every day." He added, "Wonder what her problem is. She's probably intimidated by me,"*

"Who could blame her?" Vant put on his shirt.

"So, what are we doing tomorrow night?"

"Got a date," Vant said.

"You? I'll believe that when the order falls apart. Wait—really? With who?"

"With Gordone. I have to train. My Exaltion Day is next week. They think I'm ready to become a Knight."

"What? You're joking. Did my dad agree to this?"

"I guess so."

"Before me?"

"Nope." He handed Terrii a scroll. "Special delivery."

Terrii unrolled the paper, then let loose his specialty: a vain half-smile. "That's what I thought! I didn't think they'd promote you first. Think we're going in together, for our Exaltion Day tasks?"

"I hope not. I only worry about my skin when yours is around."

"Maybe my quest will be to make an honest woman out of Shyyla."

"That would be the hardest fight of your life."

"My purpose is to maintain the elegance of this cherished home."

- Dawnrier

CHAPTER

The Master and the Mousetrap

The exterior of The Mayor's mansion dripped with pristine, manicured perfection. The estate, unlike the rest of the structures within the township, resembled an honest-to-goodness home—albeit a decadent, plantation-style mega-home. Whitewashed fences and brick walls lay behind polished wrought-iron gates.

Nauseating, gaudy lavishness.

Vant approached. A woman's voice greeted him from an intercom. "Name, and reason for visit?"

"Vant Hu'l, I'm having dinner with The Mayor." *It sounds so official,* he thought.

He sized up the premises and took note of the lack of security systems—save for the gate, which was more of a decoration than a preventative measure. Whoever lived here feared no one, and no one was around to fear them. The many thousands of Crash Town citizens knew something Vant did not: why he should stay the hell away.

"We have been expecting you. Please come in."

The gates opened.

Vant entered, walking underneath an immaculate arbor and through a magnificent garden filled with vibrant grass and lush landscaping. As he passed by one of the copious flowerbeds, he let his palm brush against a blossom to confirm a suspicion: it was as fake as the day was long. Every blade of grass, every rose petal, every tree... it was all manufactured. Vant noticed he had not seen one shred of greenery since the moment he had entered the township—not that anything beautiful could even grow in the cesspool that was Crash Town.

Vant's fingers clenched air, craving the comfort of his gauntlets. He had dropped them off, along with his mask, at a Corpo-Bot before entering the grounds. He was coming in peace, and arriving armed would surely have sent the opposite message. His only consolation was that, before storing Death's mask, he had studied the

133

mansion through its eyes in detail. Shrouded in the veil of blackness, Vant had observed many people inside the property, but none pulsed red as the thallium soldiers had in Land Escape.

He hoped this was a good sign.

Vant's robes brushed against each spotless step in his climb to the home's entrance. Impressive wooden doors glided open as he approached.

He crossed the threshold into a circular foyer. Gleaming marble floors reflected candle-lit sconces. Twin carpeted staircases, one to the left and one to the right, wrapped upward to a second tier, which featured only one closed door. Velvet curtains cascaded from the balcony to the floor.

The door closed behind Vant. And locked.

"Welcome," a voice spoke. The curtain parted slightly, revealing a woman adorned in a skintight bodysuit. Her face—save for her flawless eyes—was concealed in a bondage mask. Sheer satin flowed from the mask's hairline, creating the illusion of silky hair. Leather gloves crawled up to her elbows, and high-heeled boots hugged her thighs.

"Hi, uh, hello..." Vant stammered.

"My name is Dawnrier." She curtsied. "I am the house queen. My purpose is to maintain the elegance of this cherished home."

"Pleasure to meet you. I'm Vant."

"Yes, Master Hu'l, I am well aware of who you are. Your reputation precedes you."

"Oh. Well. That sneaky bastard *does* get ahead of me, sometimes."

The joke was met with silence. Dawnrier continued, "Dinner is not quite ready. The lord of the manor will summon us when the time has come. Etiquette dictates that I extend to you our most generous hospitality while you wait. You shall be doted upon, as all guests are. May I first offer you some refreshment?"

To Vant's left, the curtain slid partially open, revealing a wet bar stocked with multicolored bottles. Prominently displayed was a carafe of exquisite-looking red wine and one lonely glass begging to be filled.

Hell of a presentation, Vant thought. *Hell of a trap.* He experienced the overwhelming sensation that the mansion was like dog crap covered up with gallons of perfume; one could still smell shit somewhere underneath the lilac.

"Kind offer," Vant said. "But drinking usually leads me to make bad decisions. More than the usual, I mean."

"I see, Master Hu'l. Then perhaps you would delight in something sweet?"

The curtain opened further, unveiling a table stacked with delicacies. The mouthwatering treats were meticulously arranged and exquisitely crafted.

Too perfect in every way.

"And spoil my dinner? There's not a whole lot of room in here, after all..." Vant patted his flat belly.

"It seems, Master Hu'l, that you are a man of extraordinary discipline. Yet, in this house we believe in succumbing to our temptations, and in satisfying our appetites. Whatever forms they may take."

The curtain continued its path around the foyer.

Vant choked on his surprise. Behind the velvet shroud...

...were naked ladies.

Twenty of them. Statuesque. Elegant, in a "high-class hooker" kind of way. They were immaculately groomed and all stood with pageant-like hand-on-hip posture. Each female was unique; there were blondes, redheads, greenies, pinkers, blueberries, brunettes, and every body shape and shade was accounted for. The women did not talk, and they did not acknowledge their new visitor. They simply remained upright, breathed, and stared straight ahead with one purpose: to be a feast for the eyes of their guest.

Dawnrier spoke, "Are you *certain* there is nothing I may provide for you? Not even private quarters for a few hours, Master Hu'l?"

"Please, the formalities aren't necessary. Just call me Master." He winked at the girls. A few of them giggled. Vant felt impressed with himself, but noticed he was acting showy. *Nothing like twenty lady-parts, twenty derrières, and forty breasts to mess with a man's composure,* he thought.

He addressed the courtesans, "You're all very lovely. Please don't take offense. But this wasn't exactly what I had in mind when I came here tonight."

"My deepest apologies, Master Hu'l," Dawnrier said. "Perhaps I misjudged your proclivities. Let me offer you something more to your preference."

The curtain completed its path around the foyer. Behind the last quadrant of concealed temptations...

...were twenty naked men.

Their chiseled, oiled-up bodies gleamed, and their oppressively large reproductive organs hung by their knees. They did full turns in tandem, showing off the goods.

"Now *there's* something you don't see every day," said Vant.

He tapped his feet. He smiled at the men. And the women. They all remained stationary.

He was stalling.

From the moment the door to the mansion sealed him inside, Vant knew he had become a pawn in some kind of voyeuristic charade. Now the game was clear: hidden eyes were studying him, watching to see which allurement he would select. And fall victim to.

"Choose your pleasure, Master Hu'l."

He paced the foyer, taking it all in. Although his demeanor remained nonchalant, his adrenaline level had skyrocketed. His heart pumped blood behind his ears. His survival instincts kicked into gear. He tried to conceive an escape route, since the locked door behind him would not be an option, the chamber had no windows, and the only door on the second floor most likely led farther into the home's interior.

"Master Hu'l?"

The awkward silence had grown too palpable. He had to say *something*.

"I don't want to impose. I think I'll wait for The Mayor. Maybe I'll have some wine and an orgy *after* dinner."

"We stand on ceremony here. Your host will be greatly offended if you decline our generosity. I'm afraid we must insist."

From the upstairs balcony, a sconce slid downward. A mechanical arm extended from behind the compartment. Attached to it was a machine gun with its sights trained on Vant.

"You must choose, Master Hu'l."

"Well, shit," Vant said.

He contemplated. *The poison wine will stop my heart. The toxic food will melt my insides. The courtesans, of course, are in on the plot.* His mind spun, trying to deduce whether any of the choices offered a chance to walk away unscathed.

They did not. He wasn't a mouse in a maze. He was a mouse in a mousetrap.

I'll wing it, he thought. *The Vant Special.*

"So!" He clapped his hands together. A dozen of the courtesans jumped, startled. "What's your story, Dawnrier? Tell me about you. Turn-ons. Turn-offs. That sort of thing."

"I am the most coveted of the house girls. My beauty is to be preserved, and made available only on extraordinarily special occasions."

"Now, that's tempting." He pointed at her mask. "Can I peek under the hood?"

"I admire your bravado, Master Hu'l. Perhaps one day. For now, any *other* pleasure will be yours."

"What can I say, I'm a guy who likes the best of everything. So if I can't *have* you... I guess I'll just have to *take* you."

Vant lunged. He grabbed Dawnrier's satin "hair" from behind and yanked, sending her to the floor. She landed hard on her back. He pinned his boot under her chin.

"Pawn takes queen," Vant shouted to whoever was listening. "I've got your girl. Let me out of here or I'll snap her neck." He pressed down harder. Dawnrier moaned —with ecstasy.

The unmistakable twang of The Mayor rang out from speakers in the chamber. "Well, son, looks like ya made up yer mind! Dawn, m'dear, think ya can *take care* of our li'l buddy there?"

"With *pleasure*," she said.

With incredible dexterity, Dawnrier thrust her legs up like a contortionist and clamped them hard around Vant's waist. She whipped him face-first into the marble floor then vaulted up, twisted her body in midair, and stuck the landing with Vant's neck between her vise-like calves.

Vant clawed at her boots. Dawnrier giggled sadistically, tightening her grip on his throat. "Oh, *Master*. Look at how helpless you are. How pathetic."

He reached up to grab her waist. She slapped his arm away. "No touching," she vamped. "You don't deserve me."

Vant thrashed, trying to free himself. His eyes bulged from his head. Sweat poured from his brow. His face turned red. He swatted at her, but she laughed at his futile attempts.

Finally, a swing broke through her defenses—and connected with her rear.

"Naughty!" Dawnrier removed a leather strap from the lining of her glove. She whipped Vant's ass over and over. "Naughty! Naughty!" The guffaws of The Mayor boomed as she punished Vant's posterior.

He focused on the timing of her swings. At the right moment, he caught her wrist on a downward swipe and pulled hard, wrenching her to the floor. He freed his head from her legs and crawled away as she acrobatically righted herself.

"Come back here, *Master*. Come punish me. I was bad. I have to be disciplined." She slapped herself with the strap, taunting him.

"Get away from me, you nutty bitch!"

Dawnrier giggled and strutted toward Vant. She opened a slit on her mask, revealing a luscious mouth coated in lipstick. Trails of acidic steam rose from the gloss.

"Does the little *Master* want a kiss from Mommy?"

Vant backed away toward the cornucopia of naked women. They reached behind their backs and removed flesh-colored blades that matched their skin. The nearest girls took swipes at Vant. His dodge forward returned him to Dawnrier's clutches. She dropped into a leg split, wrapped a calf around his shin, and collapsed him onto his back with a tug.

Click.

A handcuff locked around his wrist.

"Now you belong to me! Now who's the *Master*?" Dawnrier dragged Vant to the other side of the room.

"What's with you?" Vant shouted. "You're the *worst*! Oh, *hell*—" He rolled to the side to evade the brass knuckles of a male escort smashing into the floor. The rest prepared to strike, but Vant twisted his arm to put Dawnrier in front of him as a shield. He kicked out with his legs. The blow inadvertently connected with her crotch.

"Oh crap. I'm so sorry—"

She shrieked. The frenzied men took swings at Vant, each looking for a piece of the action. "Stop!" Dawnrier demanded. "He's mine! I need to teach my *Master* a lesson!"

She dangled a boot-heel above Vant's face, showing off its razor-sharp interior edge. Like scissors, the heel snapped shut toward her toes. She demonstrated the castration device a few more times with glee, the blades opening and closing like hungry jaws.

She stomped at Vant's nether region—he twisted to the side. Her heel landed behind his lower back. He then jerked her connected arm downward, crashing her to the floor.

She was dazed. Disoriented.

Vant got to his feet. He curled his arms under her body and lifted her overhead with sloppy, brute strength. She flailed as he tore across the room and he body-slammed her into the table of food, demolishing it. Sweet treats rained down and melted into noxious pools beside them.

Vant pinned Dawnrier with his knee. "I've got something you can kiss." He pressed the handcuff to her mouth. Acid from her lipstick ate into the metal, and the binding split apart.

He cocked his arm back and balled up his fist. "I usually don't punch pretty things. But since I can't see your face, well, they say love is blind..."

His downswing was interrupted. Two tiny clips launched from the breasts of Dawnrier's suit. They clamped onto Vant's nipples and an electric shock flowed into his body. He hollered from the concentrated pain inflicted onto the delicate region.

"Don't you *dare* fake it," Dawnrier moaned with bliss. She rose to her feet. "I always know when someone's faking it."

Vant tried to pull off the pincers but they were locked shut. He called out in misery.

"Admit it," Dawnrier said, "you love it. Now that you're all worked up, let's finish you off."

She grabbed the carafe of wine and straddled Vant, pouring its contents all over his mouth. "Taste my juice!" she cackled. "Don't spit it out! Swallow!" She pressed the bottle to his pursed lips and plugged his nose. Several forced gulps flowed down his throat.

Vant immediately identified the chemical reaction in his belly. A heat in his innards transitioned to a sizzling acid reflux. Chemicals coursed through his veins.

His heart slowed.

Then stopped.

"Good little *Master,* drinking all of Mommy's juice." She slapped Vant on the cheek a few times.

No movement.

The clamps on Vant's nipples retracted back into Dawnrier's bodysuit.

She moved to the center of the foyer, and took a well-mannered bow.

"Ya just made me a wealthy man!" the Mayor cheered.

"I do apologize for the mess," Dawnrier said. "I'll summon the maids to remove this filthy thing from our home. I shall then come upstairs for some *real* punishment." She wrapped her mane of synthetic hair around her neck and playfully choked herself. The crowd of courtesans laughed along with her.

"*Cough.*"

Stunned silence washed over the foyer.

"*Cough!* Oh, man. This is gonna be bad. *Cough*…" Vant rolled over onto all fours, gagging.

Wide eyes from Dawnrier and her retinue.

Disbelief.

Vant shoved his finger down his throat.

And sprayed red, liquidy vomit all over the white marble floor.

A cacophony of gasps came from everyone watching.

"Hold—hold on a sec…" Vant rose to his feet and pounded on his chest. One hand was not enough—he intertwined his fingers and used both to beat against his heart as hard as he could. After the fifth thud, "There it goes!" He felt his organ lurch back to life and regain a steady pulse.

No one made a sound. The mansion's residents gawked at Vant like he was a witch. He picked up the empty wine bottle and studied it. "Must have been a crummy year for this vintage. And they say it's to die for." He smashed the bottle on the ground. Shards of crystal flew everywhere.

"What the hell are ya?" The Mayor asked from the speakers.

"You're about to find out."

"Not likely. It's game over fer you, son." He gave an order: "Lock 'er down!"

Deadbolts slid across the front door. The courtesans panicked and scattered. Some sprinted upstairs while a handful stayed down below and attempted to pry apart the front door's locks.

"Relax!" Vant shouted to The Mayor. "I only want to talk."

The machine gun rattled with the loading of ammunition.

"Don't do this!"

The gun pivoted to lock onto Vant, but Dawnrier was blocking its line of sight.

"Move!" Vant called out to her.

Too late.

The gun lit up. Ballistic rounds tore into her. She shrieked with dread.

Vant pulled her across the floor and shoved her under the bar. He dove underneath, next to her.

The machine gun fired with reckless abandon, pinning them down. Bullets chipped away at the marble flooring. Strays shattered the glass bottles. Shrapnel and smoke multiplied by the moment.

Dawnrier choked on her own blood.

"Damn it!" Vant growled to her. "Why didn't you listen to me?"

"Because… because you didn't say 'please.'" She stroked his cheek. "You should have treated me like a lady. Bad little *Master*."

She slapped his face.

Then went limp.

The sounds of artillery and the cries of courtesans filled the foyer. Two of the girls sprinted for the upstairs door. The weapon that had been trained on Vant confused their motion for his. Bullets cut through their bare skin and fireworks of gore erupted from the perforations.

The distracted gun flung bullets around the chamber, trying to pick off Vant amid the commotion. A vulnerable courtesan was struck in the stomach—she screeched, and her wound emptied thick plasma all over the floor. Another escort tried to usher her away, catching the attention of the weapon. In a blink, he too was shredded.

Vant seized the opportunity and hauled ass toward the gun. He was halfway up the stairs when it turned on him. A shot grazed his shoulder. Another scraped his ribcage. He leapt onto the armament and pulled at its bracings, rocking it back and forth while it fired spastically. It finally dislodged from the mounting hardware. Dangling limp from bent metal and loose wires, the malfunctioning armament threw bullet after bullet into the floor.

Vant caught his breath.

He assessed his wounds: they stung like hell, but he would live.

The chamber was secure.

But...

Across the room and down the stairs, the decorative arches shook.

Something large stirred.

The foyer rumbled.

This can't be good, Vant thought.

The entire eastern wall slid upward. Vant rubbed his eyes, attempting to clear out the disbelief. This was no illusion—the panel was a façade camouflaging a storage compartment.

Inside, a Peace-Keeper roared to life.

"Easy, fella..." Vant said to the mechanical biped coming online. "Let's take this down about ten notches."

The machine responded by careening up the stairs.

Vant pivoted the barrel of the dangling gun toward the Peace-Keeper, shooting it in the "face" a few times. The bullets ricocheted off its viewport and the beast kept coming. Vant dashed aside as a massive fist crashed to the floor.

He needed distance—this thing could flatten him in one move. He hopped over the banister and dropped down to the first level. He heard a bone crack as he landed —*Who needs a pinky toe anyway?* He plastered himself against the edge of the stairwell, out of sight.

The Peace-Keeper paced upstairs in search of Vant, who was busy strategizing his next move downstairs. The situation was grim. He longed for his whip gauntlets.

"Skii!" Vant whisper-yelled into his wrist-communicator. "Where are you?"

No response.

"Skii!"

He imagined her as a human caterpillar bundled up in her bed. "I hate you," he said.

The metal beast roared in protest at having lost its target.

Vant experienced a pang of guilt. Back into his comm, "Okay, fine. I don't hate you. But I am probably going to be squashed because of you. I hope you can live with that."

The walking tank thundered down the stairs past Vant, who, in a moment of misguided inspiration, vaulted onto its back. He held on while it bucked.

The kinetic movement knocked him onto the viewport. Vant reached into a crevice beneath the windshield and yanked hard on a thin, rubber device. The piece broke off.

"Ha!" he bellowed. "You're screwed now!"

The machine stopped. Gathered its wits. Then swatted overhead. A bolt on its finger snagged Vant's cloak. It whipped its arm forward. Vant flew across the room and smashed into the wall. Boney *snaps* indicated a dislocated shoulder and a cracked rib.

Vant attempted to get to his feet—and slipped. He had landed in a pool of blood seeping from the mangled body of a destroyed escort.

Disgusting.

"How exactly does removin' my windshield wiper make me screwed, son?" The Mayor asked.

"Here's how." Vant reached into the puddle and withdrew a gushing arm. He chucked it at the metal beast. It splattered across the viewport.

"Hey!" The Mayor shouted as he flailed, partially blinded. Vant lobbed a leg, which created additional carnage. He then picked up the torso and ran at the beast, heaving the leaking cadaver at its head.

The Peace-Keeper scraped its fingers across the sticky, brownish-purple slop on the viewport; the resulting gluey streaks only made things worse. "Not fair!" The Mayor whined. "Ya cheated, boy!" An access panel slid open, revealing the machine's shoulder-mounted gatling gun. It blind-fired, but Vant had already gone under the automaton and hidden behind it.

Vant's fingers trembled, but not from fear. He was straight-up pissed. He had a distaste for unnecessary bloodshed—he was an expert on the subject—and the chaos The Mayor and his Peace-Keeper cronies had created lit a burning rage inside of him.

"I'm comin' for ya, Mayor!" Vant shouted, mimicking his drawl. "I was trying to save your lives, but you had to go and pick a fight! Wrong move!"

"I ain't worried! No way out, li'l man! All the doors are locked!"

Vant climbed the stairs and moved to the limp security gun. He pointed it at the door leading further into the home and let the bullets chip away at the frame. The deadbolts buckled. Lumber splintered. A sizable hole formed.

He heard The Mayor's flustered voice: "He's doing what? Well shut 'er down, dammit! Turn off the gun!"

But Vant had already darted through the gap and into the next room.

There was a chorus of squeals from the courtesans who had taken refuge inside. They scattered away from Vant as he limped down the hallway. A peek behind the scenes revealed that while the entry hall was decorated as a lavish estate, once inside the home's guts, it turned into a series of basic rooms. Vant peered into each one as he passed by: closet, storage, bathroom...

He paused at the kitchen. It reeked of clashing spices and was stocked with the dangling carcasses of bizarre animals. A handful of cooks, preparing some sort of striped horse, looked stunned to see the stranger in their midst.

"Chefs! Take me to your leader!"

They freaked and ran for the exit. Vant grabbed one worker by the apron before he could get free.

"You! Where's The Mayor?"

The cook whimpered. "D-d-down at the end of the hall! In the g-g-game room! They never leave there!"

He let go of the man. "What's for dinner, anyway?"

"F-f-for dinner? F-f-flash-fried zebra wrapped in toucan-bacon, served on a bed of g-g-garlic pig tails with a creamy chocolate m-m-mustard sauce."

"My two-hundred-and-thirty-eighth favorite meal of all time," Vant said. He removed a double-sized meat cleaver from the skull of a sautéing lion's head. "Clear out. Things are about to get messy." The man scampered off.

Vant held the blade up to a camera he spotted in the corner. "Can somebody ring a bell? Because it's dinner time! And it looks like Mayor is on the menu tonight!"

From an overhead loudspeaker: "Har, har. Keep makin' jokes, son. See where it leads ya."

Vant caught up to several women piling into a room to hide. He kicked the door open, revealing a lounge filled with beds, couches, furnishings—and a dozen more escorts.

They gasped at the sight of the blood-soaked boogeyman brandishing a cleaver.

"Don't be afraid! You're free! You're free, whores!" Vant made a grand gesture to usher them out of the room.

They stared at him, unimpressed.

"You're free," he repeated.

"We know that," said one of the girls.

Another added, "What do you think, we're slaves? They pay us to be here."

"They—oh. So... you're okay?"

"Yeah. It's decent money," one of the gigolos said. The others nodded in agreement.

"But, your bosses... they just killed a bunch of you!"

"Sucks to be them," a skinny little blonde said between puffs from an elaborate smoking device. "Glad it wasn't my shift."

Vant scratched his sideburn. "Well, then. I guess I'll just... go?"

"Whatever tickles your pickle."

Vant slinked down the final corridor. He approached the last room at the end of the hall. Not surprisingly, it was locked.

He pounded on the door. "Open up!"

"No!" a voice answered from inside.

"Why not?"

"Because you're going to kill us!"

"That's crazy! Why in the world would I—oh, *okay*. You got me. Yeah, I'm going to kill you. I didn't want to, but you started this! Now I pretty much have to!"

"You started it! You were going to kill us first!"

"What—how—why on earth would you think that?"

"That's why *anyone* comes to the mansion!"

It's not awful logic, Vant thought. "I wasn't going to kill you! I came here to warn you about something!"

"Suuure."

"You have to open the door sometime. If you don't, you'll starve to death."

"We have reinforcements on the way. Wait there, works for us!"

"Then I'll blow up the whole damn mansion!"

"And kill all those perfectly good prostitutes? Could you live with that?"

Vant could not deal with the insanity of the conversation. "Screw this. I'm going to get an axe."

He searched room to room. Nothing. Time was wasting. Dozens of metal enforcers were likely stomping through Crash Town on the way to the mansion.

He went down into the basement, keeping his eyes peeled for anything he could use to break down the door. But, he found something more interesting: the Corpo-Cell power grid. It seemed like a good idea to pull the plug, figuring the outage might cut off communications to the reinforcements.

He switched off the first module. Several electronic hums and the temperature regulation went mute. He flipped another switch and the lights went out. He placed his hand on the last switch...

"Stop," The Mayor said over the intercom.

Vant shouted up the stairs, "Why?"

"Don't flip that switch. You can't."

"Give me one good reason."

"Jest—jest *don't,* son."

"Are you going to let me in to have a chat with you? That's all I want. A chat."

"Yessir. Agreed. We got ourselves a truce. Come on up."

"All right. I'm coming up. No tricks. Any more surprises and you may ruin my perfectly chipper mood."

Vant returned upstairs. The sealed door rattled, followed by the satisfying sound of a deadbolt unlatching. Then another. Then another.

Vant squeezed the handle of his knife.

The door creaked open.

The rancid smell of sweat, ass, and festering food hit him in the face before the visuals did.

The circular suite was dark. Every lamp was off, including those on a chandelier dangling from the ceiling. The centerpiece of the chamber, a spherical table, overflowed with food stacked ten feet high. Various animal appendages were drenched with sauces and sloppy pastries as big as watermelons cascaded from serving trays. Casks of bubbling beverages overflowed onto the carpet and containers brimming with fist-sized candies drowned in dustings of sugar.

Spaced evenly around the room were twelve elaborate devices resembling cockpits. Control panels, joysticks, and hundreds of buttons adorned their framework. Holographic visuals—each showing a different view of Crash Town—beamed above each helm. They bathed the chamber in flickering strobes of light.

Then, there were the "pilots," the people sitting in the cockpits...

Twelve revolting sacks of goo studied their new guest. Their heads blended into their necks, and their necks cascaded into rolls of fat. Stubby limbs protruded from their flab which poured over the edges of their seats. They were nude, covered only with sweat, stink, and morsels of whatever they had recently ingested—or excreted. Their loose skin jiggled as they shivered with trepidation.

These were the Peace-Keepers.

Without their remotely controlled robots, they were rendered impotent. Vant would have certainly caught them with their pants down—but they were not wearing any to begin with.

The naked servants attending to the Peace Keepers froze at the sight of Vant. He had interrupted the human-maintenance tasks they were currently engaged in. Some held wet cloths for sponge baths. Others held plates of food so heavy they could barely be lifted. Some cleaned the troughs underneath the seats of each cockpit, and some were in the midst of massaging the Peace-Keepers' body parts—using their own body parts to do so.

Vant's boots squished as he left blotchy red footprints across the carpet. He paced the circumference of the ballroom, eyeballing the drivers and their holographic displays. He noticed separate readouts on each cockpit showing numerical counters next to Corpo-Capsule icons; the Peace-Keepers were keeping track of their loot. Most values were in the hundreds of thousands, but one was in the millions.

Vant paused at the man who was most certainly the leader. He wore a ratty ten-gallon hat atop his doughy head. "Pleasure, son." He tipped the brim and smiled through rolls of saggy skin.

Vant raised an eyebrow.

"Sorry about the misunderstandin'. We get a whole heap o'trouble 'round these parts. But, hey, water under the bridge, eh? Let's make nice. May I offer ya some—"

"No, thank you. Not hungry."

"Right. Well. Welcome ta the game room, command center of the Peace-Keepers. This is where we keep our eyes on things."

"Mm-hmm."

"Somethin' ta drink, friend?"

"Sure, I'll have some more of your poison wine."

"About that... how'd ya do it? We're dyin' ta know. One drop woulda put an ox down!"

"I have a very strong constitution. Same thing that's helping me tolerate your stench."

"We don't take kindly ta insults—"

Vant blew hot breath onto his blade and polished it against one of the few clean spots on his cloak.

"Point taken, son."

"So, what am I missing? Help me out, here. I want to stick this knife into every last one of you for what you've done—for what you're doing. But there's this little obnoxious voice in my head saying, 'Hold on, Vant! They must have a reason for all this!' So tell me, Mayor. Why the twisted hookers? Why the poison? Why the guns and the psycho dominatrix and the giant robots?"

"*Hyick!* Ain't it obvious? Wagerin', son! Sometimes folks show up at the mansion, always ta rob us or git greedy with our concubines. And here *you* come inta Crash Town! Ya strut on in, dukin' it out with the hobos, puttin' up a helluva fight... we knew we had a pony ta bet on! The fun part is... which way ya gonna go out? I had my money on Dawn. *She-yit,* almost had ya there. Chuckles reckoned ya'd take the bait and put yer pipe in a puss. Our gals ain't no slouches, they woulda carved ya up good. Hoss-Hoss thought it'd be the grub, and Ol' Rosie there bet on the wine... hell, there's a dozen ways ta git yer bucket kicked inside this house! Funny enough, this time ain't none of us collectin'. No one put money on ya livin'. Sorry, sport."

Vant kept fixated on The Mayor, unamused by his jaunty demeanor.

"Ahem. Well, we gotta git back ta patrollin' the city, so if ya got somethin' ta say, now's the time."

Vant looked down at his bloodstained hand. It clutched the meat cleaver so tight that his circulation had cut off. Every last drop of willpower within him swam against the tidal wave of justification demanding he slice the necks of each worthless spud in the room.

Instead, he spoke. "Something's coming to Crash Town. Something horrible. An army."

The fetid eyes of the Peace-Keepers ran all over him. It gave him the creeps.

"It's headed here now?"

"Could arrive today. Could be a week from now. Could be ten years. But rest assured, they *are* coming. Unless we stop them."

"Ah! Well then, you and that cute li'l gal of yers have quite the job ahead of ya! Good luck, m'boy! Go get 'em!"

"I need your help, Mayor."

Twelve sarcastic chuckles from twelve repulsive flesh sacks.

Vant reasoned, "The sex, the food, the wealth... it's going to end. This evil is coming to steal you away and strip you of all your pleasures. Your whole way of life is going to be reduced to nothing. *Nothing.* Am I getting through to you?"

"Son... son. There's somethin' you should know about us, and this here town we protect."

"What."

"All of it... it don't mean *squat.*"

Vant blinked in disbelief.

"Welcome ta Crash Town. Where ya come ta crash. Life's tough, kid. Real tough. Ya got yer pressures. Ya got yer worries. Ya got yer responsibilities. Ya live, ya fart, ya die. That's a shit life, son. A shit life. Us folks, we got a better idea. We got four things on our minds. Fuckin', fightin', fun, and fuck it."

"You're not hearing me, Mayor. They're coming to *end your lives—*"

"Our lives ended the second we stepped foot in this here town. We came ta die, kid. Ta go out in a last hurrah. Ta give the middle finger ta the creator and show him that he screwed the pooch, that this world ain't worth my poopin' pot. And we ain't standin' fer it. We're gonna piss all over his masterpiece and, however the hell we die, well *she-yit*, that'll be fine with us. We figger, may as well jerk around on the way ta the finish line. We got one purpose here, son. To shove as many things in and shoot as many things out of our holes as possible."

Tornados of judgment circled inside Vant's head. Two sides loosed their artillery in a battle within his brain...

The Peace-Keepers must die!
No. I'm better than this. I don't kill the way they do.

But imagine all the people who would be liberated from their reign of terror!
Wouldn't Crash Town eat itself alive without them? Aren't they keeping the peace here, even in a sick sort of way?

They're evil! Murder the pricks!
And risk my mission? How does that help the people of Land Escape?

Killing them is the right thing to do! Do what's right!
Wait—through Death's mask, they looked normal. The thallium soldiers pulsed red, but these sons of bitches did not. Death has not marked them for elimination. There's something here I'm not seeing.

Just kill them! What's the value of a life that isn't even valued?
Who am I to make that call? Do I know more than Death?

Then, a sobering thought: *I've made a mistake coming here.*

Vant was rattled, livid, and seeing red—but only angry at one person.

Himself.

He put the edge of his knife to The Mayor's throat. "So if what you're telling me is true and none of this matters, I could kill you right now and you wouldn't give a shit?"

"Son, if ya kill me, I'll only have one regret."

"Which is?"

"If I'd a woke up jest a li'l earlier this mornin', I coulda gotten in one last pulla the pecker."

Vant shook his head. "There's more to it, you know. Than sex and money."

"Prove it, kid."

In a moment of clarity, Vant realized his judgment of them mirrored theirs of him: he perceived them as pathetic for not wanting to save their town, and they thought of him as pathetic for giving a damn.

Vant dropped the knife. The Peace-Keepers sighed with relief.

"Mayor, do me a favor."

"Name it, son."

"Don't kill me on my way out the door. I could go for one last pull of the pecker, myself."

"Obliged, kid. You spared us, we'll spare you."

"One more thing. Heard of a man named Gyse Fliyr? I'm looking for him."

"Does he have a vagina?"

"No."

"Then why the heck would I know him?"

Vant took one of the least-offensive-looking pastries from the table and said, "See you around, Mayor."

"Good luck, son. Have some fun. See the sights. Spend some money."

Vant closed the door behind him.

He walked down the hallway, past the hookers' lounge, and back into the lobby. The foyer looked like a bomb had gone off. It was wrecked with artillery shells, smoke, debris, and blood. Vant cautiously eyed the blind Peace-Keeper, which remained motionless. He stepped over Dawnrier's corpse, pausing to ponder what beauty lay underneath her mask. It did not matter now; it was destroyed. Gone, due to the itchy trigger finger of a greedy slab of man who viewed life as some sort of game.

Vant took a bite of the pastry. The sweetness overpowered his taste buds. He spat it out in disgust.

Then he had a thought.

He went back. Through the hallway. Down the stairs. Into the basement. And up to the power grid.

"I can't kill them..." he said to himself, "...so fuck them."

He switched off the power.

After relishing in the stunned silence, followed by the infantile tantrums of the cretins in the game room, Vant desperately craved perspective. He left the grounds and limped through the dingy streets of Crash Town.

Passing a Peace-Keeper sprawled out on the ground—deactivated from the power cut—he paused at a Corpo-Bot. "Need my things," he said. The bot chirped, and blasted off into the sky. Minutes later it returned, docked, and opened a compartment containing his satchel. After collecting his trappings, he located the tallest building in town, entered, found the fire escape, and climbed up to the roof.

The city looked ill. A brown haze clung to the air as the artificial sun rose in the schizophrenic sky. He observed the townspeople wandering back and forth, off to some nonsensical fetish fulfillment or vice of the week. It all seemed so meaningless —as did his attempt to save the place. *So what if these people get used for cattle?* Vant thought. *At least they'd have a purpose.* He ran his hands across his hair, which was growing fast. It reminded him of the ticking clock behind his mission. How much time was left before Death's patience would run out? Before his curse would return? Or before the citizens of Land Escape would be lost forever?

He removed Death's mask from his satchel and rolled the mysterious item around his fingers. The cold material felt refreshing on his fingertips. He looked into the empty eye sockets and spoke to the face, "Life's a bitch, huh?" He held the mask up to his head. It latched onto his skin.

The world transformed. He watched the vibrations and trails of the townspeople as they moved from place to place—yet nothing flashed red, even when he glanced back toward The Mayor's mansion. He double-checked, then triple-checked to ensure he was not missing anything. *The Peace-Keepers may be bastards,* Vant thought, *but for whatever reason, they're not drawing Death's attention.*

He started to remove the mask—but something caught his eye. "What the hell?" In the farthest reaches of his vision, he spied a phenomenon, an anomaly so insignificant he could not tell if it was real or if his transformed eyes were playing tricks on him.

He strained to see what he thought he saw. Nothing. But he could have *sworn*—

There it was.

The tiniest glint of green flickered from within the depths of the city, almost imperceptible. Much like how the townspeople glowed white, and the invaders of Land Escape had pulsed red, someone in Crash Town was sparkling emerald.

As quickly as the twinkle had appeared, it evaporated.

Looks like there's something worth seeing in this damn town after all, Vant thought.

"I can't kill them... so fuck them."

- Vant Hu'l

233 YEARS PRIOR

Of Ascension and Eradication

A delicious blend of minerals and gunpowder coated the air of the hillside chamber. The cave had a still, silent interior and held a venerable importance.

Vant, having walked past the guards protecting the stockade, turned his eyes to the spoils of hundreds of years of battles. There were blades of every shape and kind. Ancient bludgeoning instruments. Piles of explosives stored in layers of crisscrossing protection plates. And, commanding respect from its placement dead center in the cave, an anvil represented the art of blacksmithing from eras past.

Whereas Vant sipped the surroundings like wine, Terrii guzzled them like ale. He went straight to the wall of ballistics weapons where he coveted each and every gun, in turn.

"Pupils," a gravelly voice spoke. They had arrived early, but they were not the only ones there. "Congrats on this, your Day of Exaltion."

"Thank you, Cloakmaster," said Vant.

"Glad you're not dead yet," said Terrii. "I'll get to say 'I told you so.'"

Gordone smiled. "You're early, which means you're smart. I suggest you take the opportunity to gather information. One word of wisdom may mean the difference between life... and death."

Vant deduced what the veteran meant long before Terrii did. "We can ask you anything we want?"

"Yes," he answered. "But hurry. The order will arrive at any moment. One question each. Young warrior Hu'l, you may start."

"What will be the most effective weapon for my task?"

Gordone scrunched his grizzled face in thought. "Your aversion to firearms leaves you with significantly fewer options. If you ever considered reconsidering, now would be the time."

"No," said Vant.

"Vant Hu'l, you are a talented pupil, and one of our wisest. So hear me now. If you do not pick up a gun tonight, you will die."

Vant inclined his head in acknowledgment, but did not respond with words.

"That leaves my favorite student, Master Terrii the Fierce! What question do you have for your old Cloakmaster?"

"I'm good."

"Confidence without competence has a name, Terrii. It's called arrogance."

"Don't sweat it. I got this."

"So be it. May your defenses in combat be as impenetrable as your mind, Agmar-Burrian Terriforn. Best of luck, my pupils. You are both gifted in unique ways. I wish you a safe return and, thus, Knighthood into the order." The rhythm of marching came from outside the cave. *"The Knights approach. Agmar will present you with your challenges..."* there was even more ruckus, *"...and, apparently, your fans will send you off."*

Vant was the most talented student the order had ever seen, and Terrii was the son of the First Prime; as such, they had risen up through the ranks as celebrities. The entire commune was invested in their fate, and thus, they had convened for the Exaltion Day ceremony.

Agmar entered the cave, tailed by his battalion of hooded Knights. The weight of their purpose consumed the airspace. They formed a circle around the two candidates.

"Seventy-five Knights. No more, no less. That's the way it has always been, and the way it will always be. We are an army large enough to be feared, but small enough to be swift. Two of our order fell in the last battle, which means we have room for two new Knights to take their places."

Vant and Terrii stood tall. The excitement flowing through them was palpable.

Agmar continued, *"You will find no celebration here. You have come to this day, but you have not earned it. Any child can go through training. Any child can come of age by waddling around and waiting long enough. You've achieved nothing by merely showing up. Are you deserving of our respect? Doubtful. Are you as powerful as you think you are? Prove it. Walk out this cave as sniveling children, full of empty promises, but return as men. Return as warriors. Return as Knights!"*

"Knights of Rights!" the army bellowed.

"I order you to succeed. I order you! Should you fail, others will take your place. Others who would never dare to defy my command."

Cloakmaster Gordone stepped forward. *"You will travel only with weapons of your choosing and a witness—a Warrior Prime—who will confirm your victory... or demise. They are under strict orders to not interfere with your fate, under any circumstances. As for your tasks..."*

"They are here, written by my hand." Agmar handed a scroll to Terrii, and another to Vant.

Terrii tore his open, read the note, and grinned his cocky half-smile. His task would be a challenge, but surmountable. The Knighthood was as good as his.

Vant waited for permission to unravel his parchment, which Agmar granted with a nod. He opened the scroll and read the message.

His arm fell to the side.

He dropped the paper.

One word had been scribbled on it. The name of a town.

Burmose.

Terrii's elation waned when he saw Vant's expression. He turned his eyes to his father, whose fiery gaze was locked onto Vant. In this moment, Agmar could not have cared less about his own offspring. There was other blood he was far more interested in. That of Vant's, being spilt.

Vant pulled his stare to Terrii, searching for an answer he needed to know, and one he received: Terrii had no knowledge of this plot. His slack-jawed gape revealed that truth.

"Choose your weapons," said Cloakmaster Gordone. "Choose wisely for the task at hand. Choose those that speak to your strengths."

Terrii stepped right up. He snatched as many grenades as he could fit in his pockets and shouldered the biggest assault rifle in the arsenal. He wrapped several belts of ammunition around his waist and stuffed a satchel to the brim with extra bullets for good measure.

Vant paced the floor. He admired the blacksmithing tools, how beautiful they were. His mind swam as he considered the situation at hand with Agmar, as well as the impossible task before him. He was to wipe out Burmose, a city teeming with threats, and a long-standing thorn in the side of the Knights of Rights. Every attack against it had been met with failure. This was beyond a suicide mission.

"Warrior Hu'l?" said Cloakmaster Gordone, jolting Vant from his trance.

Vant approached the anvil. He studied a smithing glove in a pile of forging equipment. It was dense and weathered, used long ago to pound red-hot steel into flat blades. He slid it onto his hand. It was immensely heavy.

He walked across the floor, through the confused stares of the Knights of Rights, and up to a neglected assemblage of assorted trappings. He shouldered a dusty bullwhip, then returned to the center of the armory to meet Agmar's gaze head-on.

Agmar's heartbeat visibly pumped through his veiny frame. He gritted his teeth, as if preparing to rage, but, instead, he pointed a finger to the outside.

"Go," he ordered.

"You're already in a pile of shit. Don't make it shittier."

- Shlarky

CHAPTER 10

The Flier and the Fleeing

Vant took inventory while walking: dislocated shoulder, cracked rib, sore nipples, whipped rear, two bullet grazes, and a broken pinky toe. Damn toe. Not only that, but he was a filthy, stinking mess again. He wouldn't die—perks of immortality —but he would need a patch job. He hoped Skii had steady fingers and some skill with sutures.

"Skii," Vant spoke into his wrist-communicator. "Dammit. Where are you?"

My tummy hurts, too, he thought. The residual traces of poison were doing his insides no favors. He felt sorry for himself. And weirdly hungry.

He hoofed it back to the hotel, ignoring the invasive stares of the locals.

He knocked on Skii's door. No answer. He grumbled, then went to his room.

He peeled off his sticky robes and tried to figure out where to begin with self-administered first aid. He made his choice and, after six failed attempts, finally snapped his shoulder back into place. He whimpered like a helpless child, then burrowed into his bed.

He had barely shut his eyes when his communicator spoke: "Hey, Pops!"

"Skii! Where are you?"

"Took a walk. Gorgeous day out!"

"I thought I told you to stay in your room."

"Damn, what's up with the grump? I'm on to something. I've got a lead on my dad."

"That's great, but—"

"A few people I talked to recognized his name. Most of them run in some shady circles, though. Heh, I suppose that's not saying much, in Crash Town."

"Skii, listen to me. I could use a hand—"

"I think I know where to go next. When you're done with dinner, you should come meet me!"

"Skii, dinner was—"

"Oh. Oh crap."

"What? What is it?"

Silence.

"Skii?"

More silence. Then, muffled noises.

Vant sat upright and held the comm to his ear, attempting to overhear something —anything—that would indicate what was going on.

Finally:

"The hell you looking at? Excuse you! Look but don't touch, fellas. Hey! Get off me!"

Vant opened his mouth to speak—but shut it quickly. Her communicator was tuned to an open channel; if he spoke, whoever was harassing her would hear him and discover the device. Instead, he muted the microphone.

"Stop pointing that thing at me! No! Leave Cassidy alone!"

Vant's heart raced, listening to the abduction. *C'mon, Skii. Tell me where you are. Give me a hint.*

"I have no idea," she protested. "I haven't seen him in ages. Don't ask me, pal. How did I end up *where*? At Crash Town's most exclusive brothel? I felt like some action!"

Good girl.

He threw on his still-syrupy robes, shouldered his satchel, bolted out the door, and sprinted toward the marketplace. He paused only to ask people along the way, "Where's Crash Town's most exclusive brothel?"

"In a rush, eh?" said one random wiseguy. "I know the feeling."

A handful more inquiries revealed he was looking for "Shlarky's," located in the center of town. He followed the directions given to him while listening for clues on the communicator. Skii said, "I told you, I don't know! But if I find him, who should I say is looking for him?"

Vant continued to run, ignoring his body which longed for a break. Skii's voice appeared again, "Tell me this... are you gonna kill me, torture me, or rape me? I want to know so I can mentally prepare." A beat. "Oh. Well, that sucks. Nice place you got here, by the way, real swank. If it wasn't for the hideous statue out front, I wouldn't have even known this was a whorehouse—*hey!* Let go of—it's only a bracelet. It doesn't do anything—" A quick burst of static, then silence.

The window of opportunity to save her was closing.

Vant weaved in and out of foot traffic. He neared the center of town, apparent from the concentration of shops and eateries. His eyes darted in every direction, searching for a "hideous statue." At long last, he identified one that certainly qualified: a voluptuous naked woman riding a tiger, leaping into a flower. Beyond the sculpture lay a windowless, faux-mahogany bordello. This had to be the place.

Vant burst through the door.

Inside, a dozen men had Skii surrounded. She was gagged, bound, and being stuffed into a sack. Her eyes lit up at the sight of Vant.

The men unholstered singe pistols and pointed them at Vant.

He raised his hands. Running away would have meant a flaming bullet in the back, so, instead, as if in slow motion, he put one... foot... in front of the other...

...and walked toward the bar.

The men stared at him, baffled.

Vant hopped onto a barstool. He drummed his fingers on the countertop.

"Hey you," one of the gruffer-looking goons said.

"Me?" Vant feigned naïveté.

"Yes you, Crash trash. The hell you want?"

"I'm a customer. I really, *really* need to get laid. What do you have in stock?"

The men laughed, befuddled by Vant's gall. It granted him mere moments to assess the environment—and his predicament. The interior was dark with wooden walls and burgundy curtains, posh in a cheesy kind of way. The smell of incense and expensive tobacco permeated the premises. Unlike the main area full of the shifty fat cats, the rest of the place was empty, apparently cleared out for the day. While the men bearing down on Vant resembled nothing more than low-rent hit men, they were armed, which made them dangerous.

One thug, tightly gripping his gun, said, "This guy don't look right. He's covered in blood."

"I don't like this. Not one bit," another added.

Vant asked, "So, how does this work? Are drinks complimentary? Or do I get right to the sex?"

"Whack or thwack, boss?" a bruiser said to the largest, tackiest-dressed man. "How you want this sick-dick laid out?"

"Hold your whores," he answered. His flashy ensemble and gallons of cologne indicated this guy *had* to be Shlarky, owner of the establishment. He grinned, revealing a full set of diamonoid teeth below diamonoid-lined eyebrows. "This little ball bag knows our girl. Look at the way she's lookin' at him. No *whack*. No *thwack*. Let's *crack* open his brain and see what he knows."

"Oh, boy," said Vant. "I think there's been a misunderstanding. I'd better go. Don't worry about me, I'll take my business to the bee-jay machine down the street." Playing coy, Vant moved his hands toward his weapons...

"You're already in a pile of shit," Shlarky sneered. "Don't make it shittier."

"Guys, I just want to put my thingy into another thingy. I'm a client, I swear. I'll prove it. Bring me a woman and I'll do naughty things to her."

"That so?" Shlarky grinned. "Fine, then. Cost is three-hundy, make 'em green. Payment in advance." He held out his palm.

Vant smiled and sheepishly patted down his robes. "Oh, man. This is embarrassing. I seem to have left my capsules in my other cloak."

Shlarky polished his pistol against his inseam. "You know what kind of guy comes into Crash Town's hottest henhouse without any money?"

"What kind?"

"The dead kind." The gangsters raised their weapons. One of them broke off from the pack and closed the door for privacy.

"Okay, you got me," said Vant. "I'm not a customer."

"*Shhh*." Shlarky tapped the barrel of his gun on his lips. "Let's wait until I've pulled out your fingernails and put 'em down your throat. People tend to be more honest around then."

Skii fought against her restraints. Shlarky scolded her, "Don't mess up that tight little skin of yours. You'll be wrapping it around my customers soon enough. Once I get some loosey-juice in you, you're going to be one hell of an earner!" Shlarky's gun barrel caressed Skii's chin and slid down her chest.

"Let's make a trade," Vant said. "Let the girl go, and you can have me instead. I'll even wear her dress."

"Just don't know how to keep your yap trap shut, do you?" The minions closed in on Vant. Two restrained his arms, and one held a gun to the back of his head. Shlarky grabbed a fistful of Skii's hair and pulled her head backward. He gnawed on her neck with his sparkling teeth and said, "Just for that, I'm gonna make you watch me sample the tramp."

The gangsters laughed.

"Do it, Shlark!" a thug sneered.

"Break her hind, then blank her mind!" from another.

"Tie the sack up to her neck," Shlarky said. "I'll need an hour just on her head."

Skii's eyes shut.

Vant struggled against his captors.

The men howled with glee.

Then:

Metal pierced flesh.

"Arrrrggg!" Shlarky dropped his pistol—an embedded dagger was sticking out of his palm. He gripped the impaled hand.

More blades zipped through the air. Each gangster was tagged in the leg, the arm, or the side. One by one they collapsed, calling out in confused shock.

"What the shit!" one of them screamed as he clutched his thigh, a knife wedged into the fat.

"Where did that come from?" another hollered. He attempted to identify the source of the attack while reaching for his fallen weapon—

Crunch.

A figure dropped from the ceiling and landed on his arm, breaking it in two. In a blur, the assailant separated the men from their firearms.

Vant wasted no time. He ran toward Skii—

Too slow.

A sword was pressed to his throat.

He stopped. Raised his hands. Looked down length of the blade to find it extended from a gunmetal-gray mechanical arm. The elaborate appendage belonged to an emaciated stick of a being. Its ribs and hip muscles jutted from its frame and and extreme hunchback gave it the look of a rabid possum protecting its babies.

"The fuck is that?!" Shlarky screamed, terror spit flying from his mouth.

Circling Vant, the entity moved with fluidity, assisted by legs bending backward at the knees. A tight hood wrapped around its head and, underneath, Vant could make out red-tinged eyes, definitely cybernetic. They faintly glowed above a steel jaw that was welded to its skull. The thing had no chin or mouth, only the one chunk of grotesque prosthetic.

The sword pressed harder. Words slipped from Vant's lips: "I'm a good guy!"

In a blink, the being cut Skii's bindings to free her. In another blink, the blade was back at Vant's throat.

Skii rid herself of the loose restraints and approached, saying, "What the hell *are* you?" The entity raised a gloved hand from its normal arm, demanding silence. She obliged after one more comment: "That guy... that's Vant. He's with me."

The sword folded into the underside of the being's mechanical appendage. Replacing the blade, two foot-long fingers and a thumb extended and formed into a claw. They clamped around Shlarky's neck.

A flicker emitted from the optics of the shadowy figure's eyes, followed by a holographic image hovering in front of its face. "SHE'S MINE," the projection read. The lettering was a direct match for the warning message Skii had received earlier at the Corpo-Bots.

"Fine, *fine!*" Shlarky snarled. "It's not her we want, anyway. It's her backstabbing father!"

The cyborg dropped Shlarky and turned back to Skii. It was quick, but Skii was quicker.

She had already dived across the floor to Cassidy and had a bead on the metal-jawed menace. "Don't move!"

It raised its arms—including the unsettling mechanical one.

She approached with caution, leaning in to get a better look...

Flash!

A strobe of light blazed from its eyes. Skii dropped, temporarily blinded. Vant struggled to regain focus. When he did, the figure was gone.

"What *was* that thing? What does it want from me?" Skii was rattled, but turned full-on distraught after noticing Vant's appearance. "Why are you covered in blood, you psycho?"

"It's a long story. Wait..." He touched Skii's shoulder. Something was amiss. After being blinded, Vant had heard no sounds of the enigma exiting the premises. Furthermore, the brothel had no windows and only one door.

The attacker was likely still in the room.

Vant retrieved Death's mask from his satchel and put it on. Blackness. Pulses. Silhouettes. He read the waveforms of Skii, of the incapacitated gangsters, and carefully scanned the room.

"There!" He pointed at the farthest corner where the ceiling met the wall. The being was concealed, folded into an intricate shape. Through Death's eyes, Vant saw that the figure was not violently pulsing red. Like the Peace-Keepers, this villain was not marked for elimination as had been the body snatchers of Land Escape. Its visual signature was normal. Innocent.

With its hiding space compromised, the being used its bionic arm to swing from beam to beam over their heads. A dropkick shattered the door and it darted into the open. Catapulted by inverted legs engineered for speed, it fled into the streets.

Skii followed outside, in pursuit.

"No, wait!" Vant shouted.

"That freak knows something! I've got to catch up!"

Skii cocked Cassidy and held down the slider. The shotgun squealed as the firearm charged. When it was on the edge of overload, she let go of the pump-action, pointed the gun behind her, and pulled the trigger. The force of the burst propelled her ahead. She fired again, then again. With every blast, the momentum launched her faster and faster. Her hair plastered back from the wind as she tore through the streets after the figure. Her booted feet only tapped the ground for stability and to make course corrections.

Vant blinked in awe. "Okay, then."

He surveyed the mobsters, who looked at him for an explanation. He shrugged.

His mind focused on the task at hand. He could not leave Skii to that... *thing*, but he knew this might be his only chance to acquire intel on her father.

So, he addressed the lowlifes:

"Gentlemen! I don't have a lot of time, here. There's information I need, and you're going to give it to me. To get us past the whole 'I won't talk' nonsense, here's how this goes down." Vant activated a gauntlet. "Talk, or you get smashed in the dick."

Gulps and swears came from the mouths of the injured men.

Vant raised a thug to his feet and said, "You. I'm picking you at random. Just bad luck for you, I guess. Now, I'm going to wail on your dick. Really wail on it with this giant, iron glove. You may as well talk, because if you don't, I'll simply move on to the next guy, and the next. So, whether you spill your guts or it's another guy, one of you *will* talk after seeing all the smashed dicks. And, let me tell you something. If the fifth guy rats after four of you get smashed dicks, the four of you with the smashed dicks are going to feel pretty damn dumb. You're going to be like, 'Why didn't I just tell the dick-smashing guy what he wanted to know and save myself from getting a smashed dick?' So I beg of you, don't be that guy. Don't be the regretful guy with the smashed dick."

The men, especially the one in Vant's custody, looked stricken. "Here we go. I'm going to say this once, and only once. Tell me about Gyse Fliyr," Vant said. "Anyone?" No one spoke. "All right," he sighed. "This one's on you." He made a grand gesture, as if preparing to punch the man in the crotch—

"Stop!" Shlarky called out. "It's no secret what that shit-heel did to us. What do you want to know?"

"Everything in twenty seconds."

Shlarky spit on the floor. "That strung-out pus bucket. Gyse was nothing more than a hood biting from my business. Just a small-time thug, pimping walkers and slinging juice. I had every intention to make him a stain, but I saw potential in him. My mistake. I took mercy on his ass, cleaned him up, and showed him the ropes. He moved up fast, on account of he never talked back. Not that he could, that diseased prick. His mouth was so full of sex sores and pussy pocks that he was basically a mute. That's why we all got to calling him 'Whispers.'"

Saying the name put Shlarky in an even more agitated state. He grimaced at the dagger still wedged in his hand, but carried on, speaking with bile about his former associate. "He made good scratch for me by doing favors, dealing in my clubs, swiping secrets... anything and everything. He got big, real big. Then he got greedy. He put a group of guys together, and they ripped me off. Took more loot than you've ever seen in your life, I'll tell you that. I never should have made him what he was, that rat bastard."

"I have to find him."

"No chance. Trust me, I've tried. Whispers is as good as gone. He skipped town *years* ago. I haven't heard so much as a peep from him or his crew. They vanished proper. I thought we had a stroke of luck when that girl of yours came to town, but clearly she don't know nothing, neither."

Whether or not he spoke the truth, Skii was in danger. Vant—covered in blood, brandishing gauntlets of destruction, and wearing a glowing supernatural mask—issued a reminder to the whimpering gangsters. "Let's get something straight. If that nutjob who stuck daggers in you isn't reason enough to leave the girl alone, I sure as hell should be. Are we clear on this?"

"Yeah, yeah," said Shlarky. "You'll punch us in the dicks. We got it."

Vant darted out the door with a brain full of information sure to traumatize his companion. He filed it away under the category *I'll Deal With This Later.*

Vant spied a light pole, the tallest nearby perch. He whipped the overhang with a *crack!* and pulled himself up to survey the city.

Through Death's mask, he located Skii, a fast-moving blur pursuing an erratically moving wisp. Their rapid motions created streaks in contrast to the slow-moving pedestrians. Skii's target collided with a gaggle of bystanders, slowing its escape. She closed in.

Vant dove off the beam toward a ledge and clasped his free whip onto a nearby canopy. He alternated whip hands, swinging from rooftop to light pole to overhang to perch. While the foot chase below zigzagged through the narrow side streets, Vant took a direct path overhead.

He gambled on their trajectory and it paid off; a few swings later and he was ahead of them. He latched himself to a billboard advertising *The Wart Blaster* and dangled twenty-odd feet above where they would pass.

His heart thumped in anticipation as he watched them play cat and mouse.

He waited... and waited.

He ripped the mask off and stowed it, deciding he would need his real eyes to pounce. There were too many people around and too much movement to focus otherwise.

He waited... and waited.

They turned the corner.

Vant dropped off the perch and took a swing with a gauntlet.

He totally whiffed it.

It was not even close. The figure was *fast*. It dodged at an angle, leaving Vant about-faced. A bluish-copper blur zipped by with Skii's trailing voice:

"Nice miss!"

He cursed under his breath and swung back into the chase.

Again, he trailed overhead. He watched as Skii, using Cassidy as a turbo boost, closed in. Several times she got within grabbing distance, but the figure kept cutting abrupt paths down alleyways and corridors. Skii's high velocity had a downside: it was tough to turn on a dime. But she refused to quit.

The menace was leading Skii into the crowded Sentural Market, a swap meet for off-putting devices and cheaply made knickknacks. Vant cut across the promenade and placed himself at the end, dangling below a street sign.

He strategized from his overhang. The foot traffic was filtering through two side-by-side booths, one peddling a rubbery device called the "Stimulizer," the other selling what resembled fruit but was clearly not meant to be eaten. If he timed an interference right, he figured he might trip up the figure into one of the booths. He abandoned the idea of suppressing the foe with his gauntlets—it was too damned fast. He would have to take the impact head-on. He bristled at the stupidity of taking a full-force collision from a maniacal cyborg traveling at blinding speeds. He sighed, "This is going to suck."

The figure entered the market. It twisted, turned, bobbed and weaved. It zipped around people, slid under carts, and vaulted over barrels of wares using its mechanical arm for torque.

Skii was the opposite of deft, unable to keep up. She smashed into a cart of beer, sending suds everywhere. "Sorry!" she offered as she fired the gun again for thrust, only to be launched into a crowd of people that were none too pleased to receive face-fulls of copper hair. She gave up on using Cassidy and, instead, sprinted through the market on foot, dodging pedestrians and obstacles.

At the end of the street, the figure took a beat to glance over its shoulder at the floundering Skii. Vant seized the moment and dropped down between the booths, bracing for the impact...

...which never came.

The enigma's retractable blade sliced through the "produce stand" next to Vant. Diced fruit splattered to the ground alongside splinters of wood. Vant watched his target disappear into the streets and, to make matters worse, Skii collided with him, sending them sprawling into the adjacent display. Pink, fleshy toys toppled onto them as a salesperson screamed indecipherable obscenities.

Skii cocked Cassidy, but Vant grabbed her by the back of her dress. "Wait!" he said. "That thing's dangerous!"

"Let me go!"

"Hold on a second! I can follow him without this nonsense! My mask—"

"I don't care!" She smashed his foot with her boot, right on the broken pinky toe. He released his grip and collapsed. She was off again.

Of all the body parts Vant could have lived without getting violated *twice* on this impossibly long day, this was it. He shook it off to the best of his ability, attached himself to a flagpole, and once again donned the mask. He located the trail of the assailant as well as Skii; the chase had resumed and, yet again, he was on the ass-end of the action.

Vant's level of patience was in the gutter. His composure had turned on him. His stamina was sapped but some way, somehow, he required the upper hand. The botched attempts thus far elevated this from important to essential for his damaged ego.

It was time to fight dirty.

He swung overhead across the borough. Again, he found himself ahead of Skii and the cyborg. He lowered himself into an alleyway, one he selected for a particular reason.

He approached a Peace-Keeper in stasis mode. He knocked on its leg and the machine roared to life.

"What?" the operator bellowed from the head-mounted loudspeakers.

"Remember me? Your dinner guest? The guy who terrorized you?"

"The hell you want?" It wasn't The Mayor's voice; it was one of his cronies.

"There's a lunatic cyborg coming this way. One hundred blues if you fill it full of lead."

"A hundred pills for some target practice? You're on."

"There's a girl following behind. Hit her, and the bounty's off. We clear?"

The Peace-Keeper spun the chambers of its shoulder-mounted gatling gun in acknowledgment.

Soon, Vant heard Cassidy's blasts and saw the figure evading Skii.

Closer they came... closer...

It entered the alley.

The Peace-Keeper's cannon ignited with bullet fire—the mysterious being leapt over the robot. The moment Skii hit the alleyway, Vant shouted, "Cassidy! Growl!" Skii activated the repulser shield moments before stray bullets pelted its blue exterior.

As the artillery inadvertently hammered her defenses, the cyborg's motives were revealed. It stopped in its tracks at the sound of Skii's distress, altered course, and extended its retractable sword.

The fight was over before it had begun. The cyborg's blade slashed through the Peace-Keeper's metal frame. The robot squeezed off a few desperate rounds before the cyborg severed its gun, the slice accompanied by a shower of sparks.

"Vant, you son of a bitch! You owe me a hundred blues for this—" The attacker cut through the Peace-Keeper's auditory mechanics. Then its legs.

The metal beast fell.

The shadowy being took a beat to check on Skii. While distracted, Vant dove onto its hunchback. "Skii! Fire!" he shouted.

Skii unloaded a blast of energy toward the two of them. Vant ensured the majority of the shockwave hit his adversary.

They flew.

Impact.

The cyborg clipped a brick wall and tumbled down an enclosed loading dock. Vant somersaulted to his feet and activated his gauntlets.

The figure, disoriented and damaged, wobbled itself upright. There was nowhere for it to run, but this thing was slippery. Vant refused to blink. His gauntlets pulsed at the ready.

Skii caught up and aimed Cassidy. "Move an inch and I'll blast you so hard your face will come out your ass!"

Vant remained silent—although he made a mental note to give her hell later for that ridiculous comment. As the cyborg heaved oxygen, its hunchback rose and fell. It studied them with glassy red eyes.

Skii asked, "Why did you save me?"

The figure sized up Vant, then returned its gaze to Skii. It was either calculating an escape or considering a response. Finally, from its eyes, a holographic readout displayed the words, "FOR YOUR FATHER."

Skii shivered. Gulped air down her throat. "Where is he?"

Static combined to form the word, "GONE."

Her eyes welled up. Cassidy shook from her trembling hands.

A projection appeared: "I CAN BRING HIM BACK."

Skii's lips were pursed. Her teeth were gritted. She studied the mysterious cyborg with squinted eyes. "How?"

It took a step forward. Vant raised his fists.

The readout lit up: "RELEASE ME. IT IS THE ONLY WAY."

"I don't believe you," Skii hissed. To Vant: "Tie him up."

Vant loosed the whips from his gauntlets—

"Wait... stop." Skii noticed a projection beaming from the figure's eyes.

The image was fuzzy and corrupted, but identifiable.

"Skii," Vant said, "it's your tattoo."

"No," she said. She inched closer to the hologram. "It's my dad's."

Sure enough, the style was similar, but, instead of spirals and paths, there were shapes and symbols.

The hologram fizzled out.

Skii looked at Vant. He remained on guard, unblinking. He said to the figure, "There's information I need. Something only Gyse Fliyr knows. It's important. Lives depend on it. Everything depends on it."

The cyborg lowered its head, as if prompting for the request. Vant continued, "I have to know where an army resides. A massive force that has been invading towns and stealing their people. They wear suits of thallium armor. Can you get me that information?"

"THERE ARE WAYS." The holographic readout then projected, "IF YOU RELEASE ME."

A decision had to be made. They had backed this unpredictable thing into the corner; one wrong move and it might slice its way through them. There was no guarantee as to its integrity, so letting it go was a massive risk. But taking it out meant severing the one link Skii had to her father—and more blood on Vant's hands.

Vant tilted his head toward Skii as if to say, *You decide.* This involved her family, so it was her decision to make.

Also, he had no desire to get blamed for making the wrong call.

Skii lowered her gun. "I want to help," she said. "What can I do?"

The figure's bionic eyes studied her. Then the holographic display formed the word, "LIVE."

"I'm trusting you," Skii said. "Don't make me regret this."

It nodded, and started to leave.

"Wait," Skii said. "What's your name?"

The hologram flickered, as if malfunctioning. After a few seconds of digital noise, a name materialized:

"REDEMPTION."

Skii tapped Vant on the shoulder. He retracted his whips and switched off his gauntlets.

Skii said to the cyborg, "Bring my dad back to me. Please."

It nodded and, again, showed her the word, "LIVE."

She stepped back, providing an exit. Vant followed suit—albeit with attitude—to let the thing know who was the victor in the skirmish.

"If this is a trick," Vant said, "you'd better watch your back."

The hooded figure paused, looked with interest at something behind Vant, and responded with the words, "WATCH YOUR OWN."

Over his shoulder, Vant discovered a dagger wedged into his back. "Son of a bitch!" He had been stuck by the cyborg mid-tussle. In the blink of an eye it took for Vant to remove the knife, Redemption was gone.

Vant and Skii walked in silence, headed back to their lodgings.

Vant limped terribly and was still reeling from the horrors he had experienced at The Mayor's mansion. His bones ached and his wounds sizzled. The last drops of his adrenaline had washed away, leaving him with a hangover of cold shakes. And in one afternoon, Skii had been abducted by gangsters, attacked by a Peace-Keeper, and in a fight with a deadly cyborg. Hell of a day, for both of them.

After a time, Skii said, "Sorry I stomped your foot."

Vant answered, "Sorry I made a mechanical asshole shoot at you."

They both kind of smiled, and kept walking.

"Redemption..." Skii said, as if thinking out loud, "...what *was* that thing?"

"I've seen the type before. A deserter from Cy-Klai. A township that believes in cybernetics as the path to immortality." Vant was woozy. He stumbled, nearly kissing the pavement. Skii propped him up as best she could.

"Don't you die on me, Pops."

"I'll make you a promise. I won't die on you. Ever. You can trust me on that." She looked at him sideways. "But," Vant continued, "you're going to have to patch me up."

"No sweat," she said. "Just don't make me put on a naughty-nurse outfit. Which I'm pretty sure they sell at every damn store in this town."

At the hotel, Skii tended to Vant's damaged body. With care, she sealed his open wounds using medical supplies procured from a Corpo-Bot. She could not do anything for his broken bones—those would have to mend on their own—but he would no longer leak blood, thanks to her.

When done with the first aid, Vant rested his eyes. Skii flopped onto the bed next to him and propped her feet up against the wall. She stared at the ceiling in silence and gently petted Cassidy.

After close to ten minutes, she spoke.

"Shlarky... did he tell you anything? About my dad?"

Did he ever, Vant thought. Yet he was unsure how to answer her. What was the point in telling her the troubling news? Was the information given to Vant about Gyse Fliyr's addictions and criminal behavior even valid? Who knew if Shlarky even had an honest bone in his entire body?

Vant decided to err toward caution.

"He said a little. But not much. He was positive your father had left town. Which validates what Redemption told us. 'Gone,' he said. Not 'dead.'"

"How did he know my dad? Why was he after him?"

And then came the lie. It stuck on his lips and left a foul aftertaste, "They didn't get into that." In his mind, he tried to convince himself why it was better to go this route, but it did little to fill the new pit in his stomach. As a concession, he added, "But, they said he used to go by the name 'Whispers.'"

Skii was slipping away inside herself. She continued staring upward into nowhere.

"Skii, if there's one thing I know for certain, it's that answers don't live in the ceiling. If we want to sort this whole thing out, we'll have to keep moving. And we have to get out of this horrendous town. There's nothing here but stink."

"Yeah," she said. "I'm with you. But I've still got one lead to follow up on before we go."

"So do I. What's yours?"

"The World's Best Magician. He was my dad's obsession. I have to know if he was real, and if he could have saved my mom. Yours?"

"Some green sparkle I saw in my boss's mask." He thought for a moment. "I don't know whose lead is thinner."

"Let's call it a tie."

"Not too much longer in this worthless pit," Vant said. "Tomorrow, we beat the streets while we wait for Redemption to give us a sign. Then we get the hell out of Crash Town. Agreed?"

"Agreed," confirmed Skii. "Sounds easy enough. Can't be any worse than what we've already been through."

"Don't jinx it," Vant said.

"Nice miss!"

- Skii Tavee

233
YEARS PRIOR

Of Knighthoods and Legend

"He's back!" rang Shyyla's voice. Then another excited voice. Then another.

Word spread through the commune that the apprentices were returning from their Exaltion Day tasks. A crowd had amassed, including the entirety of the Knights of Rights.

But, they fell silent when they saw it...

Terrii's limp body dangled from Vant's arms.

"My son!" Agmar's voice roared as he stomped through the camp. "What have you done to my only son!" He pushed aside Vant, who crumbled. The last measures of his strength melted into the sod.

Pinning Vant's head with a filthy boot, Agmar pulled his scimitar from its scabbard. He pressed it to Vant's neck. "Treacherous snake!" he growled. "I'll kill you for this!" He raised the sword into the air—

"Stop," a voice called from the crowd.

Agmar turned his blade to the man who spoke out. "You dare interrupt an execution?"

"I do," said Cloakmaster Gordone. "As it's right."

Terrii coughed.

He was alive.

"He lives?" shouted Agmar. "What the hell has happened here? Where is Vant Hu'l's witness?"

"Here," said Cloakmaster Daggart.

"Approach! What is the meaning of this? What has Vant Hu'l done to my child?"

"He saved him."

Agmar's sword-hand shook as he contemplated whether or not to slay.

"Speak, Cloakmaster Daggart!" urged Gordone. *"Tell us what has transpired!"*

"Vant Hu'l has completed his task. Burmose is no more."

Another Knight spoke up, he could not help it. "How? He only had a smelting glove and a lash!"

"With patience," said Daggart. *"One by one. He eliminated every hostile in the fortress while sparing every innocent. He demonstrated unwavering discipline and immaculate stealth. The enemy never saw him, not once, while their forces fell, soldier by soldier. The heathens of Burmose shall never again be a threat to the Knights of Rights."*

A hush washed through the camp, the hush of a people who could not believe their ears. All eyes fell upon Vant. The warrior who had done the impossible was being rewarded with a face in the mud.

"After the conquering of Burmose, Vant went after Terrii," said Daggart.

"He was not allowed!"

"He swore an oath of protection to your son. Did he not?" asked Gordone.

"I cannot refuse a warrior upholding an oath," said Daggart. *"By your decree this is so, First Prime. Vant tracked Terrii to find him fallen. Your son had completed his task, but he was wounded. Left alone, he surely would have died. As had the Warrior Prime who served as his witness."*

Agmar removed his boot from Vant's head. His scimitar moved away as well—but not quickly.

"Take them to the medics," said Agmar, turning his back on his son—and his son's savior. *"They are now Knights. Treat them as such. Welcome to the order, Knight Terriforn. And..."* the words made him sick, though he said them anyway, *"Knight Hu'l."*

The crowd cheered.

Agmar stomped away.

His rage grew.

And grew.

Grew with every voice that sided with Vant, and joined in the celebration of him.

"Please. Whatever you are, let me go."

- Kram Grammie

CHAPTER 11

The Map and the Mage

Crash Town was like a cough that would not go away. A scab that would not be picked off. A cyst that kept growing back.

No new information led anywhere. Leads turned to dust almost as soon as they appeared. And no word from Redemption.

Skii, desperate for information, took to asking locals at random if they knew anything about her father. The name Gyse Fliyr always triggered nothing but blank stares, though handfuls of people recognized his pseudonym, "Whispers." Yet those who did were not exactly the trustworthy type.

Her follow-up questions were always about The World's Best Magician, and most everyone claimed they had met him. They told tales about the god of a man, tales filled with sorcery, enchantment, and adventure—or their anecdotes described the legendary show at The Spectorum Maxima, where the performer had magnificently bombed. Almost all of the stories came with a footnote that they had knowledge of his whereabouts... but it would cost pills to be led to him.

Nothing panned out.

Vant was in a similar bind. He knew the town held a secret, once indicated by the green sparkle in Death's mask, but a couple of problems presented themselves. One, he never saw the phenomenon again, and two, the process of removing the mask from his face once attached was becoming increasingly more difficult. The relic clung to his flesh if worn for too long, and it took tremendous strength to tear it off again. For fear of never being able to remove the damned thing, Vant made use of the artifact's powers only once per day, at varying times, strictly for no more than an hour. With this formula, he scoured Crash Town inch by inch.

To no gain.

Day after day passed in this fashion. Patience wore thin as the days wore on. Vant and Skii became increasingly short with each other; the majority of their conversations consisted of frustrated grunts and eye rolls. A resentment, like a fungus, started growing inside of Vant—a resentment for having trusted his young companion. *She led me to this dead end,* he often thought. *She is to blame for all of this.* And, he knew she probably thought the same things about him.

Their partnership began appearing less and less important, though neither let on about it. Admitting the end of their alliance and disbanding would have meant admitting failure. So they still met up at the end of each day to exchange information, but it was becoming more of a formality than a necessity.

Around the time they had officially lost count of their days in Crash Town—and after yet another wasted day of pointless searching—they settled in at the hotel. Vant made himself busy cleaning his weapons and Skii was poring over her notes for overlooked clues when a voice startled them and broke up their listlessness:

"Ho, there," it said.

Vant stared at his wrist-communicator, but he did not speak.

"Ho, there, Vant Hu'l," the voice said again.

Why today? Vant thought. He knew, of course, the day would come, the day where Land Escape would call for an update. But as of this moment, he had nothing to give them.

Vant responded, "Saamii Fraam. I read you."

"Sorry to bother you. Is it a good time to talk?"

Vant had the impulse to stage the sounds of an epic fight, but, instead, resigned, he said, "It's fine. How are things in Land Escape?"

"Quiet, but that's nothing new these days. How's the search going? Find our folks yet?"

"Getting closer," Vant lied. "Day by day."

"I see." Saamii's tone implied detection of Vant's evasiveness, but he did not press the issue. Instead, he offered, "Any way I can help?"

"Yeah," Vant said. "Tell me everything's fine back home."

"We're managing. Town's in decent shape. Jiino's organized things pretty good. Bomp and Fray's Zoo is quite the sight, you wouldn't believe it. Our people miss their families, though. And I can't lie to you... things are getting tense."

"How so?"

"Chaaris keeps running his mouth. He says we need to mobilize. Says we need to leave town."

"Don't listen to him."

"I never do. You know how he is. Windbag."

"Toss him over the wall." Vant was half joking.

"The thought crossed my mind! Plenty of times! Only problem is, it's been enough to rile up the others. The townspeople are afraid of the nomads, Vant. Our gates are high and we're safe for now, but, sooner or later, they're going to catch on."

"To what?"

"To the quiet. There's usually a ton of noise coming from the canopy, from all the people here. Nowadays it's dead silent, and there's only so many pots and pans the fifty of us can bang on. If the nomads find out we're vulnerable, they'll sack the city."

"How are your defenses?"

"Strong. Everything's holding, but... I don't think we have a lot of time here."

Vant pressed his palms into his temples. "Let me think."

His head swam with responsibility. Responsibility for a rescue operation currently at a standstill. Responsibility for so many lives hanging in the balance. Responsibility for Land Escape teetering on the brink.

"Chaaris has a stockpile of energy running in circles in his belly," Vant said. "It's dangerous now, but it could be diverted into a helpful direction." He considered. Then: "Here's what I want. Tell him he's right."

"I sure hope there's more to this plan."

"Tell him you spoke to me, and that I'm close to finding the army. Tell him a battle is coming, and you need to be outfitted for a fight. Put him in charge of weapons and armor. Let him train the townspeople how to shoot—and to learn himself, if he doesn't already know how. Practice tactics. Run drills. That should keep him busy for a while, and help burn off that excess testosterone."

"Got it. Thanks, Vant. I knew you'd have the answer."

"Not the answer. Just an idea. I hope it works."

An envelope slid into the hotel room, under the door.

Vant and Skii raised eyebrows at each other. Skii quickly checked the hallway, but the messenger was gone.

Vant, back into his comm, said, "Saamii, something came up. I have to go."

"Take care of yourself, Vant Hu'l. Take care of yourself, for all of us."

Vant switched off the transmission.

Skii showed Vant the envelope. It was ornate. Timeworn. Quite lovely. A wax seal displayed the symbol *W8M*.

She opened it with care. Inside was a parchment decorated with circus iconography: exotic animals, performers, tents... and, in the center of the spectacle, was a bearded, robed Adonis floating amongst the clouds. Above, him, written in calligraphy, were the words, *Tonite! ONE nite only, for ONE believer only! When the sun and moon combine.* In the corner, a small series of maps indicated a location and, in fine print, was the phrase, *100g entry.*

One hundred green Corpo-Capsules. *Always a catch,* Vant thought.

Vant assumed Skii would be beside herself but, instead, she was furrowing her brow. "It's a trick," she said. "I've been dropping his name all over town. It's no secret who I'm looking for."

Vant nodded. "Probably ten greens to make the invitation. After they rob you, they'll walk away with ninety. Decent score."

"Uh-huh." She pulled a curtain back and looked out of the hotel room window at the manufactured sky. "The sun and moon are pretty close to touching. They didn't give me much time. I'm sure that was no accident." She closed the curtain. "I'd better get ready."

"You're going?"

"Yeah, gotta."

"But you said yourself—"

"Gotta make sure."

"This is a terrible idea. You've seen what the people in this town are capable of."

"If whoever sent this letter wanted to violate me, they had plenty of chances to seal the deal. They just want money, so I'm gonna give it to them."

"Why?"

"Even though I smell a setup, I also have a hunch. You remember the mural of The World's Best Magician on The Spectorum Maxima? The one that showed a mustached man in a cape?"

"Yes. Your point?"

"This drawing is of a bushy-bearded guy in a robe. Why would he look so different, unless the person who made the flyer knew him?"

"Huh." Vant pondered. "Huh! I *never* would have made that connection. Clever girl."

"Save it, Pops. I'm well aware of how bright I am. Brighter than the sun!"

"Says the girl headed to a mugging. Oh, what am I worried about? You don't have the one-hundy anyway."

Skii's lips melted into a sly smile.

"Skii! How much did you take from the bank?"

"Relax. The fine folks of Land Escape can take one for the team. I've got enough in the bots to cover the fee. Plus, you're gonna recover the loot and pound any baddies into the ground with those big ol' mittens of yours! Right?"

"Fine!" Vant surrendered. After all, this play was in his best interest. He wished to unravel this mystery as well, in case the magician was the sparkling green shape once seen in Death's mask.

Pressed for time, they cobbled together the semblance of a plan. Vant departed first, following a hand-drawn copy of the map. After spending twenty minutes weaving through the streets to shake off any potential tails, the map directed him through an area for lizard fetishes and, eventually, to a wall near the edge of the district. He was certain he would hit a dead end but, as the map indicated, there turned out to be a passageway. It led into a darkened quadrant of the city where Crash Town's holographic ceiling was mute.

Vant inched past several sleeping hobos and made his way into the interior. The area seemed to be a warehousing section of some sort packed with high-rise structures, most likely storage facilities. He reached the map's indicated destination:

a decrepit building, once some sort of logistics center. He found a nearby ledge with a decent vantage point and tucked himself away.

"Skii," he whispered into his comm.

"Yeah?"

"I'm in position. Where are you?"

"At the hotel, getting ready."

"Still? But it's almost time!"

"It's not every day a gal gets an invitation to a show. I'm taking full advantage of the situation."

Vant shook his head. "Just hurry."

"Can't rush a work of art, Pops. Relax. It's good for a lady to keep her fella waiting."

Vant suppressed a huff and sat down.

He rolled Death's mask around his fingers. He stared into its empty eye sockets and felt its pull. A begging. A longing to be worn.

He obliged.

His insides frosted over. Dark became darker. The world transitioned into the realm of shadow. The structural details of the building before Vant faded into half opacity. Through its walls, he could see several glowing silhouettes, most likely squatters or vagrants. Innocents.

He looked around, taking in the view through Death's eyes. Vant noted a fascinating phenomenon: the farther he pushed the limits of his eyes, the more of the township he could see. Tangible structures in the foreground melted away, revealing more of the city in the background. Additional shapes of people materialized like stars pushing through a dusky sky.

He allowed himself to bask in the powers of the mask... the ability to look through walls... the ability to track the movements of people... the ability to see in the dark... and the ability he had once experienced to witness the true nature of the corrupt...

His stomach knotted as a thought appeared:

I like this mask.

He forced his mind to about-face. The guise belonged to a sadistic demon. There was no part of that creature Vant could allow himself to identify with. The mask was making him drunk on an otherworldly ability.

"How do I look?"

Skii had whispered the question into her comm. In his altered state of consciousness, Vant spotted her silhouette arriving in the warehouse district.

"Fine," Vant lied, having no idea what she actually looked like. Her glowing shape was all he could see through the mask, and he did not want to take it off. "Now, radio silence."

"Sure," she said. In the one word, Vant detected a tinge of dejection. Maybe he should have looked at her with his real eyes. Maybe he should have paid her a compliment. It was too late now. *Her safety is more important,* he rationalized.

Skii entered the building and descended into the subterranean; it appeared the "magic show" would be in the basement. Below her, Vant spied one solitary figure glowing white. The form was not pulsing red like the villains he was tasked to destroy, and it was certainly not the green sparkle he was hoping for. It was normal.

"Who are you?" Vant heard Skii say.

A man spoke to her, "I am the grand magician's grand assistant! Welcome, young beauty! We are so thrilled you have come, myself and the World's Best Magician. The show is about to begin, a special show for an audience of one. One lucky girl who will witness the mysteries of the universe, the heavens opening up, and true fantastical magics of every which kind!"

"In a basement?"

"Er, yes. In a basement. Quite private down here, is it not?"

"Sure is. And it smells like piss. Nice bonus. So, where's the star of the show?"

"Behind this very curtain, waiting for you." This was a lie. Vant could see that no one else populated the basement.

Skii sounded skeptical. "Let's see him, then."

"All in due time! But first, to business! Now, it is no great secret that summoning spirits and calling upon the forces of the unbelievable is a taxing and complicated affair. There is more to it than mere magic words and flapping one's arms about. It takes study, discipline, mystical artifacts, special potions, and let's not forget the overhead! There are assistants aplenty, living expenses, marketing and other such necessities, and so forth. This means, sadly, we cannot work for free. We would do it purely for pleasure, truly we would, but, alas, we cannot. But, I can see that you, a girl with big, luscious brains behind those modest-size bosoms, surely comprehend such things. So, I must ask—not that I don't trust you, because I do, I completely do—but I must ask, with all due respect, that I certainly must obviously need your payment in advance. You understand? Why, of course you do, my dear, sweet angel!"

"Sure," Skii said. "Here you go—"

Vant had lost patience. He spoke into the comm, "Skii, I can see from here there's no one else in that room. Don't give him squat."

"Who is that?" the man said, agitated. "You're not alone?"

"I can explain—"

Vant heard the sound of a glass shattering. Skii's silhouette flopped to the floor.

The "magician's assistant" hovered over her for a moment, then darted through the basement toward a side door.

Stupid, Vant chastised himself. *Should have kept my mouth shut.*

It took Vant mere seconds to circumvent the crook's escape. Hiding in the shadows did the thief no good; darkness was Vant's ally when he donned Death's guise. As the man emerged from the back door, Vant dropped from a ledge, tackling him.

The man stammered from shock. "What the—who the—!"

Vant, dressed in black robes, wearing a glowing mask, and brandishing iron fists, bore down on the cowering thief. "What did you do to the girl?!" he snarled.

"I'm alone! What girl?"

Vant smashed the pavement with a gauntlet. Cracks in the cement spiderwebbed inches from the man's face.

"Please don't hurt me! Okay! Okay! She's fine! Just a sleeping draught! You startled me, that's all! I thought she was alone! I heard another voice, and I panicked! I knocked her out and ran! She's probably dreaming of sugarplums and lions' dicks, whatever it is that pretty girls dream about!"

Vant leaned in closer, tormenting his prisoner. The thief trembled in front of the blinding mask.

"Please," he begged. "Whatever you are, let me go."

"Take me to her," Vant said.

"Yes! Yes! I'll take you to her! No problem!"

"If she's so much as scratched, I'm going to be a handful."

"I promise you, comrade, she'll be snoring! She'll be unharmed!"

"Get up," Vant growled. The man obliged. Vant flung a whip which twisted around his prisoner's waist. Bound and secured, he was not going anywhere.

He led Vant through the side door and into the basement. Sure enough, Skii was out cold, face-down in the cellar. Her dress was orange, reversed from the black she normally wore. Her hair was done up in a bun. She had put in effort to look presentable, and now she was a mess. Vant wished he had complimented her when he had the chance.

Vant nudged her. No response.

"Comrade, allow me. Quite a dose I gave her. I have exactly the thing to perk her up." Vant's body language was threatening. "No tricks, I swear! I'm way too frightened of you to try anything impulsive! Let me loose?"

After considering, Vant finally released the whip from the man's torso and peeled off Death's mask, storing it in his robes. He studied the charlatan, who was a stout man, most certainly not tall, with two standout features: one, his flashy eyes, abundant with cleverness, and two, a full set of gleaming, impossibly white teeth.

The trickster did a double-take upon realization that the specter tormenting him was actually a young-faced human. He fumbled about his body, attempting to locate something specific. Vant heard bottles clink together; the man carried a miniature storeroom of vials underneath his vest.

At last, he located what he had been searching for: a small tube of yellow powder. Vant shot him a look that said, *Don't test me,* and the charlatan nodded with obedience.

He waved the bottle under Skii's nose and she came to in an instant. "What the crud—? Ow, my head! Where am I? Oh, hey, Pops."

"Skii, this overzealous scumbag drugged you. Don't worry, you'll be fine."

"My cute cohort, I simply apologize for such behavior. Had I had known you have a guardian angel—or demon, by the looks of him—I would have handled the situation with much greater aplomb. But, bygones under the bridge! No harm, no foul. Yes? Yes?" He spoke with his whole body, a showman through and through. He was selling something with every word. To Vant: "My friend, I do apologize! All is forgiven?"

Though skeptical, Vant shook his hand—the con man flailed his arm with enthusiasm. In an overcompensation of friendliness, he patted Vant on the chest and stomach as if they were close friends.

"Bravo for your maturity! Now, let us begin again, this time with proper introductions. I, my dear compatriots, am the humble Kramm Grammie. Not, as you so discovered, a magician's assistant, but rather, a mere street urchin. And now that you've caught me and put my pride in the pisser, I will bid you a fond farewell and return to the streets in repentance. I shall think upon my actions with regret and begin my life anew, free of this detestable disease of petty theft."

"Hogwash," Skii said.

"My dear..."

"'My dear,' my ass! Turn out your vest, you snake. Give my 'demon' back his mask."

"Begging your pardon, but I have no such—"

Skii shoved him against the wall and put Cassidy's barrel against his neck. "Let's get this straight. First, we're no chumps. Second, I'm the scary one of the two of us. Who says I'm not *his* guardian demon?"

"Of course! Of course! I was simply testing you, that's all! I had every intention of giving it back! Here it is, you see?"

He revealed Death's mask, which he had stashed under his vest. Vant felt like a sucker; the man had pick-pocketed the relic out from his robes while patting him on the chest. He snatched it back from the thief.

"Next," Skii said, "I want my pills back."

"Clever comrade! Why, certainly! I forgot I had them! A simple mistake!" He returned Skii's purse of Corpo-Capsules.

"And now, I want you to take us to The World's Best Magician."

"Sweet cherub, there must be some misunderstanding. I am but a humble—"

"Yes, I know. A humble pain in the ass." Skii cocked Cassidy menacingly. The charlatan cringed. "The man in the invitation you gave me. He looked nothing like the one painted on the Spectorum Maxima. You've seen him. You know him. You either take us to him, or you get splattered."

He squinted at her, considering.

"I'll even let you keep the *real* pills in your pocket, and not the dummies you handed back."

Vant felt like a double-sucker. While "fumbling" in his robes for Skii's antidote, the con man had emptied her pill purse and replaced its contents with decoys. That Skii had observed the subtle weight difference was astounding.

"My dear—"

Vant interrupted, "Oh. And we'll need our communicators back."

Skii felt her naked wrist, then slapped herself on the forehead.

Kram Grammie wiggled his eyebrows playfully and smiled huge, showing off his perfect teeth. "You drive a hard bargain, companions. We have ourselves a deal! Well, come on! Off with us! Time to meet your first real magician."

He led Vant and Skii out of the warehousing center and down a back alley sandwiched between a buffet and a strip club. They approached an unmarked door that could easily have been mistaken for a utility closet. He used six different keys to unlatch six different locks, and then the door creaked open. He went in first, beckoning Vant and Skii to follow.

The dingy apartment-style hideaway was cluttered and dusty. Old books, magazines, pen-and-paper games, and outdated electronic entertainment equipment littered the space. Crumpled-up handwritten notes, diaries filled with scribblings, and other slippery obstacles lined the floor. Collages of media, crystalline displays of scantily clad women, and various other forms of "art" decorated the walls. There was no shortage of schlock, including small figurines displayed on shelves next to busts of mythological heroes. A grip of mismatched armchairs and an overused couch anchored the living room, and only a makeshift kitchen and two bedrooms down a hallway completed the dwelling.

"This way," the charlatan said. At one of the two doors he knocked and asked, "Are you decent?"

There was a vocal cacophony from behind the door. They could not decipher the exact words, but there were a lot of them, and they were passionate.

"That means yes," Grammie confirmed. "You can go in. He won't bite."

Vant twisted the knob. The door opened with a *creeeeak*.

They had barely a moment to register the man before his kinetic body movements and sing-songy voice swept them into a world of confusion. He flailed his arms wildly, stroked a mane of matted hair, and puffed out his impressive potbelly.

"*Bababoo!* My friends! My friends! Come one, come all! In fact, we should all be so lucky as to come! Now, we all know that I know you, and you may know that you know me, but in case my message is misinterpreted, let me be clear... it is always a pleasure to be in your company! Though my circumstances sometimes leave me in a holding pattern elsewhere, here we are, here and now!"

Skii's mouth was agape. Vant tried to decipher meaning in the magician's words, but, before he could, he started up again, "I'm busy from here 'til doomsday, or at least 'til I get my new show up, but I suppose that's why you're here. So, let me tell you about it! Act One, 'The Landing.' Pretty boring, actually. I disarm a guy with my wit and charm, and I try to walk through a stone wall, thinking it akin to one of my perverse Uncle Beverly's 'Library of Discontinued School Texts' secret doors. Thusly, the hidden passage performs much the same duties as a wall of stone. Enthusiasm wanes from my foibles. Act Two, it is impossible to defeat me. Act Three, buckets and buckets and buckets and buckets of blood! Act Four, we celebrate. As you know, I haven't had a drink in a really long time, but I recently imagined I'd had one. Even *that* was enough to floor me! My goodness, I'm not quite sure how we did it back then. I guess we were younger. On to Act Five!"

He continued rambling, pouring through his journals, and searching for something that likely did not exist. He wore a lightweight robe—more a bathrobe than a magician's robe—which trailed behind him as he ran from corner to corner. His slippers slid across the floor, and his soft shirt wafted at the neckline, revealing a thicket of remarkable chest hair.

Vant, in hopes of restoring some order, introduced himself to the oddity zipping around the room: "Hello. I'm Vant. Vant Hu'l. This is Skii Tavee." Skii was entranced, but gave Vant a familiar look. "Ah," he added, "and her fuzzy friend is Cassidy."

Skii waved, and showed the bizarre man her teddy bear.

"Why, there's no need for formalities. We're old friends, of course!" He scratched Cassidy behind the ear, which made Skii smile. "We all are, in fact! Peas in a pod!" He indicated each of the people in the room, "Her, me, him, you, him..." and he pointed outward toward someone missing, "...and Froggy, of course! Oh, Froggy. Always late to the party."

Vant turned to Grammie. "Can he understand us?"

"He understands us fine. I know it seems otherwise, but he's not crazy. Not in the slightest. He's just... off-kilter."

The hyperactive man turned to them in a moment of clarity. He spoke with purpose and perfect diction: "I have a nephew now. It's weird. He appears to be a regular baby, but when he talks, I don't understand what he's saying. Does this mean my nephew is a *nerd* baby?"

Vant and Skii looked at Grammie for translation. "Can I understand him? Sure can. Did I understand the last bit? Not in the slightest." He chuckled and made a polite gesture, ushering Vant and Skii back into the main room. Bewildered, they obliged.

Grammie shut the door behind them, leaving the magician to his insanity.

"Bababoo! My friends! My friends! Come one, come all!"

- The World's Worst Magician

232 YEARS PRIOR

Of Battles and Birthright

"Take it!"

"I can't."

"Do it! It's your birthright!"

A mortar exploded outside the trench. Dirt, like a waterfall, poured onto the Knights.

"My dad will kill me," said Terrii.

"No, the rockets will kill you," Vant said. "And every last one of us!"

Another explosion. The bombardments were getting closer. More accurate.

Vant put his hands on Terrii's shoulders and lowered his face to eye level. "Prime Davith has sent twenty-five Knights to their deaths. His strategy is a failure. He's sending us out five at a time to be killed. It won't be much longer before our number's up!"

"But what can I do?"

"There's a way out of this. He's not thinking clearly. He's not seeing the strategy here."

"Neither am I!"

"But I am. Terrii, I've known you my whole life. I've never misled you. Assume leadership and I'll get us out of this. Take it, Terrii! Take command! Be the leader you were born to be. Before we all die!"

Two more explosions twenty feet from the trench. The crevice wall faltered, dislodging soil and earth. If the mortars did not kill them, the dirt would soon bury them alive.

"Ba—battalion Five. Front and center," quivered Davith, the Warrior Prime leading the operation in place of Agmar. "I want you to—to spread out on the surface. See if you can draw their fire and get a bead for our snipers."

"Belay that order," said Terrii.

"What did you say?" said a stunned Davith.

"You're done. I'm assuming command."

"By what right?"

"By right of birth!" a Knight spoke up in Terri's defense. "You're murdering us all, Davith!"

And another: "I don't follow you. I follow Agmar. And Terrii's the closest thing to him right now."

Davith had no choice. He was impossibly out of his league as a commander, was facing a mutiny, and already had twenty-five deaths on his hands. "Okay," he said. "Okay. I willingly relinquish control of our forces. May Agmar have mercy on me for my failure."

The fifteen remaining Knights of Rights turned to Terrii.

And Terrii turned to Vant.

"Commander Hu'l!" Terrii said, bestowing a promotion on his friend by addressing him as such.

"Here, Prime Terriforn. What are your orders?"

"I order you to... to come up with a strategy to get us out of this clusterfu—!"

Another explosion.

"Yes, sir!" said Vant. "Knights of Rights, throw your firearms outside the trench."

"The hell we will," disputed a confused warrior.

"Do as you're told!" ordered Terrii, surprising even himself with the commanding tone.

The warriors reluctantly chucked their weapons over the lip of the shelter. There was no shortage of cursing.

"Now what?" said Terrii, in an aside to Vant.

"Run up the white flag. We're going to surrender."

Fifteen rebellious voices protested, louder than the bomb that had exploded ten feet from them.

"We're Knights of Rights," Terrii reminded his colleague. "We've never surrendered before. We don't even have a white flag. Come to think of it, I don't know if I even own anything white!"

"Who's wearing white undies?" Vant shouted to the troops.

One hesitant warrior raised his hand.

"Off with 'em!"

After insisting the rest of the Knights turn their backs, he complied.

"Now, run up the flag," Vant said, handing him a stick to serve as a flagpole.

The warrior did so.

"This plan stinks," said Terrii, tossing a glance at the sweaty underwear.

But...

The bombardment ceased.

"Battalion Five," Vant ordered, "you will surrender. You will walk out in a line parallel to the trench, hands on head. Battalions Six and Seven, camouflage yourselves." Vant chipped away at the earth with his bludgeoning glove, demonstrating how to do so.

"Then what?" asked Terrii.

"Then," Vant said, "when the captors' backs are turned, the rest of us will sneak up behind them... and snap their necks."

Vant was violating every known code of battle conduct. The white flag meant surrender, defeat, and a plea for clemency. He was preying on the enemy's merciful nature—and was planning to use it against them.

"Battalion Five, don't you dare look back. When you hear the commotion, drop to the ground and do not move. Your role is in the deception, not in the fight. Battalions Six and Seven will execute the captors, then we will all disperse and head to the rendezvous point. There, from an equalized vantage, we will march on our enemies. And kill them all."

The Knights were speechless. It was a sound—though unquestionably unethical—strategy.

"That's cold," Terrii said with a devious grin. "I love it."

The plan worked.

"Blink, and I've got your wallet—and your heart."

- Kram Grammie

CHAPTER 12

The Con Man and the Crash

"I first met the World's Best Magician when I was but a freshly sprouted man. I had just dropped my testes, and my voice cracked with manhood just arriving. I was a wandering fool, a boy finding his place without any place to place his foolishness. I made my living the only way I knew how, by telling tales and emptying wallets. I pocketed what I picked, and kept what I conned. Blink, and I've got your wallet—and your heart. Which, young lady, do I have of yours?"

"Oh, you sonofa—" Skii fumbled around for her pill purse, which was gone... again.

"Alas, enough about dear old Kram Grammie and his always-growing wealth and unmatched charm and wittishness! This is a tale about him, about he! The grand and mighty World's Best Magician! Supreme master of the unbelievable and purveyor of the impossible! Not one shred of this story is fictionalized, not one tiny teat! Everything you are about to hear is of the damnedest-be-damned truth!"

Vant and Skii settled into their armchairs, each with tall glasses of wine that Grammie had poured for them.

He continued, "One day while out in the fields, or in the storeroom, or up in a very high tree—something along those lines—a curious man came to town. He had quite the appearance, I had never seen such a fellow. His capes gleamed the greenest of green. His peepers were the brightest of brighties. He walked as if he floated, and he hummed a delightful tune. Something, dare I say, otherworldly? Of another dimension? There were full chords which harmonized with the melodies, and his tones danced on the chords. How did such musics come from the mouth of one mere man?

"I followed him closely," Grammie went on, spellbound by his own voice. "His hands moved to the rhythm. They led the orchestra behind his esophagus, and his eyes floated toward the heavens while his feet knew exactly where to go on the ground. What was his destination? Who could tell? Certainly not I! But that did not hesitate me from desiring to know one thing about him, one particular thing... where did he keep his money in those flowy capes of his?

"You see, in those days, I had a one-track mind. Now, of course, it's two tracks, what with manlihood and all. But, back then, it was profit or *pfffft*. So I did what I always did. I ran the scam!

"My companions, I knew them all. The Three-Step Charlie. The Lullaby-Lookie-Loo. The Twix-Twizzly. But, with this fantastical fop, only one such trick would do the trick. I settled on the Buxom-Betty, which any man, even one with these levels of flamboyancy, would most certainly fall for!

"'Excuse me, good sir!' I called to the strange gentleman as I summoned my faithful servants—my tear ducts—while raising the pitch in my voice to the peak of patheticism. 'Please help me! My mommy dear has vanished, and I've not the faintest where she went to! I am oh so frightened! Thankfully, I never leave home without a picture of her! Perhaps you, of such high character, can identify her, had you may have seen her.'

"And with that display of helplessness, I showed him a photo the likes of which would make any man buckle in his boots. It featured a woman with a bosom so beyond bountiful-nomical that one would be forgiven for breaking all bonds of faith and commitment right then and there. Her corset was practically bursting apart as her two attached milk sacs—"

"We get the idea," Vant interjected.

"Shh!" Skii protested. "I kinda like this part!"

"As I was saying, before I was interrupted by the bringer of good taste to the proceedings... *her tits were huge!* Any sane man would drop all pertinent business to rather quite obviously begin a hunt for this woman. Provided, of course, he still had his nutties. And fancied a lady!

"With his mind afloating in the land of sin, I had intended to pock his picket and lift all desirables as he was lost in fantasy. But this man, he did something so unexpected, so bizarre, so unanticipated, that it almost gave the whole scam away."

"What did he do?" Skii was hanging on his every word.

"He said, 'Oh, Caroville? She's a few towns over. Well, come on then! It's a couple of weeks back the other way, but a child simply cannot be without his mother!'"

"He—he knew her?"

"He *said* he did, but who could tell? At first, I thought this had to be a ploy, that he had outsmarted me. That he was bluffing. But, my lady Skii Tavee, he gave such the impression that he was acquainted with the buxom beauty in the photo—the photo of which I had harmlessly removed from a Land Escape gossip rag. I had certainly never met this lass of so many men's blind admirations, so I did the unexpected to this unexpected turn of fortunes... I followed him! For two weeks! Because, comrades, I myself wanted to meet her! Quite suddenly, I began a quest not for riches, but for hooties!"

Grammie gulped down his wine and refilled all of their glasses.

"Moving on! We quickly walked and constantly talked, although his phrasings were rarely intelligible. He told me jokes with no punchlines, and he spun yarns which changed characters and settings without rhyme or reason. I would have most definitely declared him mad, but he described my lovely lass in such tremendous detail. Furthermore, he apologized repeatedly for defiling a woman he had no clue was a mother, and one who someday would misplace her child. He said, had he been aware, he would have behaved much more gentlemanly upon completion of their communion.

"Now, at this point, there's something about him you must know. The most amazing thing about him, the most fascinating thing about him—and I beg you, compatriots and confidants, to believe me when I say this—the most incredible thing about him was... his magic. His *magic,* my chums. His magic. The man could do it."

Grammie noticed something, and paused his story.

"Does it hurt when your eyebrows burrow deep into your nose?" he said to Vant. "Why, if your chin is the destination, I'd say those two fuzzy worms were well on their way!"

Then, he was right back to it. "What I tell you is true! Truer than true! So true it's almost false! He could do *magic,* the real stuff. Sure, he could roll pills through his fingers and be tricky with card decks. But also, he could do the impossible without so much as blinking twice. He could change colors around, make people believe they were carrots, make up become down and down become left and left become backwards... things that had to be experienced to be believed—which even then, they never quite would be.

"All along our journey, I asked him questions that never got answered. And how he came to be, well, that never quite came to be. Yet, the one thing he always described in glorious detail was a show. *The* show. He was always planning a show. It would be grand, it would be gay, and it kept his top a-twitter.

"Alas, carefree companions, we arrived at a small town on the outskirts of Land Escape. Back then, if you remember, a few of those havens existed—peaceful little places before the nomads turned to organized savagery, for shame. This was a lovely place, windmills and waterfalls, flowers and kitty-cats, and all of that. Of the several shacks and cottages, our magician marched straight up to a door of no particular flavor and knocked upon it exactly twelve times. 'That's the number of her love, no one else's but hers,' he said to me. 'Don't remember to forget that soon. Very important!' And then, the blastedest thing happened. The door opened and, sure enough... it was her."

Grammie sucked in all of the air he could to steady his wobbly head.

"Majestic. A bountiful bundle of matronly mammaries. She looked upon her visitors and smiled, and then spoke words I will never forget as long as I live."

"What were they?" Skii asked.

"'Hello,' she said. 'Hello.'" He repeated the word over and over until it felt exactly right to him. It took about seven tries.

"Had she met him before?" Skii pointed to the magician's room, which had grown quiet. He must have been listening. Or sleeping.

"Oh, dearie, no. But he took her hand into his and tapped on her palm twelve times. She asked him, 'Do I know you?' He said to her, 'Yes, you don't. Of course you do, but not today.' She giggled, smitten with the stranger. He waved his hand like a fluttering bird, twisted it 'round and 'round until a trail of red came out of her heart, and with a flick of his wrist, she and I were intertwined! I'm not sure how or why, but we were embraced! My giant head fell between her giant floobies! She whispered in my ear such sweet everythings, and I cried like a child who did, in fact, find the mother he was looking for."

Vant found himself awestruck in the insanity—albeit hesitant to buy into it. *Although,* he conceded to himself, *my story, to others, would sound equally impossible. More so.*

"That was the day from whence I never left the man's side," Grammie said. "We worked diligently. We prepared for his infamous show. We did small, one-on-one gigs and impromptu sideshows to amass pills and materials. We went town to town in search of those willing to be entertained—and not murder us at the gates. Turns out, even the devout and dogmatic enjoyed a bit of magic, although we stayed away from the scary places.

"Years passed, comrades. We were inseparable, the two of us. Two gigantic peas in one gigantic pod. Over time, we built ourselves a name—well, we built *him* one— and we built our band of traveling entertainers. We played shows for wanderers happy to pay us. We paid for nomads happy to protect us. We bought animals and tanks and a militia and an honest-to-snot clown or three! We had a plan, a damn good one! We would hoof it to the wealthiest town around, which, as it so happened, was a place where I could also dampen my doodle... why, Crash Town, of course! There, we'd play the greatest show the world had ever seen, make our fame and fortune, and then, with our pockets stuffed with pills, move on and take permanent residence in Land Escape, free of our manly juices so we could concentrate on our spectacles!

"We sent promoters ahead—barkers we called them—folks paid to spread the word and put our signs up all about town. We built up the hype and reserved The Spectorum Maxima. What used to house the sweat of athletes and the might of gladiators would soon witness the magic of the unbelievable! And I, as The World's Best Manager, would be entitled to my fair share! Ol' Doubleya—that's what I call him, short for the W in his nickname—has never been too keen on counting green. Thankfully, however, I had the perfect man for the job. Myself!

"The Spectorum Maxima is gargantuan, but we sold the place out. Sold 'er out! Fifty thousand folks filled the seats. We were swimming in pills, my confidants.

Merchandise flew off the shelves. There were hats and shirts and cloaks and toy wands—mere sticks from the forest, of course—that we peddled for ten green pills apiece. The whole place chanted '*Dub-Ya! Dub-Ya!*' My friends, it was a sight to be seen. A most powerful sight. A most ass-blowing one."

Grammie caught his breath. He adjusted his level of intensity, and lowered his voice to a step above a whisper, so his roommate in the other room would not overhear.

"As I said before, confidants, I was a pup. Maybe I was in over my head. Maybe my pointer got out in front of me and I couldn't put him back in my pants. But, the truth is, I noticed something askew when I mingled with the crowd. There was wagering going on. Betting. They were betting on who would win the fight. Trouble was, no fight. You see, in Crash Town, it's either f'ing or fighting, and there wasn't anything sexy on the posters. Comrades, they came for blood. And we had none to give them.

"'But, no matter,' I thought! They would be wowed when they saw what The World's Best had up his sleeve! Real magic! Certainly he'd bring down the house! Confidants, the lights dimmed. A hush fell over the crowd. Spotlights blasted the floor of The Spectorum Maxima, enbrightening the stains of blood and the cages his opponents *should* have been cowering in. But, at the sight of no opponents, the audience took a turn.

"He walked on out. This idol I looked up to, this person of power, this born entertainer who changed every life he touched... he walked on out to center stage, looking tiny, so tiny. Just a man. Just a man. I smelled trouble, deep in my bones.

"When I saw him standing out there, shivering like a wet puppy after a bath in ice water, I started gathering all the pills I could. I stuffed my pants, my pockets, my socks, my ears, and my armpits. I got to the floor of the arena, as close as I could, and set my mind on planning an escape route. I knew, just knew, we'd need it."

Grammie downed another glass of wine. What had started out as an anecdote was becoming a confession.

"Never should have done it, put him in that arena. This town... it's possessed. It's violent. I turned a blind eye. I got greedy—"

Vant coughed.

"Okay, okay. I got greedy-*er*. I should have walked away. I should have started in Land Escape. About ten thousand 'shouldas' floated in my brain, all fighting to be the king crapper. And now, forgive me for what I'm about to say about my lifelong friend..." Grammie scratched the back of his head nervously. "He screwed the pooch. Right in the stinker."

Skii frowned. Vant had an unexpected urge to put his hand on her shoulder—he shook off the impulse.

"He tried to churn up whatever energy he usually does to begin his tricks—does this thing with his hands, you see. Problem was, nothing happened. I've seen him do his mysticisms a million times, but this time, a whole lot-o jack-o squat-o. His face...

I'll never forget it. He was scared. He was confused. Out there, all alone. He didn't know what to do. Nor did I. There we were, two self-made kings of the world, pooping ourselves like babes.

"He kept trying, kept trying. I shouted to him, but the crowd roared louder. Confidants, you've never heard such awful things. Fifty thousand folks came for blood, and damn it all if they weren't going to get some. I ran to the center of the arena where he was getting pelted with everything from popcorn to piss, and I pushed him into the escape route, down into the trenches. I moved slow, weighed down by all that loot. 'At least I'll walk away with *something*,' I kept saying to myself as I fled with my friend under my arm. He was crying, hard. Saddest thing I ever saw. No one never should have to see their hero with red puffy eyes and dirty red cheeks. Horrible shame, that. Horrible."

Grammie struggled against emotion. His voice wobbled. Skii pretended to rub her eyes, fooling no one; she was wiping away renegade tears.

He continued, "We got out of there, by the tips of our foreskins. Fifty thousand rushed the floor, out to get us. Later, I heard hundreds died in the riots. Thousands were injured. They had turned on each other, this riled-up crowd without release. Our fault, that. Our fault. Blood on our hands. No question, no doubt.

"Anyway, we hid. Tucked ourselves away. Had enough pills, plenty in fact, to rent us our lodgings, what lies before you. Not a bad place for those who don't want to be discovered. But grudges don't die easy in Crash Town. I'm sure you've seen the slander while out and about. People don't forget, won't forget. Even after all this time, it's still not safe for us. So here we are, trapped, hiding from a whole city that wants our hides."

"What happened to him?" Skii asked.

"He stayed in his room. Ate, pissed, shit, slept. That's it. But then, one day near two-and-a-half years ago, just like that, he was back to his former self. Up like a balloon, shot out like a cannon, up and speaking his usual gibberish and strategizing his next big spectacle. Been in that mode ever since, planning the show, which, compatriots, between you and me, is never going to happen. The truth is, since that fateful, ass-handing day, I've never seen him do magic. Not once. Honestly, companions, I'm not quite certain he can even do the stuff anymore."

Grammie flopped into his armchair. "I dunno. For the first time, I saw bigger winnings in the real deal than in the Sneaky-Peeky or the Freddy-Foot-Face. I thought I could make something. Create something. I was the guy bringing magic—*real* magic—to the world. Serves me right, I guess. I'm not destined for anything like that. All I've got is the con. I'm a con man, simple dimple. I'm good at tricks, but not at magic."

A long pause threatened to go on forever. Finally, he spoke again, "On the bright side, I have plenty of time to reflect, and plenty of drink to help me do so." He poured himself yet another generous glass of wine, which he slammed.

"Why don't you leave?" Skii asked.

"Well, the rent is low, you see."

"I mean, leave Crash Town."

"I'm afraid I don't quite understand, my dearest."

"Go somewhere else. Start fresh."

"Go somewhere? Else? My bony cherub... there is no *leaving* this place."

A realization washed over Vant. He had been prioritizing a departure without having truly considered the feasibility of the act.

"Just piecing it together now, are we? How long have you been here? Weeks?" Silence. "Months?" Grammie guffawed at Vant and Skii's morbid expressions. "Look at you two," he said. "Now you know why there's no mirrors in Crash Town. You're not the prettiest of sights. Face it, friends. You've crashed."

Vant fought against the statement with head shakes. "Bullshit. I call bullshit. There's got to be a way out. There's always a way."

"Plenty of ways, no shortage of them. The thing is, they all come with terrible odds. Literally, terrible odds—in the casinos, you can bet on those trying to escape. The wall is monitored and anyone that gets anywhere near it becomes a public spectacle, broadcast all about town."

Vant continued to think. Grammie broke his concentration by taunting, "Think you can get past the junkies at the gates with even a scrap o'loot? Or maybe you're nutsy enough to grapple with the Peace-Keepers. Fancy a tangle with the nomads outside the city? Or, perhaps you've taken to the notion that you'll buy a sparkling jet-bike from Corpo and fly your way out. *Hah!* That holographic ceiling does more than just look pretty. That sucker's dangerous! Get too close and you'll blow the hell up, I've seen it happen. Comrades, if you heard even *one* of the stories of botched attempts over the years, you'd get the idea out of your mind posthaste. The House, my companions, always wins."

"I know someone who beat the odds," Vant countered.

"My dad," said Skii.

Grammie turned serious. "Are you certain of this?"

Vant said, "Someone with resources has been hunting him. He's convinced the guy escaped."

"Your father was this 'Whispers' fellow, correct? You yakked about him all around town—along with my magician. Give me a few days. Perhaps I may figure out how he did it. I know people who know people who know people who know people who know people. I'll make you both a deal. I'll sniff out your father's exit... *if* you get me and Doubleya through it."

Vant knew it would be hard enough for Skii and himself to slip out of town undetected; adding a bumbling buffoon to the mix—and his certifiable friend— would certainly make it impossible.

Sensing opportunity slipping away, the charlatan kept pressing, "Let's look at the big picture here, comrades. The four of us, we have a chance." Skii shot daggers at Grammie. "The five of us! How dare I forget dear Cassidy! The truth is, I could never leave Crash Town myself, not even consider it, what with my lovable bonkers to take care of. But with your muscle and weapons and her cute little ass—" Vant turned sour. "Sorry! Habit. Just get us out into the open, and we'll find our way to Land Escape on our own. Maybe there I can make a dishonest buck in a decent place, for a change."

"No one left to scam in Land Escape," Vant said. "Some awful things went down there."

The three of them sat in silence, staring at the floor.

"Then we'll go with you," Grammie said. "Wherever that may be."

"You're joking. What would I do with a thief and a lunatic?"

"I'm quite helpful! Truly I am! Arguably, he's not..." Grammie tilted his head toward the magician's door, "...but I can contribute magnificently! What's our plan, anyway? Where are we headed? Look at this charisma! Infectious, right? I'm a natural! What's the mission?"

"Rescue a thousand prisoners from an evil army."

"The two of you? Against an entire army?"

"Well," Vant looked over at Skii, "we hadn't really discussed it. Just me, for now."

Skii rolled her eyes. Vant had no idea if it meant that obviously she was going to help, or obviously she wasn't.

"I have decided," Grammie said in a grand gesture, woozy from the booze, "to sleep on it."

Vant made no attempt to hold in the criticizing laugh that fell from his throat. He was not surprised to see the cowardice behind Grammie's pomp.

Skii eyed the door to the magician's room. "I want to talk to him."

"Go right ahead. He's harmless. He won't lay a hand on you—although he will flirt. And, he gets quite stinky, holed up in there. He'll clean up if you ask him to. He's polite, if a bit clueless."

"I'll be fine," she said.

She stood up and walked to the door. She knocked. "Mister Magician? World's Best Magician—?"

"Stop!" Grammie bounded to his feet. "Don't call him that. That's the one thing he hates. Don't ever call him that."

"What do I call him, then?"

"The World's *Worst* Magician."

"What used to house the sweat of athletes and the might of gladiators would soon witness the magic of the unbelievable!"

- Kram Grammie

229 YEARS PRIOR

Of Oath and Honor

"Hey."

"Hey."

They did not speak much these days. No reason to.

"How's your father?" Vant asked.

"Not great."

"Will he fight again?"

"I don't think so," said Terrii. "I don't think he can." After Terrii and Vant had risen to Primes, Agmar's mental and physical health had degraded significantly. And his mistrust of Vant had only increased.

Terrii continued, "I was hoping to be in battle with him at least once. But I guess you can't have everything."

"Guess not."

Terrii paced the cave. He surveyed Vant's side project. "Still working on those things?"

"I think they're almost done."

"Show me."

Vant used a pulley to lift a hollowed-out piece of metal from a barrel of water where it was cooling. The build was shaped like an inverted fist.

"It's backwards," said Terrii.

"That's the mold. I've been experimenting with metals that can be melted down and poured to harden into shape. Lets me be more exact."

"There are holes in the knuckles."

"Right." Vant pointed toward a rack on the armory wall. Dozens of rope-like strands draped from the ceiling to the floor. "They coil up inside the gloves."

"Meh. They'll be too heavy. How are you supposed to do anything useful with them?"

"Shyyla's working on that. She's figured out something interesting using Corpo-Cells for power."

"So are you two—?"

"No."

"Why not?"

Vant held his fist up to the gauntlet mold, measuring the fit. "Got my hands full at the moment."

Terrii smirked about Shyyla, then said about Vant's project, "I'm not so sure about those things. I think I'll stick with guns."

"Pulling a trigger is easy. When it's easy to take a life, it's easy to take the wrong life."

Then there was a voice from the entrance to the cave. It was weak, and dripping with spite.

"Too good for guns. Too good for all of us."

"Father!" said Terrii. "What are you doing out of bed?"

Agmar was a shadow of his former self. His boulder-like muscles were deflated. His once broad shoulders were sunken.

"You will no longer taunt me, child of Hu'l. You will no longer poison my army against me. You will never be allowed to claim revenge for the deaths of your parents!"

With a metallic sputter, Agmar's scimitar slid from its scabbard. He pointed it with sickly arms.

"Fight me," he choked out.

Vant walked past Terrii.

Moved face-to-face with Agmar.

Then dropped to his knees.

He pulled down his shirt, and presented his neck.

"Here is my neck to cut," said Vant. "I have taken an oath. I will never turn on you. I will never betray you. I will always be loyal."

"Coward! Snake! Fight me!"

Vant remained still. On his knees. Shirt pulled. Neck exposed.

"Fight me!" Agmar screamed again.

"Here is my neck," Vant responded.

"Fight me!"

Vant did not move.

"Fight me!"

No movement.

"Fight me!"

Agmar raised his sword behind his head, preparing to strike.

He collapsed.

"Father!" Terrii cried.

"I'm the pretty one! He's the smart one!"

- Clodd

CHAPTER 13

The Putrid and the Passage

"They're coming with us," said Skii.

"Out of the question," said Vant.

"Then find your own way out of Crash Town."

"What did the magician say to you? You were in his room for hours."

"Nothing. Well, a lot actually. None of it made much sense. But there's something about him. Grammie's right. The guy can do *magic.*"

"How do you know?"

"He has this way he moves his fingers. His hands. The stuff he says... It's like nothing I've ever heard before. The way he talks..."

"That's no proof of anything. These guys are dangerous. This whole thing could be a sham. They've got slippery tongues and Crash Town sensibilities. I don't trust them."

"I'm not saying I *trust* them. I'm saying I *like* them. Plus, they need our help."

Kram Grammie, snoring from his gut in an armchair, woke himself suddenly with a snort that, were they in the wild, would have alerted nomads for miles. Then he instantly conked out again.

"This is crazy," Vant said. "I'm not going for it."

"Real hero, you are."

"Let's get this straight. I'm no hero. And if you see me that way, you're making a tremendous mistake."

"I guess we're both making mistakes, then. Tremendous ones."

"Skii—"

She interrupted his thought with an obscene gesture.

Perhaps this is for the best, Vant thought. Until this point, he had not fully considered her involvement. Did he even *want* her help? What good would she be against an army? She was nimble and could hold her own in a fight, but she was not exactly a stone-cold killer.

Vant reflected deeper. He was hiding a massive secret from her, from all of them. Freeing the Land Escape prisoners was only one part of a larger purpose: destroying those marked for elimination when viewed through Death's mask. This would be a bloody, violent undertaking; could he live with dragging anyone else into the fray?

"I'm only looking out for our best interests," Vant said.

"Grammie has a plan. It's the *only* plan. What's the harm in seeing if he comes through? To me, it's pretty simple. If he finds the escape route Dad used, they get to come along. What do you say?"

Vant sighed. "Fine. *If* he finds the escape route. Only *if—*"

"Wake up, snore-face!" Skii whacked Grammie on the arm, jolting him awake. "You're coming with us. You and your magician."

Vant cracked his knuckles in protest.

"This—this is amazing!" Grammie stammered. "Thank you. Thank you! You won't regret your decision. When do we leave? How should I prepare? What should we bring? What should I wear? Gosh, I'm rambling. I guess I'm in shock—"

"Relax. We've got a lot of planning to do. And you have to deliver on your promise. If you don't, the deal's off. For now, get your affairs in order and prepare to never set foot in this ass-crack of a township ever again."

"I'm overwhelmed. To repay this astronomical generosity, I have a gift for you. I think you'll like it. I'm certain of it. I know because... it's yours." He removed an engagement ring from his pocket. It was Rii's, the one Skii always wore on the chain around her neck.

"Take one more thing from me and I'll feed you to my bear," Skii hissed as she snatched the ring out of his hands.

"No problem, no problem! I understand now, you're off-limits! Doubleya! Get out here!"

The magician, wearing nothing but a bed-sheet toga, strolled into the living room.

"Guess where we're going, old friend! Out into the world again!"

"*Bababoo!*" he howled with delight. "I plan on taking extra naps today because I know I'll be up all night not being able to sleep! I'm not going to say I'm coming, or I won't go! What kind of beer do they serve there? Ah, who cares, it's all demonic! Will Froggy be joining in on the festivities? I'm sure he will!"

Skii did her best to avoid Vant's scrutinizing gaze.

They made preparations for departure, but there was still no clue on the whereabouts of the thallium army. Vant's impatience grew with the mounting pressure. Restlessness crawled through his nerves.

He repeatedly reflected on how he came to Crash Town to find Skii's father—the one man who might know what Vant was going up against—and all he had gotten from it was an ass-kicking, a depressing story about Gyse Fliyr's history, and two tagalong deadbeats. He was failing—and failing hard—at living up to his assumed role as a liberator. Worst-case scenarios for the Land Escape hostages constantly filled his mind.

Soon, Vant ceased leaving his hotel room entirely. He sat for hours staring at the wall, chin in his forefingers, with Death's mask in his lap. Every itch he felt, every scratch, every brush against his skin seemed magnified. The gravity of the situation pressed upon his conscience while anxiety tugged at him with invisible strings. Along with the changes in his physiology, a fear took hold.

Of the one thing he could not fight.

Of the one thing he was powerless to resist.

The curse.

"Vant?" Skii popped her head into the room.

He answered with silence.

She entered. "What's up with you, Mister Moody?"

More silence.

She dropped to her knees in front of him, obstructing his view into nothingness.

"A wise man once said, 'Answers don't live in the ceiling.' I think that goes for walls, too."

No response.

"You don't owe them anything. You're doing the best you can. Why is this so personal to you? Why are you taking this so hard?"

"Rescuing a town won't even come close to making up for the things I've done in my life. But it's a start." He regretted saying the words the moment they fell from his lips.

"You don't have to do anything you don't want to. No one's forcing you."

He gave a single laugh. *If only you knew,* it implied.

"Well, this may cheer you up." She dropped the bomb: "It's time to leave Crash Town."

"What do you mean?"

"He found it. Grammie. We've got our way out."

"Let's go." Vant pushed out of his chair. His legs buckled.

"Easy, Pops. You all right? What's wrong?"

He steadied himself. "Nothing's wrong. Let's go." He needed to move forward. He feared that if he did not, he would be dragged backward. To a wasteland.

Skii tried to hit the brakes. "We've got no plan once we're outta Crash Town. Don't you think—"

"The plan is, we're going. Now." Vant stuffed his gauntlets into his satchel and packed up Death's mask. A sense of purpose washed through his veins, clearing out the poison. He would not slow down. He could not wait for one more second. He had to move forward. Always forward...

"What about Redemption?"

"Screw Redemption. That cyborg's a liar. A coward. We won, and it made up some nonsense to trick us into letting it go."

"Are you sure?"

"This is what I'm sure of. There's a one percent chance we'll find what we're looking for out there in the wild, but that's better than the zero percent chance in here."

"Yeah," Skii said. "Yeah! You're right! Damn this place. Damn Crash Town. Worst vacation ever. Let's get out of here. I'll tell the others."

Grammie and the magician were thrilled to hear the news. They did not have to be told twice to get moving. Yet Grammie was playing coy with his newfound information. He tossed around terms like *fair play, leverage, turnabout,* and *tit-for-tit* (an intentional pun) whenever pressed for particulars on their escape route. As a demonstration of good faith, however, he did make a sizable investment on behalf of his "companions and compatriots," as he was so fond of calling them. He purchased a Corpo-Bot Caller, a device that summoned a bot to one's exact position with requested supplies, or to make deposits in a pinch. It would have limited use—nomad scavengers were attracted to bots like flies—but Grammie still made quite the show of his "genius" investment, made so selflessly for his "comrades."

They optimized their luggage down to the bare essentials. Vant would bring only his whip gauntlets, Death's mask, and a handful of pills. He was already dressed for the occasion in dark robes; in the outskirts, they would need to wear muted shades to blend into the night. Skii reversed her dress so only the black was showing and utilized the sewn-in gloves, sleeves, and leggings to conceal her skin. She carried nothing more than Cassidy, a canvas blanket, and a pill purse. Grammie would bring the Corpo-Bot Caller and his stockpile of charlatan's vials, concealed under his leather vest and with "a million and one uses." And The World's Worst Magician... he wouldn't carry a damn thing, as they planned to knock him out and carry *him* while in nomad territory. His mouth had a terrible habit of running nonstop, so it would be safer—albeit heavier for Vant's shoulders—to do it this way. They tried to dress him in all black, but about this he made a ridiculous fuss:

"I know not what dark paths this would lead me down, nor what chocolate syrup and tea I would need to consume to sustain myself. I have always been of sound mind and body, but what this may do to me would rock my sanity to its very foundations! Thus begins my chronicle. I am a keeper of the peace... the piece of purple."

They succumbed to his bizarre, impenetrable logic and allowed him to wear his purple bathrobe and floppy hat.

Lastly, they all carried one more thing at Grammie's cryptic insistence: face masks.

They left the apartment.

"This is it," Vant said. "No turning back."

Skii pointed out the Corpo-Bots at the far end of town. "One more try? For old time's sake?"

"I'm game."

She approached a bot. "Any messages for me?"

It made a sad chime, followed by, "No messages."

"Worth a shot," she said.

Then, a distinct musical chime played. "Message for Skii Tavee," it stated. She took a step back in surprise.

"Play it."

"Message playback," it responded. "Message sent from: *flingleblore*. Message sent on *choobeychoo* at *diggydurrgele*." The lens cap popped open. A staticky hologram of noise and data appeared. Ten seconds later, a clear projection materialized:

An overhead image of a shoreline.

"Son of a bee," Skii said. "I know that place. That's the westernmost coast. Look..." She pointed at a marking on her tattoo. "That's here."

Vant recalled his conversation with Jiino, an abductee returned to Land Escape. The man had described the holding area for the prisoners where he had spent a short time as smelling like the ocean.

Things were coming together.

The image faded. "End of message," the bot chirped.

"Redemption came through," she said. "This means... my father must be alive."

"His brain at least." Skii glared at Grammie. "Sorry," he said, slapping his hands to his mouth. "I'll shut my yapper now."

"Show me the western coast," she said to the bot. It projected a hologram of the continent. She reached into the image, which zoomed toward her finger. She made a few adjustments and...

There was discrepancy in the sand. Like a pinhole of sun. One bright blemish on an otherwise smooth topography. Some kind of structure was there.

"I'll be damned," Vant said.

"Lead the way," Skii said to Grammie. "Once we're out of Crash Town, I'll take it from there."

They weaved through the streets. An urgency accompanied their footsteps, though the magician repeatedly fell out of step. The odor of the city increased the farther they traveled into the industrial areas. According to Grammie, Crash Town's infrastructure was composed of conglomerates that dealt with construction, utilities, and maintenance. The consortium was privatized; each branch existed for profit, not for the city's betterment. He explained that they were headed to a particularly undesirable sector within the manufacturing zone.

"Have a good, long, heart-to-heart chat with your noses," he warned. "They're about to hate you."

A horrible stench guided them to the entrance of the landfill. An iron gate was all that separated them from mountains of waste that stretched on for miles.

Grammie approached a soot-covered crane worker. "Excuse me, dear fellow. We're looking for Clodd and Blauth."

"Twenty blues," he said mechanically.

Grammie nodded at Skii. She forked over a handful of pills.

The worker scratched his rear and hocked a loogie. "Through the gates, into the dump. Go around the edge, stay to your left. Hug the wall. Don't take no shortcuts." Noticing the magician conversing with an empty barrel, the worker's eyes turned to slits. "You'll die if you wander. Watch your friend."

"Yeah, yeah. We hear you," Vant said. "Take the long way, we're going to die, etcetera, etcetera. Then what?"

"Look for the disposal. When it opens, jump in fast. Too slow, and you'll die."

"Again with the dying?"

"None of us intend to perish this fine evening," Grammie exuded with optimism. The worker was not impressed. "How will we recognize the gentlemen we seek?"

"Oh, you'll know 'em." The four companions exchanged nervous looks. "Don't worry. They like company."

Vant wrangled the magician. Grammie thanked the worker but, before they left, the man added to Skii, "Little girl, watch out for cockroaches. They eat old trash but they *love* fresh meat."

"Not afraid of a few bugs," replied Skii, coolly. She almost pulled it off... until a shiver ran down her spine. "Yeesh," she said when out of earshot of the worker. "Bugs skeeve me."

A toxic waft assaulted their nasal cavities. "Masks on," Vant ordered.

Entering through the iron gates, they stepped into the rolling hills of refuse.

They traversed the path on the fringes of the vile terrain. Vant kept to the rear and spent every thirty seconds or so grabbing the magician's robe and tugging him back into formation. They hugged the perimeter fencing and took gooey, sticky step after gooey, sticky step.

Skii cracked first. "Blech! I think I stepped on a dead rat full of maggots!"

"That's nothing," Grammie countered. "Something stuck to my foot and keeps making a wheezing sound! I'm too afraid to see what it is!"

The World's Worst Magician contributed, "Do you think I'm fat? Me too. Okay, time to lose fifty pounds!" He gagged, about to toss his lunch. He regained his composure and said, "Don't worry. That was just my soul escaping. It prefers less chunky smells and more of the variety of cotton candy mixed with sparkles."

"Let's pick up the pace," Vant insisted. "Otherwise I'm going to get sick in my face mask. Although, breathing my own puke might actually be an improvement."

They walked the edge for a half of a mile, which felt like hundreds. Occasionally, one of them would freak out about something he or she stepped in, describe the sensation, and then the others would recoil and demand the person shut their mouth.

They arrived at the disposal, a round automatic door labeled *Incinerator* that led underground. The entrance was at the base of a slope that allowed piles of trash to funnel in when the portal was opened. They got as close to the closed door as possible, which, unfortunately, was next to a pile of medical waste swarming with flies.

"When we arrive, companions, let me do the talking," said Grammie. "I'll negotiate our passage."

Vant scoffed. "No offense, but why should we trust you? This whole thing reminds me of the saying, 'If it looks like shit, and it smells like shit...' This situation absolutely qualifies."

"Frankly, my dear compatriot, my tongue is the most seasoned. The gift of gab as grandiose as mine always-nay-often leads to willing compliance. But, I'll need you all to play along. I think on my feet, and I may need to think on yours, too."

"Fine," Vant resigned himself. He reminded them, "When the door opens, jump straight in. Don't hesitate. I'll watch Doubleya."

"Just don't watch my thingy! He's shy! I never could sissy when others were watching. It may be my tremendous sense of propriety and decent taste, but who wants to see a thing like that besides the Pee-Bees of Quggly Conch?"

"Sorry, friend," Grammie said to the magician as he wrapped a gag around his mouth. "This is only temporary, and for your own good."

"Mfmm mrfermer," he acknowledged, through the fabric binding his lips.

The tunnel rumbled. Pockets of trash vibrated. Clumps of dumpings shifted.

"Here we go!" Skii exclaimed.

Vant ushered them into position.

"It's open! Jump in!"

Skii and Grammie dove into the chute. Vant gave the magician a shove, then leapt in after him. The four of them, along with an avalanche of garbage, poured into the stinky tunnel. The chute clamped shut behind them.

They slid fast down the shaft, which was slick from the lubrication of rotten waste. At the bottom, they scrambled to the side to dodge the tons of junk that followed them down. Their impulse was to clean themselves off but the crud stuck to them, affixed by slime.

They oriented themselves to the underground chamber carved into the earth. Steel pylons and walkways wrapped around its perimeter. In the center of the floor was a hatch, maybe thirty feet wide, on top of which the incoming trash heap had settled.

"And I thought my place was a dump!" joked Grammie. Even the magician rolled his eyes.

At the other end of the chamber, amid levers and machinery, two rotund laborers eyeballed the new arrivals.

They approached.

Skii spoke up first, "Are you—"

"I'm Clodd. He's Blauth," said one of them. His voice sounded like a boar's with a cold. He had nothing but a flat clump of flesh where his nose should be, as did his companion. Rotting overalls covered their oily bodies and caps held their greasy patches of hair behind their heads. Strands of armpit hair dangled down to Clodd's potbelly and Blauth's massive testicles peeked out from holes in his pants.

"It's nice—nice to meet—" Skii had trouble concealing her repulsion.

"Don't be frightened. I know Blauth's hideous. After all, I'm the pretty one! He's the smart one!" They both entered into fits of laughter choked by their lack of nasal passages. "*Snik-snik-snik-snik-snik!*"

"My dear compatriots," Grammie took over, "I am the famous inventor Shaemous T. Roddenwill of Folk Landing. These are my insurmatchable companions Trundle B. Dundle, Miss Quasar Cottonseed, and my oblivious yet loyal assistant Boo-Beer." Somehow, the magician knew to take a deep, cordial bow when introduced by his fake name. Vant and Skii awkwardly followed suit.

Clodd and Blauth looked at each other, puzzled. They attempted to return the formality, but their bodies could only bend so far because of their gigantic guts. Blauth, winded after putting himself back upright, said, "And we're the famous, um, trash men."

"But of course you are! You're the exact gentlemen we were instructed to see! You have superior reputations, my dear comrades. We hear you have quite the eyes for holes in the ground, and a *nose* for assisting others!"

"We have no noses!" Blauth smiled and clapped. "Took 'em off, we did! So we can work down here when no one else can!"

"Clever, comrade! Bravo!" Grammie swatted Blauth on the arm, which jiggled and left a smudged handprint. "Mining for treasure in the piles, I assume?"

"Yes, yes!" Blauth hopped about joyfully.

"Good man! Good men! We shall leave you to this important work soon enough. We have no designs on stepping on your toes by entering into the trash business." Clodd and Blauth glanced at their feet, confused. "We seek, my companions..." he leaned in close, "...passage. To the outside. Past the walls of Crash Town."

"We may be able to help you with that," Clodd said, puffing up his chest and sucking in his belly. "Depending on what you can do for us."

"And what would two fine folks such as yourselves require from humble, humble Shaemous T. Roddenwill, Trundle B. Dundle, Miss Quasar Cottonseed, and of course Boo-Beer?"

"Pills! And lots of 'em!"

"Why certainly, my good sirs! Miss Cottonseed, would you please hand our darling fellows your precious earnings? Don't be shy, give them every last capsule! They deserve it!"

Skii emptied her pill purse into Clodd's grubby palms.

"*Snik-snik-snik-snik!* What is this? Forty? Fifty? Cost you at least fifty-*hundred* to get through. That's what the last guys paid."

"My bosom buddies, I'm afraid fifty is all we have. But, perhaps your dear companion Shaemous T. Roddenwill, the famous inventor, has something... *else*... for you?" Grammie pulled back his vest, revealing the stockpile of liquids and powders. Blauth's eyes lit up. He lunged for the desirables.

"Ah, ah, ah!" Grammie covered up. "Not yet, my dear boy. Daddy is making a deal with your big brother, here."

"We're not brothers," Blauth said. "We're coworkers. What do those drinkies do?"

"Why, all sorts of things, my compatriot. What tantalizes you? Entrust with me your deepest desires."

Clodd and Blauth became timid. Clodd leaned in and whispered into Grammie's ear. Grammie placed a compassionate hand on his shoulder. "I've just the thing, my dearest Clodd. I've *just the thing.*"

Grammie gingerly removed a vial of pink liquid from his coat, handling it as if it were the most delicate substance in the world. "One dose of this, and anyone you so desire shall fall at your feet, madly in love with you. Or you, Blauth. Yes, you, too."

"We want that," Blauth said. "We want it."

"So we have a deal? One vial of the extremely rare Nectar of the Goddess Haven Bustybaron in exchange for safe passage out of Crash Town?"

"Plus the fifty pills."

"Why certainly, my cherished Clodd. Fair is fair."

"And you have to prove the potion works."

Grammie scoffed at Clodd. "You don't trust me? *Me?* Your dear companion and compatriot? Your friend, Clodd? Your friend!"

Blauth swatted at Clodd, upset he was botching the deal.

"I believe you!" Clodd said, backtracking. "But my coworker isn't too smart, you see. He doesn't understand certain things like I do. If you could just show us—"

"Sweet boy, the extremely rare Nectar of the Goddess Haven Bustybaron is extremely rare! A mere drop is priceless!" Grammie buried his head in his hands, then dramatically re-appeared in a display of showmanship. "I will set your mind at ease! I agree to demonstrate the power of the potion. Miss Quasar Cottonseed? Are you here?"

Skii was ten feet away. Of course she was. "Uh, yeah."

"Dearest Cotton, I must apologize in advance. It is with great trepidation that I inflict such a thing on you. But, you are about to fall truly, deeply, and madly in love with me! That is to say, if you aren't already."

"I'm not."

"Then prepare yourself! For after I put one drop on my tongue..." Grammie leaned in close and laid the scenario out for her about as obviously as he could, "...you will fall madly in love and you won't be able to keep your hands off me."

"Oh give me a break—"

"And away we go!" Grammie touched the tip of the bottle to his tongue.

He looked at Skii, wide-eyed.

He stretched out his arms.

She did not move.

"Any moment now..."

She still did not move. "Guess love potions don't work on me. Guess you'll have to prove it with Trundy B. Dundy over there." She pointed at Vant, who responded by raising a certain single digit in the center of his fingers.

"Fine! Wait..." she said. "It's working! Oh my god, Shaemous Whatsyourface! I'm losing my tits for you!"

Clodd and Blauth were riveted by the spectacle.

"I'm going to run at you now and make out with your stupid face that I hate so much but suddenly I'm in love with!"

Vant grew a conscience. He grabbed Skii by the back of her dress and simulated restraining her from the "passionate struggle" to get to Grammie.

"Let me go!" Skii fake-screamed. "If you don't, I may die! Please!"

Vant un-grew his conscience and, with a sarcastic grin, released his grip. Skii looked at Vant with murderous eyes.

"Here I come, unfortunately... ugh!"

She sprinted to Grammie, who put an arm around her waist—and a hand on her rear.

She punched him in the gut. "Whoops. Guess it wore off."

Grammie, the wind knocked out of him, managed to say, "Now you know, fine fellows, what a drop can do! Imagine a whole bottle! But, I warn you, you must only use this potion on someone you truly love! Do not squander the opportunity. Think carefully, even for years if need be!"

"Yes, yes!" Blauth jumped up and down, his balls flopping every which way. "Give it to us!"

"Our deal?" Grammie extended his hand to Clodd.

"Deal," he said. They shook on it.

Grammie handed over the harmless bottle of dyed water.

Clodd and Blauth moved to the incinerator's controls as Clodd barked instructions:

"We're gonna open the trash hatch. You go down in the elevator. Don't be scared, it won't drop you. This thing's gone on a thousand trips, and we've never needed to fix it even once! Not in twenty years!"

Vant scratched his stubble, taking in the rickety platform attached to a pulley. "You get what you pay for," he grumbled.

Clodd continued, "When you're low enough, go into the methane vent. The tunnel will split. Take the third one from the left. That one goes to the surface. And it has the least amount of cockroaches."

Skii shivered.

Clodd opened the hatch. The trash pile fell into the flames below. Vant peered over the edge; the hole ran for miles into an inferno. Fireballs of combustible fumes floated up from the pit. If there was a shortcut to Hell, they had just found it.

Blauth prepared the elevator. "All aboard!"

Vant, Skii, Grammie, and The World's Worst Magician entered the creaking platform and closed the gate—no more than a handrail—behind them. Their feet wobbled on the crosshatched floor. The spaces between the steel mesh provided a troubling view into the fires below.

Blauth flipped a lever to begin their descent. "Off you go! Take care! Bye-bye!"

Down they went.

Slowly.

The ride was not smooth. The elevator whined from the friction of wire scraping against the pulley. Every jostle shot a tinge of adrenaline through Vant's spine.

About a hundred feet down, Skii pointed out an approaching passageway. "I see the tunnel."

"This ride can't end soon enough," Grammie said.

The platform jolted to a standstill.

"What happened?" Grammie panicked.

"Apparently, it's soon enough," said Vant.

"The elevator stopped!" Skii shouted up. "Hey!"

"*Liars!*" Clodd screeched from above. "I hate you! You tricked us!"

Grammie coughed in disbelief and yelled upward, "We didn't! That's an honest-to-goodness love potion!"

"No, it's not! It's a lie!"

"How can you possibly say that?"

"Because we drank it!" Blauth blurted out.

Grammie's mouth dropped open. Vant, Skii, and the magician exchanged confused looks.

"But—I said the potion was to be used with someone you want to love you!"

"We want to love each other!" Clodd shouted down. "Me and Blauth! We want to be in love! We see each other every day, and we like the same things! It would be perfect to be in love!"

This was the breaking point for Vant. It was all too weird. He buried his forehead in his hands and laughed with resigned desperation.

Skii shook Grammie by the shoulders. "Do something!"

"I—boys—here's the thing—"

"You broke our hearts!" Blauth wailed.

"You'll pay for this!" Clodd sobbed.

A rumble from above. Vant was quick to identify the impending catastrophe. He pulled his cloak over his head. Skii and Grammie studied him, puzzled.

Then:

Gallons of trash dumped onto them.

And dumped.

And dumped.

Finally, the hailstorm of refuse ceased. They were covered in filth.

"Nasty!" Skii shouted. "Oh, *oh!* It went in my mouth!"

"Mmefeh furrber!" the magician said, elated, pointing to the gag over his lips which kept him from suffering Skii's fate. Grammie removed the fabric to free the magician's tongue.

Clodd and Blauth sealed the top hatch, trapping the four of them below.

"Nice work, Grammie. Real smooth," said Vant.

"The tunnel's not too far down. I got us close! That counts for something, right?"

"We're stuck above a pit of magma and covered in crap. How is that a good thing?"

"Could have been worse," Grammie said.

Tik-tik-tik-tik-tik-tik-tik...

A sound of tiny clicks filled the passageway.

...tik-tik-tik-tik-tik-tik-tik...

"What is that?"

...tik-tik-tik-tik-tik-tik-tik...

"I don't like this." Skii peered over the edge of the elevator.

"Cockroaches!"

Hundreds of bugs scurried out of the vent. Their foot-long bodies were fat from feasts of trash with flesh pooling out of their overstuffed shells. Their pointy legs *tik-tik-tik*'d up the rocky walls.

"Oh man oh man oh man oh man..." Skii was hyperventilating. She unstrapped Cassidy from her back with trembling fingers. Vant tore into his satchel to find his gauntlets. Grammie dropped to the floor of the platform and cowered in fear.

The magician stared with wonder.

The bugs scampered up the chute. A pack of them leapt from the walls onto the elevator. Their jagged teeth dug into the scraps of trash.

Skii cocked Cassidy and unloaded on the pests. The repeated concussive blasts scattered them. Handfuls at a time lost their grips and fell into the flames below.

Vant activated his weapons and barked orders. "Grammie! Doubleya! Kick the trash off the platform! They're attracted to the trash!"

Grammie was frozen with fear. The magician gave a hearty thumbs-up... but did nothing else.

Several bugs hurled themselves toward the elevator. Vant swung his fists. Each insect he decked made a juicy *crunch*.

The swarm grew larger. A continuous stream poured out of the vent. The platform became overrun. One of the roaches crawled up Vant's cloak. Another dove from the trench and landed on Skii's back. Grammie kicked blindly—trash and bugs —into the furnace.

Skii yelped as Vant punched a creature off her back. A roach crawling on him sunk its teeth deep into his robes. He thrashed his shoulders, but it would not budge. Another latched onto his boot and chomped away at the leather.

The conveyor groaned as their kinetic movements shifted the pulleys. The wire started to fray.

"We've got to get off the elevator!" Vant yelled.

"How?" Skii blasted away, sending insects by the dozen barreling down into the inferno. Several of them spread wings and attempted to fly to stop their descent, but their bodies were too fat. They only managed a feeble *bzzz* before free-falling into the abyss.

"We need to get into the vent!"

"*Into* it?"

"Know another way out?" Vant lowered one of his whips to measure the distance to the tunnel.

"No good!" Skii said. "It only reaches halfway!"

"That's why I have two of 'em. Hold on!"

Vant lashed a whip around the handrail and hopped over the edge.

The elevator rocked from the imbalance in weight. He lowered himself down, halfway to the vent. A strand of wire near the pulley snapped with a *thwing*.

"We can make it!" Vant shouted. A dozen pests scurried out of the passage and up toward the elevator. Two of them raised their antennae into the air, spread their wings and, smelling a free lunch, *bzzz*'d onto Vant. He felt their teeth dig into his clothes, just shy of his flesh.

"I need a distraction!" Vant yelled upward. "Ideas?"

"He—here!" Grammie handed a vial of powder to Skii.

"What's this?"

"Throw it at them!"

Vant, dangling below, used his free arm to flick a whip to Skii. The end of the coil latched onto her wrist with a *crack!* She jumped off the elevator with a squeal.

Vant swung her toward the passageway as she threw the vial at the opening. It shattered on the wall with a blinding light and a poof of smoke.

The bugs scattered from the strobe. Vant rocked Skii back and forth, giving her the momentum to swing into the tunnel. She caught the ledge and hoisted herself inside.

Next up was Grammie. He whimpered and would not budge, so Vant whipped him around his waist and yanked him off the platform.

Thwing.

Another part of the wire holding the conveyor snapped.

Grammie screamed as he arced beneath the elevator and toward the opening. Skii grabbed his flailing arms and pulled him inside.

Without a prompt, the magician took a flying leap off the edge, laughing with glee. Vant flung a whip which connected with the magician's calf. He descended head-first and swung into the cave, plowing into Skii and Grammie.

"Throw me the whip!" Skii shouted at Vant. He obliged, flicking the loose one toward her. She snatched the tip and tied the slack around her waist. Grammie tossed another vial of powder at the ground, lighting up the passageway and sending a herd of roaches scurrying.

With the coil secured, Skii threw her arms around Grammie, who threw his arms around the magician. "Hold tight!" she shouted.

Thwiiing!

The pulley snapped.

The elevator careened downward.

Weightlessness.

Vant smacked into the wall. The metal platform whizzed past his body and dropped into the fire.

The momentum from the drop jerked Vant's tethered companions toward the tunnel exit. They dug in with their feet, searching for any kind of grip on the unstable dirt. They scrambled to maintain traction.

Vant tightened the tension in the whips in hopes of being pulled upward. It had the reverse effect—the others were being dragged down. He was too damned heavy. Skii, Grammie, and the magician fought against the pull. Vant activated the thrusters in his gauntlets but there was not enough torque to raise him up. He was going down, and dragging everyone with him.

He saw their feet losing their grip at the lip of the tunnel.

He had to let go, otherwise he would kill them all.

He closed his eyes.

One for the road, he thought, taking a deep breath.

He prepared to let go...

But a blue pulse of energy whipped out of the vent. A thrust of force yanked Vant upward. Then another thrust. Then another.

Skii fired Cassidy in quick, controlled bursts. Every shot forced the bonded allies backward away from the edge—and pulled Vant up the wall.

Three more blasts and Vant was in the tunnel. His companions reached out to hug him—but several roaches were feasting on his clothing. Instead, Skii cocked Cassidy and, with some well-placed point-blank shots, sent the bugs splattering into the walls.

They sprinted down the corridor, Vant at the front, the magician at the rear.

At the crossroads of tunnels, Vant halted.

He whispered, "Grammie, do you have any more of that explosive powder?"

"Tapped out, comrade."

"Shit."

Hundreds of cockroaches flooded the corridor. They coated the floor, the walls, and the ceiling. Their legs echoed through the hallway. *Tik-tik-tik-tik-tik-tik-tik!*

Grammie whimpered. Vant charged up his gauntlets. Skii cocked Cassidy.

Closer the insect flood came, ravenous at the sight of the delicious human feast. Closer... closer...

Suddenly, the bugs halted.

Vant, Skii, and Grammie stared at the swarm. Hundreds of gleaming black pupils stared back. Yet, their attention was not drawn to the three on the front lines. The bugs were looking at what was transpiring beyond.

The World's Worst Magician held a cockroach—a gigantically obese striped one —in his arms.

"Doubleya! Drop it!" Grammie demanded with hysteria.

The bug lifted up its head, revealing jagged fangs coated in saliva. Its legs twitched in the air.

"Froggy!" The magician said to the insect. "It's you! I've been asking about you! I am so boner-fied to see you right now!"

Vant inched toward the insane man coddling the vicious creature. "Doubleya, please put that thing down..."

The magician continued, "My friends, if you know of any backyard sleds to hitch this husky to, it would give her purpose beyond struggling every day to eat more than her babies feed her. It's hard for her to live up to the past life she had as the mystical Valkyrie Queen."

A queen.

Vant revised his statement. "Doubleya, please *don't* put that thing down!"

"Oh, Froggy," he said to the insect, walking forward into the tunnel. "I told you I'd find you again. The last time we met, we were on the bridge over Jangle River. We shared a look and a moment and a smile... it was... *magical.*"

A wart-covered tongue slid out from between the roach's teeth. It licked the madman across the cheek. He giggled at the gesture.

"What's that? You want to come live with me? Well, I threw my bed out onto the sidewalk last year, but I'm sure I've got something that will pass muster."

The pests backed away, fearful of what might happen to their queen. Vant guided his allies into the passage leading to the surface. The bugs gave a wide berth to the humans, but closed in when they sensed weakness. Vant swiveled the magician to taunt them with the queen, forcing them to back away.

There was moonlight ahead.

The four of them approached the tunnel exit; the creatures kept their distance from the open air. They backed into the passageway, keeping a view of their leader. Hundreds of them *bzzz*'d in protest.

"Doubleya," Grammie said to his friend. "I think it's time to let Froggy go."

"Oh, Froggy," sighed the magician to the massive insect as he stroked its thorax. "I've found some peace in my soul in the last ten minutes. This would not have been possible if it hadn't been for you and your friends showing me you wanted me around. I may never be able to thank you for your hospitality, but I will always endeavor to make you proud of me. And, to show you that it was worth your time to save my life."

The magician lowered the queen to the ground. Seizing the opportunity, her majesty bolted back into the tunnels, trailed by the swarm of scampering drones.

Silence.

Calm.

The four companions collapsed at the tunnel exit. Skii shook out her trembling trigger finger. Grammie massaged his chest, warding off a heart attack. The magician seemed oblivious to the peril they had avoided, but Vant was well aware of it. Three more lost lives were dangerously close to being added to Vant's conscience, as well the near miss of spending eternity as ash in the earth's core.

They heaved fresh air. It had been ages since Vant and Skii had enjoyed a good lungful, and even longer for Grammie and the magician who had been in Crash Town for so many years. After a brief rest, Vant stood. He headed toward the exit.

The others begrudgingly followed even though they, too, knew it was time.

"Wait," Skii said to the entourage. "No talking, from now on. Follow in my footsteps, no matter what. No stopping. No noise. Just silence, and you shadow me wherever I go, even if it makes no sense. Agreed?" Head-nods all around. "Grammie, time for Doubleya to take his medicine."

Grammie removed a bottle of liquid from his vest.

"How long will that buy us?" Skii asked.

"Hard to tell. Couple of hours, maybe. He's a light sleeper, but this stuff's pretty strong."

"Give him all you got."

Grammie handed over the serum. The magician was overjoyed. "Ah yes! A toast! To two of the five sexes on the planet. There might be seven—I'm not sure. Or even eight. With that many to keep track of, sometimes I'm not quite certain where to put it, if you know what I mean. Cheers!"

He knocked the potion back. And collapsed to the ground.

Vant hoisted the comatose man onto his shoulder.

They took their first steps onto the surface.

"Time for the hard part," said Skii.

"Cockroaches!"

- Skii Tavee

PART
FOUR

EXPOSED

"This Spider's hungry. This Spider's thirsty.
This Spider's caught you in his web."

- Ranchula

CHAPTER 14

The Web and the Wizard

The night was thick with frozen mist and scored by a symphony of crickets. Visibility was horrendous. Rolling fog masked any trails the moonlight would have illuminated.

Skii led the group, moving swiftly. Vant carried the magician and Grammie trailed close behind. With no discernible direction offering the sanctuary of cover, they had to risk the open. Skii's body language exuded tension alongside heightened awareness.

Vant wanted nothing more than to slap on Death's mask to identify hidden predators, but he feared it would do more harm than good. It glowed brightly when worn and, even if he pulled his hood over his head, there would be a pinhole of light that could be seen for miles.

So, they braved the unknown.

Skii found a mound of raised earth. She plastered her body onto it and brought her companions in close. She made hand gestures that said, *Stay near. Run fast.*

On her signal, they sprinted across the empty field.

Skii darted like a fox. Vant bobbled, weighed down by the magician. Grammie's lungs wheezed, fighting for air. The sound of his huffs grew quieter as he fell farther behind, struggling to keep up.

There was no cover anywhere.

They were totally exposed.

It felt all wrong.

Skii stopped.

Vant caught up. She clamped his cloak in her hand and pulled him down to her level. Her mouth was so close it grazed his ear. She whispered, "It's over."

Vant studied her face. It was frostbitten with fear.

His own internal proximity alarm kicked in. He swung around to find shapes melting in and out of the shadows. Dozens of silhouettes began to manifest from within the surrounding darkness. People, hundreds of them, stood shoulder to shoulder. They had formed a circle of containment. It was closing in from all directions.

Vant laid the magician on the ground and noticed someone missing: Kram Grammie. Vant assumed the con man had sensed danger and disappeared, tail between his legs. Or maybe...

Maybe he had planned the whole damn thing.

Maybe he had set them up. Maybe he worked with Clodd and Blauth on an elaborate scam. Vant chastised himself for his naïveté in believing their "secret" way out of Crash Town was actually a secret.

He stifled his anger and focused on the threat before him. The circle of bodies continued to constrict. Vant scanned the surroundings for any kind of escape. He inched his fingers toward his weapons—Skii put a hand on his forearm and shook her head.

The perimeter tightened... tightened...

Vant pointed overhead, granting Skii permission to use Cassidy to propel herself out of the trap. Skii made a gesture indicating she would be gunned down. She then pointed at herself, then Vant, then the magician, and drew a line across her neck.

We're all dead, it implied.

The circle tightened. And tightened...

Finally, they set eyes on what had them ensnared.

Nomad hunters.

The predators were decked out in trappings pillaged from robberies and raids. All of them brandished weapons looted as spoils of conflict: swords, axes, machine guns, machetes, rifles... one muscled warrior lit a flamethrower. Another loaded a bazooka.

One by one, the nomads activated head-mounted lamps, chest-mounted lights, spear-like torches, and perimeter floodlights. The glare was blinding, contrasted against the dark of night.

No one spoke.

No one dared.

The nomads were waiting on something.

But then:

"There you all are!" Vant exclaimed. "We've been looking everywhere for you!"

Skii's eyes widened with shock.

Stunned stares came from the circle of warriors.

Vant continued, "We want to join up! We're very excited about joining a tribe. We heard yours was the best. Ultra-classy, more into taking prisoners than executing them, that sort of thing."

Three hunters with identical bolt rifles converged on Vant and Skii, pointing the weapons at their heads. A huntress emerged from the ranks, a wiry, mean-looking thing. Veiny muscles coiled around her twig-like body and she wore a vest strapped with an array of knives. She approached and confusedly kicked the magician, who was still out cold.

Vant said, "So, how do we sign up? Is there paperwork to fill out? An interview process?"

She pressed a knife against Vant's cheek. "Seal them lips or I slice that head." She removed Vant's satchel and passed it to one of the nomad scouts. Skii squeaked the tiniest of squeaks when they separated her from Cassidy.

"So you wanna join us? You wanna be a spider?" said the huntress.

Vant pointed to his sealed lips.

"Open them and speak!"

"Yes, please. It's been my lifelong dream."

The huntress withdrew a ceremonial dagger from her vest. It was dull, coated with layers of dried blood. She dropped the knife in the dirt between Vant and Skii.

"Then kill."

"Sorry?" Vant said. "I don't follow. Who are we supposed to kill?"

"Each other," she said. "Strongest joins the web. Weakest gets dead."

Skii shot Vant a look that said, *Don't you dare...*

"Oh, you'll want both of us. All three, in fact. We're powerful warriors. Even the sleeping guy. You don't want to miss out on any of us. Surely you can make an executive decision, being the leader and all."

The perimeter of nomads burst into laughter. The huntress herself cackled hard. "You think me, Widow, the leader? I not the leader. Ranchula the leader."

The tribe began to chant...

"Ran-Chu-La. Ran-Chu-La."

Vant shrugged. "My mistake. Can I speak with him? Do you mind?"

The chanting grew louder. "Ran-Chu-La! Ran-Chu-La!"

Widow smiled. "Only way to talk to leader is to challenge him."

"So, to be clear, my choices are to die, kill my friends, or fight your leader?"

She grinned a confirmation.

"RAN-CHU-LA! RAN-CHU-LA!"

Vant cracked his neck. Cracked his back. Cracked his knuckles.

"I'll fight him."

A concealed hunter exploded from the dirt. The force of impact took Vant to the ground. His oily body dripped clods of dirt as the beast of a man pinned Vant by all four limbs. Vant struggled, but the hunter was packed with muscle and twice his size. He smiled, revealing rancid teeth underneath a face adorned with scars in the shape of a spider.

He bit into Vant's neck.

And ripped out a chunk of flesh.

Skii shrieked in terror.

"RAN-CHU-LA! RAN-CHU-LA!"

Ranchula snarled, blood dripping from his lips, "This Spider's hungry. This Spider's thirsty. This Spider's caught you in his web. Buzz away, fuck-fuck fly. Try to buzz away."

Vant was incapacitated. Blood spurtted from his jugular. The hunter laughed. His breath smelled like rotted compost.

Skii lunged for the ceremonial dagger. Ranchula kicked a pressure point in her forearm, paralyzing it. Then he drew her in, fingers clamped around her windpipe.

"Only reason you live, little fly... soon you'll carry my eggs in your sac."

The crowd cheered. Ranchula let go of Skii to devour the adoration from his tribe.

Skii gasped for air, rubbing her damaged throat.

Ranchula rose.

Widow handed him Vant's satchel. "Lots of treats!" the huntress said. "Special treasures!"

He searched through it, finding the pill pouch. He popped a blue capsule, then dropped the rest in the dirt. "This should cover fuck-fuck fly's funeral." Laughter from the crowd. Three underlings scrambled to pick up the discarded loot.

Ranchula removed Death's mask from the pack. "Scary, scary! I need this to protect my pretty face. I'm a fucking beauty... now my spider cunts won't try to rape me in my sleep!"

"I still gonna try!" Widow catcalled.

More uncontrollable laughter from the tribe. Ranchula tossed the mask to one of his lieutenants. "Shavious, cover that shit. No one wants to see your fucking face." The perimeter hooted and hollered. Shavious smiled with the half of his face that functioned—the other half dangled loosely. He held the mask up to his head and gave a tribal salute.

Vant tried to stand, and faltered.

"Hey, fuck-fuck. Only reason you still breathing is, this toy needs explaining." A dip into Vant's satchel brought forth the whip gauntlets. "Heavy damn things. Good for breaking faces, I think." He shook them and peered into the hand-holes, failing to identify the hidden activation switches. "Hey, dead fuck. Tell your friend. How these things work?"

He raised a barely functioning Vant to his feet. Ranchula leaned in and closed one eye, as if listening *extra* hard.

"It's easy," Vant wheezed. "Shove 'em up your ass and wiggle."

The crowd booed and hissed. *As last words go,* Vant thought to himself, *those weren't half bad.*

The chieftain slammed into Vant's ribcage, taking him to the ground. He pinned his arms with his knees, raised his clenched fists, and pounded his face.

Again.

And again.

And again.

And again.

And again.

With each blow, more bloody meat flew.

Skii wailed.

"RAN-CHU-LA! RAN-CHU-LA!"

With one arm, Ranchula raised Vant and held him suspended by the hair. He used the other to pummel his ribs and intestines. "Smart face! Smart face! Stupid fuck-fuck had to run his stupid face!"

Ranchula raised a finger to the crowd. They obediently silenced. He wrapped his mitt-like hands around Vant's skull and placed his crooked nose against Vant's tenderized face.

"This fly's dead now. So long, smart face."

He twisted Vant's head. With a *snap,* neck separated from vertebra.

His destroyed body crumpled into a heap.

Skii covered her eyes.

The crowd went wild.

"RAN-CHU-LA! RAN-CHU-LA!"

Vant lost control of all bodily functions, save for his eyelids. He fought to keep them open, fixed north on Skii, even though his body pointed south.

"And now, The Spider eats the rest of the maggots."

Skii clamped her mouth shut when it hiccupped a sob.

"Why you cry, little fly? Don't you like The Spider?"

She looked away. The crowd laughed.

"I like *you.* You good enough to eat. I think I'll try a bite."

He lunged for Skii—

"*Bababoo!*"

The crowd hushed. The nomad chief stopped cold. "What you say, fly?"

The World's Worst Magician was wide awake and on his feet. "I said, 'Bababoo,' of course. It's what I always say after a nap."

Widow held a blade to the magician's cheek. "You fuckin' crazy? What you thinkin'?"

Skii looked up at the magician. She whimpered, "Do something. Please."

He put his hand on her shoulder. "Ah, yes. Something *would* be quite something. But sometimes nothing means everything. Depending on where you're sitting. Like the toilet."

"Ranchula," one of the nomads in the crowd spoke to the chief, "I recognize this freak."

"Me too," someone else called. Another agreed. And another.

"This is the World's Best—Worst—Magician," said the nomad. "I saw his signs all around Crash Town before."

"He's right," another hunter in the circle stepped forward. "I seen his show. This guy's a joke. Can't do nothin' except piss himself and talk nonsense. I seen it."

The magician shook his head and mumbled to his crotch, "Don't get sad, hiding pecker. Don't listen to them."

"Help us," Skii said to him, while the nomads conferred.

"How could I possibly help? All I do is put on shows and make dreams become less irksome."

"Then put on a show!"

"A show?" The magician looked around and sniffed the air. Then suddenly, "Of course! A show!" He planted his feet, bent his knees, and thrust his hands into the air as he exclaimed, "Dearest friends! Bid farewell to getting ripped off by unscrupulous show-mongers! For I am here to mystify and entertain the likes of you! Prepare yourselves! For I—with a turd-on-the-highway realness and a shit-kicker sensibility— am the best damned magic man that ever was! Owhow! *Bababababoo!*"

"This fly's brain-fucked," Ranchula said as he backed away, joining the nomads in the perimeter.

"What I say is true! Nothing is exaggerated for effect, all is pure reportage! I *will* dazzle your razzle! I don't want you to come unless you're fully satisfied, and if you are, you'll come regardless!"

"No more shit!" said Ranchula. "Spiders in the web! Show them fangs!"

They raised their weapons.

"Oh, forget it," the magician said, deflated. "I'm feeling mushy. I thought I could sparkle, but now I don't want to. What a weird world."

"You can do magic," Skii said. "I believe it."

He scratched his rear, then smelled his finger.

"Squash the fucking flies!" screamed Ranchula.

"*I believe it!*" cried Skii.

A hell-storm of gunfire let loose.

Electrical blasts from bolt rifles arced toward Vant, Skii, and the magician. Bullets flew. There was a spray of flame. Two bazooka shells exploded. Another twenty bullets. Five more elctro-bolts. A grenade went off. Two shotgun shots. Another grenade. Six rounds thudded from a magnum, followed by the click of a needed reload.

Silence.

Charred terrain.

Bits of debris plunked to the soil.

The smoke cleared.

Vant, Skii, and the magician had not been hit. Not once.

"The fuck?!" Ranchula ran at the magician. "The Spider's gonna fuck you!" He threw a punch. It missed. Another swipe. It flew past his head. A right cross. A left jab. Both failed to connect. An attempted tackle put the nomad chief face-down in the dirt. He looked up, over his shoulder. Confusion coated his stunned eyes.

The World's Worst Magician shook his head at the man on all fours in front of him. "Stopping to smell the roses," he spoke with perfect diction, "gets you butt-fucked bad."

And with that, everything got weird.

The World's Worst Magician raised his hand like a claw, and a wisp of green mist materialized from the trail it left. He used his other hand to slice through the smoke, splitting it in half. He manipulated both clouds into fast-moving spirals of particles.

The effect was hypnotic. The crowd gasped. Several fell over each other, running away from the sight of such impossibility.

Faster and faster he swirled the smoke overhead. More and more of it materialized. The spirals grew larger—they were now twice the size of his body.

"I need a volunteer from the audience! How about you, fine fellow?" The magician bore down on the nomad chief, who backed away. "Don't be shy! Are you allergic to magic? I almost forgot—I certainly am! *Awah-hah... hawah-hawah-hah...* hold on, I'm gonna sneeze... *ah-hawah-hawah-hawah-shit!*"

With the fake sneeze, The World's Worst Magician ignited the spirals into spears of light. Firework-like fragments flew through the crowd. The tribe screamed—but then relented upon the realization that the explosion was harmless.

While they were distracted, the magician had begun his next trick. He held his claw-like fingers level with Ranchula's chest; a green fluid poured from it into the magician's hand.

"He's killing him! Shoot the bastard!" one of the scouts yelled. Several nomads raised their firearms. With a *slap*, the magician yanked the green fluid toward one of the gunmen, hitting him square in the chest. The impact dislodged a purple, pulsing shape. *Slap.* He flung the glow into another man, and another, and another.

Magic illuminated the night. Most of the nomads panicked, but a few ambitious warriors fired their weapons. They could not hit their target—not because he was out of range, but because, somehow, their aim was completely off.

The crowd dispersed, save for their leader and the victims of the magician's powers. They were not dead—far from it. No one had been hurt. They were catatonic, lying flat on their backs, staring up at the sky.

Smiling.

The vibrant colors soon faded. The trails of charms melted into the aether. The night was silent again. Even the crickets were speechless.

The magician took a deep, courteous bow. Then, he lay back down on the ground.

And fell back asleep.

Skii dropped to her knees next to Vant.

"Can you hear me?" she said. She tried to touch him, but fear forced her trembling hands away. He was mangled beyond recognition.

Vant, helpless, felt a surge of emotion. There was so much he wanted to say to her, but now it was too late. *Sentimentality,* he thought, *is no match for practicality.* And, with that thought, he summoned his final shred of strength to speak.

"Skii..."

She nodded. Sniffled. "I'm here, Pops. I'm here. What is it?"

"Don't cremate me."

She looked at him, confused.

He died.

"Bid farewell to getting ripped off by unscrupulous show-mongers!
For I am here to mystify and entertain the likes of you!"

- The World's Worst Magician

226

YEARS PRIOR

Of Prizes and Primes

It was Vant's turn.

He entered the tent. No fire was lit.

He saw Agmar's body.

He circled the casket and approached Terrii, who sat in Agmar's old armchair.

"I offer my deepest condolences for your father," Vant said. "He was a fierce warrior."

Terrii rubbed his temples with his palms. "What's in the box?"

Vant handed over a meticulously finished wooden parcel. "For the new First Prime. A prize worthy of a leader. My life's work."

Terrii lifted the immensely heavy package into his lap and opened it.

His face contorted with disdain and he violently shoved the box away. Two polished gauntlets toppled out, thudding onto the floor.

"Isn't my father's death enough?" Terrii's voice quivered.

"Terrii..."

"A reminder of your parents' execution on my day of Ultimate Exaltion?"

"No, it's not like that—"

"Get out of my sight!"

"It's not a taunt. It's a gift!" Vant dropped to his knees. "I don't want you to share my parents' fate. I have created the perfect weapon for you. For my friend. For my leader."

Terrii was silent. He looked upon his deceased father, then returned his attention to Vant. "I'm sorry," he said. "I'm sorry. You've always been there for me. You're better than me. Better than me in every way."

"No," Vant spoke, still on his knees. "That's just not true."

Terrii eyed the gauntlets sprawled on the floor. Their heft had dented the hardwood.

"How do they work?"

"Try them on."

Terrii slid the weapons onto his hands. "They're heavy."

"Yes," Vant acknowledged. "They can only be brandished by the truly powerful. Run your index fingers along the lips at the top. Feel for the hidden switches. Flip the ones on the edges."

The gauntlets activated and roared to life. Terrii buckled from the shift in weight. "Son of a bitch!" he said.

"They can only be wielded by the truly clever. You have to move your arms in tandem with the throttle grips."

Terrii waved them around, admiring the symbiosis of the thrusters and gyroscopes. "Shyyla made the electronics work?"

"She did."

"Smart and sexy. Are you and her—?"

"No."

"Good. Because I'm going to marry her. Perks of leadership." He waited for a reaction. Vant gave him none. "And the whips?"

"My favorite part. Slide the throttle while flicking your wrists. Snap them down, otherwise you're going to put holes in the tent."

On the third attempt, the coils unraveled and slapped the floor with a crack!

"They can only be flourished through the will of a warrior," Vant said. "Anyone can pull a trigger, but not everyone can look an enemy in the eye before extinguishing their light. The whips bring them in close, and the gauntlets end their lives. That's true strength—to acknowledge a foe before you destroy them."

Terrii retracted the whips and turned the gauntlets off. He placed them on a wooden end table.

It collapsed from the weight. Vant and Terrii shared a laugh.

"I'll treasure them," said Terrii.

"Don't treasure them. Use them. Let them be a reminder that you are willful, clever, and strong."

"Thank you. Oh! Before you go, I would like to make my first executive decision as leader."

"Ready for your orders, First Prime." Vant stood at attention.

"Send in Cloakmaster Gordone. It's about time someone cut that geezer loose."

Vant breathed. He did not move.

"Is there a problem, Prime Hu'l?" Terrii was testing him. His famous smirk appeared. But this time, the smirk was different. It was... empowered.

"I have taken an oath," said Vant. "I shall follow your command."

"Good." Terrii stretched, and slinked into his father's armchair—his armchair—like royalty. "Bring him in."

Vant left the tent to collect his mentor, an ancient, loyal veteran, who was about to be banished on Terrii's self-righteous whim.

"Walk into the light and you'll meet a demon."

- Vant Hu'l

CHAPTER 15

The Truce and the Truth

Blackness.

Then:

Vant cried out.

He attempted to move his body, but his limbs disobeyed his commands. When he tried to sit upright, his head flopped over in a weird way.

The flashes and strobes of returning consciousness waned. A puzzling view took their place. Brown surrounded him with a patch of gray overhead.

He managed to kick out his left leg, causing his torso to pivot. His head bobbed into a position from which he could decipher his surroundings.

He was lying six feet deep in a dug-out grave.

Morbid, he thought.

His eyes travelled up the damp soil walls of the burial plot to cloudy skies. He coughed out dried blood until he could speak—albeit from disfigured vocal cords. "Hello?" he croaked. "Is anyone there?"

Silence.

"Hello? Anyone?"

He heard the sound of a spit-take, and then a head appeared. Saucer-sized eyes stared down at him.

"Holy son of a doodle, this is impossible! Vant! Vant, my dearest companion! Are you alive?"

"Grammie," Vant coughed some more. "Yeah... I'm alive."

"This—this is crazy! I've seen a whole pile of nutter-butt in my day, but nothing like a man who can come back to life! You aren't a zombie, are you? After my brain and my balls? Which part does a zombie eat first? Ah, hell, let me get you out of there, my not-dead companion! Doubleya! Get over here! Come give me a hand!"

The World's Worst Magician and Grammie hoisted Vant from the grave. The wizard expressed a polite enthusiasm at the sight of Vant, as if he had returned from a brief vacation. "I should have known you'd be the least of my worries. Leave it to you to find the tunnel back to the forgotten realms. What I want to know is this, how many people are supposed to use that passage in a day?"

Grammie could hardly contain himself. He said, "We were just toasting your memory before giving you a proper send-off. Skii's going to be thrilled you're huffing and puffing and not pushing up daisies. Poor thing's been down as a dog over your untimely dust bite. She's off doing some hunting and—toasted ball sack, you're a mess! You're going to need a hospital. A nice big-titty nurse to rub the life back into you! I've heard tell of a township that can swap in new parts for broken ones, that sort of thing. Maybe we should take you there?"

"I'll be fine," Vant wheezed. "Just need some time."

"Well, if you don't want to go the clinical route, we can take a more *holistic* approach..." He nodded toward the magician.

"Yeah. Sure. Do me a favor, first?"

"Name it, comrade."

"Anything of mine pointed in the wrong direction... point it right." Vant groaned. Even the words sounded painful.

"Take this first, my compatriot." Grammie procured a vial of syrup from his vest.

"To numb the pain?"

"Quite the opposite! You'll feel every sensation tenfold."

"Why would I want that?"

"Because it also turns the pain into pleasure. And you're about to feel a *lot!* So this should prove to be quite the treat!"

Vant swallowed a gulp of the narcotic. For the hell of it, Grammie and the magician took swigs as well. The magician scratched his crotch. Grammie cracked his knuckles. "This is going to hurt you more than it's going to amuse us," he said.

The magician held Vant down while Grammie got a grip on the first twisted appendage. Vant closed his eyes and mentally prepared. History's most bizarre chiropractic session commenced. Every bone realignment elicited screams from Vant —first of misery, then of pleasure—and uproarious guffaws from the magician and Grammie. Vant's tears of pain turned into tears of laughter, and Grammie and the magician began making bets on which bones would pop the loudest when shoved into place.

Soon, Vant resembled a normal person again, though the biological numbing agents and narcotics in his bloodstream overran his senses. He began to succumb to the soothing slide of consciousness loss. But, moments before blacking out, he witnessed one last thing. The magician, in a trance, stood over him. Green smoke poured out of his fingers and coated his body in a gentle, hazy glow.

Vant could hold on no longer.

He drifted into an endorphin-soaked slumber.

He dreamed of Death.
Peeling his skin.
Flesh from bone.
Bone from body.
Laughing, "Meh-heh."
He saw his love.
Taken. Fearful. Crushed.
Betrayed.

"Welcome back, Pops."

Vant blinked at Skii.

She tapped him on the cheek. "No, please, don't get up on my account. I'm going to tell the others you're awake. Hungry? Thirsty?"

"Tursy," Vant mumbled. "Tur—thurr—"

"I got the idea. Be right back."

Vant tried to sit upright but ended up on his side, face-to-face with a snail. "Hi," he said.

The snail said nothing.

Skii returned and knelt beside him. She dribbled water onto his lips, which he lapped up. Like a river, tactile responsiveness flowed back into Vant's body. He wiggled his fingers and toes, and blinked until his vision was no longer blurry.

"Thanks for trying to save us," Skii said coolly. "Wish you had listened, though. You would have avoided getting beaten up. And killed." Any elation Skii may have been experiencing about Vant's return was being concealed by a layer of caution—and perhaps fear.

"Told you I wouldn't die on you," he said. "Made you a promise, didn't I?"

"What the *hell*. I buried you. You hadn't taken a breath for days and, all of a sudden, here you are. What *are* you?"

Vant changed the subject by rising to wobbly feet. He scanned his reconstructed frame, healed weeks—maybe months—ahead of schedule. "That magician is quite the guy, isn't he?"

"He can do *magic*. The real stuff. He saved us."

"I saw."

"You know what this means? My dad was right. He could have healed my mom. He *could* have."

Vant stretched. A few dawdling bones cracked into their default positions.

Skii continued, "Grammie told me he can move energies around. He's been filling you up with the stuff from all over... trees, plants, animals, even us. It feels so weird. Speeds up the healing process, something like that. Did he bring you back to life?"

"No. There's more to it."

"Well, what, then?"

"Yes, please, do tell." Grammie plopped down with a plate of food for Vant.

The numbness inside of Vant subsided, allowing room for mistrust to reappear. Without a filter, the words just slid out: "Where did you go during the fight?"

"Well, my companion, the answer is complicated, and in your weakened state—"

"You left us to die."

"I did feel quite bad about it. Why do you think I dug you this lovely grave? Don't I get a thank-you?"

Vant squinted at him. The others watched the awkward tension unfold from the sidelines.

Grammie insisted, "Go ahead, say your piece. Don't hold back. Good ol' Grammie knows when he's on the receiving end of an accusation. He's no fool."

"I just want to know where you went," Vant said. "I don't think that's too much to ask."

Vant studied Skii's expression. She had the same look in Land Escape when she defended Vant from the hotheaded Chaaris—except, this time, Vant was on the other side of her scowl. She was siding with Grammie.

Grammie laughed. "You think I set you up, don't you? You think I ran a Triple-Cheese-Charlie and I'm some grand mastermind who coordinated an elaborate plan involving Skii's mysterious father, two mutant trashmen, a legendary mystic, and a few hundred rabid savages. You've got me all figured out, comrade. All figured out."

Words eluded Vant.

Grammie continued, "For our best interests, let us clear the air. I am *not* here to fight. I'm not a fighter. I'm here to profit. I'm a profiteer. I don't use my fists, I use my brain." He tapped the side of his head twice. "Fists are for brutes, the mind is for those with more intellectualary pursuits. Some of us always choose to die another day... without *actually dying,* that is. Also, being sneaky has its own rewards..." He nodded toward a stockpile of equipment, weapons, and raw materials. "Found their camp, comrade. Took what we needed—along with a few pills for our trouble, of course. Half for me, half for the rest of you! Fair is fair! Oh, and one more thing..." Grammie withdrew Death's mask from his vest. "I recovered it from the nomads. Thought you might want it back."

Vant walked up to Grammie. Towered over him. Pulled the mask out of his hands. "All right," he said, "you've had your say. Now let me have mine."

Grammie shifted uncomfortably. "Why, sure, my comrade. That's only fair."

The tension between the two men was thick. Skii nervously buried her face into Cassidy's fur.

Vant spoke:

"I'm the asshole."

Skii's head popped up and her eyes widened. Grammie choked on his surprise.

Vant was ashamed. Deeply. He felt guilty for asking so much of Grammie. Did he really expect one man to rescue them from a militia of tribal mercenaries? Hell, the guy was *smart* to stay away. The truth was, charging in and running his mouth would have probably gotten them all killed—not just Vant. Not everyone had to be a warrior, a brawler, a fight-to-the-finish-and-then-some soldier. Grammie was a person who was masterful at something *else*. And the whole group was alive because of him.

Furthermore...

They were all alive because of each other. No one of them could have made it on their own to where they were now. In the last few days they had all taken turns saving each other, each in unexpected ways.

Vant extended his hand to Grammie. "Allies?"

"Compatriots," Grammie said. They locked hands and shook on it, like gentlemen.

"Thank you for your help," Vant said. "We made it out of Crash Town because of you. And you, Doubleya. You were magnificent." The magician appeared nonplussed, swimming around in his own psyche. There was no acknowledgment of the praise. Or that he knew what he had even done.

"Pops," Skii said, "there's something you should see." She stood and approached the nomad stockpile. "Grammie found it in a box."

"Under lock and key, where the best things usually are," he added. "Thankfully, I'm as good at undoing locks as I am brassieres."

Skii found what she was rummaging for. She handed Vant a helmet.

"Son of a bitch," he said. Then, truly realizing what he had in his hands: "Son of a *bitch!*"

He cocked back his arm to throw the helmet across the dirt in frustration—but stopped himself. "Thallium," he said. "This means the nomads have seen the army we're looking for. Look at the neckline. Like it was ripped off. Someone fought the soldier who wore this, and they won. They kept this helmet as a souvenir."

"I know how they got it," Skii said.

Vant's eyes conveyed, *If you've been holding out on me...*

"It's not like that," she said. "A while back, you asked if I left Crash Town alone or with others, when I was a little girl. The truth was, it was with nomads. I ran with a tribe for a while."

Grammie gasped.

"But *not* like Ranchula's. We were tough, but nothing like them. Everyone knew the stories, though, about how something attacked him and his people."

"And you didn't think to bring this up?" Vant scowled.

"Ghost stories," Skii said. "I never thought to believe them as true."

"Well if they are, Ranchula's been hit hard. And, apparently, he's rebuilding. Hell, he tried to recruit *me* before he sucker-punched me."

"Sucker *killed* you," said Grammie.

"It's a safe bet that the thallium army stole his warriors. And, somehow, he avoided capture." Vant paused, then added: "That bastard."

"Why is he a bastard?" Skii asked. "Besides killing you. And trying to impregnate me?"

"Because if he'd fought fair, I would have won. And if I had won, I would have found out this information and could have helped him find his tribe. Bastard!"

"Calm down," said Skii. "The nomads were scared off by our magician, but maybe we can wait for them. It's a good bet they'll come back when they think he's gone. Their trap outside Clodd and Blauth's tunnel is way too good to resist."

"We can't wait," Vant said. "Too much time has wasted already."

Grammie interjected, "Now hold on a moment, my cavalier comrade. Before we go any further, and without pressing my luck... we still don't understand *you,* it would seem. You, our dear outcast from the afterlife. Is there something you wish to confide in us? Anything at all?"

Vant thought. Then thought some more. Finally, he tossed the helmet aside. "Okay." he said. "I'll come clean."

All eyes fell upon Vant, waiting for an explanation.

"I need a drink, first. We got anything?"

The charlatan dug into the nomad stockpile and removed two bottles. "*Now* who's your best friend?"

"Pour the wine," Vant said. "We're going to need it."

Grammie filled four mugs with a brownish liquid. "It's certainly not wine, but we're going to put it in our faces anyway!"

Night fell. They lit a campfire.

"Where to begin..."

Vant wrestled with his point of entry. Portions of his past were untouchable. Unforgivable. And might sever any bond he had with his companions.

He decided to start with his love. With Rii Tavee.

"Skii, I first met your mom when she was three."

"Three whats?"

"Three years old."

Skii did a double-take with confusion.

Grammie hooted, "I like this story already!"

She punched Grammie in the arm. "Keep talking, Pops," she said to Vant.

He continued, "I was living in Land Escape at the time. I saw her on the playground. She was a funny-looking thing. Huge head. She made me laugh. Something I hadn't done in quite a while." The corners of Vant's mouth felt odd—he was smiling. He put a stop to that immediately and went on, "I watched her grow into a toddler. A little girl. A teen. A woman. It was nothing weird. I just... had lots of time on my hands. I'm older—"

"Older than you look," Skii finished his sentence. "You've said that about fifty times now."

"It was a harmless pasttime, keeping tabs on her. But, something happened. Something changed. She started to... captivate me. She was driven. Smart. So quick. She was a lot like you, Skii."

Skii accepted the sentiment silently, but earnestly.

"I never could say anything to her," Vant went on. "I watched her for so long, but speaking to her... that took a courage I just didn't have. One day, though, she spoke to *me*. I couldn't believe it. And my feelings came pouring out. I blathered on, like a fool."

"What did you say? What did *she* say?"

"Is it really important?"

"Uh, yeah."

"Ugh." Vant took a massive sip of liquid courage. It was not enough. "Really?"

"Yes!"

"Fine! She asked if I needed pills. I guess I wasn't keeping up appearances at the time. She handed me a bunch, she thought I was a beggar. I was embarrassed as hell. And then, it just slipped out. Instead of, 'Thank you,' I said, 'Love you.'"

"Aaaaaawk..." the magician hollered like a bird. They looked at him, puzzled. He completed his thought: "...ward."

"She asked what I meant. I told her I'd been watching her, and that I was in love with her. I told her I wanted to get to know her better, but she *really* didn't want to know me. 'I'm a monster,' I said. 'I've done terrible things. I'm the devil. But when I look at you, I'm in heaven.'"

Vant took another swig. "But she didn't run away. Instead, she smiled... a smile that was improbable. Impossible. And she said words I will never forget."

"What were they?"

"She said, 'It's nice to know I can take the devil to heaven.'"

Vant rubbed the back of his neck with embarrassment. "She accepted me. Somehow. I still don't know why. We spent a lot of time together, after that. I was with her for three years."

Vant swallowed more drink, which burned on the way down. "But something took hold of me. Pulled at me. Forced me away from her. I didn't get to say goodbye... I can only imagine what she must have thought. One day I was there, and the next, I vanished."

Skii stared at a rock. Her glassy eyes reflected the campfire licking the air.

"I should have stayed away from her. Being with Rii was a mistake, I know that now. I knew at the time that I would outlive her, and that I must have been breaking the rules by loving her. I was right. I was taken away and forced into a hell of isolation. Forced to suffer, day after day. I was living a life that should have ended long ago, but it didn't. It wouldn't. It doesn't. Ever. Every time I die, I come back."

Skii and Grammie could not conceal their body language. They were in the company of either an immortal who had touched the very edges of darkness, or a completely delusional man. Vant knew they would have gravitated toward the latter conclusion, save for the compelling argument that he *had* just returned from the grave.

"If that's so," Grammie said, "then tell me. What happens when you die?"

"Blackness. That's all."

"Can you feel anything?"

"No. Yes. Kind of. It's like an infinite tunnel. Time doesn't work. It lasts forever and no time at all, simultaneously. Limitless waiting in the black."

"No white light? That's what they say, right? 'I'm going into the light!'"

"Oh. That."

Vant tossed Death's mask next to the fire.

"Walk into the light and you'll meet a demon."

They stared at the eye sockets of the relic. Its importance drew their focus toward its lifeless visage.

"I didn't know it at the time, but I was being drawn to Death. And I found him." Anxiety bubbled up from Vant's insides. He feared the hulking demigod would suddenly materialize and strike him down for discussing his existence. Thus, Death's true power was demonstrated: the mere thought of what the creature could do to him—and to his companions—adjusted Vant's attitude to one of subservience.

Although it felt like a risk, Vant showed the others the symmetrical scar where Death's scythe had sliced his head clean off. "Beheading. Even Death couldn't kill me. So, instead, he's using me."

The group fell silent. They were drawn to the supernatural mask, which seemed immune to the fire's reflections.

They stared at it. And stared.

Unprompted and in unison, they all gulped down their "wine." The coincidence created a tension-breaking laugh between them.

"What's Death like?" Skii asked.

"You don't want to know," Vant said.

"I remember him," the magician said. "I've met him."

"Oh?" said Vant.

"Yes. I got the feeling he needed a hug. But, I was worried if I gave him one, we'd brush cocks. So, that was out."

"Good thinking!" Grammie humored his friend. "So, how long have you been alive, compatriot? In total?"

"Couple hundred years."

Skii asked, "And before you met my mom? What's the story there?"

Visions. Flashes. A hole in the chest. Friends destroyed. Righteousness. Betrayal. So many dead. So many...

This topic was off-limits.

Vant pulled himself together and said, "A tale for another time. I was a different person, back then." Vant drank deeply from his cup. "So, yeah, when I wear that mask I can see through Death's eyes. It shows me another realm."

"Mind if I take a look-see?" Grammie asked.

"Knock yourself out. It won't work, nothing personal. It only seems to like me."

Grammie picked up the mask and ran it through his fingers. "Heavy thing, isn't it? Smooth thing. Quite gorgeous. Wonder what she's worth!" Vant rolled his eyes. Grammie pressed it to his face and... nothing happened.

"Here, I'll show you." Vant took the mask and held it inches from his nose. It leapt from his hands, latched onto his skin, and beamed a piercing white.

"Well, stuff my pisser!" said Grammie, bolting upright. "Got a mind of its own!"

"When I look at you, I see vibrations, but nothing crazy. When I look at Skii, it's the same thing. Same for Doubleya—"

But it wasn't. The magician's silhouette pulsed bright green. The green of the energy he moved with his fingers. The green Vant had observed as a faint glimmer in Crash Town.

"Something's different with him, isn't it?" Skii asked.

"Yeah," Vant said. "He's green."

"Doesn't surprise me none," Grammie chuckled. "He's a special one. Fella's a space alien, for all we know."

"I'm not an alien!" the magician demanded. "Although my grandmother was. Her name was Phoeba. She smelled of stale tulips and made love like a wild boar!"

The magician had been manipulating a ball of concentrated flame encased in green smoke. Upon noticing he was being observed, he put his hands behind his back. The smoke dispersed, and the combustion evaporated. When he stopped doing magic, his unique color in the mask reverted to a calm white.

Vant pulled the mask from his face. "The visions I see while wearing the mask all mean something. When I looked at those things that overran Land Escape, I had the drive to destroy them all. I have to do what Death tells me. I'm on the hook, here. If I don't, I'll be answering to someone who doesn't care for excuses—and, frankly, who doesn't like me all that much to begin with."

Grammie joked, "I've heard of some awful bosses in my day, but this one takes the cake!"

Skii was quickly piecing things together. "So that means this rescue mission, it's actually—"

"Both," Vant said. "A mission of death, and a mission for life. I have to wipe out an army, and hopefully save the Land Escape citizens in the process. Two birds, one stone."

"Two massive birds," Skii corrected.

"So, there you have it. I'm immortal. I'm cursed. I'm Death's stooge. And I'm going up against an entire army in hopes of rescuing a thousand hostages. Anyone want to come along?"

The World's Worst Magician leapt up and howled, "*Bababoo!* You're gyaddamn right I do! My jimmy just put a hole in the roof thinking about it!"

"I guess that's one," Vant said.

"They say risk is directly proportional to reward," Grammie pontificated as he poured a fresh helping of hooch to the brim. "If that be the case, our rewards are going to be *gorgeous!* Here's to war profiteering, and the pleasures such pursuits provide!"

Grammie filled Vant's mug. They clunked them together and downed their fill.

"That leaves two," Vant said to Skii... and Cassidy. "How about it, ladies? Been fun so far, right?"

"*Fun?*" Skii protested. "Cockroaches, nomads, abductions, armies, and evil dickheads? Fun my buns! Ever since I met you, everything wants to kill me! And, not all of us have the luxury of returning from the dead, you skeevy freak!"

"You don't have to come," said Vant. "None of you have to. I'm the only one of us who has a reason to fight."

"The hell you are." Skii kicked dirt in Vant's direction. "Those soldiers sacked my home and sucked up my mom's remains in a vacuum. Those shiny pricks deserve to get castrated." She scratched her teddy bear behind its ears. "What do you think, pretty girl? Want to pick a fight?"

Cassidy's crooked eyes twinkled from the flickers of the campfire.

"Why do I even ask? Of course she's in. She loves a good scrap. As for me..."

She looked over at the magician. A spiral of smoke circled above his fingertips. It transformed into a letter. A number appeared. Then another letter.

W8M.

"I'm in," said Skii.

After a boozy hiccup, Grammie locked arms with Doubleya and said, "In honor of this memorious occasion, I'd like to protose a moast. To the best damned team of misfits I've ever had the pleasure to enjoy misfortunes with!" He guffawed himself into a dogpile with the magician, then drunkenly passed out.

Vant raised an eyebrow at Skii. She rolled her eyes.

And they both grinned a little.

"What do you think, pretty girl? Want to pick a fight?"

- Skii Tavee

223 YEARS PRIOR

Of Power and Purpose

Seventy-five figures faced a white palace in the distance. Their cloaks whipped in the wind. The elements pushed hard against them. They pushed back.

The view of the mansion did not intimidate them. Under new management, the Knights of Rights had yet to lose a battle—or even one warrior. They had become precise. Exacting. Their skill in battle was beyond unmatched. The hooded warriors stood in formation behind Vant, their prized commander, and Terrii, the First Prime.

Terrii devoured the building with his eyes. "Give the devil an inch and he'll take a mile. Give him miles, and he'll turn them into Hell."

Vant held steady.

"My father dreamed of taking this place down," Terrii continued, "but he never had an army skilled enough to do so. Now we do. After this night, The Shift will finally be complete. The strength of our forces... the power of our weapons... finishing Agmar's work... it's all thanks to you. I suppose you're the true hero, here."

"I'm no hero. And if you see me that way, you're making a tremendous mistake." Vant leaned in to Terrii. "You've trusted me with your warriors as you've trusted me with your life. That's a choice you made. You. You're the leader, I'm just a soldier. And..." The words stuck on his tongue, though he said them anyway, "...your friend."

Terrii's skeptical squint hinted at years of suppressed feelings. That word, friend, *had become all but extinct. As time progressed, the rift between the two of them had grown deep. Terrii had banished Vant's mentor, Cloakmaster Gordone. He had forced Vant's colleague, Shyyla, into marriage. He had numerous rash decisions and nearly mismanaged the order into oblivion. It was not until Vant was sworn in as a Second Prime that the Knights of Rights fully recovered. But it was in Vant's astounding competence and, in return, the admiration of his peers where Terrii tasted the bitterness of jealousy.*

"Awaiting your command, First Prime," said Vant.

"Give them the battle speech."

Vant faced his loyal warriors.

"Ignite."

Seventy-five pairs of whip gauntlets roared to life. The sonic shockwave displaced the air and traveled with the wind, bending the grass toward their target.

"Tonight we set things right," said Terrii. "Go."

In a flash, seventy-four of the most ferocious warriors in existence sliced through the open air and converged upon...

The White House.

It was a vestige of a bygone era, sheltering the last bastion in a regime of greed. The most devious and dangerous elitists dwelled inside, those once in power who shunned Corpo's new economy and resisted the status reset created by The Shift. Behind its fortified walls were officials who were no longer official. Leaders who had betrayed their followers. Faith-peddlers who had preached complacency for profit. And those who had nearly destroyed humanity a hundred times over in their wars over fuel.

They had collected their trinkets, trifles, and symbols of wealth and barricaded themselves inside to wait. To defend themselves. To rebuild. To regroup. And to re-emerge when the time was right, in hopes of returning things to how they used to be, when they were in charge, and they pulled the strings.

But this could not happen. They could never again be allowed to seize control. The Knights of Rights had come to break their unbreakable defenses.

And to break them.

Six groups of ten split off to their breach points through windows, side doors, and the basement. Ten others scaled the walls of the compound and took apart the helicopters on the roof, eliminating any chance of escape. Four of the highest Primes, led by Vant Hu'l, gauntlet-smashed the front door and stormed the interior.

There was gunfire.

And screams.

But mostly screams.

Terrii, full name Agmar-Burrian Terriforn, son of the fierce warrior Agmar and leader of the legendary Knights of Rights, watched the storming of the keep safely from the hillside.

Safely, in his cowardice.

A snail inched through the mud, near his feet.

He charged up a gauntlet.

And smashed it in disgust.

"We're approaching the basin."

- Skii Tavee

CHAPTER 16

The Grief and the Gravestone

The World's Worst Magician was a liability. He spoke up when they needed him to be silent, and was silent when they needed his feedback. He constantly chased his hat whenever the wind blew it off his head, which was often. His flashy robes and jingling trinkets—handmade from branches and stones discovered along the way—made him a visible and audible target.

Kram Grammie was rife with challenges as well, especially at night. His snoring was so oppressive that anyone in the area could be forgiven for thinking a maniac lumberjack was on the loose.

Something had to be done.

At a resting point, Vant pulled Skii aside. "We're really pushing it with these two. How far until we reach the outskirts?"

"Depends. We've got to get southwest, but nomad territory stretches for a hundred miles in that direction. Heading due west would mean half the time in danger, but it would triple the mileage of the entire trip."

"If we go that far west, we'll hit the cliffs."

"Right. We'd follow them south all the way from there."

Vant's blood turned cold. "We can't go that way."

"Why not?"

"Because..." He could not put it into words. He did not *want* to put it into words. "Look. I have my reasons."

"Such as?"

"We just can't go that way, understand?"

Skii was visibly thrown by Vant's sudden bite. "The only thing I understand is that you're being a weirdo. More than usual, I mean. What's the deal, Pops?"

"You said you'd take me where I needed to go. That was our arrangement."

"Right, but I didn't say you could pick the path."

Vant scratched his stubble in frustration. He filled his lungs and opened his mouth to protest, but only an exhale came out.

Skii continued, "We have to get out of nomad territory. We *have* to. We barely survived one attack, we can't risk a second. We'd never walk away from it, no one's that lucky. Ranchula's tribe isn't the only one out there, you know."

"I promised myself I'd never take the cliffs again unless I absolutely had to."

"Well, guess what, pal?" Skii glanced over at Grammie and the magician, who were rubbing their calloused feet. "You have to."

She was right and he knew it. While the verbal agreement never came out of his mouth, he managed to muster a reluctant nod.

So, she set them on a course designed to circumvent unnecessary attention. She soon developed a sense for which routes would prove too challenging for her inexperienced companions and, weeks in the making, their footsteps finally found a natural pace. The magician's desires to explore soon resolved into a discernible pattern, as if an internal clock dictated his wanderlust. And, on a hunch, Vant put Grammie in charge of the group's breaks; this somehow extended the out-of-shape con man's stamina and energized him through a primordial desire to show off. They soon fell into a rhythm and were, at last, making good time.

The extra mileage added to their trip was a daunting prospect, but the upside to leaving nomad territory was a freedom to converse and the ability to camp in more pleasant conditions. They risked small pleasures such as admiring the landscape, sharing stories about their lives, and singing songs from their hometowns. Vant and Skii, both of whom had lived at various times in Land Escape, knew similar tunes— mostly children's songs—though Vant refused to join in. Grammie's and the magician's hymns from Crash Town, however, skirted the edge of sensible taste:

I dream of my maiden so fair,
With her lush flowing mane of long hair.
It gleams like a mare's,
And it's strong like a bear's,
It's too bad all that hair is down there!

Occasionally, the magician soloed. The verses were nonsensical but magnificent, decorated in resounding melodies from seasoned vocal chords. When he sang, the party would fall silent, knowing the treat could stop at any time, for any reason, interrupted by the tiniest of stimuli.

Vant grew quieter the farther they got into the outskirts. The familiar topography had triggered a perpetual meandering inside his head, something that was cryptic to the others. Skii often tried to break him from the spells of introspection; at first, just calling him "Pops" did the trick, a teasing reference to their first meeting, when Vant believed he was her father. She had yet to let him live that down. But eventually, the effect wore off. Next, she took to placating his ego by asking his expertise on subjects in which he was well-versed. It worked for a time, but his manner soon turned even more distant. Finally, she resorted to a basic, recurring check-in to see if he was okay. He always said he was fine.

But he wasn't.

His ice-cold demeanor, over time, completely chilled the rest of the group. They grew hesitant to speak with him. Soon, however, Skii had to...

"We're approaching the basin," she said. "We'll go around it."

"Through it," Vant insisted.

"What's with this guy?" she asked the others. Then she turned back to Vant. "I can't figure you out. Stop being crazy."

"The basin is safe," Vant said. "The nomads keep away from it. Let's go through it, then head due west."

"The nomads keep away from it because *everyone* keeps away from it. It's not the nomads I'm worried about. There are *way* worse things in there."

"We can't take the cliffs."

"And we can't go through the basin. Grammie and Doubleya will never make it out alive. I can't be any clearer than that, Vant."

She called him "Vant." Not "Pops." It sounded off, the way she said it. Like it was not his real name.

She added, "Unless you have a damn good reason for putting us all at risk, we're going around it."

He had a damn good reason.

"Speak now," Skii said, "or forever hold your peace."

He said nothing.

Skii took point, going the way she wanted to go. Grammie and the magician trailed behind.

Vant followed them. Slowly. But he followed.

Skii led them to a hidden trail angling slowly but steadily upward. It was skinny, winding to the west and hugging a mountainside. Soon, a serrated cliff appeared to their right, dropping into a gully of jagged rocks and boulders. They carefully traversed the lip.

At peak elevation, the terrain leveled off. And to the east, the forestry melted away. A gradual slope cascaded into a valley.

"Look," Skii said.

She, Grammie, Vant and the magician stood in reticent awe of the view before them.

An ancient, rotting city stretched for hundreds of miles through the basin below. A marsh, like a mossy lake, enveloped its base and crawled up the rusted skeletons of skyscrapers. Outcroppings of infrastructure in the final stages of biodegradation protruded from pockets of wetland as if clawing their way out of quicksand. Patches of bog coiled in organized spirals, evidence of what had once been highways running between the crumbling structures.

The forgotten metropolis was being swallowed by time. It was losing a battle against nature and being reclaimed by the earth. The landscape told the story of the world that used to be, before The Shift. A nuclear bomb had gone off, but there had been no explosion. The bomb dropped was free energy, distributed by Corpo. Power in the form of Corpo-Cells and sustenance in the form of Corpo-Capsules was provided for free, to all. The result of these baseline human needs being met was a shockwave sent around the globe.

Faith was no longer needed. Theologies disintegrated, lost from the temporal nature of the objects that had recorded their views. Industry was replaced by bots, and global commerce was rendered obsolete. Corpo soon handled it all, and, when it did, everything changed. Everything.

With unlimited energy at everyone's fingertips, the burden of carving out a living had fallen away. The concept of individual purpose based upon skill-set had been reset. Governments only perpetuated outdated systems and served no further purpose. The very foundations that organized society had been built upon had been eradicated.

Which led to an Armageddon.

Freedom had been the apocalypse.

People of like minds banded together, created new ideologies, and turned insular against the outside world. They holed up in sanctuaries—townships—and became rigid in their beliefs. Dogmatic. And they toiled away at whatever they believed could extend their lives. In the age of plenitude, life extension became the last great commodity worth chasing.

But those who resisted The Shift—those who clung to their old ways, defended their status, upheld their superiority, and coveted their now-obsolete symbols of wealth—they were executed.

Executed by the Knights of Rights...

...and Vant Hu'l.

Vant tore himself away from the view, wishing he could also tear himself away from the part he had played in The Shift.

They traveled south for two more days letting the cliffs be their guide. They skirted the edge of the dramatic drop-off until they reached a hollow of flatland. The trees had been cut. The grass was patchy. People had lived there at one time.

Skii, with great courage, disrupted Vant's impenetrable silence by asking, "What is this place?"

He answered her by leading the group across a field and to a cave carved into the hillside.

They entered.

The floor was encased in a layer of dark crimson. In the center was an anvil. Unyielding. Unmovable. It was a reminder of the cave's prior purpose as the arms cache for the Knights of Rights.

"This place skeeves me," said Skii. "Awful things happened here, didn't they?"

A surge of vehemence rose up from the crimson on the floor, entered Vant's legs, passed through his groin, and overfilled his gut. His heart began pulling apart, thread by thread, artery by artery, muscle by muscle. He wrapped his arms around his chest and squeezed. Not to comfort himself—to crush himself.

He was losing his grip. He had to get out of the cave. He summoned enough strength to blow past his friends.

Outside lay a lush green country, full of rolling hills.

And upon a small hill, there was a stone. A black stone. Worn and crumbling.

Vant stood before it.

His knees buckled.

He hit the dirt.

His head sank into the grass.

His hands clasped the grave of his dearest friend.

"Awful things happened here, didn't they?"

- Skii Tavee

222

YEARS PRIOR

Of Bloodlines and Betrayal

"I've come to say goodbye."

"What do you mean?"

"I'm leaving the commune," said Shyyla. "And I'm leaving him.*"*

"Tell me what's wrong." Vant crossed through the cave and approached her. "Tell me."

"Terrii's nightmares… they're getting worse. He repeats his father's name, over and over."

"They're just nightmares."

She moved her hair away from her neck, revealing bruises where fingers had once gripped.

"He did this to you?"

"He rages at night. In his sleep. He… he didn't mean to. I know he didn't. But… I can't take this anymore."

"Tell me what I can do to help."

Shyyla offered her hands to Vant.

He did not take them.

"I hardly see him," Vant said, turning away. "He's avoided me ever since we took down the White House."

"The time of the Knights of Rights is over. Two hundred years of fighting have ended, thanks to you. It's time to move on. Come…" she struggled with the words, "…come away with me."

"I will never defy our leader."

"Our leader? The man who hoards our food and capsules? The man who banishes our Cloakmasters? The man who spits on the Hu'l name and degrades his own wife?"

"*Quiet!*" *Vant's demand echoed through the cave. He had spent countless days in the armory with Shyyla, building whip gauntlets and dismantling firearms. They had shared so much together. But this... this was the unshareable. This was treason.*

Shyyla said, "You asked what you can do to help. I'm telling you. You can be with me. It's what I need. It's what you need." She offered her hands, yet again. "You have to choose, Vant. It's Terrii... or me."

There was no delay, nor hesitation, nor the slightest pause in his response:

"*The war is over, but my oath lives on. I swore to protect him. I cannot break my oath.*"

She fell into his chest, wrapping her arms around his waist. Vant refused to give her the embrace she was desperate for.

"*Take her!*" *Terrii's voice shrieked as he entered the armory. "Take the backstabbing bitch!"*

Shyyla released Vant and lifted her hands, betraying the guilt behind her actions. She approached her husband. "Terrii, it's nothing!"

"*Nothing? This man is a traitor! He has stolen my glory, he has stolen my father's legacy, and now he is stealing my wife!*"

Shyyla put her hands on Terrii's chest. "I can explain!"

His gauntlets activated. He raised his fists—

Crack! Vant whipped Terrii's weapons and yanked them from his grip. He revved the thrusters on his gauntlets as Shyyla ran behind him.

"*Stupid son of a bitch!*" *Terrii screamed. "Threatening me? Me? First Prime and leader of the Knights of Rights?"*

"*I'm not threatening you,*" *Vant said with icy calm. "I'm protecting you. From yourself.*"

"*I don't need your protection! I need you to get the hell out of my life!*" *To the outside: "Knights of Rights! Form up!"*

The battalion of hooded warriors entered and stood at attention.

"*Now this is loyalty! This is my army! They give allegiance to me! I'm the one who feeds them! I'm the one who shelters their children! I'm the one who keeps them safe and rich! Not you! You're a deceiver, hell-bent on revenge!*" *Terrii addressed the Knights of Rights: "This bastard demon, this child of treasonous parents, he has seduced my wife and plotted against our order! He must be executed for his schemes! My father was right! We must sever the bloodline of the betrayers! The Hu'l line dies tonight!"*

The army's whip gauntlets activated, turned against their creator.

Vant stung the ground with the tips of his lashes. "Don't do this," he said to the Knights. "Don't."

"*Kill him!*" *Terrii screamed.*

They charged.

"And those guys."

- Vant Hu'l

CHAPTER 17

The Fortress and the Found

"There, there," said a familiar voice. A hand emanating inexplicable amounts of compassion patted Vant's back.

He looked up to find The World's Worst Magician smiling down at him.

"They're dead because of me," Vant said. "It's all on me."

"You're not alone in this. You know that, don't you?"

"What do you mean?"

The magician took a long look at the seventy-five gravestones spanning the hillside. "All of them... they're with you. They're relying on you. And it's not only *their* destinies on the line. It's the destinies of *every single soul on the planet.*"

Vant's eyes widened.

"Yes, sir." The magician folded his arms and looked about as if surveying the entire world. "I daresay there's a lot on your plate. Or is it your lap? Either way, everyone everywhere is riding on it. Your lap, that is. You can't ride on a plate."

Vant blinked.

"There, there," The World's Worst Magician said again. He smacked Vant on the rear end as if he had given him The World's Best Pep Talk.

As per usual, what he said made little to no sense. But, through the sentiment, suddenly, somehow, purpose returned to Vant. Whether it was the Land Escape hostages relying on him—or that there was something more in the mix, as his delusional companion had suggested—either way, there were lives on the line.

And they were waiting on him.

Vant rejoined his companions. "You okay?" Skii asked.

"Yeah. My past just caught up to me, that's all."

"Comrade," Grammie offered, "if we're going to get into a 'who's past is pissier' pissing contest, I'm afraid all we're going to have to show for it is a whole lot of piss."

Vant nodded.

"So, what's the plan?" Skii asked. "Change of scenery?"

"This is the point of no return," Vant said. "Make no mistake, we're going to raise hell. And hell will most certainly be fighting back. No one has to come. Everyone makes their own choice. Last chance to bow out."

"Nuts to that, Pops." Skii cocked Cassidy. "Let's go to hell."

"Time is money," Grammie said, "and money's wasting."

"Covering one's shame is an option," said the magician, "but I, instead, will fly my unmentionables in the wind."

"Then it's unanimous." Vant said. "Let's get moving."

They travelled faster than they ever had.

The green of the terrain gave way to amber browns. The geography relaxed, settled, and stabilized. A hillside descent was accompanied by a new quality of air, one with a sour aroma of salt riding on its breeze. Seagulls flew among the low clouds, singing to one another grand tales of fish they ate. Their songs mixed with a steadily increasing ambient *whoosh*.

Skii saw it first. She dropped her gear and broke into a run, bounding across the sand. The magician followed like a spirited dog thrilled for the excitement. The two of them waddled into the surf, then dove headfirst into the sea.

Grammie shrugged his shoulders at Vant, then joined the amusements at the water's edge. He wet his head and dipped his toes into the frothy tide while Skii and the magician were engaged in an epic splash battle. Eventually, however, temptation became too great to resist; Skii and the magician muscled Grammie into the water, to his tremendous protest.

Vant lowered himself to the sand and observed them. Their joy was strange to him. Foreign. Like a language he had forgotten—or perhaps he never knew. He zoned out to the whitecaps floating in a give and take against the tide. Serenity overtook his mind. *What else is there in the world?* he thought. *I should hang this whole thing up. I'll start a new life, a quiet life, and just fish for a living. All I need is a few rods and a hut on the beach. That's all I need.*

He had the feeling, however, that a certain decrepit sonofabitch living in the wasteland would have something to say about this.

Damn you, Death.

His career as a fisherman would have to wait.

Shoom.

The unmistakable sound broke his trance. The resonance was faint, nearly imperceptible. It barely rose above the white noise of the ocean.

A few minutes later: *shoom*. Coming from the north.

Vant walked the water's edge. His companions filed in behind him.

The resounding grew louder the farther they went up the coast. Vant's suspicions were confirmed; he saw the hint of a smoke trail in the sky. Somewhere nearby, a Corpo-Bot had flown.

After another hour of walking, they saw a glimmering light. It seemed as if the rays of a second sun were beaming out from the sand.

They moved closer to the anomaly.

It grew larger and more powerful.

Soon, the phenomenon was explained:

It was a stronghold on the beach. Grand, even from their considerable distance. The complex craftsmanship of its framework was striking, and the structure was a marvel of engineering. It reflected the sun like a blinding fireball.

Vant searched his satchel, then held up the piece of thallium scavenged from the destroyed suit of armor in Land Escape. Sure enough, the quality of light bouncing off of it matched that of the fortress.

"We have a winner," he said.

They got closer, but not too close. The fortress was large. Damn large. It appeared impenetrable, with rock-solid construction, no windows, and only one main door. The only other accouterments were two cylinders that stretched from the structure into the ocean. One had a propeller churning water—some kind of filtration system —and the other, perhaps a sewage pipe, dumped liquid back into the sea.

"It's a dogmatic township," Grammie said, looking at the edifice through a spyglass. "See for yourself." He offered the telescope to Vant, but Skii snatched it from his fingers.

"Too slow!" She peered into the device. "Grammie's right. They have a big wank-off sign out front."

"What's it say?" Vant asked, pawing at her for the scope.

"Those arrogant jerks. It says, 'THE IMMORTALS.' Real subtle. Who do you think's inside?"

"Let's find out." Vant withdrew Death's mask from his pack. A forearm's length from his head, the relic leapt from his hands and sucked onto his face. It was desperate for flesh after weeks of neglect. The force knocked Vant back a step.

The world transformed into the realm of mesmerizing blackness. Vant saw through Death-centered eyes what lay beyond the glimmering walls of the fortress...

Pulsating dots of red. Hundreds. Thousands. Their vast numbers blended together into one spastic blob.

"The asshole-detector is going nuts," Vant said. "Wait. There's something else."

His heart raced at what lay within the subterranean of the structure. The sparkling white life forces of a thousand or more innocents were creating a cloud of magnificent energy.

"They're here. The people of Land Escape. They're underground. They're alive." Shockwaves vibrated Vant's body with every heart thump. "Time to make a call."

He mashed the buttons on his wrist-communicator. "Samii Fraam?"

A beat. Then, "Ho, there, Vant Hu'l."

"We found them."

Stunned silence.

"You still with me?" Vant asked.

"Hold on a second. Don't go anywhere. Where's the mute on this thing..."

But he did not press the right button.

"Hey everyone! He found them! He fucking found them! That wonderful, weird son of a bitch! He did it!"

There was an outpouring of celebration from the Land Escapers in the background. Skii, through a giggle fit, said into her communicator, "Hey! I did most of the work! Pops just tagged along!"

"Oh, hell!" Saamii said. "You could hear me? Ah, screw it. I'm thrilled. We all are. Thank you, you two. What does this mean?"

"It means we're getting closer," Vant said. "They're still prisoners, but hopefully that's only temporary. Are you all safe back home?"

"For the moment. There's been two nomad attacks, but we held them off with the turrets. We're keeping them at bay, but if they organize, we'll be in trouble."

"We're sending help," said Vant. "Hang in there."

"We are?" asked Skii.

Vant shoved her in the forehead and gave her a look that said, *Throw me a bone, here.*

"Whoops!" She smacked her hand to her mouth.

"Don't worry," said Saamii. "We'll protect the town. Holler if there's anything we can do to help. Oh, and if you see my wife before I do... give her my love."

"I will." Vant clicked off.

He turned his attention back to the structure, and its inhabitants. Using Death's mask to visually penetrate the building's exterior, he observed how the peaceful human shapes in the basement remained motionless. Vant assumed the prisoners were secured or bound—that much seemed clear—but unexplainable was how the souls marked for elimination by Death were somehow moving through the environment as if hovering. If these were the thallium soldiers last seen in Land Escape, something was off. They were winding midair, in motion patterns far too smooth for bulky armor.

More troubling: so much time had passed since the invasion. Vant wondered how many white dots were missing—his fault for taking so damn long. The pressure weighed on his back, but he forced himself to reconcile those feelings with the importance of not rushing into a losing situation. That was a mistake he had made far too many times in his life, and one he could not risk now.

To his companions: "We've got a lot to discuss."

A purple dusk fell. They huddled around a campfire. Vant kicked off the brainstorm:

"Here's what we've got. A stronghold on the beach. Only one door in, and no idea what's on the other side besides bad news. A giant pipe funnels water into the structure, and a filtration propeller grinds up anything in its path. What else?"

"Tons of sand. Fresh air and sunshine. Sea gulls and a couple of hermit crabs," Grammie added.

"And underground," Skii said, "a snot-ton of innocents held captive."

Shoom.

"And those guys," Vant said. A mantis-like Corpo-Bot flew overhead, headed toward the fortress.

"So," Vant continued, "the task at hand. How do we march in, kill everyone bad, and rescue everyone good?"

Silence.

"This shouldn't be too hard to figure out, right?"

More silence.

They pondered. Grammie nibbled his fingernails. Skii petted Cassidy and stared into her crooked eyes. The magician played with a ball of earwax.

Vant drew upon his mental archives of combat lessons. He ran through battle plans, infiltration strategies, and warfare techniques. Utilizing the small amount of experience garnered from his melee against the thallium soldiers in Land Escape, he tried to emerge victorious in hypothetical scenarios fighting against their entire army. Each time, however, the outcome was a fast and ruthless defeat.

He wanted nothing more than to storm the fortress. *For shit's sake, I'm right on the enemy's doorstep,* Vant thought. The hostages were right there waiting for him—*right there.* But he hadn't the foggiest idea of how to get to them.

"We could go through the Corpo-Bot access in the roof," said Skii.

"It's hundreds of feet high, and those walls look slippery," Vant said. "Plus, they'd spot us climbing. And the location of the portal would drop us right into the lion's den."

"You can't die. Could you go through the filtration system?"

"It would take eons for my body to heal itself after being ground to pieces."

"Can we blow up the whole damn thing? Wait—bad idea. We might kill the Land Escapers in the basement. Could we dig a tunnel or something? I dunno. Burrow underground?"

"My dearest compatriots," Grammie cut in. "You're going about this all wrong. There's a key to every locked door, and each of us has it."

"I don't follow," Vant said.

Grammie stuck his tongue out, flat and wide. "Your tongue can unlock any door, so long as there's someone on the other side for it to be used upon."

A synapse fired in Vant's brain.

"Grammie, tell me more. About a con."

"The gist is rudimentary, my beloved companion. A con is, at its most basic, the acquiring of goodies or services from a mark using only deception as due impetus. Make sense? Simple dimple!"

"I'm lost," said Skii.

"To put it another way, I offer you a coveted desirable. While you're predisposed with the particulars, I'm already in the process of securing my bounty and leaving your pockets liberated from the burden of occupancy."

Skii scratched her scalp. "So, you give them something, and they give you something in return?"

"No, my dear darling, that's called shopping! There is a difference, with a con. You see..." he held up a seashell procured from the beach. Skii's eyes lit up at the perfect specimen. "I have something that piques your interest. And, you have something that I'm hankering for... a kiss!" Grammie shoved his chin into the air with a gigantic grin. Skii snorted, rolled her eyes, and smooched him on the cheek loudly and melodramatically. With panache, he tossed the shell to her, which she gladly caught.

He went on, "This, my lovely love, is called a transaction. Although I'm a peck richer, I'm also missing a shell, and therefore, I spent to get. This cannot do! We are not lowly salespeople, for titty's sake! We're masterminds of the profit business! A con, sweet pea-pea, would be my regaling you with tales of a decadent gift from the mermaids, convincing you that you absolutely had to have it, you giving me the peck on my pecker—er, cheek..." Skii gagged. "...And then me disappearing without you ever having received your keepsake. Then, I would be one up on you—pun definitely intended."

"So what do *they* want?" Vant nodded toward the fortress on the beach. "And how can we convince them we have it?"

Silence.

Then, from the magician, "How many believers do you have to sacrifice at the altar before you realize your smelly temple is never going to be worshipped at?"

Vant rubbed his eyes. For the first time in, well, ever, he deduced meaning from the magician's words. Or, maybe he was listening harder out of desperation. "Doubleya, you're a genius!"

The World's Worst Magician did a dramatic pirouette. "Come on. If I made sense all the time, wouldn't it be sort of Plippy the Clown of me?"

"What am I not getting here?" Skii asked.

"They want what every dogmatic township wants. What everyone wants—"

A raspberry from the mouth of the magician interrupted Vant.

"Okay, everyone except *you,* magic man. Immortality. Whatever secret they have in there, it's put them on Death's shit list. They're breaking the rules. But, it occurs to me, they can't be immortal, even if their sign says they are. I know this because I killed one in Land Escape."

"There's nothing lower than an imposter," Grammie said. He received three sets of raised eyebrows. "*Ahem,* takes one to know one, after all."

Vant continued, "What if there was a way for them to do it? To be *truly* immortal? Maybe we could convince them of the possibility." Vant thought for a moment. "I think I know how to make that happen."

"How?" Skii asked.

"I'll give them me. I'm the key. I'll show them I can't die, and pretend I have the newest breakthrough in everlasting life. They'll think I've brought it straight to their doorstep."

"Bing bang!" Grammie exclaimed. "That'll get you through the front door to ding their dongs! And all you'll have to do is die to do it!"

"Easy," Vant said. "I'm good at getting myself dead."

"Once you're inside, then what?" asked Skii.

"Then, I'm going to need some assistance from our loyal band of oddballs." Vant shot a half smile to the enthusiastic con man, the teenager cuddling a shotgun teddy bear, and the magician putting sand down his pants.

They smiled back.

"Let's get to work." Vant said. "Who's got a knife?"

Skii handed him a hunting dagger she had made from flaked river rock.

"Thanks," he said. He touched the blade to his skin. "Time me."

He slit his wrist.

Blackness.

Then:

Vant arose.

"How long was I out?"

"Two days," they all said at once.

"Not bad. Now I need one of you to strangle me."

Each initially jumped at the opportunity—but once they had their fingers around his neck, conscience overrode their capabilities.

Grammie insisted, "Forget it! I refuse to take the blame for the one time we do this and you don't come back!"

"Too skeevy," Skii said. "End of discussion."

The magician offered, "I only kill things that are already dead inside. Like lemurs. Those cocksuckers."

So instead, Vant hanged himself.

Blackness.

Then:

His entourage had taken the liberty of cutting him loose after his brain had shut off and all the twitches shook from his feet. They noted the duration until his resurrection: one day.

After being satisfied with the data acquired from the experiments, the four of them put the final pieces of a plan together. It wasn't perfect—hell, it wasn't even a *good* plan, or even a halfway decent one for that matter—but maybe it would be enough.

The next day, Vant sat on the beach, focusing on a side project. He tinkered with a bolt rifle—a spoil acquired from the run-in with Ranchula's tribe—which he had withdrawn from storage using the Corpo-Bot caller. Vant had the firearm disassembled and its parts were spread out on a blanket next to his whip gauntlets.

Skii plopped down, intentionally jostling the loose items. "What are you up to?"

"Removing the core. Want to learn how?"

"Meh. Things that kill things aren't really my thing."

"Useful skill. Take a look." From the guts of the rifle, he slid out a small engine connected to a bundle of intertwined wires. "Since Corpo won't do it, each township manufactures its own weapons. But their cores are almost always energized by raw Corpo-Cells added after the fact. The cells are tiny, but powerful. Completely self-sustaining. Little micro-nuclear reactors."

He emptied one of many pellet-sized orbs into his palm from the stock chamber and handed it to Skii. She rolled the glassy sphere between her thumb and forefinger.

"Back in the day," Vant continued, "people used all kinds of bizarre contraptions to generate power. Fire and fuel, gears and grinders... that sort of thing. Corpo invented the microcell, started distributing them for free, and all that other nonsense went away. In the case of our rifle here, the combined output of the cells in the chamber is harnessed by the turbine. That creates electricity, which is fed through the barrel."

"Fascinating." Skii fake-yawned.

"Watch." He placed the scrap of thallium near the chassis of the firearm. After removing an insulated tube from the gun's barrel, he stripped the end, touched the lead to the shrapnel, and opened a tiny gate in the carbine. Arcs of electricity crackled across the metal's surface.

"Whoa," Skii said. "Okay, I'm moderately impressed."

Vant showed Skii the shrapnel. It was untarnished, as if nothing had happened. "This stuff's highly conductive. Those thallium soldiers must be powered by electricity. Our bodies work the same way, with electrical pulses going from our brains to our spinal cords. Remember how their armor was filled with water? I think they're propelled by conduction through the liquid."

"So, this means?"

"Ever seen what happens when you toss a billion volts into seawater?" He dropped the shrapnel into a half-full bucket of water. He connected the wire to the scrap's edge and opened the gate in the engine. Electricity blasted across the surface of the metal and particles of spray burst from the container.

"Son of a bee!" Skii applauded. "So you're gonna—?"

"Exactly." He pointed at his gauntlets. "Should make some sparks fly."

Vant put his items aside for a moment. The two of them watched the waves tumble over each other. It was peaceful. Addictive. Skii took fistfuls of sand and let them drain between her fingers.

She asked Vant, "Are you afraid?"

The question washed over him, along with the cool breeze.

"Yes."

"But why? I mean, you can't die. Who cares, right?"

"It's new."

"What is?"

"This fear."

"Let's say you're ground up into a million pieces. Or someone lops your head off —*again*. Or they use you as a punching bag until they get bored of smacking you around—although why would they? Eventually, you're good as new, right? Just gotta wait it out!"

"It's the time that concerns me. When Death took my head, it took me twenty years to come back. That's how I lost your mom. And, this go-round, there are so many lives at stake... including one I truly don't want to lose."

Skii's eyes widened. "That's..." Her pupils darted around, and then she slyly squinted. "You're talking about me, right? Damn, Pops. Sappy, much?"

Vant kicked sand onto her boots. He walked away, in a huff.

"Wait! Come back!"

"No. You ruined the moment."

"Aw, come on! Get back here! I'll pretend to be moved this time!"

"No. You ruined it. I'm going to say the same thing to Grammie. He appreciates me."

Skii threw her arms around Vant's waist from behind. She was so little compared to him, reaching just above his lower back. "I promise to make you laugh, even if you do get mushed up. I'll even save you in a jar."

Vant shook her off his back. Skii overtook his stride and led their way back to camp. After so much time spent traveling together, they had a natural rhythm that took only moments to rekindle.

"I'll even sing to you and stuff. It'll help you grow faster. Like a little plant."

Vant balled up his fist and jerked his body as if he was going to sock her in the shoulder. She flinched, then laughed. "You ass!" She punched Vant's arm in retaliation. He chuckled. But it hurt.

She was stronger than she looked.

The next morning, preparations were complete.

Skii slinked up to Vant. With a furrowed brow, he was studying the sky. It was the perfect hue of blue.

"What's wrong?" she asked.

"Usually there's lightning and thunderstorms before all hell is about to break loose."

"Today's forecast, piss-perfect. Good sign? Bad omen?"

"No idea. Let's find out. You ready?"

"Nope."

They stared at a cloud lazily floating by.

"How about now?" Vant asked.

"Nope."

"How about now?"

"Nope."

"How about now?"

"Oh, *fine* already!"

Vant walked. Skii followed. Grammie and Doubleya watched them; Grammie's eyes were large, in a state of disbelief that the day was actually here. The magician said nothing... a first.

They made their way to a small patch of trees where the beginning of the path to the habitable zone took shape. Vant stopped. Skii stopped.

She spoke, "What you said earlier, about being afraid to die... what if a person doesn't have it? That fear? Because I don't think I do. I don't want to die, but I'm not afraid to."

"Everyone handles death in their own way. Our final statement in life is how we face death."

"What did you do?"

"I fought," Vant said. "And I will continue to. Every chance I get."

"I don't think I will." Skii looked at a lifeless bird resting on a bed of leaves. "Peaceful. Quiet. Not so bad."

"Just don't be in a rush to get there. You get dead and I'll be left in that fortress with my pants down."

"Right. Let's avoid *anything* that involves your pants being down."

"Skii... you've got the hardest task of all of us. What I'm asking you to do, it's like... like trying to move a mountain."

"I have my ways."

"Don't be too attached to the outcome. If things take a turn, just get out of there, okay? Live to fight another day. Hope for the best, but expect the worst."

"Story of my life. But don't worry about me. Cassidy will protect me. She always does."

Vant nodded. He took a long, deep breath and handed over his satchel containing Death's mask and his weapons. "Okay. Go. Be careful."

"Yeah, yeah. I heard you the first time, bucko." She started off toward the forest.

"Skii, wait…"

"Shut it! I'm on a mission! Let's go, dingus and doofus!"

Grammie and The World's Worst Magician caught up to her. Grammie nodded at Vant as he passed by, and Vant gave him a friendly salute. The magician expressed *so long* with flatulence; whether the discharge was real or simulated was anyone's guess.

Vant kept his eyes on them until they were dots on the horizon. He knew all three were heading toward fool's errands; they were about to face danger, resistance, and life-threatening scenarios. Yet this was far safer than the alternative: going into the township where Vant was about to start some shit.

Days and nights came and went. Vant trained his body, optimized his weaponry, rehearsed strategy, and got all the rest he could. He also performed minor surgery on himself, as the plan required.

Eventually, he counted the exact number of nightfalls Skii, Grammie, and the magician were allotted to reach their destinations.

The plan had officially commenced.

Vant took a breath.

And walked toward the fortress of The Immortals.

"Let's get to work. Who's got a knife?"

- Vant Hu'l

PART
FIVE

SANCTUARY

"Onward, into wherever the hell."

- Vant Hu'l

CHAPTER 18

The Keys and the Consciousness

Vant moved to the water where the waves licked the sand. The golden powder transitioned into glossy gray muck. He let the tide lap at his boots.

The structure grew larger as he approached. He had yet to be this close; this thing was *huge*. The fortress had been intentionally placed in a bitch-to-find location, but at this range—and hundreds of miles from the nearest habitable zone—it was not the slightest bit shy in showing off its brilliance. Light bounced off its exterior, with each flawless panel reflecting a vision of the beaming sun. The sleek surface allowed the salt in the air to slide right off. It was eerily beautiful.

Vant put himself in the mindset of a traveler stumbling across the gleaming marvel. The ostentatious signage promised everlasting life while the sophistication of the structure backed up its claims—the whole package would be too tantalizing to resist. The fortress was designed to lure in anyone who might pass by. To suck in strays.

Vant passed underneath the glimmering letters which spelled out, "THE IMMORTALS." He wanted to release the sarcastic chortle in his throat, but he had to stifle it. At this point he did not know who—or what—was watching him.

He stepped onto a concrete slab in the sand and approached the front door. A gemstone-like button, set between decorative polished spirals, practically begged to be pressed.

So he obliged.

Hissss. The bottom of the six-inch-thick steel door scraped away sand that had built up around its base as it slowly opened.

Onward, thought Vant, *into wherever the hell.*

He entered a hexagonal lobby. The area was sterile. Industrial. Ocean water rushed underneath a grated metal floor. The walls were adorned with floor-to-ceiling chambers bubbling with a phosphorescent blue liquid. Thick rubber piping lined the glass containers and ran along the edges of the floor. A closed portal stared at Vant from across the foyer; it appeared to be the only way farther into the compound. Behind Vant, the entrance sealed itself shut.

"Deserter presence acknowledged," a voice emanated. The vocalization was synthesized. Exact.

"Hi," Vant responded.

"Remain still for vitality assessment."

"Sure. Go for it."

A transparent scanning commenced. Vant felt nothing out of the ordinary. While waiting, he reminded himself of Grammie's *Keys to the Con,* the tactics he would be using to, hopefully, achieve access to the interior of the compound. He was currently entering *Phase One: The Titty Tweak.* Grammie insisted that the first step to every scam was grabbing the attention of a mark in any way possible. To do so, Vant would have to use a powerful weapon: his mouth.

The synthesized voice spoke, "Body composition normal. Heart rate normal. Cell count normal. Antibodies normal. Oxygenation normal. Subject is in optimum health."

"Thanks for the check-up."

"Foreign object detected: nano-transmitter behind right scapula."

"A what?"

"Tracking device. Embedded within subject's muscle tissue."

"Sorry, disembodied voice. Your scanner must be on the fritz." He was being honest. Vant had nothing of the sort inside of him—that he knew of.

"False. Bio-scanner functioning with maximum efficiency. Object shall be removed before integration. Additional foreign object detected: metal splint in left arm."

That was true. "Don't mind that," Vant said. "That's just the bomb I smuggled in here."

"Explosive quantity minimal. Projected damage negligible. Object shall be removed before integration as a precautionary measure."

"The bomb's not for you. It's for me."

"Explain, deserter."

"It's to blow myself up and wash away with the tide." Vant tapped the metal grate beneath his boot, the barrier between himself and the ocean.

"Provide further explanation, deserter."

"I'm here for someone you've stolen."

"Then you shall be reunited. All those who enter here become part of the mass consciousness of The Immortals."

"There seems to be some sort of misunderstanding. Let me be clear. In your possession is someone I want returned to me. I want this person *out* of the mass consciousness of The Immortals."

A pause. Then:

"Process the deserter."

"Yes, 'process the deserter.' Great idea. And make the biggest mistake of your so-called 'immortal' life."

The portal leading to the fortress interior opened, revealing five thallium soldiers.

At least I know I'm in the right place, Vant thought. He said, "I'm not looking for trouble."

The soldiers surrounded Vant. Two placed their hands on his biceps and lifted him off the ground.

"I've come to barter," Vant said. "I have something you'll want."

"There is nothing a deserter could offer The Immortals. We are rich in our one purpose: everlasting life."

"I think you'll like what I'm offering. I'll make you a trade. One life for mine, straight up. You should know, there's something special about me."

"Explain, deserter."

"I can't die. Ever."

The voice was silent. Vant, still suspended by the soldiers, dangled his feet. *Keys to the Con Phase Two: The Hooker,* had begun. Grammie referred to it as the moment a fish nibbled on a baited hook.

"Yeah, I know. Hard to believe," Vant said. "Process that."

"Explain further, deserter."

"My name is Saamii Fraam," Vant lied. "You've stolen my wife, Laamlielle. She goes by the name Laam Fraam. I want her freed. In exchange, you get me, an honest-to-goodness immortal. And, here's the kicker. I can show you how to do it. How to live forever."

"We know how to do it. We are The Immortals."

"I'm not here to argue semantics. I'm just telling you that I also have a method. Any harm in knowing two ways?"

"An immortal who would be killed by a bomb?"

"I didn't say it would kill me. I said it would blow me into bits. I'll float downstream and start a new life under the sea. I always come back as soon as my body has all the pieces reassembled. I've never started from microscopic chunks mixed with saltwater before, so it may take a few eons to regenerate—I'll probably grow a set of gills or something—but, hopefully, it won't come to that."

Am I pushing too hard? Vant wondered. Conning was Grammie's forte. He assumed he was doing okay, but the ambient voice fell silent. *Good sign? Bad one?*

"Prove your worth."

"Not a chance. You don't get jack until I see my wife walk out of here on her own two feet."

"Prove your worth or be processed, deserter."

Batons slid out from the wrists of the soldiers.

"Hold on. Let's hammer out the details."

Keys to the Con Phase Three had started. *The Fancy Finagle.*

"Here's what I propose," Vant said. "First, you show me my wife. Second, I die. Third, I come back to life. Fourth, you get an erection. Fifth, you let Laam go. Then sixth, I tell you my secrets."

"Death first. Then you see your wife... should you return."

He took a pause for dramatic effect. Then, "I can live with that. Get it? Okay, now for a few provisos. These are non-negotiable."

"Proceed."

"When I'm dead, no hacking me up, and no trying to remove the bomb. The hardware is wired to blow if tampered with. And no experiments on my body or shoving anything weird into anything sacred. Touch me on the outside if you must, and examine me by sight, but that's it. I don't want to wake up with a newfound love of anal probes. Next, I pick the method of death. There's a reason. The worse you break me apart, the longer the recuperation period. I don't have a lot of time here— or I should say, my wife doesn't. I don't want her freed with only enough years to enjoy knitting doilies and picking petunias. Kind of defeats the purpose of rescuing her. I love her, and I want her to have a full life."

"Die as you please, Saamii Fraam."

"So, we have a deal?"

"Confirmed."

"Aces! Let's get started, then." Vant rubbed his hands together. He was anxious to get things moving, but was dreading *Keys to the Con Phase Four: The Testicle Tickle.* Giving the mark a tease.

"You said you can monitor my vitals, right? Well, go ahead and keep your eyes— or whatever you have—on them. Hey, fella..." Vant tapped the shoulder of one of the soldiers. "Do me a favor? Choke me to death. I don't mind, I like it rough."

The enforcer did not have to be told twice. Metal fingers clamped around Vant's neck, squeezing the air from his throat. Small crackles accompanied muscle and bone giving way in his esophagus.

Vant's survival instincts kicked in, resisting the inevitable. His heart struggled from deprivation. His gut spasmed, desperate to draw in oxygen. His insides panicked. His muscles twitched.

His hands attempted to pull the soldier's fingers apart and his legs flailed, pushing against the armor in an attempt to break free. Urine dripped down his leg. His ego experienced shame—not only for pissing himself, but also for his body defending itself without permission.

The world became fog. A squealing filled his ears. His frame rhythmically convulsed, searching for air in every pocket of his anatomy. It discovered none.

His brain understood before his body. A release of serotonin alerted all physicality to surrender.

Blackness.

Then:

The sound of rushing water. Cold metal on his face. Cognitive faculties and motor skills inched back into him.

Vant's eyelids resisted—not to open, but to close; he had died with his eyes peeled. They were dried-out, and a crust was holding them expanded.

"Muhrgerfer," Vant declared.

"Welcome back, Saamii Fraam."

"I'mno Samerfurr..." His brain was not fully online. He was fairly certain he had just admitted something he should not have—but he was also pretty sure no one would understand what the hell he had just said.

His arm worked again, so he smacked some sense into himself. He manipulated his eyelids and pulled delicious oxygen into his lungs, which helped reboot his system.

His breath tasted horrible.

"Ow," Vant said, wrestling with gravity to get to his feet. His head throbbed to an insane degree.

"You are a fascinating specimen. Your vitals ceased, and your body flatlined. This is confirmed. Yet, more data is required. One incident does not establish a pattern."

"What do you—how can you not—"

"To rule out deception, you will die for us again."

"That wasn't part of the deal!"

"As an incentive, we shall procure your wife."

The phosphorescent liquid in the tubes bubbled. Something was moving—being moved—through the fluid. A figure floated into one of the glass enclosures.

A woman. Hairless. Naked. Below her forehead, two goggle-like cylinders were screwed into her eye sockets. A breathing apparatus protruded from her mouth, secured with bolts through her cheeks.

"What the hell!" Vant ran up to the chamber to study the imprisoned woman. She was emaciated, floating with limp limbs. Her hairless head bobbed with the current. "Let her out *right now!*"

"Her freedom is contingent upon you."

"What *is* this place? What have you done to her?!" Vant pressed his teeth into his knuckles and bit hard. He was reacting from his gut, but he needed to hurdle over his emotions. He had to stick to the plan.

"Laamlielle Fraam," the cutting voice spoke to the prisoner, "your husband is about to die. If he returns, you go free. If he fails to do so, you shall become a widow. Though, do not dismay. You will enter into another union... a permanent union with The Immortals."

The thallium soldiers advanced on Vant. He was seething, yet he managed to get out one key sentence, "Fine, kill me. I don't give a shit. But, whatever you do, don't slit my throat. I need my blood to—"

"Slit his throat," the voice demanded.

Suckers, Vant thought.

One of the soldiers extended a hard-edged metal finger. Another two grabbed Vant from behind. He struggled, enough to make it convincing.

While constructing the plan, he and his companions had assumed there was no way The Immortals would settle for one demonstration of death. If this were to be the case, Vant had to control the scenario, somehow. Thanks to his experiments at camp, he knew how long it took to come back to life from suffocation, and from open veins. *Keys to the Con Phase Five: The Sucker Suck-In* had worked.

"Goodbye, immortal impostor."

The soldier slit Vant's throat.

The symmetrical scar given to him by Death was now re-opened. He choked on loose fluid and attempted to shut the flap of skin. Blood leaked from his neck and his legs buckled. He fell forward onto the tube containing his "wife." She recoiled in fear, trying to look away. Vant's bloody hand slapped on the glass, leaving a smudged print as he lost his footing. He reached out to her again, pressing his fingers onto the chamber. His eyes bulged and welled up.

Laam struggled to shield her view, shaken and confused. *Sell the lie,* Vant willed to her in his head. *For your sake. For everyone's sake. Sell the lie.*

Vant slapped his syrupy palm on the container, once again.

She pressed her hand against the glass, on top of his.

Good girl.

He smiled at her.

Then blood spewed from his gash, splattering all over the glass in front of her face.

She cowered.

He died.

Blackness.

Then:

The smell of seawater came back first. Then the shape of the room.

A thought appeared in Vant's head: *I hate dying so very, very much.*

His nerve endings tingled. Senses returned in random order.

He heard the portal open, followed by the clank of armored boots on metal flooring as the soldiers entered the foyer. Vant then became aware of something damp covering his body, like a shivering blanket of icy flesh. A woman was clinging to him, her arms draped around his shoulders.

"Sir? Sir?"

Vant snapped into cognizance. He looked at his hands, which he expected to be stained with red but had, somewhere along the line, been cleaned, as had the rest of him. He felt his neck, which now had a fresh, clotted wound being held together by brass hooks.

"Sir?"

"Shu—" he tried to speak. "Shut your—"

"Are you okay?"

The woman was hairless and naked, shivering in goose-pimpled skin. Her eyes were bruised, scarred, and sunken—a byproduct of the goggles unscrewed from her skull. Her cheeks had holes in them and her lips dangled loose, devoid of shape from the months attached to the breathing apparatus.

Vant rubbed his temples to stimulate his senses. He willed himself to think faster.

"Sir, who are you?"

This was supposed to be his wife, but she was inadvertently telling her captors the truth: she had no idea who Vant was.

"Honey," he said, "it's me, Saamii."

"Who?"

"Your husband! Don't you remember me?" Vant grabbed her arms. Hard. If The Immortals discovered the lie about their union, he would be in some serious shit.

"I'm sorry, I've never seen you before."

"We've been married for years!" He shouted upward, "What have you done with her? Why doesn't she recognize me?" He hoped his hosts could not monitor theatrical abilities the way they could vital signs.

The voice from above said, "Your wife has been connected to our unified mind for a significant period of time. There are side effects to detachment. Her individuality will return to her, with time."

Vant swallowed. Thank goodness. Too close.

He felt the staples on his neck, holding the flap of skin shut. It made him queasy. "We attempted to expedite your healing, Saamii Fraam," said the voice.

"I've died twice for you. I've done my part. Now, release her."

"As you request. She is free... or so you believe. You have bought your wife mere moments before her inevitable extermination. Off she shall go into a world of disease, chaos, and violence. She will not last a day in the wild before suffering enslavement, rape, or murder at the hands of savages. If by some miracle she should she make it to the doorstep of a dogmatic township, she will be treated as a deserter, spit upon, and tortured until assimilated and forced to believe their empty promises. This is your final opportunity to reconsider. Here, we offer sanctuary and a peaceful, unified consciousness. Here, she may exist without the burden of external threats and internal torments. Here, we offer peace. Choose her fate, Saamii Fraam. Everlasting life in our paradise, or suffering and death in the outlands."

"No question. Option B. She walks, I stay. I'd rather she live with five minutes of freedom than suffer a lifetime of imprisonment."

"Acknowledged," the voice conceded. "From this moment on, she receives no assistance from The Immortals. She is now a deserter from our ways. Let her live—and die—by that designation."

The fortress door opened.

Laam shaded her eyes from the daylight. The best smile her numb lips could manage appeared when sunshine fell upon her face.

"Go," Vant said to her. "Perhaps one day, all of this will make sense." He leaned in to kiss her—she gave him the cheek. So much for a romantic moment.

The soldiers restrained Vant to prevent him from darting out the door. He did not struggle. He had no intention of leaving.

"Walk due east," he said to Laam. "Use the ocean and the sun to get your bearings. I left a stash of capsules for you in the woods near a tree that looks like a Y. Find the tree and you'll have all the food and water you need. Good luck, my love. It was fun while it lasted."

"Thanks," she said. "I do appreciate it, sir." She walked out of the front door, into the open.

And now, Vant thought as he watched her go, *Skii has my signal.*

He hoped she was out there to receive it. Should Laam follow his instructions, she would walk straight to a rendezvous point where safety awaited.

In theory.

Daylight disappeared as the fortress door sealed.

"Alone at last," Vant said.

"It is time to deliver on your promise, Saamii Fraam."

"Call me Vant. Old fraternal nickname. But, before I show you the secret to immortality, I need the grand tour. I've got to know what I'm working with. My process is complex—it has a lot to do with energy, feng shui, that sort of thing."

A pause. Then, "Your request is granted."

The portal opened, revealing the interior of the fortress.

"Now *there's* something you don't see every day," said Vant.

"Welcome to the sanctuary of The Immortals."

Vant took in the sight of the sprawling environment, bright as day from synthesized ultraviolet light. Hundreds of glass pipelines ran throughout the expansive domain, like a liquid-filled mega-highway. Millions of tons of glowing blue solution flowed through the winding water tunnels. Walkways zigzagged on multiple levels: access-ways for bipeds. The inhabitants, however, did not need the platforms, as Vant discovered when laying eyes on them...

Thousands of submerged humans in various age stages floated in the liquid. As with Laam Fraam, they were naked, save for goggles screwed into their eyes and breathers bolted to their mouths. Some were fully developed. Some were highly atrophied. Others resembled children whose growth had been grossly stunted. Still others were incredibly old, with bones so frail their appendages wafted in the water like empty sacks.

Their heads turned toward Vant.

Thousands of goggled gazes fell upon him.

These were The Immortals, corrupted humans who had made the ultimate sacrifice of forfeiting their humanity for the promise of everlasting life.

They propelled themselves through the currents as though flying. A few of the nimbler specimens zipped around, pausing at various points to check variables. They stopped to investigate fluctuations in the temperature, vitals of other Immortals, or imperfections within the pipes. The phenomenon Vant had witnessed through Death's mask outside the fortress now made sense; he had thought the beings inside were hovering, but they were not. They were floating. Floating in the waterways.

Vant descended a flight of steps, noticing the rubber tubing that ran across every platform. He traversed the catwalks and paced the edges of the pipelines trailed by a security detail of thallium soldiers. Vant could not help but be drawn in; he studied the Immortals with morbid curiosity. "Can they hear me?" he asked.

"*We* can hear you," the synthesized voice replied. "We are all connected."

"How did you do this?"

"Arduous research and experimentation have yielded a vast understanding of organic processes." Vant halted to study a sophisticated device churning away at the water as the voice continued, "Water is the foundation of life, and we have harnessed its true potential. Ocean water flows into our environment, where it is cleansed, treated with chemicals, and enhanced by ionic particles and stimulants to create ideal conditions for a neural network. To sustain our physical forms, we have adapted to accept nutrients through osmosis."

Vant's ears perked up at the word *nutrients*. An important part of the equation was missing. Perhaps detecting this, the voice changed the subject: "The electric impulses of our brains manipulate the currents to allow for multidirectional travel within the pipeline."

"Why go anywhere?" Vant asked. "Why not just sit still?"

"We must exercise our bodies to prevent atrophy. While our consciousness is unified and our psyche is regulated, each Immortal retains a portion of independent thought to self-administer bodily requirements."

Vant was impressed. Disgusted, but impressed. He climbed a flight of stairs parallel to the glass channels, taking it all in. He paused at an Immortal hovering in a quadrant quarantined by sectional dividers. She was delicate, like a wilted piece of paper. Her fingers looked like deflated balloons and her head was pointed in the wrong direction.

"What's with this one?" Vant asked.

"Faulty hardware has resulted in a miscalculation of atmospheric pressure. The equipment is under repair and the Immortal will soon return to full functionality."

Either that, Vant thought, *or this was attempted suicide. A tedious, self-administered execution carried out over hundreds of years.* Vant—who had been tortured, abused, and killed in a myriad of ways—felt nauseated at the idea of this endurance test of self-destruction.

"Quite an operation you've got here," he said. "Most impressive swimming pool I've ever seen."

"Let us proceed."

Vant continued his walk from one end of the habitat to the other. All the while, not one of the Immortals took their goggled eyes off of him.

At the far side of the expansive chamber, a cargo door lifted.

Vant and the soldiers entered the armory.

An enormous quantity of thallium exo-suits stood lifeless. Their casings were empty of liquid filling and missing their helmets. They were organized with precision, stored in symmetrical rows. Ultraviolet light glinted off their superbly constructed shells.

Vant approached the front lines and poked his head into the neck-hole of a suit. It was hollow. No controls, no mechanics... nothing. Vant turned his gaze upward to intertwining rubber tubes dangling from the rafters above the armor. Several dripped moisture onto the steel floor, their purpose clear: to fill the suits with The Immortals' treated liquid concoction.

Vant surmised that indoctrinated Immortals were inserted into the casings, and they used their thoughts to send impulses to power the currents within. This would move the thallium suits, similar to how they manipulated their movements inside the liquid pipelines. It made sense why the protective shells appeared devoid of humanoid assistance in Land Escape; Vant had overlooked the tiny Immortal that would have been controlling the suit from inside the helmet.

"Our protection," the voice said.

"Your army," Vant responded.

With the security detail in tow, Vant entered a mechanical foundry.

"These machines sustain our infrastructure," the voice said. Assembly lines of robotic arms were constructing suits of armor, polishing glass panels for the liquid highway, cutting rubber tubes, and assembling looping pieces of material with the same properties as the massive hose that had sucked up the people of Land Escape. Vant also noticed Corpo-Bots zipping in and out of a small hole in the roof, arriving with raw materials and presumably departing for more.

Continuing through a water-treatment area, Vant observed automated laboratory setups mixing chemicals and pumping them into the liquid. One particular machine stood out; it churned a thick, soupy pool of organic material—perhaps the "nutrients" of which the voice had spoken.

"This concludes the walkthrough."

Vant knew an underground stronghold containing a thousand captives lay beneath his feet. *Guess that's not something worth seeing,* he thought with sarcasm. In a similar vein, he noticed one final cargo door at the far end of the foundry, secured with more protective measures than the rest.

"What about you?" Vant asked. "When do I get to meet you?"

"We are a unified consciousness."

Vant coughed the word *bullshit,* then added, "You said your psyche is regulated, so someone has to be adjusting the dials. Oh, and back in the lobby, you were giving orders to your shiny soldiers. Proof of a hierarchy, if I've ever seen one."

Silence.

"Come on. You can't fool me. I've been around the block a few times."

Then:

"Aren't you clever," the voice spoke. With those words, the façade was finally dropped.

"I can smell a dictator a mile away," Vant said. "Open that door and let's meet face to face."

"No man has ever laid eyes on our eldest Immortals."

"I'm more than a man."

"So you say."

Locks unlatched. Motors whirred. Sensors disabled. The final cargo door lifted.

Vant entered.

He descended into a glass tunnel. Water surrounded him on all sides; it was a habitat like an elaborate aquarium. Within the liquid were hundreds of decrepit humans—if they could even be called that. Their deteriorated bodies ranged in size, though none was larger than an infant. All were saggy. Wrinkled. Many lacked key appendages. Unlike those in the main area, these Immortals existed without goggles and breathers. Decades of submersion must have allowed them to adapt for survival in the liquid formula without mechanical assistance.

Vant proceeded down the aquatic tunnel and continued to eyeball the ancient Immortals. One of the beings was missing half of its body. Another's phallic part unceremoniously broke off and floated away. Yet another's noodle-like arm had somehow ended up in its own mouth and was halfway down into its transparent belly. Each one was more pathetic than the next.

Vant arrived at the end of the corridor. He exited the glass passageway and paced to the far reaches of the chamber.

A fifty-foot pod stood at the apex. It was filled with The Immortals' liquid concoction, yet was seemingly vacant. It was isolated from the other quadrants, save for one pipeline connecting it to the elders' tank. While mostly glass, it appeared to be impregnable. Dozens of rubber tubes ran from the back of the pod into the floor and walls, like dreadlocks of piping.

"Approach," the synthesized voice said, "and greet your Overlord."

Vant moved closer. There *was* something in the tank. Something floating. Something the size of a nectarine.

A foot from the glass, Vant understood what it was.

It was a head.

A shriveled head, more resembling a fetus than an elder. Its eyes were concave, sunken into its forehead. A skin-sealed mouth had taken on the look of a grimace, frozen into position from a vast number of years without use. Dangling from the bottom of the head were fine strands of tissue, like hair, hinting at where a body was once attached.

"I look forward to studying you," said The Overlord, clearly the source of the synthesized speech. It somehow transmitted the voice through its thoughts, as, even when speaking, its permanent scowl never changed. "You, my fascinating new specimen."

Acidic bile rose up into Vant's trachea and he was overcome by nausea. "I'm sorry," he said, "it's just that you're horribly ugly. I don't mean to be rude. But you're vile."

"Appearances are trifles."

"No, see, you don't understand. You're *hideous*. I can't believe I'm not puking. The fact that I'm not is a compliment. You're welcome, actually."

"You will see things differently when unified with my consciousness. As all do. As all will."

"What do you mean, 'all?'"

"This world requires unification. I shall make it so."

A floor-to-ceiling panel slid open, revealing a gigantic, panoramic window. Behind the glass lay the vastness of the ocean—the chamber they were in was below the surface. Beams of sunlight cut through the salty waters and towers of kelp ebbed with the currents.

"Great view," Vant said. "Corner office is the way to go."

A school of fish nibbling on a pocket of coral merged into a formation and swam up to the glass. They stared at Vant, as The Immortals had done in the liquid highways, and as the Immortal elders were doing now.

"How are you doing that?" Vant asked. "Your chemically treated fluid?"

"Yes."

"You're dumping it into the ocean?"

"Yes."

"So the water in this fortress, it connects you to the water out there?"

"Yes."

"In an evil plot to control the tuna?"

The school of fish smashed into the glass. Their faces flattened and their bodies bent, killing them instantly. They sank to the ocean floor.

"In a quest to control *everything*," The Overlord said. "This planet is predominantly water. I shall modify its entire supply and, as a result, dominate everything alive. Life shall have a unified consciousness. A single consciousness. Mine."

"Impossible. To treat all of the water in the ocean, that would take an eternity," Vant said.

"An eternity is something I have."

"You'd have to surround everything on the surface with water."

The thallium soldiers symbolically stood at attention. Vant understood the implication; inside their armor, The Overlord's concoction surrounded the beings, thus controlling them.

"Those connected in my waterways keep my mind fresh. Organic material harnessed from the living sustains my physical form. And you... you will provide me with the key to regeneration. Thanks to you, I shall repair my body and continue to extend my reach."

"Sounds like a plan," Vant said. "I'm on board."

"You are *not*."

Vant swallowed.

"You have brought me nothing but lies alongside your special ability. You forget, I possess the capability to monitor bodily functions. I can see inside of you and detect when your heart rate elevates. I know when you are not being truthful. When you are *lying*."

Vant tried to wrest control of his heartbeat to hide it from The Overlord. Doing so was impossible.

"I know that woman was not your wife. I know you have another purpose for being here. None of this is of my concern. All that matters to me is your everlasting life—the one thing you *have* been truthful about."

Vant stared out the window into the sea, wondering how far The Overlord's grip already stretched.

"Like everything which crosses my path, I regard you merely as a specimen. One whose attributes are to be studied, learned from, and harnessed. There is no hope for you, other than what I make for you. You belong to me, now. Your choice is not whether or not you wish to help me fulfill my purpose. It is whether or not you wish to be a lab rat. Your choice is between cooperation... and dissection."

Vant's plan was unraveling. Besides The Overlord's detection of his deception, he was supposed to have received a signal by now. His troupe had discussed a gunshot, a cannon, or some sort of earth-shaking force to let him know they were out there. While they had not calculated the signal to the minute, they had planned for enough of a buffer to grant plenty of time. By this point, the milestone had long since passed. Something must have happened to his friends. To his compatriots.

No help was coming.

Time for Plan B, he thought. *I'll have to wing it. Once again, 'The Vant Special.'*

He picked truthful words while simultaneously maintaining the charade. He knew his pulse would rise with one false phrase, so he chose his words with care:

"I don't wish to be dissected."

"Excellent choice."

"I made a discovery."

"Go on."

"I found something in the desert, in the middle of nowhere. An artifact with supernatural powers."

"An artifact?"

"A mask. It does incredible things."

Doing good, Vant thought. *So far, no lies.*

"Where is this mask?"

"In storage with Corpo. If you let me use a bot, I'll get it for you."

"Do so." Vant noticed the wretched head bobbing in the water, excited. "Corpo-Bots make their deliveries in the foundry. Access one. Bring this artifact to me."

"Roger that, big guy."

Vant passed through the aquarium of Immortal elders and exited the habitat. Although he was in great peril, he was not afraid for himself. His thoughts drifted to Skii, and to his other companions. He was worried he had sent them to their doom.

He entered the foundry and located the Corpo-Bots dutifully zipping in and out of the small opening in the roof. He approached a docked bot.

"Hi," Vant said. It chirped an acknowledgement. "Need my satchel, please."

The bot chirped cheerfully and launched out of the skylight.

Vant used the time to survey his surroundings. Besides the five thallium soldiers keeping watch over him, there were no other identifiable defenses in the compound. No turrets, alarms, motion sensors, or any other protective measures. Of course, there was the armory; if The Immortals managed to activate even a handful of additional soldiers, he would be subdued, and fast.

Shoom.

Minutes later, the Corpo-Bot returned and docked into kiosk-mode. It chirped politely and opened a storage compartment, revealing Vant's satchel.

"Thanks," he said.

His adrenaline boosted. Head spun. Fingers itched. Heart raced.

This is it...

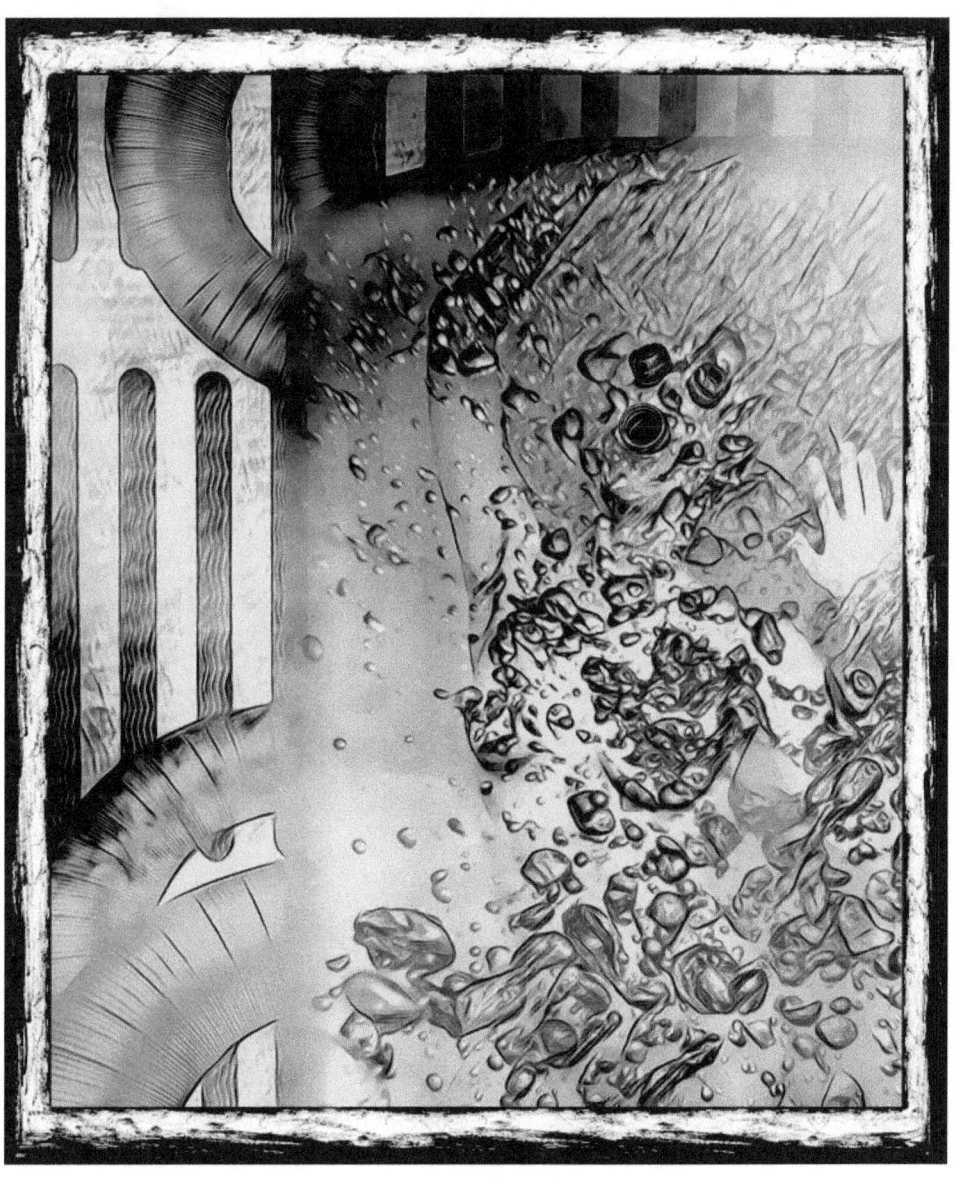

"You will enter into another union... a permanent
union with The Immortals."

- The Overlord

222 YEARS PRIOR

Of Iron and Lead

Steel clashed with steel. Lashes flew. Wails accompanied every bashed jaw, every shattered ribcage, every dented skull.

Vant, too, screamed. Screamed with the agony of splitting apart his friends.

One by one, every Knight fell to Vant Hu'l. Every Knight, but one.

"Drop your weapons." Vant said, sucking air.

Terrii's trembling rage became the cold shakes of defeat. He had underestimated Vant's sheer talent as a warrior and had sent the Knights of Rights to their deaths. Vant had defeated Terrii's army. Vant was *an army.*

Vant wiped a sleeve across his face, making a skin-colored streak in the coat of blood. "I'm smarter than you, Terrii. I'm faster than you. I designed the very weapons in your hands. You cannot defeat me. Drop your weapons."

Terrii's gauntlets clunked to the floor.

Vant dropped his, as well.

Shyyla held Vant from behind, her body pressed into his back.

"Thank you, my friend," Vant said to Terrii, in exhaustion. "It's over."

"Yes, Vant." Terrii removed a concealed handgun from his cloak.

"It is."

He cocked the hammer back.

Vant closed his eyes.

Terrii pulled the trigger.

The bullet cut through Vant's heart.

The same bullet, in its trajectory, exited his back.

And pushed through Shyyla's skull.

"I've stood against worse."

- Vant Hu'l

CHAPTER 19

The Commander and the Corrupt

Vant dove into his satchel, drew out a flare gun, and fired a shot through the Corpo-Bot access in the roof. He slapped on Death's mask and activated his whip gauntlets.

"Deceiver!" came the voice of the Immortal Overlord.

The thallium soldiers charged.

Vant loosed his whips and toggled on the weapon's upgrades. Lightning spilled from the gauntlets' knuckles and crackled down the lashes.

He whipped a soldier across the face and another across the chest. Blue arcs blasted over their armor and engulfed them in a storm of electricity. They crumbled to the floor, convulsing in overload.

Another soldier lunged. Vant sidestepped and whipped it around the torso, sending thousands of amps into its thallium frame. It thrashed from the electrical reaction as its insides cooked. Vant tightened the slack and flung it into the remaining soldiers. They collided, creating an explosion of kinetic discharge.

Vant blinked at the sizzling pileup of armor, then looked at his weapons. "Not bad," he said. "Oh, who am I kidding? That was *stellar!*"

"Foolish terrorist!" screamed The Overlord. "What do you hope to gain from this outburst?"

"You're overdue for an appointment with my boss."

"I control an army with my will! You dare stand against me?"

"I've stood against worse."

Within the armory, dangling hoses spurted liquid into the headless exo-suits. Once a suit was full, *plop,* an Immortal dropped like a bowel movement into the neck hole. A robotic arm then bonded the helmet to its armor and the newly functioning soldier sprinted into the foundry. Seven approached fast.

I have to preserve my energy, Vant thought. *Have to stay alive as long as I can.*

He latched his whips to a hunk of assembly equipment and pulled tight. The gauntlet thrusters roared as the gear bent, buckled, then snapped. The pylon flew overhead and careened into the soldiers.

It was a solid move, but the situation was dire and it had only begun. Ten more soldiers replaced the fallen ones. Batons slid out from their wrists as they streamed into the foundry.

Vant eviscerated two with electrified lashes, but the other eight closed the gap. His whips were useless at close range—he zipped them back into the gauntlets and blocked the solders' baton swings. He jabbed the helmet of one and dented another with an uppercut—but one from behind got a fist full of cloak. Vant tumbled to the ground.

From the floor, he defended himself with iron fists as batons struck out from every direction. They ignited on his knuckles with vaporous discharge.

One arm pinned.

But Vant kept fighting—

Two arms pinned. Then his legs.

He thrashed with defiance.

A thallium boot pressed down on his chest, securing him.

A soldier's arm cocked back, raising a baton.

"It is time to put this rat in its cage—" said The Overlord, "—forever."

BAH-DOOM!

An explosion rocked the fortress.

The environment shook.

The thallium soldiers halted, confused.

The smoke cleared, revealing a hole in the fortress wall.

And in the center of the breach, was a man.

He shouted:

"Fuck-fuck flies are about to die!"

Ranchula tore into the fortress, a smoking bazooka in one hand and a four-sided axe in the other.

His tribe of nomad hunters followed after him, stampeding into the foundry. They unloaded automatic weapons on the soldiers surrounding Vant. Their shots punctured thallium armor and water, like crystal blood, leaked from the bullet holes.

"Eat the dick! Eat the dick!" Ranchula growled from his scarred face. Swings of his axe gashed the helmets of the last remaining soldiers and pulverized the tiny Immortals inside.

The foundry was secure. Vant leapt up and bolted toward the armory.

"What the shit? Where's my thank-you?" said Ranchula.

"Give me a second!" Vant got to the other end of the room and whipped the cargo door. He pulled hard, sliding it manually downward. "Hold them off!" he shouted. Ranchula relayed the order to his tribe and they opened fire on the thallium soldiers behind the door.

A guttural wail came from Vant's lungs as he drove the gauntlets' thrusters—and his muscles—to their limits. The gate moved inch by inch as more and more soldiers fell to the nomads' weapons.

"Fuck-fucks about to come through!" Ranchula shouted. "Hurry that skinny ass!"

A final tug and the door sealed. A handful of soldiers slammed into it from the other side.

Vant struck the door's control panel with his electrified whips, short-circuiting it. "That should buy us some time," he said, sprinting toward Ranchula.

The chieftain slapped his hands on Vant's shoulders and smiled, showing off his blotchy teeth. Then he head-butted Vant. "Good to see you, smart face!" Vant shook off the "affectionate" greeting as Ranchula added, "Got a message for you. From General Grammie."

"*General* Grammie?"

"He says you know where my stolen spiders be. Where my people at?"

Vant had been right; the thallium helmet Grammie had stolen from the nomad's stockpile hinted at Ranchula's past. He had, in fact, seen this army years ago—they were the ones who had hijacked his tribe.

"They're here," Vant said. "Fight with me and you'll get them back."

"I'll fight with you. I'll squash with the undead warrior who comes back to life. But first... how you did that trick? I killed you dead, but here you are, with your balls and everything!" He bluffed a grab at Vant's crotch—Vant covered up. The tribe guffawed.

"Spider! We got shit comin'! Listen! Listen!" said Ranchula's wiry huntress, Widow.

There was commotion behind the cargo door. Using the inky infrared of Death's mask, Vant peered into the armory. Grips of soldiers beat against the door, and even more were coming online.

"More of those things are on the way," said Vant. "Every second we wait means more we'll have to deal with."

"Can I help?" a voice came from outside the hole in the fortress wall. "Ho, there, Vant Hu'l."

"Saamii Fraam!"

The kind-eyed civilian entered the foundry. He walked slowly, weighed down by a repurposed Land Escape turret strapped to his body along with a backpack of ammunition. Vant pulled off Death's mask and sprinted toward him.

"Many thanks for saving my wife," Saamii said.

"Least I could do."

"One thing, though. Not that I'm complaining—and please know that I'm very, *very* appreciative—but, see... Laam can't remember me. And she thinks... *you're* her husband?"

"Ha!" Vant punched Saamii collegially in the arm—who buckled from the force of the iron glove. "Sorry, friend. Had to borrow your name. It's a long story. Don't worry, she'll remember you soon enough."

Saamii smiled. "I've got a present for you." He strapped a wrist-communicator to Vant's gauntlet.

"Vant here. Come in."

"Vant, my cherished companion! It's so greatly good to hear your voice!"

"Well if it isn't *General* Grammie!"

"How do you like your army of ferocious fighting nomads? You winning the war down there or what?"

"We need more men. Come on in, the water's warm."

"What a generous invitation! Though I must politely decline. I'm quite satisfied watching from afar, protected by my loyal band of Land Escapers! After all, we can't allow anything bad to happen to our general, now, can we?"

"How many troops are with you?"

"Forty—well, forty-and-a-half, if you count Doubleya. Forty of Land Escape's finest!" Vant heard them cheer at Grammie's words. He was a natural. But a natural *what?*

"I also have twenty folks here for support and medical assistance," Grammie said, "but they're not fighters."

"Send in the infantry. All forty."

"Ten are my personal bodyguards. I can't spare 'em. They stay put."

There was no time to argue. "Send in thirty. But if I call for the others, you damn well better oblige."

"No promises! What's the point of a battle if no one's alive to profit from it? Good luck, my cherished! Win us some spoils!"

The Land Escape reinforcements entered the foundry. Three more, like Saamii, were outfitted as walking turrets. Vant recognized Jiino, an ally crucial to the rebuilding of Land Escape; Lyyra, who had assisted Skii with the bank break-in; and several other familiar faces.

The nomads traded out the civilians' pistols for burly assault weapons, safeties toggled off. The pounding of the door continued; every thud on the barrier caused a fearful twitch in the Land Escape troops, who were virgins to battle. Their firearms quivered in their hands.

Vant ordered, "Turrets! You're in the corners for support fire only! Crossfire is your deadliest enemy—kill one of our own, and I'll kill you myself! Land Escapers! You're in the back! Form a wedge of protection. That's our safe zone for escape cover!"

There was no part of Vant that would allow himself to stand anywhere but on the front lines. He took point and commanded, "Spiders, fall into a diagonal formation behind me! Bolt rifles in the front to stun them, assault weapons in the back to shred them!" The nomad hunters formed a line, staggering themselves and training their barrels at the cargo door. "Check your sights! Shoot straight! Ranchula, you're up here with me!"

"Where the fuck you think I was gonna be?" He and Widow joined Vant at the head of the pack.

The Immortal Overlord spoke: "Like a virus, you have multiplied. I now address the new arrivals. If you seek death, then resist. I shall use your bodies as nutrition. If you seek life, then submit. I shall grant you the peace that comes from eternal subservience."

The voice rattled the already nervous troops.

One of the Land Escapers panicked.

And fled.

Vant had to boost morale before he lost any others. He looked at them, these people who had come to support him, to fight with him, and to follow his lead. For the first time in centuries, Vant found himself leading an army.

And he wanted a fierce one.

It was time for the battle speech.

He looked at his troops.

They looked at him.

He cleared his throat.

And said:

"Pile 'em up!"

The troops cheered.

"Damn good speech," said Ranchula.

The door caved in. Thallium soldiers poured into the foundry.

Vant dealt overhand strikes from his lightning-charged whips. Ranchula hacked away at anything metal. Widow threw razor-like daggers with terrifying accuracy into helmets.

The infantry held their triggers down and pelted the soldiers with artillery. Bolt rifles electrified conductive armor and bullets ate away at their casings.

But the thallium soldiers were tough. Damn tough. They pressed hard against the onslaught and broke off to the sides to avoid direct fire, converging upon the troops on the front lines. Vant threw himself into a skirmish, parrying baton attacks to protect three overrun nomads. Two of them scrambled to safety but the third—a lunatic with a death wish—fought back. He unholstered a hand cannon and unloaded shots at point-blank range into thallium helmets, creating liquid eruptions where their faces should have been. The nomad took out four soldiers, but the remaining two landed baton strikes, caving in his skull and breaking his back.

Vant retaliated. His punch broke the arm off a suit of armor, emptying it of its fluid. A second blow crushed another soldier's helmet—he heard a tiny Immortal's death rattle from inside the casing.

A turret fired—*thip-thip-thip*—and bullets whizzed past Vant's head. They cut holes through a thallium soldier who had snuck into his perimeter. The suit of armor collapsed. Vant waved *thanks* to Saamii, who saluted back.

Vant scanned the battle.

Close to thirty thallium soldiers were down. Forty were fighting in the foundry. Fifty more were coming online in the armory. Their activation rates were far surpassing the speed at which Vant and his forces could take them out.

"Spiders!" Vant shouted, "Pull your weapons from the doors and concentrate on the hostiles inside! Turrets! Relocate to protect the wedge!"

The troops shifted positions, falling back. Most made it to safety, but several fell to batons.

Ranchula pulled his axe from the leaking chest of a soldier and pointed it at Vant. "Zombie fuck! Make a plan or die!"

Vant shoved the axe away from his face. "That's not helping! I have to go through the armory. There's a room on the other side where these things live. I have to shut them down at the source!"

"Get gone! Squash your flies!"

But Vant had no way to reach the liquid highways. Thallium soldiers kept piling into the foundry, and even more were on the way within the armory. Vant strained his brain for ideas.

Nothing came to mind. Not a damn thing.

Twenty soldiers charged. The turrets gave them everything they had, but the opposition was too great. After two impacted nomad heads and a Land Escaper's snapped spine, Vant was in a fistfight with ten foes. He acted with pure instinct, letting his combat training take over.

Right cross. Uppercut. One-two combo. Floor-slide. Parry, parry, parry.

He felt his energy slipping away. The breath in his lungs thinned. His strikes became slower. Weaker.

Jab-jab-jab. Backhand. Parry. Parry—

A soldier grabbed him from behind, locking up his arms. Vant lifted his legs and kicked an incoming foe in the chest. He pointed his gauntlets down, activated the thrusters, and let go. They launched into the grappler's feet, flattening them. Water emptied from the split metal—the soldier released its grip. And collapsed.

Vant slipped the gauntlets back on as three batons flew at him. He raised his weapons to defend, blocking all but one, which clobbered his chest and laid him out. Desperate, he risked electrocution by swinging a whip in a circle over his head. The lashes struck thallium and the soldiers fell.

Vant tried to recover the wind knocked out of him as he surveyed the blurry battlefield...

Five of the armored demons converged on an outnumbered nomad and pulled his body apart. A Land Escape woman dove in to protect an ally and got her face bashed in. Jiino unloaded a hailstorm of bullets into an enemy wrapped around his waist as two more approached from the rear. A metal boot crushed the head of a fallen nomad. One room over, a stream of Immortals dropped from tubes into armor.

Hopeless.

Totally hopeless.

But then...

"What the crappin' butt is going on here?!"

A blur of blue and copper dropped from the Corpo-Bot canopy into the center of the skirmish.

"Skii!" Vant sprinted to her, dodging several soldiers. He shoved her behind cover as a nomad tossed a grenade. It detonated, sending shrapnel flying.

Vant hugged her. She flicked him on the forehead of the mask. "Cut that out, creepy face!"

Ranchula noticed them sharing a moment. He shouted, "Fuck her hello! Real man fucks a girl hello!"

They ignored him. Vant said, "It's good to see you, kid."

"You too, Pops. What a mess!"

"We're overrun—" a flying baton nailed a Land Escaper in the neck, laying him out, "—and we're outmatched. We need to regroup."

"I've got friends on the way. We just gotta sit tight. Plus..." she cocked her shotgun, "...Cassidy's hungry."

She fired a burst of energy under her feet to launch into the air. Mid-arc, she cocked the gun several more times to charge it and landed a few feet from the collapsed cargo door leading to the armory. Repulser blasts shockwaved from Cassidy into the soldiers. Their armor splintered at the seams and slammed into the walls and floor.

"Here's your problem," she shouted so Ranchula could overhear. "You brought a spider to the fight. What you needed was a *bear!*"

Handfuls of soldiers replaced those fallen, but Cassidy's discharges toppled groups at a time. They kept coming, but Skii kept dishing out punishment.

Vant latched onto an overhang above the doorway and pulled himself below it. "Skii!" he shouted. She used Cassidy to boost herself upward; Vant whipped her around the midsection and dangled her above the threshold.

As the soldiers entered the foundry, she fired blasts straight down, flattening them with direct impacts. Over and over they filed in. Over and over she crushed them into a mess of debris, liquid, and chunks of dead Immortal.

The counterattack bought enough time for Ranchula's hunters to secure the foundry.

They cheered for Skii.

Vant looked into the armory—his heart leapt into his throat. He flung Skii away from the door, put himself in front of her, and shouted to the others, "Get down! Take cover!"

One hundred newly activated soldiers fired batons at the wall that separated the armory from the foundry. The combined steam-powered explosions crumbled the divider. Now with plenty of room to enter, they stormed into the foundry while another fifty came online and took aim with their batons.

"Skii?" Vant said.

"On it! Time to growl, Cassidy!" Skii held down the shotgun slider. A blue glow appeared on the barrel along with an ascending charge sound. She squeezed the trigger.

A burst of sapphire energy encapsulated Vant and Skii as a hailstorm of batons flew into the foundry. Several exploded on the repulser shield, but many more tagged the human fighters behind them.

Skii shouted into her wrist-communicator, "Where's my damn backup? We need you now!" Cassidy's shield began sputtering out. "Now, now, now!"

A voice from the other end said, "Don't get yer panties in a pinch, li'l lady! You'll get a rash! Here comes the cavalry! *Yip-yip-yip!*"

Ten mechanical beasts careened into the foundry from the hole in the fortress wall. Metal clashed with thallium as the Peace-Keepers, led by The Mayor of Crash Town, blitzed the army. Their robotic arms swatted at the soldiers and their shoulder-mounted cannons spat armor-piercing bullets.

"You did it, Skii!" Vant exclaimed. "You actually did it!"

"Damn right, I did!"

The shrill racket of metal thrashing metal was so overpowering that Vant had to yell into his comm, "Well, if it isn't The Mayor himself!"

"Vant, m'boy! Still dumpin' shit on every township ya come across, I see!"

"I never thought I'd say these words, but *damn* it's good to see you!"

"*Hyick!* Well, here we are! Me'n the Peace-Keepers are loaded up on uppers and we're ready fer a thrashin'! My pecker's gettin' slurped on as we speak, jest ta keep my nerves nice'n calm! Now quit yer yappin' and go rescue yer folks! These li'l gnats just met a coupla' big ol' flyswatters!"

The Mayor scooped up three soldiers in each fist and clenched, spraying water and chunks of Immortal into the air. He winged the lifeless thallium suits into the armory, smashing a dozen more.

Vant gazed downward, using the power of the mask. A thousand Land Escape and nomad prisoners were beneath his feet, but he had no idea how to get to them.

"Mayor, I need a way into the catacombs below!"

The Mayor sprinted to Vant's position and unloaded artillery into the ground. The bullets created a dent, then a crater, then a hole.

Skii shoved Vant out of the way. "Ladies first, Pops. *Always* ladies first." She hopped in, using Cassidy to slow her descent.

"Hold this," Vant said to The Mayor as he wrapped a whip around the robot's finger. He loosened the slack to lower himself down. The Mayor let go when Vant hit the end of the coil—he landed on his ass. Skii tittered at his misfortune and helped him up.

Her laughter was cut short once they took in their surroundings:

Rows upon rows of naked, hairless hostages were submerged in a water tank—a massive, liquid prison. Harnesses held the prisoners stationary, and goggles and breathing apparatuses were fastened to their faces.

The captives were mid-assimilation into The Overlord's consciousness and in the process of adapting to the underwater conditions. Yet they were still *them*. Death's mask revealed their true nature: innocent, non-corrupted, and resisting forced indoctrination.

"Look..." Skii pointed to a massive container that funneled into a grinder. Within the receptacle was a mixture of flesh: human corpses, fish, animals, and most likely the remains of the Land Escape graveyard sucked up during the raid. The top layer of people, naked, soiled, and intertwined, appeared to be alive—barely. Vant drew the conclusion that the live subjects were those The Immortals deemed rejects for whatever reason. Inferior specimens? Or, perhaps, they were superior. So much so that they outright rejected assimilation.

The grinder led into a churning soup of biological matter. The processed concoction fed into the pipelines. "Nutrients for The Immortals," Vant said.

Skii looked away. "You really know how to sniff out the horrendous, don't you, Pops?"

Vant peered through the mask at the innocents in captivity, their life forces flowing naturally, harmlessly. He then glanced up toward the battle, witnessing the mess of chaos and violence spasming like manic fireworks. The Immortals were so corrupt and committed to their way of life that they had inflicted their will upon others. The Overlord was brainwashing them, stripping them of their humanity, using them, and grinding up the rejects to be used as food.

All for one reason: to keep on ticking, no matter the cost.

Vant looked into the farthest reaches of the basement and identified the mammoth-sized hose that had been used to suck up the citizens of Land Escape—and the nomads before it. It would most certainly be used again, if The Overlord were allowed to continue the quest for planetary domination.

"Over here!" Skii fiddled with a hydrant. "Help me with this!"

Vant snapped to. He pummeled the regulator with a gauntlet and the water level of the tank began dropping.

From his wrist-comm, The Mayor shouted, "Vant! Git yer ass up here! We got a situation, son!"

"Skii, it's up to you. You have to get these people out."

"There's a thousand of them! Maybe more! How?"

Vant spoke into his comm, "Grammie! You there?"

"Here!"

"Don't argue with me. Send in the ten reinforcements to help Skii with the evac."

"But they're my personal bodyguards! If you take them, I'll be all alone! Then who will laugh at my jokes?"

"Grammie, if you don't send them in *right now,* when this is all over, I'm giving Death a freebie."

A pause. "You drive a hard bargain, comrade. They're on their way."

"Tell them to go straight to the catacombs. Saamii, you there?"

"Here, Vant!"

"Guard the hole for the incoming troops. Move any active turrets to that position."

"Right!"

To Skii: "I'm outta here. You got this? Once they're out of the water, you'll have to wake them up. Pull off their breathers and goggles. They'll be disoriented—"

"Just get upstairs and finish those monsters off!"

"On it!"

Saamii and Jiino were damaged, ravaged, and soaked with crystalline blood. Yet they relocated their turrets and laid down a covering fire for the reinforcements sliding down a rope into the catacombs.

Vant climbed back up and returned to the battlefield.

The situation was horrid. Two Peace-Keepers had been taken out, overrun by thallium soldiers. The nomads and Land Escapers were halved in numbers. Vant's army was scrambling for survival.

"If ya got a plan, son, now's the time!" the Mayor barked at Vant, over his own gunfire.

"You've got to get me through the armory. They have no defenses in there. They'll be easy pickings."

"Hoss-Hoss!" The Mayor called out to one of his flock. "Wanna go fer a stroll?"

"Shit-chyeah!" he answered.

Vant turned, recognizing a droopy-faced nomad from his encounter with Ranchula's tribe outside of Crash Town. "Shavious! Got any grenades?"

"Two left. Make 'em count." He handed the orbs to Vant, who pocketed them in his cloak.

"Mayor, you ready?"

"Ready as a cleanie-weenie in a whorehouse!"

The Peace-Keepers rushed full tilt into the armory. Vant trailed the metal beasts as they steamrolled through a tidal wave of thallium. Running with their robotic heads down, they threw arms and elbows at every soldier in their way.

Vant stole a glance over his shoulder. Near a hundred soldiers were on his ass. He increased his speed as armor flew above him, around him, and to the sides from the Peace-Keepers' avalanche-like charge.

They reached the end of the armory. The Mayor and Hoss-Hoss barreled through the cargo door and about-faced to fight off the impending forces—but the thallium soldiers disengaged once Vant and his squad hit the room. They turned their attention back to the foundry.

"What the heck?" said The Mayor. "How'd ya know they'd do that?"

"I didn't," Vant said.

"Holy moly, guacamole!" The Mayor bellowed at the sight of the Immortals floating in the glass pipelines. "Ugly sonbitches! I know I ain't much ta look at, but these li'l goobers take the cake!"

Hoss-Hoss, from his remote cockpit hundreds of miles away in Crash Town, spoke to someone else in the room with him: "Naw, honey, it ain't you. You're doin' fine. These disgusting grubs just make my constitution soft, that's all."

Every goggled eye was upon them. "They're lookin' at us, Vant," The Mayor whispered. "Creeeepy."

Vant said, "If stares are their only line of defense, we're in good shape. Let's take 'em down."

All lingering doubts about committing mass genocide disappeared when, through Death's mask, Vant saw the turbulent red shapes of The Immortals. These were not people; they were too far gone. They were violent. They were indoctrinated. They were corrupt. And each of them—each and every one—had been marked for elimination by Death.

Vant charged his gauntlets and cocked his arm back. The Mayor and Hoss-Hoss spun the barrels of their gatling guns and took aim.

"Your forces are all but destroyed," said the voice of The Immortal Overlord. "I suppose I should thank you for bringing them to me. They will provide me with excellent nutrition. As for you, Vant..."

There was a strange hiss—the sound of water traveling through a contained space. The black rubber tubes that ran across the floor were expanding. Filling.

"It will be easier to study you in pieces. You squirm too much."

The hoses broke loose and shot upright, twisting like snakes. Their nozzles aimed at Vant and the Peace-Keepers.

"Ah, hell!" Vant dove away from the rubber serpents.

They spat pressurized streams of acid.

The beams of liquid exploded into clouds of mist on the wall behind him, leaving seared, wet holes.

The goggled eyes of The Immortals continued to track him.

The Mayor and Hoss-Hoss tried to flee, but they had nowhere to go. Acid blasted the machines. Chunks of metal dislodged, circuitry melted, and both robots collapsed into malfunctioning heaps.

"Sonofanasstickle!" The Mayor shouted. "I'm done for!"

"Shit on a shitter! So am I!" said Hoss-Hoss.

Dodging to escape a close call put Vant face-to-face with the gleaming nozzle of a writhing hose. It spat as he flung himself behind the collapsed shell of The Mayor, taking cover. The snakes congregated and spewed liquid ammunition at the wreckage.

"Vant..." The Mayor's voice crackled through the speaker in the Peace-Keeper's broken head. "I'm toast, li'l buddy. I can't... I can't hang on no longer. This is the end... for The Great Mayor... of Crash Town."

"How can you die? You're hundreds of miles away."

"Oh, shit, yer right! *Hyick!*" The Mayor laughed at his own prank. "Guess I'll jest have ta pull one of my backup machines out from storage! Now git outta here and finish the job! Mayor signin' off! My fightin' may be done, but my cockle's ready fer fun!"

Vant knocked twice on The Mayor's busted head to confirm completion of the conversation.

The snake-like hoses dripped acid. Vant needed reinforcements. He was pinned down. Trapped.

"Skii!" he yelled into his wrist-comm.

"Kind of busy at the moment!"

Next idea: "Ranchula, come in!"

"Fuck you!"

"Saamii?" Nothing. "Jiino? Anyone?"

He was answered only by the sounds of battle.

He was out of options.

Wait... Vant thought. *No, I'm not. There's one left.*

"Grammie, you read me?"

"Here, comrade."

"I need our remaining half-a-man."

A pause.

"He's no soldier. He doesn't know where he is most of the time. He's currently snorting ants."

"Shit!" An acid spike drilled through Vant's metal protection and sliced a gash in his side. His nerves hollered out from the sting.

"Listen to me, damn you! Send him in the front door!"

"But—"

"*Do it!*"

"Okay... okay. He's on his way. This is on you. I take no responsibility for the consequences."

Vant abandoned his fortification and rushed through The Immortals' environment, winding around the glass pipeline. The snakes hissed steam and spat acid at him. Liquid projectiles burst at his feet.

From behind, a snake capitalized on a moment of Vant's unsure footing. A water stream cut into his shoulder, sending him into a roll down a flight of stairs. He allowed his body to go limp to lessen the damage. At the base of the steps, he righted himself and forced his body to push on, avoiding more hydrous projectiles.

Nearing the entryway portal, Vant pulled the pin from a grenade and tossed it. A fiery explosion knocked the divider off its hinges. He pushed a gauntlet forward and plowed fist-first into the barricade, collapsing it into the atrium. A second well-placed grenade blasted the front door open, letting in the sunlight...

...and a schizophrenic lunatic.

"You asked me to come, so I came! Happy to do so! After all, we're consenting adults."

"Doublya, I need you to use your magic."

"They say *all* life is magic. I say, the people who say that should be flayed."

"You're not hearing me. Everyone is going to die!"

"Well, then they should have eaten more carrots!"

Vant brought The World's Worst Magician in close and looked deep into his eyes. "Please hear me. I'm going to take you into the fortress. You and your friends are going to be killed unless you do magic. A thousand lives are on the line. Do you understand me?"

The magician sighed. "When I kill hundreds of men and you only kill twelve, what the hell am I paying you for? Seriously."

He whistled a sarcastic tune and sauntered into the sanctuary.

The floating Immortals pivoted to look at their new guest. The snake-like hoses aimed in his direction.

Vant recoiled, tensed, and mentally prepared to be shredded.

"I didn't want to say anything," The World's Worst Magician spoke to the goggle-eyed goblins, "but when I'm fully erect and you just stand there watching, well, you're sort of acting like pervs."

They remained fixated on him.

He walked, pausing at a particularly decrepit Immortal. "You've probably heard this before—I know I sure have—but your ding-dong shows though those invisible clothes."

The Immortal Overlord spoke: "This ends now. You shall not take what is rightfully mine. These bodies belong to *me*. They are mine to do with as I wish."

The magician perked up at the voice. He responded, "You cannot win, voice in my head. If you slay me, I will become more powerful than you can possibly comprehend. Even if you can comprehend a lot. Because you are on the evil team. The skins."

"I shall enjoy slicing you up," The Overlord said.

"Froggy," the magician quipped back.

The room shook.

Vant felt his legs drop out.

A massive creak coursed through the environment... as if it were bending.

The rubbery snakes spat spears of water. Vant flinched, protecting himself...

But none of the shots came anywhere near him, or the magician.

Vant took in the spectacle; liquid from the nozzles crisscrossed midair, making a spectacular pattern.

The World's Worst Magician churned his hands, digging into the aether. Spirals of particles materialized along with wisps of emerald smoke.

Pop. An Immortal ruptured in the pipeline. *Pop. Pop.* Two more. Then ten more. They burst into puffs of bloody mist, then dispersed. Vant watched through Death's mask as their pulsating silhouettes evaporated, one by one.

Luminous smoke poured out of the magician's hands and flowed through the waterways. Like he were a musical conductor, the mists followed his movements. When their trails passed over a crumbling Immortal, additional smoke appeared, magnifying the reaction and disintegrating the decrepit being in the process.

The liquid bubbled with vigorous force. Currents whipped through the tunnels. A new sound arose, a slow, moaning wail. The sound did not originate from the Immortals; it came from the structure—it was destabilizing. The disruption of the water inside the glass pipes was causing their anchoring braces to buckle.

"Um, Doubleya? You're destroying the building. Which may end up killing us all. Kind of defeats the purpose."

"Sometimes pixie dust can be confused for juju balls," he replied. He closed his eyes and fell into a trance, magnifying the reaction even more. A jagged crack appeared in the glass. Then another. Then another.

"Not good," Vant said to himself. "Skii!" he shouted into his communicator, sprinting back toward the armory. "How's the rescue going?"

"Total disaster! We've got most of them unplugged, but they can barely move. There's no way we're getting them out!" Her tone shifted suddenly, "Uh, Vant?"

"What?"

"Perhaps you'd like to tell me why the *roof is leaking!*"

Vant looked back at the magician. One of the glass pipelines had sprung a leak and was dumping hundreds of gallons of water per second onto the floor.

"This place is going to flood! You've got to get everyone out!"

"Yeah, okay. I'll just put a thousand people on my back and carry them out."

"I have a better idea. Maybe it's worse. I'm not quite sure."

"I'm all ears."

"Flip the switch, throw it in reverse, and toss 'em in the vacuum." He was referring to the hose that had sucked the people out of Land Escape.

"I'm thinking... yep, got it. Terrible idea. We have no clue where the other end leads!"

"So jump in and find out!"

"Nuts to that!" Skii's voice was drowned out by bedlam as Vant re-entered the foundry. It was pure anarchy. Vant's army was in shambles. The Peace-Keepers, some with handfuls of thallium soldiers clinging to them, blind-fired at anything that moved. There were more dead nomads than live ones. The Land Escapers hid behind the walking turrets, which were sputtering with a lack of ammunition. The floor contained a mixture of shrapnel, flesh, and corpses.

Yet...

The creation of new soldiers had ceased. The damage being caused by The World's Worst Magician was putting a massive kink in their system. The dispatching of the Immortal grubs was stemming the flow of new thallium soldiers. Vant experienced a warm, gooey sensation in his stomach: joy. The tables had turned.

"They're shut down at the source!" Vant shouted to his troops. "We've got this! *We've got this!*" A boost of morale filled the room. Bullets instantly seemed more lethal. Punches more accurate. The nomads, Peace-Keepers, and Land Escapers had been running on fumes, but their fire was now rekindled.

Back into his wrist: "Skii, we have no choice! Jump in the vacuum and find out where it leads! Or throw Saamii Fraam in there!"

"Hey!" Saamii protested from the other end of the communicator.

"Not a lot of takers for the suicide mission," Skii said. "How about you, Vant? Want in on this?"

A voice came from behind: "I'll go."

Vant turned to see Shavious, bloody, sweaty, and smiling with the half of his face that could.

"You're a brave man," Vant said.

Shavious blinked at him. A few times. Before Vant realized he was winking.

"Skii, you've got a hero incoming. Give him a wrist-comm and toss him in the sucker."

"On it. And you?"

"One more loose end to tie up."

"Which is?"

"Gotta pop a zit."

Vant rushed toward the cargo door leading to the habitat of the Immortal elders.

A soldier got in his way. Vant decked him so hard the helmet ripped off. Three more lunged for his feet. He leapt, they collapsed in a heap, and he smashed their torsos until they leaked. The door was getting close. Two soldiers were holding Lyyra at point-blank range with batons aimed at her head. Vant whipped her foot—*thwip-crack!*—and pulled her to safety as they fired their weapons. He darted across an open area... and came upon twenty soldiers on top of a fallen Peace-Keeper. They stared at Vant. Vant stared at them. Then he whipped the Peace-Keeper around the wrist and shot lightning through his lashes. The destroyed biped flared up into a cacophony of bolts as electricity flowed through the metal frame and into the soldiers, frying them.

The coast was clear.

Almost there...

The floor wobbled beneath Vant's feet.

A rhythmic tremor shook the environment.

Then another.

And another.

Vant knew what was coming.

"Ugh," he groaned.

The semblance of a wall separating the armory from the foundry was decimated.

By the Thallium Titan.

The gargantuan overseer of the army, the one who had singlehandedly breached Land Escape's gates, crushed mechanical equipment and armor casings as it ran into the fray. Two Peace-Keepers assaulted the giant with their gatling guns, but it crossed to them in one massive stride, swung its hammer-hands, and flattened them into piles of scrap.

The remaining human resistance scattered.

The titan stared at Vant. It rammed its hammers together in an impatient taunt.

Vant sighed. Stretched. And returned the sentiment by knocking his own fists together, as well.

And then he charged.

The titan pounded the ground. Vant dove away from the collision, somersaulted back to his feet, and struck its shin with an electrified whip. Sparks bounced off the surface—the armor was far too thick to conduct electricity into the liquid within.

A club hand arced overhead and collided with the floor mere feet from Vant. The impact sent him into a roll. He righted himself, whipped the arm of the giant, and propelled himself onto its shoulder.

Before it could react, Vant flung another whip. It twisted around the neck of the titan. He swung behind its back, around its midsection, and onto its foot. In a confused rage, it swung downward. Vant vaulted off at the perfect time—the titan's hammer connected with its own foot. The force of the blow severely dented the thallium appendage.

It stumbled forward, landing on one knee.

Vant ran underneath the giant's midsection. He latched a whip onto a crease in the armor and pulled himself upward, dangling beneath its crotch. He stabilized himself by pulling the tension on the whip, then drew back his fist as the giant flailed and twisted, searching for him.

In a little-guy-big-guy fight, Vant thought, *the little guy gets to smash the big guy in the dick.*

Vant repeatedly pummeled the titan's underside. The barrage of punches chipped away at its thallium. Particles splintered and a dent formed. The tiniest crack appeared, and a few dots of water dripped from the blemish.

The titan struggled to stand. Vant held tight, dealing blow after blow.

The gargantuan foe bucked like a wild animal. Vant's whip lost its hold. He thudded to the ground.

The titan raised a hand, preparing to squash the tiny nuisance giving it so much trouble. Vant, on his back, pointed a gauntlet upward and flipped the function switches inside. With an ascending sound, the power cells charged to capacity.

Vant held his breath to steady his arm.

He took careful aim.

The titan began its downswing...

Vant activated the thruster and released his grip. The iron fist rocketed out of his hand and smashed into the giant in the exact spot where the crack had formed. The collision with the weakened area caused the seam to split open.

A stream of liquid flowed from the giant's groin.

Vant pulled the whip. The slack recoiled and the gauntlet zipped back into his hand.

"Get clear!" said a Peace-Keeper.

Vant darted away from the damaged titan. "Fire!" he shouted.

Gunfire erupted from the weapons of the remaining infantry. The Peace-Keepers rattled off shot after shot. They concentrated their attack on the hole, which widened with every hit. The gap became the size of a boulder, and the giant lost all internal stability from the decrease in water pressure.

It staggered back...and forth...

Then collapsed.

Vant's army roared with victorious cheers as the fleshy Immortal pilots poured out of the hole, twitched, and died on the floor.

Vant made it to the cargo door separating the foundry from the domain of the Immortal Overlord. He holstered his gauntlets by whipping around his waist and letting them dangle at his sides. He jammed the buttons on the door's control panel, but it was on lockdown.

A knife whizzed over his shoulder and stuck into the manual override.

Vant spun around to find Widow standing behind him. He stared at her with confusion.

"Ah, shit," she said. "Thought you tryin' lock it. Not open it. Heh."

Vant pocketed the knife and shouted, "Need a hand!" to the two remaining Peace-Keepers. They lifted the door, breaking the deadbolts in the process.

Vant ducked inside.

The door slammed shut behind him.

He walked past the glassy gazes of the Immortal elders in their aquarium and approached the floating head in its containment pod. It stared at Vant with its revolting, frozen grimace.

"Funny thing about a fortress," Vant said. "With a few modifications, it easily becomes a tomb."

"You will suffer for resisting the will of your Immortal Overlord!"

"You are *not* immortal. Let's cut that out right now."

"I have lived for ages! And I shall continue to do so!"

"See, that's the thing," Vant interrupted, shaking his pointer finger at the pod. "Just because you haven't died *yet*, that doesn't mean you're immortal. It just means you're old as fuck."

"I *am* immortal."

"No, you're not. Hop on out of that tube. I'd bet my right nut that if you did, you'd die on the spot. Here's another idea—let me reach into your tank and squish you between my thumb and forefinger. I'd wager you'd pop like a cherry, and that would be the end of you."

"How dare you—"

"How dare *you!* You call yourself immortal? You're not immortal. You're a vile little turd who found himself a bath to keep warm in for a few eons. Immortality means you cannot die, but I'm watching you expire right here, right now, as we speak. And, mark my words, when you're nothing more than a pebble of shit in a water tank, I'll still be alive, cruising along."

"*Rrrr...*" The Overlord was making a strange noise—either stammering, or growling.

"You're like everyone else. You're temporary. You're *mortal.*" Vant tapped on the glass with Widow's knife. The head flinched. "Huh, little fishy? All you've done is found a way to hack life and bend it to your will. You're cheating the system. You're sidestepping the grim reaper. But you can only dodge him for so long."

The tiny head bobbed in the water, in protest. "What gives you the right to destroy my way of life?"

"Orders from the top. You've overstayed your welcome. You've got to go."

"How was this decision reached? I bring peace to my inhabitants! I strip away all that is unnecessary! I grant lifetimes upon lifetimes to my loyal subjects! And soon I will extend that blessing to the entire planet!"

"Word of advice, short stack. If you have to force people into your way of life because no one's into it, then your way of life chugs wang."

"So this is a cleansing based upon judgment? I am evil, and you represent the good?"

"Let's get this straight. I'm not the good guy. I'm the bad guy. But you're the *worse* guy."

Vant sliced a gash into his own shoulder with Widow's knife. He let out a shrill cry as he shoved his hand into the wound, dug through tissue, and located the implanted bomb.

He ripped it out.

He pressed a button on the detonator.

"Have a nice afterlife," he said.

He tossed the explosive at the Immortal Overlord.

The hoses behind the pod detached and swatted away the bomb. They twisted like enraged serpents and their nozzles hissed steam. They fired blasts of liquid at the explosion, reducing the fire to vapor.

Before Vant could react, a hose shot out and wrapped around his neck.

"Insolent pest!" Vant was lifted off his feet and pulled to the pod's glass, forcing him eye-level with The Overlord's grimace. "I no longer wish to study you. I wish to destroy you! The satisfaction gained by flushing you into the ocean will last me a millennium!"

Two hoses fired pressurized acid near Vant's legs.

"But first, I need to know if there will be more of you coming to my door. Reveal your identity to me and be spared dismemberment."

The streams inched closer... closer...

Vant pushed his hands into the gauntlets by his side, activated them, and batted at the coils around his neck. The struggle was pointless; they were far too thick, and the rubber was far too malleable. His weapons had a flaw—there was nothing sharp to cut with. Vant's eyes rolled into the back of his head as the staples sealing his neck wound began to break apart from the tension.

The Overlord spoke again, "Tell me now. Who sent you?"

The slack loosened so Vant could speak.

"Death," he choked out.

"Your reckless tongue damns you. Your failure to cooperate has cost you a leg."

The beams of acid sizzled through Vant's thigh.

His leg dropped to the floor and landed with a chunky plop. His screams filled the sanctuary.

"I shall ask again. Tell the truth to keep your other leg. Who sent you?"

"Death!"

"Two limbs for two lies."

The Overlord sliced. Clotted blood emptied from Vant's new stump as his other leg dropped to the floor.

"Next, I shall show you what it feels like to lose your manhood." A hose aimed below Vant's waist. "Speak of who sent you! This is your last chance to utter words that are not preposterous!"

Vant stifled his agony. Composed himself. Cleared his throat. And said:

"Life's a bitch... but Death is worse."

Crack!

He whipped the metal nozzles and blasted lightning into them. The electrical current travelled through the liquid inside the hoses and into The Overlord's pod. It became a sizzling cesspool of sparks and shocks.

The tiny head twitched. Then it squirted fragments of meat from its ears, along with an oily bile. Vant kept his grip firm and poured even more voltage into the water. The Overlord's skull collapsed on itself—there was a gentle, bloody poof, and all leftover remains dispersed into the liquid.

The electrical current flowed from The Overlord's pod into the aquarium of Immortal elders. The smallest of them simply evaporated, while the larger ones cooked until they burst.

When all were dispatched, Vant deactivated the electricity. The water became calm again, with nothing more than small bubbles and stray tissue floating by.

The hoses de-pressurized and dropped Vant. He landed on his amputated stumps and crumpled into a heap.

Shock took over. His body pumped numbing agents into his bloodstream. He fought against stasis when reality hit: a battle was still carrying on, and a rescue mission was still in progress. The Immortal soldiers, as The Overlord had explained, retained a portion of autonomy and were most likely still fighting back.

He pressed his comm to his lips. "Skii?"

Nothing.

"Any Peace-Keepers, come in. Ranchula? Saamii?"

All silent.

Vant surveyed his ravaged body. His flesh sizzled from acidy wounds on his side and shoulder. His legs leaked globs of meat. His neck was a mixture of bent hooks, blood, and pus. His shoulder was torn open. His insides were soft; he was most likely bleeding internally.

Consciousness was slipping away. Each blink was longer than the last.

Then, a voice on the comm: "Ho, there, Vant Hu'l."

"Saamii! What's going on out there?"

"The vacuum leads to safety. We got the prisoners out, but the enemy is still fighting back. We're barely holding on. There's only a few of us left and—wait. What is that? What the hell is *that*—"

Silence.

"Saamii?" Nothing. "Saamii!"

Keep moving, Vant urged himself.

He scooped up his floppy legs and dropped them into his satchel, along with his gauntlets. He gripped the grated floor and pulled himself across the room by wiggling his torso. He moved through the glass passageway and up to the sealed cargo door.

There was no way to open it. He flattened his hand against the barrier. It was cold and unyielding.

But then...

The door slid upward.

Water flooded in and rushed over Vant. He coughed from the face-full of liquid, trying to keep his head above water.

A razor-sharp sword appeared. It pressed against his throat.

Vant looked up past two inverted legs and a stick-thin body. Two red eyes above a metal jawline stared back.

"Oh, great," Vant said. "Of course you're here, you psychotic can opener."

Redemption studied Vant's mangled body.

"I beat you in Crash Town and now you've come back to finish the job. So get to it, then. I don't give a shit. Go ahead and kill me when I'm unarmed. And bloody. And missing my damn legs."

The cyborg only stared back, its hunchback rising and falling with each breath.

"Do it! Do what you came here for!"

The sword swished...

A thallium soldier collapsed, cut in half.

Redemption launched backward and landed between a pack of soldiers. Its blade flashed through their armor. Torsos slid from waistlines, then helmets from necklines. The foes fell into the knee-high water.

The cyborg retracted its sword, scooped Vant onto its back, and rushed him through the flooding foundry. It leapt over armor fragments, avoided dead bodies, and skirted falling obstacles.

Vant heard a cough, almost imperceptible among the noise. Within a mess of debris, an arm rose up.

"Wait!" Vant shouted. The cyborg about-faced and dashed in the direction of the drowning victim. Vant clasped his hand around Ranchula's forearm and pulled him from the wreckage. "Got him! Go!"

Redemption sprinted with the two wounded men on its back, searching for an escape route. The doors were blocked. Glass fell from the shattered pipeline. There was only one way to go: down. They dove into the whirlpool swirling above the hole to the catacombs. Redemption propelled them deeper into the icy waters. *I hate suffocating,* Vant thought as he felt the familiar heart palpitations from the initial stages of drowning.

They caught a current. It pushed them toward the vacuum at the other end of the catacombs. Their momentum increased. The suction pulled them into the tube. They twisted and turned, whacking the walls but never slowing down. Redemption went limp, allowing the currents to take over. Vant did the same.

They hit perilous speeds. Vant's lungs begged for air. Ranchula convulsed under his arms. *Just hold on,* Vant willed to him.

Finally...

The three launched out of the hose and touched down onto a soft, sandy beach.

Ranchula was not breathing. Vant pushed him onto his back and pounded on his chest. Again. And again. After a good hard thump, the nomad chief hacked up the water trapped in his lungs and rediscovered his breath.

Vant rolled over, turning to Redemption. "How... how did you find me?" Vant wheezed.

The cyborg activated the holographic display: "I TOLD YOU TO WATCH YOUR BACK."

"You sneaky bastard. The Overlord said I had a bio-tracker in me. You implanted it when you stabbed me in Crash Town, didn't you?"

Redemption answered with an inclination of its head.

Vant peeled off Death's mask. He shut his eyelids.

Wet hair in the warm sand. A cool sea breeze. The whisper of the ocean.

The Immortals were destroyed. The hostages had been freed.

"Hell yeah," he said to himself.

Then he passed out.

"Pops!"

The nap had lasted nineteen seconds.

Skii yelped with delight. "Holy skizzbutts, we did it! I can't believe we made it out alive! Whoa. Whoa! Oh, *nasty!* Where are your legs? Oh, man, I'm going to throw up!"

"Way to kick a man when he's down," Vant said. His eyes were half closed.

Skii looked at Redemption, piecing together that it was responsible for Vant's rescue. "Thanks," she said.

The cyborg stared back through infrared optics. Its eyes beamed, "RECKLESS. I THOUGHT I TOLD YOU TO STAY ALIVE."

"You said, 'LIVE.' Living isn't the same thing as staying alive."

Its metal jawline seemed to twitch, and it gave a look resembling a scowl. Then, "I HAVE A MESSAGE FROM YOUR FATHER."

"Not interested. If he has something to say, he can say it to me himself. I'm tired of chasing him. Maybe he should chase *me* for a change." Skii turned her back on Redemption and added, "I'm right here. I'm only hard to find if I *want* to be."

In response, the enigmatic figure absconded from the beach. It vanished in moments from the powerful strides of its mechanical legs.

Skii dropped to her knees next to Vant. She put her hand on his heart. "Strong thing, huh?"

Vant felt it beating, though slowly. "Guess so. Doesn't know when to quit."

She pulled the wet strands of his hair off of his forehead and out of his eyes. Vant reflected on their first meeting. He had been bald then. Now he was shaggy.

She stroked his hair. Vant noted how long it had been since he had been touched by anything that was not blunt or sharp, and traveling at high velocities. It felt good. Familiar.

It was something Rii used to do to him.

But his mind would not allow him peace. Not yet.

He said, "The hostages. Are they—"

"They're safe. Most of them. We couldn't... we couldn't save the ones in the grinder. The water flooded the basement, and—"

"They're resting now. We did all we could."

"They must have drowned. Is that a good way to go? Did they go peacefully?"

"Yes, Skii. It's the best way to go," he lied to her. "You don't feel a thing."

Vant's eyelids became impossibly heavy. He could not convince them otherwise, they were insistent on calling it a day. He was tired of fighting. He had done enough for a lifetime. For several lifetimes.

So he let them win.

"Pile 'em up!"

- Vant Hu'l

222

YEARS PRIOR

Of Blood and Stone

So many bodies.
Maimed, split, torn, slit.
Terrii stood frozen amongst the dead. In their silence, the deceased spoke of his atrocities. He tried to walk, but blood glued his boots to the floor. It forced a reflection upon his crimes...

He had turned his army against their respected commander...
...and forced them into an unnecessary fight.

He had pitted them against a foe who far surpassed their abilities...
...and sent them all to their deaths.

He had let his jealousy poison his insides...
...and taken a wife who did not love him.

He had banished a prized Cloakmaster...
...and run the commune like a master doling out scraps to peons.

He had sided with his bloodthirsty father...
...and murdered his best friend.

And murdered his wife.

Terrii pulled his gaze from the destroyed Knights of Rights to Vant's body, lying on a bed of red. Terrii had gunned him down, in cold blood, when he had been unarmed.
A lifetime of loyalty terminated with a slug through the heart.

He looked upon Shyyla. Her corpse was a mess. Her skull was chipped. Her body was sprawled and bent.

Emotions exploded up from Terrii's belly and into his throat. So many at once. Angst. Upset. Rage. Guilt. Loneliness. Guilt. Sadness. Guilt.

He un-stuck his boots and ran. Ran away from every death that was his doing. Ran away from every decision made from a place of born-into righteousness. Ran away from his life, in ruins.

He ran out of the armory. Past the commune. Toward the cliffs.

As he stared at the rocks hundreds of feet below, self-judgment appeared in the form of an executioner. Terrii, the leader of the Knights of Rights, had taken an oath to be a paragon of virtue. A bringer of justice. A defender of rights.

But he had not been.

He had been a mockery.

A failure.

A villain.

The leap off the cliff was an effortless decision.

"Come back, Vant," he said as the ground approached at breakneck speeds. "I trade my life for yours."

The ten thousand winds of gravity pushed him into the jagged rocks below. And split his spine in half.

"A deal's a deal."

- Vant Hu'l

CHAPTER 20

The Debts and the Deals

Hours later, everything was calm, yet everything was in motion.

The vacuum had spit them out a half-mile north of The Immortals' fortress. The sun had set. Bonfires peppered the beach.

A makeshift base camp had been established. The rescued hostages—naked, wet, and debilitated—received aid in the form of blankets, food, clothing, and medical supplies thanks to Grammie's Corpo-Bot caller. The supplies were paid for out of Skii's account, which was, somehow, much larger than she had been letting on.

And then there was Vant.

With Skii's help, they had lined up his severed legs with the stumps, doused them with sterilizers, and secured the appendages with brackets and bindings. They had also sealed his open wounds and flushed the acid from his injuries. He would be on his ass for a while, but everything in his vast repertoire of injuries would heal as they always did: over time. The magician's "holistic" treatments would help, too, of course.

Vant, immobile, was miserable in the role of the great liberator to whom homage should be paid—a role given to him by the freed hostages and their loved ones. Word among the people spread that he was the one responsible for the rescue, so it became "the thing to do" to collapse at his feet, sob, and swear allegiance to him. His ego did not mind the admiration at first, but after a few hours, it grew overwhelming.

Yet one particular visitor stood out.

"So there you are," an old lady said to him. She was frail, weakened from the months of imprisonment. Her eyes looked ancient underneath the scars where the goggles had been screwed into her face. But beyond the shadows were sparkles. She stood as tall as her elderly bones would allow and said, "You never paid your tab."

She was the innkeeper from Land Escape. Someone who had showed Vant extraordinary kindness when he had arrived in town.

He was speechless.

She grinned as big as she could and added, "All right... *fine*. It's on the house."

Soon, the band was back together. Skii, Grammie, and The World's Worst Magician sat in a clump babysitting Vant, to his chagrin. But Grammie broke out the wine, and, as they were wont to do, they enjoyed a half-dozen drinks. Each.

Grammie told tales of his "heroism behind the scenes," insisting he was crushed that his companions never got to witness these deeds. The way he and the magician recruited the nomads was a grand tale full of plot twists and exciting turns, with fact nearly impossible to separate from fiction. Skii hinted at her adventures as well, but left out huge chunks of the story. When asked how, specifically, she convinced The Mayor and his Peace-Keepers to come along for the ride, she said simply, "I challenged the size of their stones. I said they didn't have the rockets in their pockets for this kind of work." But the way she said it, Vant knew she was leaving something out.

The World's Worst Magician was another matter altogether. He seemingly had no clue of what he had actually done during the battle. When asked about his contribution, he said, "I was only there for a few minutes, but it felt like at least a few more."

"Well," Vant said, "even if you almost killed us, I can't thank you enough for saving us."

The magician was visibly upset at the praise. He leapt up and thrust his hands toward the heavens, shouting, "Would you thank King Croy for rescuing you from the clutches of Satanne DeVile? Would you thank the Champion of Ersed for freeing you from the Realms of Injustice? Would you thank Steely Charr for helping you overcome the Plague of Scaraff?"

Vant considered his answer. "Yes?"

"No, you wouldn't! Because they would be off to their next adventure before you could even begin the words! They know that every moment they spend so pleased with themselves is a moment they could be helping someone else in need—or getting sucked off!" The magician burped, then flopped face-first into the sand. The snoring was the only indicator he had not dropped dead.

The eccentric wizard clearly had no handle on the scope of his deeds. With no more than a few flicks of his wrist, he had wiped out thousands of villains and manipulated the elements to wreak havoc in a hostile environment. He had shattered glass, redirected weaponry, and rearranged biological matter to single-handedly stop The Immortals from creating more troops. He was a savior—but a dangerous one. He was a man with magnificent celestial powers, but one who could barely put a coherent thought together. Vant forced himself to be cautious of the man. Like a smart bomb with a fried microchip, if pointed in the wrong direction, he had the potential to cause a cataclysmic disaster.

The evening progressed. Every minute brought a new star to the brilliant, twinkling sky. But along with the peace came a permeating melancholy. Reflections turned to loved ones lost, and realizations that those missing were officially gone for good. Soon, a wail filled the air. A wail Vant was familiar with. A wail that meant grief.

It was Widow, in the distance.

Moments later, Shavious approached Vant. His demeanor read as shell-shocked. He murmured though the functioning side of his mouth, "Ranchula... the Great Spider... he dying. He wants to see you."

"We can't move him," Grammie said, referencing Vant's weakened condition.

"Yes, you can," Vant insisted.

Skii, Grammie, and a handful of nomads carried Vant to a secluded portion of the beach. The nomad huntress was crying over the ravaged body of Ranchula. His battle wounds were beyond repair.

"That you, zombie fuck?" Ranchula groaned.

"Spider," Vant said. "I'm here."

"I killed you," he said. "Don't forget that. I'm a better hunter than you. If I die now, I'm still better than you."

"You are," Vant said. "Better than me in every way."

"Especially fucking," he said. He laughed himself into a coughing fit. Finally, "See you in Hell, zombie fuck."

He fell silent.

The huntress let out a scream that pushed the wind aside, and the ocean back.

Back at Vant's camp, Shavious said, "We'll bury Ranchula. Him and the others we lost."

"I led him to his death," Vant said. "Was it worth it? Were your missing people rescued in the evac?"

"Not many," he said. "The ones we saved, they're sick. They were stolen from us almost ten years ago. Too long in the water. Way too long. They're going to die, I think."

"You probably lost more people than we saved. And I killed all the nomads who had become Immortals. Their deaths are on me."

"To us, they're more than just bodies. They're spirits, too. They're no longer prey in a cage. That is the worst fate there is, for hunters. Their bodies may be gone, but their spirits are now free. And those of us left... we are in your debt. You led us here, to our new home, the place General Grammie promised us. It was everything we hoped it would be."

The charlatan pretended to be preoccupied. Nonchalant was not his strong suit.

"Oh, *hell*," said Vant. "What did the *General* promise you?"

Shavious pointed toward the former fortress of The Immortals. "Beachfront property. Not a bad home for our tribe. He said we could have it."

Vant scowled at the charlatan for making a deal like that. For conning them.

"Well," Grammie said, "it *would* be a shame for it to stay vacant..."

Shavious said, "We had no idea the place would have such machines. Like the ones that make fresh water, and bring in fish. We will never starve, or die of thirst. General Grammie promised us shelter, but you, Vant Hu'l, led us to salvation.

"Nomads are hunters," he continued, "but we are not savage. We fight for loyalty. For survival. And for freedom from dogma. But above all else, you let our Spider fight for greatness. For that, Ranchula's spirit will rest, eternally grateful."

Vant shook his head at Grammie. Grammie smiled back. "What the hell, right?"

"What the hell," Vant said, turning the con into a transaction. After all, the fortress was not really his to give—the nomads could just take it by force, if they so chose. So, Vant thought, it was better to use the situation for diplomacy rather than letting it devolve into a territorial dispute.

There was opportunity here.

"The place is yours, Shavious. Yours, and your people's. Under two conditions."

"Tell me."

"One, it becomes a safe house for *all* nomads. *All* tribes. Everyone is welcomed. Everyone gets food and water. No exceptions."

"Of course. Next condition?"

"You're the new chief."

Shavious stared at his feet. "I don't think that's a good idea."

"Why not? You're perfect."

"I..." Embarrassed of his abnormality, he touched his fingers to his face. "I can't."

"*Pshh!*" Grammie interrupted. "If looks made the leader, *I'd* be the one in charge!"

"You fight with courage," said Vant. "You have heart. You think clearly. You're selfless. And, if it's your appearance that's bothering you..." He removed Death's guise from his cloak and showed it to Shavious, "...then wear a mask."

With the half of his face that was not paralyzed, Shavious smiled. He reached out to take the mask.

"I didn't mean mine," Vant said. "Get your own."

They shared a laugh.

"And now, my companions and compatriots," Grammie piped up, "before the sparkling shack on the beach becomes nomad property—which, granted, is a wondrous and wonderful thing—Grammie must first be allowed to do what he does best! To sniff out the loot! We had a deal, remember? Those Immortals were doing quite a fair share of trade with Corpo, and good ol' Grammie's gonna help himself to their stockpile of pills—provided he can find it in the wreckage, of course! There has to be a mattress in there somewhere, under which they stashed all their booty!"

Skii socked Grammie in the shoulder. "One-track mind, Kram."

"Two tracks," he said to her with a lecherous wink. She fake-vomited in the sand.

"Deal?" Grammie asked.

"A deal's a deal," Vant agreed.

And, Vant reflected to himself, he had completed *his* end of a different deal, as well. He had been sent on an errand for Death, and now it was complete. He had earned his freedom.

Silently toasting to his own future—whatever it might be—he downed his wine.

A week passed.

It was time for the return trip to Land Escape.

The survivors had their strength, and were reacclimatized to independent consciousness. Supplies were divvied up and dispersed, and a palpable buzz grew in the anticipation of the expedition. Most of the Land Escape citizens had never seen the outside world, and now they were getting an armed escort back to safety by the very nomads that would have attacked them. In a twist of irony, the ordeal was a kind of blessing, as the majority of the townsfolk would have lived their entire lives without so much as a glimpse of the outskirts.

But... Vant was in a state. He had no clue as to how the hell he was going to travel; his legs were in an extremely delicate condition. As the time of departure drew closer, Skii busied herself with packing while Vant pestered her.

"I can't walk. How am I supposed to make it back?"

"Such a baby! Relax, Pops. Don't you trust me?"

"Uh..."

"Don't answer that. And don't worry. I managed to get you a ride."

"A ride?"

"It'll be here soon. Calm your bomb."

"Fine," Vant huffed.

During the wait, Saamii Fraam, arm-in-arm with his wife, approached Vant and Skii. "Ho, there, you two," he said.

Vant shook hands with Saamii and smiled at Laam. "Glad you recognize your *real* husband," he said.

"I never believed you for a second. After all, I couldn't have married you." She smooched Saamii on the cheek. "I only go for *strong* men!"

"Hah. Well, thanks for playing along. We're all here because of you. So, what's the update, Saamii?"

"We're all set. Everyone's ready for the journey. Jiino's organized everyone into teams with accountability systems in place, so no one will fall behind. We've dispersed wrist-comms to coordinate from group to group, and we're good on supplies and have the wounded covered. Anything I'm forgetting?"

"One thing," Vant said. "Is Land Escape... still there? Who's protecting it?"

"Ah. That. It's still there. It's in good hands with our most ferocious protectors... Bomp and Fray."

Skii laughed. Vant choked. "*Children?*"

"And one adult. One stayed back. Someone who refused to fight."

Vant thought. *Who was missing?* Then: "Chaaris."

"Our favorite blowhard. All that talk, challenging you, puffing out his chest... he disappeared the night before we left for battle. We figured he could stay at home with the kiddies."

"We were better off without him."

"I just spoke to Bomp. The town's safe. He asked if he could still shoot off the turrets when this thing is all over. We taught him how to fire them into the air every few days to scare off threats. He loves it. I think he found his calling in life."

"I can't thank you enough, Saamii. For everything. There's little more powerful than a level head. Thanks for lending us yours."

Saamii nodded, his eyes shining.

Skii interjected, "Oh, hey, we're in luck! Looks like you won't be left behind after all, Pops. Here comes your mighty steed, now!"

A brand-spanking-new Peace-Keeper crested a nearby hill. Then another. Then five more. Over a loudspeaker: "Well, I'll be a bee's cunt! Look at ya, Vant! Last time I saw ya, you were cowerin' in yer own piss next ta my broken body, weepin' for yer ol' pal, The Mayor!"

Skii patted Vant on the head. "See? I told you I'd take care of you! I'd never leave my buddy behind!"

He fought off her affectionate assault as the remote-controlled enforcers sidled up to the encampment.

Vant said, "Back so soon, Mayor? Sorry, there's nothing left to stomp or shoot. I guess my winning personality will have to keep you entertained."

"Gonna be a long ride ta Land Escape, and it looks like I'm yer horse! Ya best be good company, lest I drop yer ass and make ya crawl home!"

"I appreciate the lift. But, one thing I don't understand—why all the kindness?"

Skii opened her mouth to head off the answer, but it was too late. "Kindness? *Hyick!* There ain't no kindness here! We're doin' it fer payment! Ya didn't think we were in this outta the goodness of our hearts, did ya? Yer lady friend promised us quite a lick'a loot fer our services, and we're keepin' *yer* busted bones as collateral until we're paid up!"

The Mayor's guffaws trailed him as he stomped down the beach with his cohorts.

"Paid up?" Vant squinted at Skii.

"Okay, so, don't get mad, but remember when I broke into the bank in Land Escape, and you told me to only take enough for necessities?"

"Yeah?"

"Turns out, one of our necessities was to hire a fleet of mechanical men to kick some ass."

"Skii! How much did you take?"

She could not help but smile. "All of it."

"*All of it?*"

"Aren't you glad I did? It bought you an army! Plus, it was pretty great being the richest woman in the world." She added a purposeful, but ironic, "Tee-hee."

Vant and Skii shared in the sight of contented people, no longer captives of a corrupt dogmatic township, no longer restrained and forced into liquid captivity. They saw Saamii Fraam holding his wife, overcome with love. Children snuggled with their liberated parents. A captive audience crowded around The Mayor and the Peace-Keepers as they boastfully showed off their gear to *oohs* and *ahhs*. Hundreds of similar sights dotted the sparkling beach. Everything seemed just fine.

"Know what's funny?" Skii asked.

"Tell me."

"Everything's different now." Her attention was focused on one of the bald, emaciated children roughhousing with a nomad whose gun lay neglected in the sand.

"Why funny?"

"That's not the funny part. The funny part is who's responsible. Look at the dregs who changed the world. An undead freak—"

"Thanks a lot," said Vant.

"A lunatic magician. A con man. Some sex-crazed maniacs. A gaggle of nomads. And me."

"Apparently, you're the normal one of the group."

"Apparently, *we* are," she said as she smooched Cassidy and rubbed her mangy belly. "Always heard the good guys save the day. Not this time, huh?"

"Looks like the world ran out of heroes. I suppose we were the best it had. A pack of psychos and some hired guns. Whatever works, I guess."

"Whatever works."

One of the strongest nomads was dog-piled by a grip of rowdy kids in fits of laughter.

Vant continued, "I guess freedom does have its price. I hope the bankrupt Land Escapers consider it money well spent."

"Damn right, Pops. Damn right. Plus, a deal's a deal. You said it yourself."

"A deal's a deal. Pay the Peace-Keepers. How much do we owe them, anyway?"

"Best not to know. You've died several ways since I've met you. Let's not add 'dying of shock' to the list."

Vant raised an eyebrow. Skii gave her sly smile.

Hours later, the caravan departed. The convoy was a spectacular sight. Droves of high-spirited people were organized into groups, each protected by a detail of nomads and a Peace-Keeper for good measure. They began the long walk home as Skii led the way, certain of the most efficient, yet beautiful, route back to Land Escape.

Two of the mechanical bipeds broke off from the pack and headed in the direction of the fallen fortress. They would act as reconnaissance, provide muscle for manual labor in the repurposing of the structure, and salvage the destroyed Peace-Keepers for parts. A handful of nomads, led by Shavious, went with them to oversee construction of their new home. They were also under strict orders to dismantle any traces of The Overlord's schemes, including halting the flow of the mind unification formula being dumped into the ocean. While The Overlord was no longer around to exert control, Vant did not want anyone tempted to follow in The Immortals' footsteps.

Two more people, as well, began following the caravan back to the fortress: Grammie and Doubleya. "A fond farewell, my dearest companions!" Grammie shouted back to Vant and Skii. "I have led our forces to a sublime victory, and now it is time to collect my reward! Please ensure they spell my name correctly in the poems and songs that will be written about me!"

The World's Worst Magician added, "I congratulate ourselves on predicting the future so well! More than a few were skeptics, though they must have been impressed with our ability to know the outcome after only having seen it twice before. And now... off to the abyss! Begun, our adventures have! Has. No, have!"

Vant, strapped to the back of The Mayor in a makeshift carriage, took up the rear. They started walking and The Mayor started yammering. But, before they had gone too far, Vant stopped him.

"Wait. Turn around."

"I'm sorry, son?"

"Turn around, Mayor. I just thought of something. Something important. Take me back to the fortress."

"Ya sure? Ah, hell, if you insist. I know better'n ta argue with the likes'a you!"

They broke off from the group and went a half-mile south, returning to the structure. Vant pointed The Mayor toward the ostentatious signage that still declared, "THE IMMORTALS."

Vant gave a very specific order.

"Heh! Obliged, son."

The Mayor's gatling gun rose from his shoulder mount. He blasted away. Sparks bounced from the metal and pieces of scrap flew from the sign. The letters weakened and frayed and, with unceremonious *thud*s, the *I* and the *M* dropped to their final resting places in the sand.

"Nice touch," said The Mayor.

"Thanks." Vant said. "Now let's catch up to the others."

They departed from the fortress on the beach with the sign now reading: "THE MORTALS."

"The funny part is who's responsible. Look at the dregs who changed the world."

- Skii Tavee

222

YEARS PRIOR

Of Death and Rebirth

Blackness.

Then:

Terrii's eyelids opened.
Sunlight scalded his pupils. Breath pressed into his constricted lungs. His frame pulsed with shock. A flock of buzzards scattered from his body.
He was at the base of a cliff. The one he had thrown himself from.
His spine was straight.
His wounds were healed.
He was alive.
"Not me. Not me!" He buried his head into his arms and rocked back and forth.
Eventually, he rose. He scaled the serrated cliff with bare hands and a weakened body. He crested the lip and walked through the commune of the Knights of Rights. It was empty. Stripped. Only naked fields remained.
Weeks must have passed.
He entered the hillside cave expecting to find the remains of his soldiers. But they too were gone. All indicators that this space had once been an arms cache had been removed—save for the immovable anvil at the cave's center.
And the floor...
It would forever be stained with darkened crimson.
Outside, Terrii paced among the dead laid to rest. Tombstones dotted the landscape, monuments for each of the Knights of Rights—and one for his wife, Shyyla. Although she had never become a Knight, those who buried her honored her as one.

One monument stood out. It was twice as tall as the others, carved out of a polished black stone. It was at the forefront of the burial plots, as if leading the battalion even in death. And bonded to the top of the tombstone were the very items that had represented the man, in life.

Vant's whip gauntlets.

Terrii dropped to his knees in front of the grave. He clawed at the grass, shredding it, and the soil, disrupting it. "You brought back the wrong man," Terrii said to whatever force had resurrected him. "The wrong man. The wrong man."

The tears subsided. His fingers stopped tearing at the grass, and, instead, started smoothing it down.

Terrii turned to the sky. "If you won't bring him back, I will."

He threw his shoulder again and again into the gauntlets sealed to the gravestone. They broke loose, and he slid them onto his hands. He activated the thrusters. The power cells sang Shyyla's song.

"Vant Hu'l is alive!" he shouted to the storm clouds gathering. "I take on his name, now and for all eternity. I will carry his weapons as a reminder of the man I should have been, and the man I must become. Agmar-Burrian Terriforn is dead. Vant Hu'l lives within me!"

He revved the engines of the gauntlets.

He loosed the whips, which crackled taunts to the heavens.

"Here I stand!" he declared with the might of an immortal warrior.

"I am Vant Hu'l!"

"I have to say goodbye."

- Vant Hu'l

EPILGUE

The Dead and the Damned

Vant could have been the king of the city, if he so chose. The Land Escape citizens treated him as such. They offered him comforts of every kind, material goods, and any home he would have wanted anywhere within the township.

But he stayed at the inn.

He liked the innkeeper. And he *loved* her food.

The days came and went. Sunrise, sunset, rinse, repeat. He spent his days walking the streets, taking meetings with newly appointed defense volunteers, and cleaning his weapons for unforeseeable battles. Life was simple.

But sleep... sleep was the one thing that would not come easy. The dreams were always the same. Always.

He dreamed of Death...

On a nondescript evening, he abandoned the idea of slumber altogether and, instead, stared at the ceiling, wide-eyed.

It was too damned quiet.

He felt impatient. Stagnant. His heart took on a rapid *thump-thump-thump* and would not relax. Claustrophobia set in. The walls were so tight.

So tight.

He decided to take a walk. To clear his mind. He strapped on his wrist-communicator and grabbed his satchel, as was habit, and left the inn.

Land Escape was a whisper at this hour, yet it still felt oppressive. The streets seemed too narrow, and the buildings too overbearing. He needed space. Open air. The vastness of a star field to look upon.

He approached the main gates. Being the savior of the city came with special privileges, including the ability to come and go as he pleased, no questions asked. The guards on duty nodded to Vant, watching him through sunken eyes scarred by the goggles once forced into their brows by The Immortals.

They cracked the gate for him.

He left Land Escape, and walked into the open.

Day broke, then night fell again. He still needed more damned space. *Maybe the mountains,* he thought. They looked so peaceful, so calm.

He tried to alter his course.

Teeth of fire gnashed at Vant's skin. A ravenous devil inside slashed at his flesh.

He howled in pain and quickly course-corrected. He could not turn. He was ensnared.

Ensnared, once again, by the curse.

The return trip to Death's lair had begun.

His feet moved slowly, weighed down by his heart, which had sunk deep into his stomach. A prickly tingling formed in his chest around a hollow core, a core that was filling up fast with bitterness, remorse, and frustration. He remembered the last time he had experienced this sensation, almost thirty years ago, when forced to leave Rii for reasons he did not, at the time, comprehend. The feeling now reappeared, this time for someone new he was leaving behind.

"Skii," Vant spoke into his comm. "Skii."

No answer. It was very late—early. Dawn. Light was just beginning to break. It was cold and hazy.

He heard a click and some ruffling on the other end of the line. "Do you have any idea what time it is?"

"Skii..." He could not find the words. They were blocked by a barrier of heartache.

"What?"

"I have to say goodbye."

Silence. Then: "What are you on about, Pops?"

"He's calling me back."

A long pause. "Fight it."

"I can't."

"You said you'd fight every chance you got. You *said* that." It was an accusation, but underneath the statement was sorrow. Skii's mother had been taken away from her because of an illness. Her father had abandoned her on his failed quest. And now, her best friend was leaving due to a force too powerful to resist.

"Skii, I want you to know something."

"Don't. Don't do this. I don't want to hear any of this."

"Skii..."

Nothing.

Vant's eyes became wet. He had no idea if she would hear his next words, but he said them anyway. "I will come back. I will. I just... don't know when." A pause. "Tell Grammie and Doubleya I'll see them soon, too."

Dead leaves crackled underneath his rhythmic footsteps.

He picked up the pace.

More than a year passed.

When he arrived at the center of the wasteland, his heart was filled with poison. The venom of anger had surpassed the mire of heartbreak. He was coming in hot, with glassy eyes and a pounding pulse behind his ears. He could see Death's awful form in his mind's eye, and all he wanted to do was tear into him.

Vant dropped into the hole leading to Death's lair. Blackness enveloped him, isolating him from everything but his raging emotions. He waited impatiently for his eyes to adjust.

He stormed through the delicate cavern and halted at the torturous tunnel. Dropping to his knees on the mound of dusty bones, he dug into the pile of human remains to unearth a handful of energy and moisture pills. He greedily ingested them, then searched through the expedition gear of the crumbling bodies in hopes of finding one more thing, which he did: a bundle of rope. It was quality stuff—frayed but not rotted—and plenty sturdy. He threw the coil in his satchel and activated his whip gauntlets.

He sprinted beyond the tunnel of disfigured carvings gasping for his life force. He entered the piercing passageway, this time well aware of its secrets. He smashed the razor-sharp spikes that were no match for his fury, leaving behind a pile of rubble. He entered the antechamber attempting to keep his wind; his lungs were desperate to squeeze air from the micro-thin layer of oxygen in the vast emptiness.

He navigated the the black labyrinth, turning in circles, searching for "the face." Eventually, the blackness waned, and he could make out the mountainous formation in the shape of Death's mask. He made a beeline for its mouth, the opening to the throne room, hoping to pass by unnoticed—

A guardian golem dropped from the eye socket of the monument and blocked his path.

"Dammit," Vant murmured to himself.

The childlike brute took a slow but powerful swing at Vant, who sidestepped the attack. He knew that if he shattered the creature, two more would appear in its place; he had learned that the hard way during his first visit.

He flipped switches inside his gauntlets, reversing the whip orientations and giving the coil some slack. Within the hand-holes, he twisted the ends of the lashes around his knuckles and got a tight hold.

The golem lumbered toward him, stupid thing.

Vant activated the thrusters. The gauntlets launched from his arms in the direction of the beast. They impacted with its chest, sending it tail over tits into the dirt. Vant tugged on the whips, zipping the weapons back into his hands.

"Easy boy," Vant said. The bone beast groaned, attempting to figure out how it had ended up on its ass. "I have a present for you."

Vant wrapped the legs of the golem with the rope. He pulled tight, then bound its arms, as well. It was not going anywhere.

Vant entered the palace.

Death sat motionless, his hulking body sunken into his throne.

"Miss me?" Vant asked.

Death did not move. Not one inch.

Vant pressed harder. "I can only assume you summoned me here to lift my curse. So, let's get to it, then." He knew it was unwise to taunt a demigod, but he was pissed. His sweaty palms gripped his whip gauntlets. His fingers rested on their thrusters.

Death did not stir.

"We had a deal," Vant said. "I've done your bidding. I've wiped out The Immortals, hideous wretches that they were. Now release me." Vant removed a hand from a gauntlet, reached into his satchel, and tossed the mask across the floor. The relic tumbled to a rest near Death's massive boots.

"No."

The word stabbed Vant in the gut.

"Excuse me?"

"Finish the job," Death said through his raw rasp.

"I have."

"Your job is all of it. *All* that you see through my eyes. Look deeper into the mask. Expand your pathetically limited mind. Do my bidding."

"Do your own bidding," Vant declared.

"*Tsk, tsk.* Such behavior. I suppose, rebellious child, it is time for your... *spanking.*"

Death rose.

Vant revved the thrusters in his gauntlets. "Death," he said, "Before we get into this, I have something to tell you. Something important. Something you should know."

"Speak."

"You're a cock."

Silence. Then, "Meh-heh." That condescending laugh. "Now, immortal babe, the time has come for you to learn gratitude. We shall begin by draining your blood. I suspect we shall discover how grateful you were for it, once it is gone."

Death moved like a specter. He was everywhere. He was nowhere.

He brushed past Vant, his magnitude leaving a gust of wind. Vant swung his iron fists where he hoped to find the beast—but hit nothing. Again, he swung. Again. Death's hideous laughter assaulted Vant with every failed punch.

For a moment, Death seemed to linger. Vant charged in with both fists. The form was a mirage. Vant ended up sprawled out on the floor. He leapt to his feet and let loose the whips. Their stinging impacts sent oscillating echoes throughout the black palace. He swung the lashes recklessly, hoping to at least catch an edge of his foe. He connected only with air.

Death was toying with him. This was not a fight. This was a lesson.

"Only the foolish would challenge the very end of all things," Death said.

"You're a coward! Face me!"

"There is no victory over death!"

He leveled Vant with one blow. Vant's body went limp. The wind shot out of his lungs. He collapsed to the floor.

Vant wheezed. Got to his shaking feet. Dug into his body's energy reserves and, in a calculated move, flicked a whip at the mask on the ground, sending it into the air. He rolled underneath it—it latched onto his face during the descent. The already dark surroundings shifted into an even deeper darkness, and Death was rendered as a violent, pulsing red shape before him.

Vant could now see his foe.

"I don't want to defeat you," Vant said. He retracted the whips and juked left, faking Death out. "I just want to punch you in the face." He swung right.

His gauntlet smashed the creature's face. Death crumpled for a moment, then retreated.

In his long life, it was the greatest feeling Vant had ever experienced. He laughed aloud, even though he knew what would come next. He was about to get dismantled. He did not care. In his mind, he had won. He had decked a demon.

Vant stared at Death, whose silhouette was outlined in spastic pulses. The figure had the most volatile reddish form he had seen since donning the mask. As if...

...as if Death himself is also marked for elimination, Vant thought.

The inevitable moment arrived. The terrifyingly beautiful chime of steel rang in the dark as Death unsheathed his scythe.

Vant maintained focus and kept his masked eyes on the beast. Death weaved swiftly, leaving a glowing stream of red everywhere he went. With the newfound ability to track Death's movements, Vant pivoted and twisted to avoid the monster lunging at him.

Out of nowhere, Death struck out. His weapon flashed faster than physics should allow. Vant raised a gauntlet in time to parry. Sparks flew from the clash of polished steel on unyielding iron. Death swung again. And again. Vant deflected each blindingly fast strike.

The speed of Death's swings increased with every attempt. The attacks were coming far too fast to comprehend. Vant let go of his thoughts and moved with the intuition of hundreds of years of battle instinct. It had become a dance of showmanship, the relentless gleams of Death's mystical blade blocked time and again by the sturdy weapon of a hardened fighter. Vant surrendered his mind and flowed with the tide of combat.

Faster and faster the scythe swished.

Vant felt his focus slipping. In the tiniest moment of hesitation, the blade penetrated his defenses and connected. The edge slid across Vant's chest. His stomach. His thigh.

Blood spilled from the incisions.

Vant needed distance. He swung at Death's face, forcing him to dodge, which granted a brief opportunity to shift backward to surer footing. He extended the whips and activated the electricity modules. Lighting flowed from the gauntlets into the coils. Arcs of energy filled the blackness as Vant flicked at the beast over and over, forcing Death to disengage.

Vant brandished the weapons without respite to keep the demon at bay. Flashes of light revealed beady eyes beneath the hood, studying Vant's attack pattern.

Death sensed a weakness.

He lunged.

Vant adjusted by crouching and rotating a fist in a circle above his head, creating a propeller of protection. He kept his eyes trained on Death, who crept at the edges of the defensive radius.

"I'm through!" Vant shouted as the blood in his body puddled at his feet. "I've killed enough! No more!"

"I will say when you have killed enough."

"How many have to die? *How many?*"

"All must die, when the time is right." Death paced Vant's perimeter of defense. "And, if they refuse, they shall deal with *you.*"

"I'm not your enforcer! I'm not your slave! You can no longer force me to kill. I won't trade one form of torture for another!"

"Foolish child! I'm not *torturing* you." Death vanished upward. "I'm *teaching* you!"

Then he crashed down onto Vant's one exposed area—his arm above his head, near the apex of the propeller where there was no electricity protection. In the one swift stomp, Vant's arm crumpled into his torso, and his torso into his ribcage. His spine cricked out of alignment. His body tumbled into a broken heap.

"Have you learned *nothing?*" Death said. "Have you not seen the corruption of those who rebel against their expiration? Has your run-in with The Immortals not shown you *why* those who flee from death must be taken? Destroying them is an act of mercy!"

Death's gloves wrapped around Vant's limp body and lifted him up. He squeezed, wringing out Vant's vital fluids into a sopping mess in the dirt.

"Are you not grateful now for the blood that was once in your body? Do you now not long for it? Today, it seems, you have learned both empathy *and* gratitude. Shame you had to learn the hard way."

Vant's vision went in and out. Death dragged him through the palace and into a long, stone corridor, speaking: "It is time for your next lesson. It is time to expand your horizons. Time to give you a... *new perspective* on life."

At the end of the tunnel, an underground stronghold stretched for miles.

Death tossed Vant into the expansive room. He landed with a *thud*.

"Rise, ignorant child, and look upon your fate."

Vant attempted to prop himself up. The world spun. His body trembled as he stood as tall as his broken frame would allow.

A sweeping array of alcoves were carved into the stone walls—prison cells with no bars. They were stacked high and ran deep into the nothingness.

Vant struggled to make out the shapes of those trapped within...

Black wisps of liquidy smoke.

A moan emanated from one of the ethereal beings. It was cry of suffering—deeper than suffering. A vocalization that came from the place inside of truest misery.

Another cell burst into wails.

And another.

Then ten more. Then fifty more. Then a hundred. Cries, bellows, retching, begging, screaming. A chorus of unbearable sadness.

Vant pressed his palms into his ears, but the resounding was far too pervasive. Thousands called out in the dark, their voices bellowing with the profundity of their anguish. Death's mask tightened on Vant's face. Tightened. He tried to pull it off, but it refused to let go.

Vant cried out, "Stop this!"

"Meh-heh." Death paced through the stronghold like a victor in an arena.

The soul-penetrating screams were more than Vant could bear. The sound vibrated his nerves and dislodged his fragile insides. He shrieked with the captives. The scream would not stop. It went. And went. It severed his larynx.

"Witness the repercussions of your insolence!" Death lifted Vant off his feet and held him up, parading him like a trophy. He called out to those trapped in the alcoves, "Meet the one who took you against your will. The one who destroyed your human forms. The one responsible for the end of your precious lives!"

Suspended from Death's grip, Vant looked closer at the vaporous beings. They resembled those lost from his past. He recognized Ranchula, fighting for liberation. He identified The Mayor's house queen, Dawnrier, ripping herself apart from the shame of having lost her perfect physical form. He recognized the Knights of Rights, his heart shattering at the sight of the loyal troops he had sent to their deaths. Countless numbers of the recently dispatched, fetus-like Immortals begged for mercy, as did the nomads and Land Escapers who had fallen under Vant's command. Shyyla, his wife, whom he had carelessly gunned down in his rage, melted into the structure in agony, a mere fragment of her former self.

And...

...there was Rii.

Vant reached a trembling hand out to his love.

She screamed at the sight of him and recoiled, as if he were a monster.

Which he believed himself to be.

Death brought Vant in close, meeting him eye to eye. Vant looked upon his naked, maskless face—a wrinkled, crackled visage of chalky skin and charcoal veins. His saucer-like nostrils flared with hysterical hatred toward the immortal in his grasp and his tiny, black eyeballs reflected like mirrors. In them, Vant saw his own, mangled form.

Death smiled. "I have kept them here, in purgatory. Saved them for you. I refuse to transition them to the netherworlds where they would find peace. Defy me. Continue to rebel. Do as you wish. It is no concern to me. I shall watch them suffer alongside you. You, my favorite... *plaything.*"

He dropped Vant and pointed at him, in view of the tortured souls. "Your fate is now tied to his! This insolent, untamable, unyielding lump of flesh is your only hope for salvation! Do not beg me for release. Your pleas fall upon deaf ears. Beg him! Beg this foul excuse of a man for mercy, for only *he* may set you free!"

The cries of the souls permeated Vant's core. Their melancholy was infinite. Vant wrapped himself into a fetal position, covering up with his robes. His physiology, pushed far past critical condition and emotional capacity, kicked into a grisly autopilot. Without his permission, his head bashed into the ground over and over in an attempt to kill itself. His fingers dug into his scar, trying to separate head from neck. His body was horrifyingly, mechanically doing everything it could to end itself.

And then, Death's words came. Words that cut through Vant, straight to his core. Words that carried with them a heinous purpose.

"Why so... *grim,* my little reaper?"

Vant looked upon himself, dressed in black robes, wearing a mask like a skull, and surrounded by the souls he had harvested for Death. He saw what he was becoming—what he had become.

The Grim Reaper.

"Just figuring it out now, are you? You *will* go back into the world and continue to harvest the damned. So long as you reap, we *both* shall live. The souls of the dead give me the strength to survive... *and* the strength to keep your curse at bay."

Vant shook his head.

Death kicked him across the floor. "Ever the obstinate child! Though this is the very reason you are here. Because of your consciousness of violence. Because you are the lowest of all creatures. Because you have committed atrocities based upon your whims. That is why I chose you, because you have never failed to *kill* what gets in your way. I suppose, in that respect, we are quite similar. Meh-heh!" Death poked at Vant, taunting him. "Meh-heh-heh!" He spat a hunk of phlegm onto Vant's back. "Meh-heh-heh-heh-heh!" Death's sadistic laughter fused with the screams of the trapped souls, screams that turned into a thundering cacophony of despair.

Vant was drowning in the deafening roar. His sanity was melting away...

...but something caught his eye.

Tucked away in a far-off corner, one apparition did not cry out. It did not wail, and it did not succumb to the turmoil. Instead, it stood tall, with folded arms.

It was the spirit form of Vant Hu'l—the first Vant Hu'l—who had lived before Terri had assumed his name.

The apparition gazed with a purpose unbreakable by any force, and beamed the same compassion he had always bestowed upon his best friend. It was a compassion once given to a child born to a warmongering father. A compassion once given to a teenager who had lost himself in jealousy. A compassion once given to a leader who had created a reign of cruelty because he knew no different. And a compassion now bestowed upon a warrior living into a legacy that had begun centuries ago.

The spirit inclined its head in acknowledgment of his friend. It was a simple gesture, but it implied *everything*. Unification. Power. Honor. Strength. Integrity. Valor. Love.

The look infused every atom inside Vant's broken body with strength.

He rose.

Ripped off the mask.

Locked eyes with Death, and stared him down with defiant rage.

The screams of the spirits hushed as Vant lifted the mask high.

Then, with his other hand...

...he gave Death the middle finger.

The imprisoned souls erupted into ferocious cheers, united with Vant in rebellion.

Vengeance was sworn.

"All must die, when the time is right. And, if they refuse,
they shall deal with you."

- Death

THE REAPER WILL RETURN

LEGENDS of GRIM #2

COMING SOON

Let's take *Mortal Enemy* to the next level!

Only together can we bring Vant Hu'l, Skii Tavee, Kram Grammie, and The World's Worst (or is it Best?) Magician from the page to the screen!

If you'd like to see this book developed as a feature film / television show, you can pledge your support by signing the online petition!

Signing only takes a couple seconds, and it means *everything* to the author, and the entire cast and crew. Thank you so much for joining our cause!

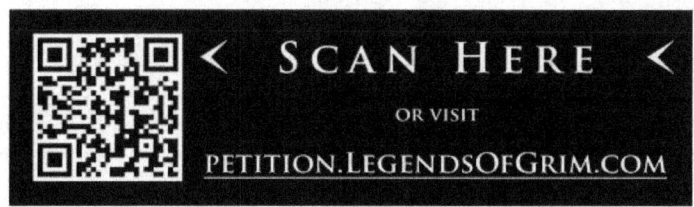

ACKNOWLEDGMENTS

An astounding number of people have demonstrated vast and unfathomable generosity to the development of this project. Because of them, I shall now and forever know what it means to be authentically collaborative, unapologetically bold, and fiercely creative.

I am forever grateful for:

Patrick J. Adams, Keegan Allen, Christa B. Allen, Angela Alvarez, Baxley Andresen, Emily Babbitt, Ken Baker, Robert Baker, Mel Banick, David Bartis, Sean Beavan, Crispian Belfrage, Troian Bellisario, Anderson Blackman, Harrison Blackman, Katherine Blackman, Neal Bledsoe, Phil Boucher, Amanda Bradbury, Austin Bradbury, Cynthia Abad-Bradbury, Jonathan Bradbury, Adam Bravin, Pierce Brown, Renee Buckley, Sean Bury, Emma Clark, Nicholas Daly Clark, Joshua Close, Noell Coet, Perri Cohn, David Crocco, Jane Cross, Adrian Cruz, Sanaz Dahi, Flora Demirchian, Laura Dewey, Brett Dier, Timothy Dowling, Michael J. Dowling, Heather Dowling, Joel Drazner, Michael Dunn, Holiday Evans, Huntington Evans, Kara Evans, Brenda Felbinger, Doug Felbinger, Justin Felbinger, Ranya Fezzani, Stefan Fletcher, Lenka Fucikova, Juan Garcia, Christian Gecosala, Phil Gevaux, Hester Gevaux, Millicent Gevaux, Anthony Gonzales, Ian Gotler, Darcy Graham, Anthea Graupner, Sarkis Gringorian, Steven Griswold, Jesse Gros, Bill Grveles, Malcolm Guess, Tina Guo, Jamie Harris, Rebekah Hendershot, Billy Henehan, Brendan Hines, Ron Hodge, Edouard Holdener, Eric Holdener, Isabelle Holdener, Selkie Hom, Elise Diamond Howard, Gary Howard, Jayke Howard, Jeremy Howard, Lorin Howard, Emma Howie, Ron Hulnick, Mary Hulnick, Johanna Jenkins, Kira Johannessen, Elspeth Keller, Devin Kelley, Rob Kerkovich, Nicholas Knudson, Anita Lashkari, Kamran Lashkari, Kian Lashkari, Shawn Layton, Derrick K. Lee, Sonya Lee, Lynne Lees, Meagan Lopez, Deborah Lurie, Willis Lurie, Adetokumboh M'Cormack, Jason MacRay, Kira Mamula, Lavena Mathrani, Craig Maurer, Marshall McCabe, Lily McKay, P.T. McNiff, Emily Mefford, Mark Meloccaro, Gretchen Menn, Mary Menninger, Meg Minker, Bob Mitsch, Matt Morton, Allie Moulton, Usman Mustafa, Rolando Nadal, Jordan Nelsestuen, Negar Nosrat, Eric Christian Olsen, Ophelia, Michael Patterson, Babar Peerzada, Molly Peters, James Petix, Cara Petry, Chris Pine, Robert Pine, Anjali Prasertong, Charlotte-Ann Riffey, Chris Riffey, Lesley Robins, William Rowel, Joseph Rubinstein, Simon Russel, Riegan Sage, Benjamin Salisbury, R.A. Salvatore, Rosa Nadine Xochimilco Sánchez, Jasper Savage, Chuka Schneider, Lucia Schneider, Valentina Schneider, Brenda Schneider, Dave Schwep, Reid Scott, Cela Scott, Peter Seibert, Michiko Sellars, Stacey Sellars, Amir Sharomi, Fatima Silva, Anakin Skybarker, James Slainmann, Scott Michael Smith, Erinn Sosa, Stephanie Spiegel, Julia Stewart, Ramu Sunkara, Satsuki Takahashi, Steve Tavaglione, Andru Thomas, Barrett Thornbury, Lyla Thornbury, Lucas Thornbury, Angelina Tracy, Vreny Van Elslande, Amanda Walsh, Eric Wegener, Kaitlin Weichsel, Carrie Wick, Victor Wilde, Mark Wildman, Julisa Wilson, Sarah Wright Olsen, Lillia Wylie, Karen Yee, Justin Zsebe.

And so many, many more.

CAST: THE NOVEL

Character Live Reference
Baxley Andresen: *Dawnrier*
Emma Clark: *Laam Fraam*
Nicholas Daly Clark: *Thallium Soldiers & Titan*
Michael Dunn: *Shlarky*
Malcolm Guess: *Vant Hu'l*
Ron Hodge: *Clodd, Blauth*
Selkie Hom: *Skii Tavee*
William Rowel: *Kram Grammie*
Rosa Nadine Xochimilco Sánchez: *Kryystin, the Innkeeper*
Chad Harrison Waylon: *Death*
Mark Wildman: *Ranchula*
Justin Zsebe: *The World's Worst Magician*

CREW: THE NOVEL

Story
Nicholas Ryan Howard: *Author*
Babar Peerzada: *Story Editor*

Edits
Joel Drazner: *Editor*
Rebekah Hendershot: *Editor*
Rosa Nadine Xochimilco Sánchez: *Additional Edits*
William Rowel: *Additional Edits*

Artwork Design
Nicholas Ryan Howard: *Designer*
Joseph Rubinstein: *Photographer*

Artwork Production
Emma Clark: *Camera Assistant*
Nicholas Daly Clark: *Thallium Soldiers & Titan Design*
Emma Howie: *Assistant Costume Designer*
Emily Mefford: *Makeup Stylist*
Bob Mitsch: *Costume Support*
Rosa Nadine Xochimilco Sánchez: *Production Coordinator*
Dave Schwep: *Thallium Soldiers & Titan Photography*
Stephanie Spiegel: *Prop Master*
Kaitlin Weichsel: *Costume Designer*

Production Affairs
Keegan Allen: *Author Photo*
Derrick K. Lee, Esq.: *Legal Services*
Meagan Lopez: *Public Relations*
Mark Meloccaro: *Legal Rights and Clearances*
Meg Minker: *Social Media Support*
Rosa Nadine Xochimilco Sánchez: *Manager of Creative Affairs*
Chuka Schneider: *Marketing Support*
Satsuki Takahashi: *Associate Producer*
Julisa Wilson: *Social Media Support*

CAST: THE AUDIO EXPERIENCE

Narrators
Reid Scott: *Narrator*
Devin Kelley: *Narrator, era of the Knights of Rights*

Performers
Patrick J. Adams: *The Immortal Overlord*
Keegan Allen: *Agmar-Burrian Terriforn, era of the Knights of Rights*
Christa B. Allen: *Dawnrier, Shyyla*
Baxley Andresen: *Mother of Vant Hu'l, era of the Knights of Rights*
Robert Baker: *Death, Bad Luck Peace-Keeper,Right-hand Man, Shlarky's Crew,Father of Vant Hu'l, era of the Knights of Rights, Land Escape Riot Squad Officer, Nomad Hunter*
Crispian Belfrage: *Blauth,Compassionate Knight, era of the Knights of Rights, Gigolo in The Mayor's Mansion, Jiino*
Troian Bellisario: *Skii Tavee*
Neal Bledsoe: *Vant Hu'l, era of the Knights of Rights*
Joshua Close: *Crash Town Wiseguy, Excited Nomad Hunter, Land Escape Prison Guard, Rebellious Knight, era of the Knights of Rights*
Brett Dier: *Land Escape Interviewer, Land Escape Riot Squad Rookie, Antsy Thug, Shlarky's Crew, Ancient Nomad Hunter*
Timothy Dowling: *Chaaris*
Michael Dunn: *The World's Worst Magician, Shlarky,Shavious, Thiio,Prime Davith, era of The Knights of Rights, The Mayor's Chef, Crash Town Crane Worker*

Justin Felbinger: *Bomp, Young Agmar-Burrian Terriforn, era of the Knights of Rights*
Ian Gotler: *Land Escape Gate Guard*
Jamie Harris: *Clodd, Cloakmaster Gordone, era of the Knights of Rights, Impulsive Bruiser, Shlarky's Crew*
Brendan Hines: *Saamii Fraam*
Edouard Holdener: *Fray, Young Vant Hu'l, era of the Knights of Rights*
Adetokumboh M'Cormack: *Ranchula, Cloakmaster Daggart, era of the Knights of Rights*
Eric Christian Olsen: *Vant Hu'l*
Sarah Wright Olsen: *Kryystin the Land Escape Innkeeper, Widow, Sarcastic Courtesan in The Mayor's Mansion, Corpo-Bot*
Chris Pine: *The Mayor*
Robert Pine: *Agmar, era of the Knights of Rights*
William Rowel: *Kram Grammie*
Reid Scott: *Redemption*
Amanda Walsh: *Laam Fraam, Land Escape Traumatized Survivor, Smoking Courtesan in The Mayor's Mansion*
Chad Harrison Waylon: *Hoss-Hoss*

CREW: THE AUDIO EXPERIENCE

Babar Peerzada: Director / Producer

Music
Deborah Lurie: Composer

Musicians
Tina Guo: *Cello*
Gretchen Menn: *Guitar*
Steve Tavaglione: *EWI*

Music Support
Emily Babbitt: *Score Technical Producer*
Phill Boucher: *Additional Arrangements*
Stefan Fletcher: *Additional Arrangements*
Peter Seibert: *Additional Arrangements*
James Slainmann: *Additional Arrangements*
Scott Michael Smith: *Score Recording Engineer*

Audio Production - A.G.E. Post
David Crocco: *Executive Producer of Sound*
Rolando Nadal: *Sound Supervisor / Re-recording Mixer / Dialogue Recordist / Sound Designer / Dialogue Editor*
Christian Gecosala: *Dialogue Recordist / Sound Designer / Re-recording Mixer*
Sean Beavan: *Sound Designer*
Eric Wegener: *Re-recording Mixer / Sound Designer*
Vreny Van Elslande: *Dialogue Editor*
Cela Scott: *Audio Post Operations Manager*

Production Support
Nicholas Ryan Howard: *Executive Producer / Assistant Director*
Rosa Nadine Xochimilco Sánchez: *Line Producer*
Perri Cohn: *Production Assistant*
Noell Coet: *Production Assistant*
Flora Demirchian: *Production Assistant*

Production Team
Keegan Allen: *Photographer*
Emma Clark: *Camera Assistant*
Emily Mefford: *Makeup Stylist*
Joseph Rubinstein: *Photographer*
Jasper Savage: *Photographer*
Dave Schwep: *Photographer*
Kaitlin Weichsel: *Stylist*
Julisa Wilson: *Photographer*

Production Affairs
Steven Griswold: *Associate Producer*
Shawn Layton: *Associate Producer*
Derrick K. Lee, Esq.: *Legal Support*
Lavena Mathrani: *Associate Producer*
Mark Meloccaro: *Legal Rights and Clearances*
Meg Minker: *Social Media Support*
Chuka Schneider: *Marketing Support*
Satsuki Takahashi: *Associate Producer*
Julisa Wilson: *Social Media Support*

ABOUT THE AUTHOR

www.NicholasRyanH.com
@NicholasRyanH

Nicholas Ryan Howard is an author, philosopher, and expert in the field of creativity. He was educated at the University of Southern California in Communications and trained as a master facilitator in Spiritual Psychology at the University of Santa Monica, where he later served as a director. As a media producer and content creator he has worked on such properties as *The Bourne Identity*, *Harry Potter*, and *Star Wars*, and in the technology sector he has overseen projects for corporations such as Mattel, Sony, and Panasonic. He is the visionary behind the epic *Legends of Grim* saga, the best-selling poetry collection *Mercenary at Midnight*, and the acclaimed podcast *Of Tears and Blood*. Currently he spends his time dreaming up new worlds, counseling individuals on their expansion of consciousness, consulting with organizations, and speaking around the globe.